THE WAKE

Nicola Faulkner

IONIC
PUBLISHING

The Wake
© 2025 Nicola Faulkner

All rights reserved.
No part of this book may be reproduced, stored in a retrieval system,
or transmitted in any form or by any means—electronic, mechanical,
photocopying, recording, or otherwise—without the prior written
permission of the publisher, except for brief quotations used in reviews
or scholarly works.

This is a work of fiction. Names, characters, places, and incidents are
either the product of the author's imagination or are used fictitiously.
Any resemblance to actual events, locales, or persons, living or dead, is
purely coincidental.

ISBN: 978-0-473-75074-9
Cover design by: Ayesha pilots_gfx
Published by: Ionic Publishing
First Edition

For my dad,
who never left me behind—
except that one time…

CHAPTER ONE

Claire holds Lily's hand too tightly as they push through the crowd. Her eyes dart from strangers' faces to oversized bags, scanning for dangers she knows aren't there. The ship looms ahead, vast and gleaming, both escape and entrapment.

Lily bounces beside her, a ball of energy, barely tethered by Claire's tense grip. She stomps like a dinosaur, scaring no one. Claire doesn't laugh. Not yet. Not with this many people pressing in on all sides. She forces a smile, but her grip doesn't loosen. The child's enthusiasm is as exhausting as it is contagious.

Claire whispers, trying to soothe her own nerves. But Lily is untroubled. Her small feet skip through the terminal, while Claire wonders what it means to be afraid.

"Lily, sweetie, stay close." Claire's voice barely carries over the noise. Her grip tightens.

"I'm a big T. rex!" Lily roars, full of spirit. Her steps are quick and uneven, more a hop than a walk.

Claire smiles despite herself, trying to match Lily's pace. The ship looms above them, immense and intimidating. Claire feels its shadow, a reminder of both the vast ocean and the small cabin waiting inside. She isn't sure which frightens her more.

"Mummy, we're going on an adventure!" Lily's declaration draws looks from other passengers. They smile at the tiny whirlwind.

"We sure are. From Southampton all the way to Canada." Claire assures her. "But let's find our room first." Her eyes linger on the faces around them. Families, couples, strangers all moving toward the same destination. The crowd presses in, and Claire swallows the feeling rising in her throat.

She leads Lily onto the ship, through boarding, immigration, and security checks and onto a deck buzzing with excitement. Music plays somewhere, cheerful and distant. They pass shops and restaurants, not stopping, not yet. Claire only wants to find their cabin, to catch her breath in private.

The hallway to their cabin feels endless. The carpeting is too soft, the air too clean. It unsettles Claire in a way she can't name. She clutches the boarding card like a lifeline; eyes fixed on the numbers as they walk. Lily skips alongside, unconcerned with the journey or the people they dodge.

"It's just around the corner, Lily," Claire says. Her voice betrays more hope than certainty.

"Did we find it? Did we find our room?" Lily asks, bouncing on the spot as they finally reach their door.

Claire double checks the name on the envelope in the mail slot outside the door, then opens it to find two sail pass cards and taps one on the door lock. The light turns green, and she lets out a relieved sigh. "Here we are," she says, opening the door with a flourish. Lily rushes inside. Claire follows, closing out the noise and the world.

The cabin is compact, cheerful. Too easy. Too calm. Two twin beds and a small couch occupy most of the space. Muted blues and beiges create a soothing atmosphere. Claire finds them comforting, in their own way. She sets the suitcase down, the tension easing from her shoulders.

Lily surveys the room with wide eyes. "Look, Mummy! It's our home on the big boat!" she exclaims, spinning in a circle as if claiming the space.

Claire laughs softly.

"It is. What do you think?"

"It's roarsome!" Lily says, her excitement a force of nature. She grabs her backpack, and dumps out a mess of dinosaur toys and her beloved ragdoll cat, Thomas. "This is my spot," she declares, arranging them on the bed with the seriousness only a three-year-old can muster.

Claire watches her daughter settle in. She tries to match Lily's enthusiasm—but can't shake the feeling that she's missed something. That she's forgotten to double-check something important.

Lily is in her element, content with the simplest of comforts. "I love it here, Mummy. Look at my dinosaurs!" she says, holding up a plastic Stegosaurus, her eyes shining.

"I see," Claire replies, unable to hide her smile.

"You've got quite the collection."

She thinks of the weeks spent planning this trip, of the countless doubts that nearly kept them from it. She looks at Lily and knows it was worth every hesitation.

Together, they turn the compact room into a temporary home. Lily chatters nonstop, her words a gentle soundtrack to Claire's thoughts.

"Can we go swimming, Mummy? Is there a pool? Are we going to eat tiny toast for breakfast?"

Each question reflects Lily's boundless enthusiasm—each one answered with quiet, patient love.

"Yes, there's a pool," Claire says, folding the last of Lily's dinosaur-print dresses.

"And yes, we'll have tiny toast." She sits on the bed, the exhaustion of worry giving way to relief. Lily's joy is infectious, washing away the last of Claire's anxieties.

"Mummy, I'm going to see sea dinosaurs," Lily announces.

"I'm going to see everything." She climbs onto the bed, nestling among her toys and Thomas.

Claire reaches over and gently smooths Lily's soft curls.

"We'll see it all," she promises.

Her voice is calm now, the earlier tension gone. She leans against the wall, letting the cabin's warmth settle over her like a blanket.

She locks the door.

She checks it again.

They've made it here, she thinks. Together, always together.

Claire sits on the bed, each spring giving way beneath her weight and her thoughts. Lily's voice fills the room, her words blending into a hum like the soft vibration of the ship beneath them. Claire watches her daughter and sees her life in fast-forward: from tiny infant to fierce, joyful three-year-old.

Her own history flashes back at her in fragments. A proposal, perfect until it wasn't. A loss, swift and silent. A determined choice to do it alone, or at least with Lily.

Lily's exuberance breaks through the memory. Claire inhales it like oxygen.

With intense concentration, Lily arranges her toys. "This one's named Steggy," she announces, pointing to a green Stegosaurus. "And this one's named... Steggy!" She erupts into giggles at her own wit, then begins to roar in her sweet, tiny way.

Claire smiles, her eyes distant, half-lidded. "Both named Steggy?" she teases. "What happens if they get mixed up?"

"They never get mixed up," Lily replies confidently. "Steggy always knows who's who." She returns to her play. Claire leans back, letting the exhaustion of the day settle over her.

The room's soft colours blur at the edges of her vision. Uninvited memories press in. They settle beside her like unwelcome guests, stubborn, impossible to ignore. She sees her fiancé, the ring, a future that once felt certain. Then the cold echo of a doctor's words, and the emptiness they left inside.

"I'm going to have tiny toast for breakfast," Lily declares, rolling onto her back and hugging her dinosaurs to her chest.

"Croissants," Claire murmurs. "They're called croissants." But Lily doesn't hear, her world too full of adventure to notice.

The phone buzzes beneath Claire's fingers, not with a message, but everything it holds. The screen glows as it finds her face, lighting up with photos of Lily. Her life, from newborn to now, flickers past in colourful little squares.

Claire wonders if it was wrong to keep Lily from him, even after he walked away. Would he have wanted to know? Would he have cared? Questions echo, not as sharp as they once were, but still there, a dull throb.

"I think we'll see sea dinosaurs," Lily says suddenly, already swept up in her next excitement. "Swimming, swimming!" Her energy is relentless, a bright flare against the heaviness of Claire's thoughts.

They had drifted apart so quickly. She'd known they would, after the miscarriage, after he'd stopped talking and she'd stopped hoping. Still, the abruptness of his disappearance shocked her. His absence was sudden and total, as if he'd vanished from the world, not just from her life.

"Sea dinosaurs, Mummy!" Lily shouts, sitting up and jolting Claire from her reverie.

"From the balcony," Claire agrees, offering a smile. But Lily's already back in her game.

She watches the photos multiply, each capturing a fragment of their shared life. A first birthday. Their old apartment. The park where Lily fell and scraped her knee and didn't cry. Claire had never planned to do it alone. But here she is. Here they are.

She wonders if she'll always be alone. She looks at Lily, who has never made her feel lonely. And yet, beside her, there's a space her daughter can't fill. Would it be so terrible to let someone else in one day? Would she even know how?

Claire wants to hold onto this moment, this trip, to make it last forever. But the future looms, uncertain, uninvited. Beyond this cabin, this vacation, this year, she doesn't know what is waiting. She's not sure she wants to find out.

Lily stomps her feet. "I'm a big dinosaur! And Thomas is a dinosaur too!" She tosses the ragdoll cat into the air and catches him with delighted clumsiness.

"Thomas? A dinosaur?" Claire's voice is mock incredulous.

Lily nods, solemn. "Yup. A big dinosaur." She leaps into Claire's lap giggling, her tiredness forgotten in this final burst of play.

Claire holds her close, feeling her daughter's small heart beating against her own. She knows this won't last, that children grow, their needs change. But for now, Lily is hers. Entirely. Claire rests her chin on the soft curls, breathing her in, unwilling to let go.

"I love you, Mummy," Lily whispers. A declaration. A universe.

The past dissolves. The cabin becomes everything. Small. Safe. Enough. The ship hums around them like the blood in their veins. Like life. Claire kisses Lily's head, closes her eyes, and holds onto the now.

Claire and Lily step out from the cabin, taking their first tentative strides into the ship's sprawling maze. Claire's gaze sweeps the endless corridors, plush carpeting muffling each footfall and brass fixtures gleaming like hidden treasure. A subtle sway beneath her feet reminds her of the vast ocean just beyond the walls. She tightens her grip on Lily's hand, as if the ship's immensity might somehow pull them apart.

But Lily is uncontainable. She breaks free, darting to the windows, pointing gleefully at the sea. Claire reels her back in, held together only by nerves and love. Together they venture deeper into the ship.

The enormity is overwhelming. Claire feels like an ant in a floating city, insignificant among the passing families. They drift by some with crying infants, others with trailing teenagers glued to glowing screens. They all look happy, Claire thinks—or at least content.

"Mummy, look!" Lily tugs her toward a window, eyes wide with wonder.

Claire lets herself be led. The sign of the endless sea tilts her balance, its vastness dizzying.

"I see, Lily. It's the sea," she says her voice softening with awe.

They stand quietly, the two of them against the world. Lily's nose nearly touches the glass, fogging it with her breath. Claire's sees her own reflection, translucent and fragile. For a moment she sees herself as Lily must, a mother stitched together with hope and uncertainty.

"Are there sea dinosaurs, Mummy?" Lily asks, eyes still on the waves.

"I don't know," Claire replies, hiding a smile. "Maybe we'll find out."

They step away from the window. Lily bounces with each step, brimming with energy. Claire matches her pace, but tension creeps back in as they re-enter the crowd. She clutches Lily's hand, needing the contact more than her daughter does.

Lily pulls out of her grasp and runs ahead, fearless. Claire stays close, counting exits. At the muster drill, she watches other parents talk casually, unbothered. How do they do that? How do they trust this place?

They sit, Claire's mind racing with what-ifs and maybes. She didn't expect this, the crush of people, the weight of the ship's isolation pressing down on her.

A young man steps to the front, commanding attention. "Welcome aboard," he says, his voice calm, slicing through the noise. "I'm Adam, one of your activity coordinators. Let's go over safety procedures."

Claire studies him, his enthusiasm striking. She sees the way Adam presents himself, each movement precise, each word relaxed. The way she wishes she felt.

Lily squirms beside her, eyes wide, trying to take it all in. Claire wraps an arm around her, gently pulling her close. Lily pushes away—not with defiance, just wanting to roam.

"We're going to cover what you need to know in case of emergency," Adam continues. His instructions are clear, a stark contrast to Claire's overwhelmed thoughts.

Claire tries to focus, to gather the pieces of the presentation, but her mind drifts—to the hum of the engines, to Lily's restless energy, to her own unease.

"Are we done yet, Mummy?" Lily whispers loudly, drawing amused glances from nearby families.

"Almost," Claire murmurs, smoothing Lily's hair in a gesture meant to soothe them both.

Adam's voice rolls smoothly through the mic—clear, practiced, even a little charming—as he points to the emergency exits and demonstrates the life jacket with effortless confidence.

Just before dismissing them, his eyes scan the crowd. They land on Claire then Lily.

They don't move.

Only for a second. Two, maybe. But long enough for Claire to notice.

Then, just as quickly, he smiles—a pleasant, professional smile—and turns back to his clipboard.

Claire hesitates, one hand resting on Lily's back. Probably nothing. Just the way people look at kids. But something about the stillness of it —the quiet click in her chest—didn't sit right.

"Mummy, let's go!" Lily exclaims, her enthusiasm never once dimmed.

Claire follows, as always, trailing in her daughter's wake, grateful for the momentum. The noise fades behind them, replaced by the ship's hum and the wide-open promise of their adventure.

CHAPTER TWO

The ship's buffet hums with life. Laughter and cutlery echo off high, shell-white ceilings. Wait staff in crisp uniforms dart between tables, encouraging guests to buy a dining package for the specialty restaurants. Oversized windows spill the grey light of Southampton across linen and glass, the Atlantic waiting out of reach.

At a table for two near the window, Claire Holloway prods the last sliver of quiche on her plate. She's not really hungry—it's a prop, something to keep her hands busy. Across from her, Lily delivers a spirited lecture on which dinosaurs would have enjoyed "tiny sandwiches."

Lily's voice carries. She's three, and hasn't yet learned to modulate for indoor acoustics. Her favourite shirt—green, with stegosaurus spines poking out from both shoulders—already sports a splotch of butter. The crusts of her second sandwich remain, untouched, arranged like broken dinosaur bones on her plate.

"T. rex only likes the ones with ham. Not cheese. Cheese is yucky for 'ty-wan-o-sauruses'," Lily's declares, nose scrunched, index finger wagging.

Claire sets her fork down carefully. "What about stegosauruses?"

"Steggy eats leaves, Mummy." Lily's tone is patient and instructional. "You have to read more books."

Claire smiles. The tension coiled in her shoulders at the start of lunch begins to ease. The first meal had felt like a gauntlet—five hundred strangers, ambient noise loud enough to drown a thought, and the subtle but constant pitch and roll of the ship beneath her chair.

She glances around. Most tables are occupied. Nearby, two elderly men whisper conspiratorially over teacups. Farther down the aisle, a family in matching cruise shirts poses for a photo, the father trying to

9

wrangle two boys into submission with promises of 'no dessert tonight'.

Claire looks at her daughter, crumb-dusted and radiant, and feels a clean line of affection slice through the white noise.

Lily notices the pause. "Can we take a picture? Of me and Steggy and the tiny sandwich?"

"We sure can." Claire retrieves her phone and wipes a smear of something, possibly jam, off the lens. "Smile, Lily."

Lily bares her teeth like a T. rex instead, sandwich in one hand, her battered green dinosaur in the other. Claire snaps three photos in quick succession. Each one captures Lily's earnestness: unblinking eyes, defiant forward lean, the fierce resolve to be seen and remembered.

Lily demands inspection. Claire hands her the phone. Lily flicks through the images and nods in approval. "That's a good one." She pivots the screen to show Steggy, pressing its threadbare nose to the glass. "See? You look so nice."

"Very nice." Claire sets the phone face down on the table.

A server glides past with practiced grace. "How was lunch today?" Her accent is Baltic, and her name tag says LINDA.

Lily answers for both of them. "Roarsome! I liked the ham best. He liked the leaves." She hoists Steggy as proof.

The server's face softens. "I'm glad. Would you like some dessert, little dinosaur?"

Lily's eyes widen. "Is there chocolate pudding?"

"There is," Linda replies, "but only for good dinosaurs who finish their sandwiches."

Lily's face falls—just for a moment. Claire sees the calculation of effort versus reward. Lily squares her jaw and devours the sandwich halves with near-heroic determination.

Claire suppresses a laugh. She glances up at the faces around them. No one seems disturbed. In fact, the men at the next table watch with open amusement. One raises his mug in a silent toast. Claire returns a quick, sheepish smile. Not pity in their eyes, she notes, nostalgia and warmth.

She thinks of her own childhood lunches—stiff, formal affairs punctuated by reminders to sit up straight and use the correct fork. Her parents had cared deeply about "proper behaviour." Raising Lily on her own, the rules are different. Maybe there aren't any.

She watches as Lily offers Steggy a dignified bite of sandwich before finishing it herself. There is no pretence in Lily's world, only the instinct to share joy the moment it is felt. Claire makes a quiet promise to learn from that.

Linda returns with a bowl of chocolate pudding balanced on a doily-lined tray. "For the brave dinosaur," she says with a half-bow.

Lily claps, vibrating with excitement, then attacks the pudding with a spoon clutched in her fist.

Claire sips her water and lets the sounds of the room wash over her. The din is bearable now. She tunes into what matters—Lily's exclamations, the soft encouragements from passing staff, the muted pulse of ship engines underfoot.

She wonders if she'll get used to the motion, the public-ness of it all. Maybe. She's learning, too.

A few tables away, a phone rings. A child shrieks with delight. Lily, echoes it—twice as loud. Claire shushes her, half-heartedly, smiling.

The pudding vanishes. Lily licks the spoon, then wipes her mouth with the back of her hand. "All done, Mummy. Can we go look at the ocean now?"

"In a minute," Claire replies, checking her watch. There's nowhere they need to be. The whole afternoon stretches out like a blank page.

Lily wriggles out of her booster seat and lands on the floor with a triumphant "Ta-da!"

The two men at the next table chuckle. One leans over, smiling. "She's quite a handful."

"She is," Claire agrees, gathering her bag and Lily's tattered green friend. "But I wouldn't have it any other way."

Lily grabs her mother's hand, her own is small and sticky. Together they weave through the maze of tables and out into the corridor. Claire glances back. The buffet glows with a kind of diffuse warmth. She saves the image—Lily, Steggy, chocolate pudding; the sound of laughter over cutlery; the feel of her daughter's hand in hers, anchoring her to something solid and bright.

Outside, it's quieter. The carpet muffles Lily's footsteps as she hops along the inlaid pattern, counting the diamonds aloud. "One, two, three… so many!"

She stops at a porthole and presses her face to the glass. Beyond, the harbour stretches blue and boundless, churning with whitecaps.

Claire crouches beside her, arms around Lily's shoulders. For a moment, their reflections overlap in the glass. The same jaw. The same eyes. Except Lily's are unclouded by memory.

Claire feels a flush of pride—not just in Lily, but in herself. They made it this far—past the doubts, the worries, the well-meaning advice from everyone who thought they knew better.

"Ready to go exploring?" she asks.

Lily grins, baring dinosaur teeth. "Roar!"

It's answer enough. Claire stands, straightens her shoulders, and together they head down the corridor, side by side, their steps steady in the warm, comforting glow.

Lily's laughter carries across the kids' club. Claire watches as her daughter's shyness gives way to giggles and shrieks. A green-haired girl leads Lily by the hand, the two of them conspirators in the secret world of children. Claire captures the moment with her phone, the camera a shield against worry and doubt.

Petra approaches, explaining that it's open day today—embarkation day—and they will need to register to attend sessions starting tomorrow. Claire listens, unsure if she can let go, but promises to return. Lily runs to her, breathless and grinning.

"I have a new friend, Mummy!"

Claire holds her tight, afraid to blink and lose it all.

The kids' club is bright and loud—chaos wrapped in warmth. Claire hadn't been sure how Lily would handle it. So many children, all new and unfamiliar. But Lily surprises her, jumping into the fray with determination. Claire snaps photos, capturing each cautious step and then the joyous leap as Lily finds her place among the others. Her phone fills with images, tiny fragments of a day that she doesn't want to lose.

Petra smiles, watching the children. "You see?" she says, her Hungarian accent soft and melodic. "She is having fun. Tomorrow, we have so many activities planned."

Claire nods, hesitant. "I think we'll come back. Just... tomorrow." She clutches her phone like a lifeline, unsure she's ready to let go, even for a few hours. She doesn't register Lily yet, but she feels herself opening to the idea.

"Mummy, can we stay?" Lily's eyes are wide, pleading. The green-haired girl waves, calling her back.

"Soon, sweetie," Claire says, smoothing her daughter's hair. "We'll come back tomorrow. Promise." She hopes Lily doesn't notice the reluctance she's trying to hide.

They eat lunch from a kiosk near the pool: burgers, fries, and a lemonade on the side.

The pool deck is crowded but inviting, the air filled with the sounds of splashing and laughter. Claire watches as Lily's small body arcs through the water, buoyed by a life jacket. Sunlight dances on the surface, and Claire can't stop taking pictures. Each click of the camera is a reassurance, a way to hold onto Lily's confidence as it blossoms before her eyes.

Lily squeals, delight mingling with mischief, as she kicks her legs and sends a wave splashing toward Claire.

"Mummy, I'm a fish!" she shouts, giggling.

Claire wipes water from her eyes, laughing. "A very wet fish," she replies, snapping another photo. Lily's face radiates pure joy, the weight of earlier fears washed away.

Other families play and relax nearby, their presence oddly comforting. Claire notices them, their togetherness reflecting something she thought she'd lost. A sense of belonging, slowly returning.

Lily climbs out of the pool, a bundle of dripping energy.

"Look, Mummy! I can jump!"

She doesn't wait for an answer, leaping back in, fearless and free.

Claire captures the moment, storing it away like treasure, a piece of happiness to revisit when doubt returns. The distance is closing, not just between her and Lily, but between her and a world she thought she no longer belonged to.

Mini-golf is an explosion of colour and laughter, each hole a new adventure. Claire struggles to keep up with the whirlwind that is Lily, who attacks the course with relentless enthusiasm. The putter is too long for her small hands, but she insists on doing it herself, undeterred by the challenge.

"Can I do it, Mummy? Can I do it?" Lily's voice is a constant stream of determination.

"Of course, you can," Claire assures her, bending down to help adjust her grip. She watches, heart swelling, as Lily swings with all her might and finally connects with the ball.

It wobbles its way toward the hole—a small but mighty victory.

"I did it! I did it!" Lily cheers, jumping up and down, the golf course her stage for triumph.

Claire's camera is never still, each photo a testament to Lily's spirit. She's creating a visual diary of their day. Every moment feels monumental. Every snapshot a story of where they've been and where they're going.

They explore the ship like it's a new world, Lily's excitement the map they follow. Claire documents it all: Lily conquering a giant chessboard where the pieces tower over her; darting through an arcade full of flashing lights and loud noise; leaving her mark with pink boots and dinosaur shirts.

Her stamina seems endless. Her joy unstoppable.

"Mummy, look at me! Look at me!" Lily's voice rings out like a song that Claire never tires of hearing.

She no longer feels out of place. Not here. Not with Lily. Not among the smiling families who nod as they pass, recognising her as part of something bigger.

Claire reclines on a deck chair, the world warm and bright, Lily's steady breathing a lullaby beside her. She scrolls through the day's photos; each image a time capsule, a moment she can't afford to lose.

Flashbacks rise like waves: relentless, deep. Bringing Lily home, her newborn eyes wide, already a mirror of her own. Celebrating a first birthday in quiet solitude, joy and loneliness braided together. Watching as her business grew, wondering if she'd ever fill the void left by a love that slipped away. She looks at Lily and sees their whole world.

The pictures blur into a montage of laughter and smiles, a day so perfect Claire can hardly believe it's hers. Behind each image lies a history; the path they've walked to reach this moment. So much she's had to release. So much she's had to learn to hold.

She pauses on a photo of Lily at the pool; her face lit with discovery. The image pulls her back, unbidden, to another kind of pool, another kind of light. A hospital room: sterile, stark. Holding Lily for the first time. The same place where he had left their relationship. She remembers the way he looked at her, or rather, how he didn't. A goodbye, spoken and final. His departure from their bond that preceded his departure from her life. A beginning, unexpected and entirely hers.

Lily was so small then, her weight almost nothing, her presence everything. Claire felt raw and unformed, her life cleaved into before and after. She brought Lily home, the nursery unpainted, the crib hastily assembled in the corner of her room. She paused at the apartment threshold, knowing this is the first step of a journey she was terrified to take alone.

She swipes to another image: Lily at mini-golf, her excitement echoing that first year. Just the two of them in the old apartment. Balloons. Cake. A birthday no one else would remember. Claire sang "Happy Birthday," her voice cracking. Lily beamed, smashing icing into her curls. Thomas the stuffed cat sat loyally by her side.

Claire wiped frosting from the floor, trying to ignore the hollow space in her heart. It was a celebration, and yet, the emptiness touched every corner. She hadn't expected to do this alone. Cradling Lily, she vowed her daughter would never feel the same absence that haunted her.

The images continue, a living chronology. Claire scrolls through, the years when everything felt impossible. She sees the day they moved into the new apartment, the one she found once her business grew. She remembers the long nights and early mornings, filling orders between feedings and naps, balancing exhaustion with resolve.

It took years of tight budgets and tighter schedules. At first, she hadn't realised she needed more than money, she needed independence, proof that she could build a life on her own. She remembers booking the cruise, her hands trembling with fear and exhilaration.

Each memory cuts sharp and deep. Claire feels them all at once— pride, grief, gratitude. She's built something real from the ruins of what could have been. Still, the ache remains for the family she imagined, for the certainty she once believed was hers.

She returns to the photo of Lily at mini-golf, her small hands gripping the putter. The image is a window to everything before. Lily, vibrant and fearless. Claire, reflected in her daughter's eyes, still learning to release dreams that never came true.

Beside her, Lily stirs, blinking in the soft light. She sits up, a sleepy smile spreading across her face, the afternoon sun painting her hair gold.

"Hi, Mummy," she says, her voice still heavy with dreams.

"Hi, sweetie," Claire replies, brushing a curl from her forehead. She looks at her daughter and sees not just the three years of Lily's life, but a lifetime of love and struggle in that tiny frame. "Did you have a good nap?"

Lily nods, stretching, Thomas still clutched tight. "I dreamed about dinosaurs."

"Of course, you did," Claire laughs, her heart swelling. The sound of her own joy surprises her, like hearing a melody she'd forgotten.

Lily stands, shaking off sleep, already ready for the next adventure. "Can we play more, Mummy?"

"Always," Claire promises, packing away the memories she'd just unpacked, holding each one close.

Lily leaps into her arms, her energy infectious, her spirit unstoppable. Claire kisses her cheek, a gesture rich with meaning. The day isn't over. Neither is their journey.

She carries Lily across the deck, her steps lighter than they've been in years. The past still lives within her, the dreams that never came true still echo but they no longer define her.

She's something new, something more. And so is Lily.

Claire watches the sea—vast, uncharted—as Lily chatters in her ear, a symphony of childhood and possibility. She feels the truth of where they've been, the promise of what's ahead. And in this moment, it is enough.

They linger over dinner at the buffet, Lily's cheeks flushed from sun and excitement, Claire watching the life and energy pour out of her like an endless fountain. She wonders how much more her heart can hold, how much more the universe can give before it takes away. But she doesn't dwell, not tonight, not when everything feels so complete.

The sun dips low, spilling gold across the deck and painting the world with a light that exists only for this moment. Claire captures it with a click: Lily in her dinosaur sundress, her hair bobble bright against dark curls. The perfect end to a perfect day. She clings to the memory as they return to their cabin.

Lily's eyes droop. She leans into Claire, soft and pliable, her tiredness a warm weight. Claire tucks her in, pulling the covers tight, Thomas never leaving her side.

"I love you, Mummy," Lily whispers, a half-asleep confession that fills the room.

"I love you too, sweetheart," Claire replies, brushing her a kiss to her forehead. She watches her daughter drift into dreams, her own heart light and untethered, floating on the promise of what might come.

Claire steps onto the balcony again, the night air cool and bracing. She gazes at the horizon, at the water stretching endlessly, like a road without a map. It excites her now. A testament to how far she's come, to the resilience she's discovered within herself.

The ship's gentle sway rocks her, its motion a lullaby, the waves a soothing chant. Claire breathes deeply, taking it all in, a part of something greater than herself. She's learning to let go, to trust that everything won't fall apart the moment she relaxes her grip.

She opens her phone; the screen lights stark against the dusk. The photos are vibrant, alive—capturing Lily's laughter, Claire's joy. A narrative she once believed could never be hers. The weight of it is immense, but it's a weight she carries gladly.

Gratitude wells up inside her, fierce and insistent. It spreads, warm and unexpected, a counterpoint to the dark spots of her past. Claire is finally ready to dream beyond what she thought she deserved, beyond the walls she'd built to protect her heart.

She scrolls back, through birthdays and milestones. Lily's first steps, a tottering triumph. Her second birthday: laughter, cake, new friends. The first day of daycare: a tiny backpack, a smile stayed strong, even when Claire's didn't.

Each image is precious, a testament to their journey. Claire can trace the arc of their love, the line they've drawn through time and hardship, unwavering even when she couldn't see where it led.

The setting sun reflects off her phone, casting a soft glow across the images. She looks at one last photo of Lily's smiling face, its radiance nearly blinding. It's a beacon. A promise. Of more days like this.

She closes her eyes, letting the moment settle in her bones. Uncertainty lingers, soft and familiar, but now overlaid with the colours of hope. Claire is buoyant, lifted by the life she's built, ready to meet what comes next.

Her daughter sleeps soundly. The ship moves steadily. Claire's heart beats in time with it all. She steps inside, leaving the vastness behind and drawing close to what's hers.

CHAPTER THREE

Breakfast the next morning is on the balcony, the early sun dazzling, the air cool and salted. Lily eats 'tiny toast' with crumbed fingers and excited squeals, an explorer in dinosaur pyjamas, pointing at seagulls, ships, and a world made new.

Claire watches, holding these moments like secrets. The horizon stretches before her promising everything she once believed was lost. Time feels fluid, like the ocean, endless and kind.

"Look, Mummy, look!" Lily's voice pulls her back, and Claire laughs at the fierce joy in every gesture. Her daughter is life, uncontained. They talk about the day's adventures, Claire struggling to keep pace with Lily's whirlwind of ideas. She mentions the art class, and Lily interrupts with her own agenda.

"We have to see sea dinosaurs! And and and..." Her voice is bright and relentless.

Claire smiles, the feeling soft unfamiliar, like the morning itself.

"You think we'll find sea dinosaurs?" she asks tucking Lily's hair behind her ears. The day feels wide open, like the horizon, like the love she once locked away. Lily's face is a map of excitement, traces of crumbs still clinging to her cheeks. She's all motion, a bundle of plans and exclamation points.

"Yes yes yes," Lily says, words almost colliding.

Claire breathes it in, this joy, this light. She watches Lily's eyes sparkle with the reflection of the sea. This is happiness, she thinks. Unexpected. Pure.

The ship's rhythm lulls her thoughts. She watches Lily devour her breakfast with the appetite of a pirate.

"Careful, sweetie," she says as crumbs scatter across the deck, but Lily is too enraptured to notice. She stands on her chair, her small hand shielding her eyes as she scans the horizon. Her dinosaur pyjamas hang loose on her thin frame. Claire watches the bounce of her curls with the ship's sway and aches to remember it all, every second of this trip, of this day.

It's been so long since she let herself believe in this.

"We're going to see everything," Lily insists, a declaration of truth.

Claire nods, letting herself be pulled into the tide of her daughter's enthusiasm.

"We're going to see everything," she echoes, knowing the promise is for both of them. She watches the seagulls drift alongside and Lily as she conquers the morning. The breeze carries the scent of salt and something else—possibility.

"And the pool, Mummy?" Lily adds, eyes wide, demanding the world.

Claire nods again, catching Lily's spark.

The breakfast tray is nearly empty, the remnants of their meal a quiet testament to Lily's spirit. Claire takes a piece of croissant, bites into the sweetness, tastes the memory of her own joy. She leans back, watching Lily's mind leap from the sea to the art class to the pool and back again.

She doesn't know how Lily holds so much energy, so much joy. She doesn't know how she got so lucky.

"It's roarsome, Mummy," Lily declares.

Claire looks out over the vast ocean and sees their life reflected there —the future as bright as her daughter's laughter.

She doesn't notice the shadow creeping at the edges of her world. Doesn't see the loose thread about to be pulled. Right now, she only sees Lily, this moment, this perfect day.

"It's roarsome," she agrees, her voice soft with love and the feeling of everything finally being right. The horizon stretches out, endless and welcoming. The morning sun glints off the water, and the future opens wide.

One of the bars is hosting a parent-child art class. It's a world of cheerful chaos, bursting with children's voices. Paint-spattered smocks and smudged hands fill the room. Claire helps Lily into a chair, settling her with brushes and a colourful palette. She watches Lily dive in, her face a study in concentration as her paintbrush dances across the page. It becomes a green-and-blue tangle, wild and unexpected, the way children see the world.

"It's a sea dinosaur," Lily declares, her enthusiasm bigger than the creature itself. Other kids look over, curious. Claire sees the old shyness melt away as Lily shares dinosaur stories and new friendships begin to form.

Paint streaks Lily's cheeks like war paint, and Claire smiles at her daughter's bright determination. She helps wash small brushes and cups, marvelling at the vibrant chaos. She watches as Lily commands attention, her voice full of certainty.

"Triceratops have THREE HORNS," Lily shouts, making sure no one can miss it. Other parents nod and smile at Claire, charmed by Lily's energy and the sheer volume of her dinosaur facts.

"And and and... they have frills too!"

Claire laughs, hears the social barriers crumble, and knows this moment matters more than she can say.

Adam, leading today's activity, circles the room, and pauses to admire Lily's creation. He places his hand on her shoulder.

"What a wonderful imagination!" he says. Lily beams with pride.

"It has a happy face!" she declares, pointing to a wide, yellow smile that takes up half the page. Claire feels the warmth of the compliment; sees it light up her daughter's eyes. The paper is full of colour and life, blue and green and purple and orange, and something like a dinosaur but more like a dream.

Lily is full of words, the excitement spilling out, pure and sweet.

"It's for our cabin!"

Claire takes a moment, lets the happiness rise and swell. This is how far Lily has come, from the shy days to these bright bursts of confidence. Claire remembers the shy child, the worry that Lily might be like her: too afraid to reach out. But now Lily is here, in the centre of it all.

Claire helps her gather the supplies and makes sure the precious painting is safe and dry. It means everything—this triumph, this courage.

"Can we hang it up now?" Lily asks, her voice insistent. "Please, Mummy, right now right now right now!"

Claire relents, too filled with love to say no. She hugs Lily close, kisses her paint-smudged face.

"Alright," she says. "Let's hang it up."

They leave the room with Lily's new masterpiece, their shoes tapping down the corridor like a song. Other children call goodbye, and Lily waves, her face bright, full of hope and plans.

They reach the cabin, and Claire finds tape to stick the art to the wall. Lily arranges it with the seriousness only a three-year-old can muster. She stands back, hands on hips, surveying the transformation of the room into their own gallery.

"It's roarsome!" Lily announces, running in circles, the energy of the morning carrying her away. Claire watches, breathless with pride, swept up in the speed of Lily's spirit. She holds these seconds tight, too afraid to blink.

She remembers Lily's first steps into daycare, how her heart ached, but how Lily took off like a shot.

"I knew you'd like it," Claire says, her words barely carrying above the storm of her own emotion.

She sees the art on the wall, the vivid proof of Lily's certainty, of her place in the world, and knows how much that means.

Lily can't stop talking. Her words tumble out, tripping over themselves like a race. The painting, the children, the compliments—each thread woven into the story of her day.

"I told them about Steggy! I told them everything!" Her eyes shine, and Claire wonders if she's ever felt this proud, this full of love.

"You did, sweetie," Claire replies, her voice thick with feeling, filled with everything they are and everything they've been through.

This is love, she thinks. More than anything she dreamed. It is Lily. It is life. And it's about to change.

The café is quiet and intimate. A small world suspended between ocean and sky. The windows frame the sea, each wave a gentle reminder of the vastness beyond. Claire watches Lily climb onto a chair, determined to order for herself, to be bigger than her three years. The menu wobbles in her hands like a paper giant—but she's firm: a grown-up sandwich, please, not the kiddie one. Claire laughs, loving her daughter's certainty. They sit close, the table a stage for Lily's animated theories. Crumbs scatter as she gestures, her words as wild and unexpected as the sea dinosaurs she imagines.

"Mummy, did you know that 'plee-zee-o-saurus' could swim super deep?" Lily asks, her eyes wide with possibility. Claire smiles, encouraging Lily's enthusiasm. She asks questions, feeding her imagination. "What if they're still down there?" Lily continues, almost breathless, her voice rising with each sentence. Claire reaches across, gently touching Lily's hand, grounding her excitement. She loves these talks; loves the way her daughter's mind races ahead. A nearby elderly couple looks over, smiling at the scene. Claire feels noticed, connected, part of a world that had seemed unreachable for so long.

Lily tackles her sandwich with determination, her hands barely able to hold the grown-up choice. She laughs as the filling spills onto her plate, unconcerned about the mess, only the adventure. Claire watches, her heart full, seeing the fearlessness she wishes she had.

"It's too big!" Lily giggles, crumbs flying. Claire leans in, savouring every moment, tasting joy and contentment with every bite. She can't believe this is hers, this life, this happiness. She can almost touch its fragility, almost feel the edges starting to fray, but she pushes that fear away.

"I think it's roarsome, Mummy," Lily declares, still fighting with the sandwich but refusing to let it win. Her face is smeared with dressing, her smile wide and unconcerned. Claire wipes her chin, laughs softly, catching the eyes of the other diners sharing the moment. It feels new, this being seen, this belonging. "Tell me more about the dinosaurs," Claire prompts, wanting to stretch the seconds into forever. Lily obliges, her theories coming faster than Claire can follow. Her hands wave, the whole café a witness to her spirited narration.

Claire notices the volume, and tries to rein it in, her voice gentle. "Maybe not so loud, sweetie." But she's not upset, not when she sees Lily so alive, so unguarded. Lily nods, her expression serious before launching back into stories of undersea adventures. "Did you know there's a mosasaurus?" Lily asks, not waiting for an answer. "He's big and he's fast and maybe he's out there!" Claire watches her daughter's determination, sees the light in her eyes and wonders if she was ever that certain, that bold.

Her own childhood creeps into the edges of her thoughts, unbidden memories of being small and timid, never daring to be this sure. She marvels at Lily; at the strength she sees in someone so young. It awes her, the way Lily trusts the world not to let her fall. Claire feels old fears stir but clings to the moment, knowing it might be the best one she'll ever have.

The sandwich is finally conquered; crumbs scattered like a map of Lily's spirited effort. "I did it!" she shouts, triumphant and uncontained. Claire smiles, wipes sauce from Lily's fingers, feels the echo of her daughter's voice in her heart. They share the last of the meal, Claire's love stretching across the table, across time. It is a new kind of freedom, fragile and fleeting, but she holds it close, unwilling to let go.

* * *

The pool is a kaleidoscope of summer and sound. Claire holds Lily's hand as they find a spot to leave their things, the air thick with chlorine and excitement. Children splash, the deck a blur of wet footprints and laughter.

"Ready, sweetie?" Claire asks, adjusting Lily's floaties.

"I'm ready I'm ready!" Lily replies, a tornado in a pink bathing suit. They jump in, water crashing around them. Claire stays close, protective even in play. Lily kicks and laughs, a bright echo that draws smiles.

"I'm a dinosaur!" she shouts, fierce and fearless. Claire teaches her to swim, and to trust.

Claire wades through the shallow end, cool water swirling around her waist as Lily kicks beside her, arms flailing with wild joy. The partially inflated floaties make her clumsy, but she doesn't care, she's laughing, cheeks flushed, hair slicked to her forehead.

Claire smiles. For the first time in days, her muscles start to unknot. The sun reflects off the surface in shimmering waves, the buzz of holiday chatter blurring into background noise.

"Careful," she says as Lily lunges toward a patch of sunlight.

"I'm a dolphin!" Lily squeals, disappearing beneath the water with a splash.

Claire laughs. It feels good—real.

She watches the ripples fan out.

And then they settle.

Too quickly.

"Lily?"

No answer.

Claire turns in a slow circle. The water's clear, shallow. Empty.

"Lily?" Her voice sharpens. She scans the pool, no tiny head, no pink floaties. Her heart surges into her throat.

She turns around again. Faster. Calling louder now. "Lily!"

Nothing.

Then—

A giggle.

Claire turns. Lily's crouched just outside the pool, behind the towel rack, wrapped in a striped towel like a cape, eyes bright with mischief.

"You didn't see me get out!" she beams.

Claire rushes to the edge, breathing hard, water streaming off her arms. She hoists herself out, grabs Lily close.

"Don't do that," she whispers, clutching her. "You scared me."

Lily snickers, clearly proud of herself. "I was hiding like a turtle!"

Claire forces a laugh, presses her lips to Lily's damp forehead.

But her hands won't stop shaking.

Claire helps her rinse off, holding her daughter's hand as they head to the showers. Lily chatters nonstop, the words tumbling over themselves in excitement.

"Did you see me? Did you see me swim?"

Claire wraps Lily in a fluffy towel, her voice soft and full.

"I saw you, sweetie. You were amazing." She kisses Lily's wet curls, holds her close, never wanting to let go. The exhaustion of the day hits, but it's the best kind of tired.

"I swam like a champion dinosaur," Lily insists, her eyes bright even as they begin to droop. Claire laughs, a sound so free and rare she barely recognises it as her own. They head back to the cabin, the ship a cradle that rocks them gently. Lily holds Claire's hand, her voice still strong but her steps slower. The promise of tomorrow is in her eyes, but Claire knows today is what matters. She feels the old fears loosen their grip, feels herself floating on the joy of Lily's presence. It's all she's ever wanted.

They are back in the cabin, wrapped in the ship's soft lullaby. Claire sits with Lily on the balcony, pizza boxes open, the air fragrant with cheese and possibility. The sun sinks lower, turning the sea to gold.

"What was the best part?" Claire asks, brushing sauce from Lily's chin, hearing her own voice gentle and full. Lily can't decide, her words colliding—everything important all at once.

"The pool and the dinosaurs and the paint and my friends!" She stops for breath, a rare moment of quiet before the day catches her again. It's as close as they've ever been.

"I think you had a roarsome day," Claire says, trying to keep up with Lily's breathless recounting. Her daughter is full of stories and energy, unwilling to let exhaustion claim her yet. Claire listens, letting the words wrap around her like a blanket. She feels safe, more than she ever thought she could. The pizza disappears, one slice after another. Claire notices the first stars and the first twinkling lights of the ship as night falls. She sees the tiredness growing behind Lily's excitement.

"And the man who likes dinosaurs!" Lily adds, her face bright with every remembered detail. "Remember, Mummy? At the painting." Her voice is eager, demanding agreement, too big to ignore.

"I remember," Claire assures her, smiling at the persistence. She knows these moments won't last, changing as quickly as they come. She watches the sunset's glow fade, watches Lily's expressions, her energy slowing at last. The comfort of it all fills her with an unfamiliar peace.

Lily stands, holding a piece of pizza aloft like a victory flag. "Tomorrow I'm going to tell him more about Steggy!" She grins, convinced the new friends will be forever. Claire thinks of the kids' club, of letting go even for a little while. It's not easy, but maybe, just maybe, she's ready.

"Would you like that?" Claire asks, her voice betraying more uncertainty than she means. "Would you like to go play at kids' club tomorrow?"

Lily nods, sauce on her cheeks, hope in her eyes. Claire wipes her face, laughs, a sound that feels free and unafraid. "I love you, sweetie," she says, the words carrying all that she can't express. Lily wiggles into her lap, warm and soft, her last burst of energy holding her awake. "I love you too, Mummy," she replies, her voice still strong but edged with sleepiness. Claire sees the day catching up, sees Lily finally letting tiredness take hold.

"I had a roarsome day," Lily repeats, quieter now, as if saying it less loudly might make it last longer. Claire hugs her, feeling the shape of her daughter's contentment, her own heart echoing it. She thinks of how much has changed, how much Lily has changed her. The night deepens, the horizon stretching—endless and full. She sees the shadow at the edges of her perfect world, but it doesn't touch her yet.

It's the happiest she's ever been, and she's too in love with this life to see anything else. Claire closes her eyes, taking in the sweetness of the moment.

"Let's see what tomorrow brings," she says, already certain it will be as wonderful as today. She watches Lily's tired, happy face and wonders if her heart can hold more. She wonders what she did to deserve this love. She wonders what waits, just beyond.

Lily's eyes droop, heavy with sleep and the day's fullness. Claire tucks her in, Thomas nestled beside her, the cabin dim and peaceful. A nightlight casts gentle dinosaur shadows on the wall.

"More sea dinosaurs tomorrow?" Lily whispers, her voice soft, an echo of her waking self. Claire smooths her curls and kisses her cheek.

"More adventures," she promises, the words a lullaby, fierce in their certainty. Lily's breathing steadies, soft and even. Claire watches, holding the moment close, unaware of the storm waiting beyond. Right now, it's perfect. It's everything. It's enough.

Lily's dinosaur pyjamas feel soft against the covers, her small body snug and safe. Claire sits by the bed, listening to the ship's gentle hum. A lullaby for them both. She watches the slow rise and fall of Lily's chest, feeling the same rhythm in her heart. It amazes her, the life they've built, the love that's grown around them.

"I love you, Mummy," Lily mumbles, half-asleep, but Claire hears it, feels it, holds it like a promise. She feels complete, as if nothing can touch them, nothing can break this spell.

She stays by the bed, afraid to move, afraid to miss a single second of Lily's dreaming face. Her own dreams were once so small, so fragile. Now they are as big as Lily, as bright as the love filling the cabin. She sees their perfect day, unfolding again and again, each moment a piece of happiness she never thought she'd own. She remembers the early years, the struggle, the way she grew alongside her daughter. Every step was with it.

Claire thinks of all they've done, the laughter, the closeness. She recalls the art class, the pool, the lunch, the pizza on the balcony. She remembers Lily's stories, her breathless excitement, her sleepy confessions. It spins around her, a beautiful dance. It's what she wished for, what she fought for.

She trusts it enough to dream again. Claire rises, watching Lily sleep, feeling the pull of the horizon beyond the cabin walls. It's as close as they've ever been, as sure as she's ever felt. She kisses Lily's forehead—the soft warmth a beacon in the dim light. She feels safe. She feels home. She steps onto the balcony, letting the night wrap around her. The ocean is dark and vast, the ship's motion a gentle reassurance.

Claire stands alone, letting herself feel the vastness of the world, the vastness of their love. She sees the future as an open sea, endless, uncharted. She doesn't know what's coming, can't see the change waiting just beyond her vision. Right now, it's all she wanted, all she worked for. She takes it in, feeling the thrill of hope.

"Let's see what tomorrow brings," she whispers into the night, believing it will be bright, believing it will be theirs.

She returns to the cabin and closes the door on the uncertainty outside. Claire takes one last look at Lily, watching the peace of her daughter's sleep, the rise and fall of her small body, the trust in it. She sees the art on the wall, the colours vivid and new, a reminder of their perfect day. She holds onto it, wraps herself in the memory. She knows it might never be like this again, but she believes it will be.

CHAPTER FOUR

Claire holds Lily's small hand as if the world might pull her away. Her daughter's breathing slows; curls spill onto the pillow like ripples of brown water. Claire pulls the blanket tight, careful not to disturb her. It's the happiest she's ever been, but she can't let herself trust it, can't let herself blink. Her anxiety, persistent since she found out she was pregnant with Lily, has finally begun to wane. Claire sits, still, listening to the ship and Lily's soft breaths. She's never felt so deeply in love with this life.

A flyer catches her eye: a notice for an Elton John tribute show in the ship's theatre. She hesitates, desire battling instinct.

One hour, she reads. She looks at Lily, back at the paper, back at Lily. The debate rages inside her, protective instincts alive like a living thing. She's never left Lily alone on the ship. Never imagined she would. The thought is terrifying and thrilling all at once.

One hour, she thinks again. The words pull at her, seductive. A chance to be more than just a mother. But can she really do it? Can she leave Lily here? Claire's fingers tremble on the flyer, the tension pulling her in two.

Lily shifts, hugging Thomas closer. Claire waits; afraid her daughter's dreams might shatter. But Lily stays asleep, so perfectly, so peacefully. Claire's heart aches with love and fear. She reaches out, strokes the soft curls, feels Lily's breath, soft and sure. It eases the tightness in her chest, a little. She wonders if she could have this—just this one thing. She imagines slipping back before Lily even stirs, before anything changes, before she loses it all.

Her own needs creep into the edges of her thoughts. She sees them like shadows, half-forgotten. She can't remember the last time she did something like this. Something that was hers alone. She can't remember wanting it so much. Claire's hand drops to her side; the paper clutched like a secret. She lets the longing wash over her, a guilty thrill. It's only an hour. Lily won't even know. She'll never have to know.

Claire stands, watching Lily, the rise and fall of her small chest. She's never seen anything more beautiful, more fragile. But she has to do this, for herself. The decision is a tremor, a ripple, but it's there. She lets it take shape; lets it steady her. She's going to the show. She will be back before Lily misses her. Claire repeats it like a mantra, her own kind of lullaby.

Guilt blooms, but Claire pushes it down, burying it under the weight of her own need. It's a risk, but it feels manageable. Just this once. Just this one time. She takes a deep breath, lets it out, filling the room with resolve. Her heart pounds with the enormity of it, with the terrible excitement. But she's decided. She holds the paper like a lifeline, clinging to the possibility of more.

One hour, she tells herself, eyes locked on Lily. She sits on the bed, sitting with her uncertainty. The room is full of the ship's hum, the sound of Lily's dreams. Claire's doubt softens, making room for the indulgence. It's an experiment, a taste of something long denied. She lets herself imagine the freedom, the weightless feeling of being away. She lets herself believe she can do this.

Lily stirs, but it's only a murmur, a tiny movement. Claire feels her own heart echo the quiet, echo the slow, even breaths. She can almost see herself at the show, a person she hasn't been in years. A person she might want to be again. Claire closes her eyes, seeing Lily's sleeping face, imprinting it on her mind. Her choice is fragile, new, but it holds. She's doing this. She's really doing it.

Claire sets the flyer down, letting the temptation rest. She scans the room with methodical precision, ensuring the universe won't take this from her. She checks the balcony door's child lock, tugging it twice. The main door follows, a cautious pull. Satisfied it's too heavy for Lily's hands. Her eyes sweep the room, a searchlight. Her hand adjusts the nightlight, a lighthouse casting comfort. Blues and beiges mingle with the ship's gentle sway. Claire feels the floor beneath her feet, the nerves beneath her resolve. Returning to Lily's side, she brushes a curl, and whispers, "Sleep well, sweetheart."

Her heart skips at the words, at the audacity of her own voice. She pulls the balcony door again, noting the distance from the ground to the lock. There's no way Lily could reach it. No chances. No letting her guard down. Excitement and terror tremble through her. Claire breathes deep, watches Lily's soft breathing, feels the familiar fears grip her heart. She fights them back, holding certainty tight. One hour, she thinks. Only an hour. What could possibly happen?

She turns to the corridor door, the barrier between Lily and the vastness of the ship. Her hand grips the handle and pulls. The weight is satisfying—a reassurance that her daughter is safe, that she's still a good mother. Claire releases it, hears the latch catch with a solid thud. Instincts battle resolve, a storm of worry and hope. She breathes, slow and measured, anchoring herself to the moment. Doubts creep in, uninvited. She pushes them away, forcing herself to believe this will be okay.

She goes to Lily, needing one more touch, one more connection before she trusting herself to leave. Her hand brushes the soft curls from her daughter's forehead. Lily murmurs, a tiny sound that tightens Claire's chest. She's going to the show. She tells herself again and again, as if repetition will make it true, as if saying it will make her brave. Claire bends down, kisses Lily, the warmth of it more than she can bear. She whispers, softer than breath, "Mummy will be back before you know it."

Like a spell, a promise. Claire stands, watches Lily sleep, feels the enormity of what she's about to do. She knows she'll be back, knows this is as safe as she can make it. But the fear nags. A familiar companion she wishes to leave behind. She watches Lily's chest rise and fall, it fills and overwhelms her. Claire turns to the door, one last look, one last second to hold on. She steps out, leaving her heart behind. The lock clicks, firm and final.

Claire makes her way down the ship's long hallways, as if walking could push away the guilt. The harsh fluorescent lighting casts a sterile glow. She feels the ship sway beneath her feet, matching the nerves fluttering inside her. Other passengers pass by, dressed in evening attire, the embodiment of her doubts. Claire feels out of place, painfully self-conscious. She checks her watch, calculating the time away from Lily. The enormity of her choice grips her, almost turning her back. But she keeps going, the muffled sound of pre-show music growing louder. She repeats her mantra, as if it could make the decision less impossible.

Each step pulls at her, a tether stretched too thin. Claire notices the happy couples, the parents who have left their children behind without a second thought. She wonders if she's the only one who feels this torn, this alone in a sea of people. The ship's corridors seem endless, each turn like a test of her resolve. Her heart races, loud and insistent. Claire feels like an intruder in her own life, like she's stealing something she doesn't deserve.

She checks her watch again, frantic; the numbers blurring together. How long since she left the cabin? How much longer can she bear this? Claire almost turns back, almost runs. But she thinks of the flyer—the promise of something more, something hers. Determination keeps her moving, a small, fragile spark. She clings to it, even as her fears claw at her. One hour, she whispers in her mind. One hour.

The music seeps through the walls, a distant rhythm pulling her forward. Claire's steps quicken, her own kind of march, her own kind of rebellion. She wants this, wants to remember how it feels to be someone else. Someone besides Lily's mother. But the price feels too high, too dangerous. Doubt shadows her, but she pushes on, trying to outpace the weight of what she's doing.

Claire reaches the theatre, a cavernous space that makes her feel both small and insignificant. The tiered seating stretches out, the rich burgundy curtains a stark contrast to the clinical hallways. The grandeur of it all fills her with awe—and fear. She's forgotten how to be part of this world, forgotten how to belong. Her excitement battles guilt in an uneasy truce that leaves her breathless.

She finds a seat at the back, as close to the exit as possible. Claire sits, her body taut with the strain of her decision. She can't believe she's here, can't believe she's followed through. The plush seat is a strange luxury, a curious comfort. She sinks into it, letting herself feel both thrill and terror. Her eyes flick to the door—her escape route. But she stays, holding herself to the choice.

The chatter of the audience fades; a hush settles over the room. Claire feels the ship's hum even here, feels her heart echo it. The lights dim gradually, and the first notes of "Rocket Man" fill the air. The music wraps around her, unfamiliar but welcome. Claire lets herself relax, the tension easing just enough. She's here, she's doing this.

Spotlights illuminate the stage, a burst of colour and sound. Claire's worries shrink, just for a moment. She holds onto the image of Lily's sleeping face, holds onto the promise that this is possible. It's freedom. It's fear. It's more than she ever thought she'd dare. Claire watches the show, her heart divided, her life on the edge of something unpredictable.

CHAPTER FIVE

Claire's thoughts drift like confetti amid the theatre's noise. Each song cuts a tether, lifting her away from the anxious, anchored mother she's always been. The freedom tastes sharp, strange, and sweet. The music stuns her, loud as longing, full of abandon and reckless joy. For the first time, she nearly remembers how to feel like herself. The performer croons his way through "Goodbye Yellow Brick Road," every word and note heavy with nostalgia. Claire lets the music swell, rising like a swell against the life she's trying to forget.

The theatre holds her in its dim glow, a plush cocoon of red seats and shadows. The crowd's excitement wraps around her, amplifying the release. It's another world, a universe away from Lily and the constant tug of worry. Claire sinks into the softness, into the anonymity of being one among many. She feels the music vibrate through her chest, a soothing pulse syncing with her heartbeat. The ship's motion, usually a reminder, now feels distant and unimportant. She loses herself in the moment, letting the rare indulgence wash over her.

Claire wonders if it will always feel this strange to let go, if the weightlessness will ever stop feeling like a betrayal. But for now, she leans into it, savouring the release. Her mind, usually cluttered with fear and love, begins to clear. The final note fades into silence, and the room erupts in applause. The performer offers a tired, grateful smile and a quiet bow, then steps offstage, swallowed by the dark wings.

Claire claps with the crowd, but her hands slow before the rest. Around her, people remain seated, waiting, hopeful, maybe, or just unwilling to break the spell.

But for Claire, the moment has shifted.

It's the space after the set, before the encore, before anyone knows the night is truly over. A breath held too long.

Her chest tightens. She should go.

She checks her watch. Forty-seven minutes. Not even an hour stolen, but it feels like something.

The exit signs glow faintly, unnoticed by most.

She stands and walks toward them, swift and sure, the noise of the crowd dulling behind her.

She doesn't wait to see if the performer returns.

She's already halfway to the cabin in her mind.

The world tilts with Claire's hurry, each step like a leap into thin air. She races for the exit, her mind already at the cabin, but the ship jerks her sideways—a sudden betrayal. Her shoe catches on the stair carpet. She reaches for anything to steady herself, but it's too fast. Her purse flies from her grip, its contents scattering like a constellation around her. The ground falls away. Then crashes back with a hard edge. A dizzying blur. The last thing she feels is the sharp pain when her head hits the floor and the echoing sound of the encore fading like a dream.

Help. Help. Her voice? Someone else's? A rumble of panic from the crowd. A man shouts and a woman cries. Claire can't tell where she is anymore. It's all noise, pain, and sickening dark, and she feels herself slipping away.

Her own name. Lily. Her mind clings to it, a desperate last hold. Then even that fades, the dark like water, like drowning. She drifts in it, through it, away from it. Far, far away.

CHAPTER SIX

A flash of colour, then the sterile white of a room that isn't hers. Claire's mind scrambles for purchase; Lily's name forms like a cry in her throat. She blinks against the light, against the pain. A bandage pulls at her temple. Her fingers grip thin blankets, and her breath quickens. Dizzy and terrified, Claire sits up. Memory floods back with brutal speed.

A doctor appears, calm and composed, her voice cutting through Claire's haze. "You fell down the theatre stairs."

Claire remembers the fall—the terrible arc, the name she'd held like a lifeline: Lily.

"Where am I?" Her voice is strained.

"The ship's medical bay," the doctor replies, her tone practiced, reassuring. "I'm Dr. Reyes. You're going to be alright."

Claire's heart hammers, each beat loud as a drum. "How long have I been here?"

Dr. Reyes glances at her clipboard. "You lost consciousness after your fall. Possible mild concussion. We just need to observe you for a few hours." She completes her physical exam.

The words cut sharp and unbearable. Hours stretch wide, impossible. Lily, alone. Claire sees the cabin in her mind, Lily's small form, trusting and unaware. Her fingers twist the blanket, her panic rising like floodwater.

"You'll be fine," Dr. Reyes assures, eyes on Claire's face. "I know you want to leave, but—"

"But I can't stay," Claire blurts out, the desperation raw in her voice. Dizziness swells; the room tilts dangerously.

Dr. Reyes frowns, watching Claire's agitation and nervous hands. "Is someone waiting for you? Family?"

The question hangs heavy. Claire avoids it, avoids the doctor's eyes. She's made it this far; she can't risk everything now. "I—no," Claire lies, a tremor in the word. Thoughts circle back to Lily, the fear a gnawing thing. Vision blurs, unsteady as her heart. "My daughter," she adds reluctantly.

Dr. Reyes hesitates; her expression softens. "Worried about the kids' club hours? You'll be out before they close at two. There's an hourly charge after ten, but we can waive it because you're here."

Relief strikes like electricity, propelling Claire's mind. She nods, frantic. "Yes, yes. That's it." She clutches at the reassurance, clutches at anything that will get her back faster.

"I'll have you sign a release form," Dr. Reyes says, the words like an opening door. "But you must be careful. Rest. Watch for signs of—"

"Thank you," Claire interrupts, already halfway to the cabin in her mind. Back with Lily.

Dr. Reyes leaves the forms and a pen on Claire's lap, the papers a bridge to freedom. Claire grabs them, her hands shaking with urgency. She fills in the blanks, the letters uneven and hurried. Her breath comes fast, too fast.

Dr. Reyes returns, watching Claire struggle with the pen. "Take it easy," she warns, concerned.

Claire barely hears. The need to leave consumes everything else. She pushes the papers toward Dr. Reyes; each second is an eternity.

Dr. Reyes signs off, her own movements calm and measured. "Keep an eye on these symptoms," she advises, her voice distant to Claire's single-minded focus. "Headaches, nausea, dizziness—"

Claire nods, barely; her world a pinpoint. "I will."

The words are rote, a ritual she can't bother to attend. She swings her legs over the bed's side; the floor is a challenge she won't refuse. Gripping the bed rail, she fights the rush of blood and pain. Unsteady, her body a foreign thing, but she's standing. Moving. Her heart pounds with each step, the beat matching her thoughts. Lily, Lily, Lily.

Her purse snags on the door handle as she pulls it open. The white walls close in around her. Claire breathes, just once, then leaves the room—and everything but Lily—behind.

The ship's corridors stretch before her, endless as doubt. Claire rushes through them, ignoring the pain, the dizziness, the body that refuses to obey. Panic propels her forward. Love propels her forward. She clutches the wall for balance, indifferent to the stares of strangers. Her mind races—lost time, Lily, what she'll find. A young mother with a baby passes by, and Claire can't breathe, can't bear the thought of never seeing Lily again. She reaches her cabin, trembling hands fumbling with the key. Seconds stretch into eternity. Fear feels eternal.

She lurches away from the wall, forcing herself faster. Each step sends a jagged echo through her skull, a reminder of the fall, of how swiftly everything can change. The ship's gentle sway twists into a monster, turning the floor to liquid, blurring the corridor. She can hardly tell where she is or isn't—but it doesn't matter. Only Lily matters.

Her purse clasp snags on her sleeve as she searches for her sail pass card, tugging at her, feeling her panic. It dangles like a shackle. A reminder of the hours she's lost, the fear filling every second. She nearly stumbles as a couple passes, their eyes wide with concern. Claire knows how she must look; knows the terror she cannot hide. She pushes on—pain, dizziness, all nothing compared to the hollow ache of being away.

Her breath comes in ragged bursts; her heart a relentless drum. She can't remember how long she's been gone. She can't remember what it feels like to not be desperate. Only one thought, one need, keeps her moving. She must see Lily. She must be there. Now. Now.

The corridor seems to lengthen before her, the door to her world slipping away with every frantic step. Claire's eyes blur with unshed tears, with panic. The blue and beige walls close in, tightening around her, and still she moves, faster than she should, slower than she must.

At last, the door to her cabin. Claire's hands shake violently, the sail pass card a slippery thing in her grip. It falls once, twice, the small sound like a scream, like defeat. She snatches it up again, adrenaline and fear making her clumsy, making her a stranger to herself.

The lock light flashes red, then green. She almost cries out with the agony of it, with the unbearable thought of what she might find inside. Her heart races, the final beats before a fall. She swings the door open, the distance between her and Lily like a chasm she can't cross fast enough.

CHAPTER SEVEN

The noise of the hall fades away. She holds her breath. The cabin waits. She waits. It's a trick, a mistake, a terrible dream. Claire wills the world to snap back—but it won't. The only snap is the breaking of her certainty; brittle and unforgiving. She braces herself, fragile, her body reeling as she steps inside. The air is empty. Her heart pounds with denial. The room is still, indifferent. Lily is gone.

The door slams into the wall, sounding like a gunshot, and Claire flinches. It must be a dream. A hallucination. Her heart pounds with the force of truth. She can't believe it. Can't see it. Can't trust it. "Lily?" Her voice is hollow and afraid. Only silence. The bedsheets are taut like accusations. Claire grips the wall, waiting to wake, waiting to remember. But the emptiness won't give, won't let go.

Blood rushes in her ears. The room blurs, the world she built unravelling around her. Her head swims, the ship sways, and Claire is drowning in it. She holds her breath, again, again. Her pulse races, impossible, the rapid thrum of panic and denial. Her mind screams, and the silence screams back. It's the silence that breaks her.

She cries out, fierce and raw. It's the sound of tearing, of losing. She searches with frantic hands and wild eyes, upending every corner. No child under the bed. No child in the closet. The air is empty and cold and gone. The balcony door remains locked tight. "Lily, please!" Her voice cracks, and so does she.

Her legs give out, folding her to the floor. She's slipping, slipping. Her vision narrows to a tunnel of grey and fear. Her fingers clutch the air where Lily should be. Her breath comes fast and shallow, desperate. The truth hammers at her, louder than the ship, louder than anything she can bear. She rocks alone, an orphaned mother. Her head spins with the empty cabin, the universe collapsing in, a sea of blank and gone.

She closes her eyes against it, forcing herself to breathe, to breathe. Once more, her voice—a last gasp: "Lily." It is an end and a beginning. Claire knows what she must do, but can't remember how to move. She doesn't know where to start, only that she must. Her will claws to the surface, fighting through the wreckage. She staggers up, a survivor of her own broken life, and stumbles back to the world.

Claire lurches into the corridor, shouting—a noise that shocks even her own ears. Doors open around her. Her mind shuts down. All that's left is panic and the sound of bare feet on carpet. She calls again, louder. The call of something broken. Her head throbs with each heartbeat. "Lily!" She grabs at the walls, runs blind, runs desperate. The ship is a labyrinth. It breathes. It sways. It taunts. It takes. The hallways blur, a watercolour of blue, beige, and fear. Claire is drowning. She must keep moving. She must not drown.

The long corridor stretches, longer than before. She runs, frantic, calling out, shouting. Passengers appear like ghosts or dreams, watching with wide eyes and open mouths. Some look concerned, others annoyed. Claire sees none of it, hears none of it. Only her own voice, her own terror, the unbearable panic of her own love. It drives her, her pulse, her feet. She calls again, waiting for the one voice she must hear—her daughter's.

Her breath comes in shudders. Her hands reach for support, finding only the emptiness. The ship is a monster, consuming everything— consuming her. Claire keeps running, past strangers and emptiness. Her voice rises, hoarse and desperate, then falls, lost, unheard. The ship's mechanical hum fills her mind and the world. An engine of despair.

She's losing track, losing hope. Her head pounds with blood and fear. Her legs ache; the slap of her feet is a punishing rhythm. She can't tell how long it's been. Can't tell how far she's gone. She pushes on, searching for any sign, any sound. "Lily!" A howl. A prayer. The only thing keeping her going.

The hallway is infinite, impossible. It never ends, never stops. Claire's vision blurs, softening at the edges. Dizziness and panic combine, a cruel force. She clings to the walls, the universe spinning beneath her hands. She can't give up, can't let herself collapse, not here. Her will is a thin thread, but it holds. She must find Lily. She must.

An alcove. A door. An endless line of blue, beige and dread. Claire wrenches it open, checks every shadow, checks every space. No child. She cries out, louder, her voice cracking like the ice around her heart. "Lily!" Still nothing. Her hands grab at the air. She moves on. More ghosts watching. More time slipping away. She doesn't know how much longer she can do this. Her mind is a whirlpool, pulling her down. But she doesn't stop. She can't.

Claire loses herself, the floor and walls a nightmare blur. She tries to go back, back to the beginning, back to the last place she saw Lily. Her breaths are harsh, painful. Her chest heaves with exertion and fear. A couple stands in her path, shock on their faces. They ask if she's alright, if she needs help. Their words are as distant as stars. Claire brushes past, unaware, uncaring. Nothing matters but finding her daughter. Nothing matters but Lily.

"Where is she?" Claire's heart wails, and her body wails with it. Her calls grow ragged. Her feet slow but her thoughts race, a frantic loop of panic and what-ifs. Her stomach clenches, tight and raw. "Where is she?" Her voice drops to a whisper, a sound swallowed by the ship, by the emptiness. It can't be true, but it is.

Her steps falter, slower now, a dream in reverse. Dread wraps around her like a second skin. Claire moves through it, a thing underwater, a thing without air. She reaches the hallway's end, an end with nothing in it. She turns, desperate, unsure where else to go. Only knowing that she must keep moving, that she must find her way. Every step is agony. Every step is despair. "Lily." A word. A memory.

Her mind splinters, her heart breaks. She doubles back, legs weak, spirit weaker. "Lily," she calls again. Unsure if she ever stops. Unsure if she even exists beyond the need, the panic. It consumes her. It's all she is.

The ship's hum vibrates through the walls, through Claire, matching her fear, beat for beat. The sound is everything. She is nothing. A blip. A small, scared thing. She lurches forward, moving without thought or direction. Her mouth is dry, limbs leaden. Still, she pushes. Still, she fights.

A blur of faces and noise. She wants to scream but has no strength or voice. Her hands tremble; her body is an anchor. The world tilts, but she holds on. She keeps going, though every step feels like the end. Seconds bleed together, lost and running, lost and gone.

Claire reaches the cabin. The place she fears most. Her last hope and worst nightmare. She slams the door, feeling it in her bones, the hurt and the nothing. The absence and the pain. She's alone, lost, and falling apart. "Lily!" she calls. The echo is a terrible answer.

She collapses, her legs no longer hers, no longer anyone's. Her body a stranger; her life a stranger. Her world unravels, tighter, tighter. Claire grabs the phone, a lifeline, a plea. Her hands shake, her heart shakes. She punches the security button—desperation a scream she can't stop.

The line rings. Each ring confirms her worst fears. "Security," she pleads, the word an unbearable hope. Her grip tightens on the receiver, on the last piece of everything she has. "Please." It hangs there, a prayer. A wish. "My daughter. She's gone." Claire's voice breaks, an ending. A beginning she can't survive.

CHAPTER EIGHT

A uniformed woman stands outside Claire's door. Claire doesn't remember anything since she picked up the phone. Her hands tremble. The woman introduces herself as Security and asks her to follow. Claire doesn't hear the name. She only hears the words, "You've searched the room? Please come with me, ma'am."

The ship's corridors lurch and twist, every light too bright, every shadow too dark. Her head throbs in time with each step. She wonders if she's still concussed, if the world can look like this inside a broken brain. She asks, "Did you find her?" but the woman only replies, "Let's get you to the office."

The office is smaller than Claire expects. A wall of screens monitors different parts of the ship, a patchwork of halls, decks, and empty rooms. The fluorescent lights are merciless, humming louder than the air itself. A plain metal desk stands at the centre, nothing like the massive stations on TV cop shows. Behind it sits a man with short dark hair and a crisp blue shirt, too new for the frayed chair beneath him. The name tag reads DANIEL JACKSON. He looks up as Claire enters.

"Have a seat," Jackson says. His voice is tired, but not unkind.

Claire sits. The metal chair is cold through her skirt. The dizziness flares and subsides like a tide. She grips her hands, feeling her pulse pound as if it might explode. A second man, younger and olive-skinned, types away at a computer. He never looks up. His name tag reads CARL TORRES. He's the only person in the room seemingly unaware of Claire's panic.

Jackson leans forward. "Let's get some details. Your name?"

She struggles to find her voice. "Claire Holloway."

"Good. You said your daughter is missing? What's her name?"

"Lily," Claire manages.

Jackson waits, patiently. "Her full name?"

"Lily May Holloway. She's three. She—" The words catch. Claire breathes in, shallow and sharp. "She was in bed. I left the room for— I came back and she was gone."

Jackson's pencil moves in careful, even strokes. "When did you last see her?"

Claire tries to count time, but it slips away, refusing to be measured. "I put her to sleep after dinner. Maybe eight? Then I went to the show." The numbers feel meaningless; time is a thing that only matters if you believe in clocks.

Jackson nods. "Can you tell me what Lily was wearing when you left?"

"Dinosaur pyjamas. The green ones." Claire closes her eyes, holding the image. "She had a dinosaur hair bobble. Stegosaurus. She always wants the green one." Her breath quickens. "If she got up, she might have taken her rain boots. She likes the pink ones. And she never sleeps without Thomas. He's a fluffy ragdoll cat."

Jackson's lips twitch, the hint of a smile, but he just writes. "Thomas the cat. Got it."

Claire sees her hands, knuckles white from gripping so tightly. She tries to let go, but can't.

Torres finishes his typing and finally looks up, his eyes blank, almost bored. "Was the cabin locked when you left?"

"I think so." Claire's voice is uncertain, like failing a test she didn't know she was taking. "I always check. But maybe— I don't know. Maybe I didn't."

Jackson nods, as if this was the answer he expected. He turns to Torres. "Radio the patrol. Code Adam. Sweep of the deck, elevators, stairs, common areas. Pull the CCTV."

Torres lifts the radio, speaking in half-code, half-urgency. Claire hears her heart pounding between the words. She stares at the wall of screens, searching for Lily in the thousands of pixels. No movement. No dinosaur-print pyjamas. No brown curls. Only empty corridors. Only places Lily isn't.

Jackson stands walking around the desk, to sit closer on the edge. "Miss Holloway, we'll find your daughter. This is a safe environment. Children don't just disappear on cruise ships."

The words should comfort. Instead, they make her want to scream.

"I only meant to leave her for forty minutes," Claire says. "I never—I've never left her alone before." She expects judgment, but Jackson only nods.

"Most likely she woke up, got confused, went looking for you." He gestures to Torres. "We're spreading the word. These ships are big, but there's nowhere to hide for long."

Claire swallows the questions she can't ask. What if she fell? What if she slipped outside? What if she's with someone who doesn't care about Thomas or the green bobble or the pink rain boots?

Jackson says, "Let's get a photo out to all staff. Do you have one?"

She reaches into her bag for her phone. It's not there. "I must have dropped my phone in the theatre," Claire explains.

"Okay, I can file a lost property report. Can you describe it?" Jackson asks.

"It's a silver iPhone, latest model." Claire's words rush out, fingers tracing the air as if trying to find it. "Clear case with little blue stars." She swallows hard; the phone feels vital, a lifeline to Lily she can't lose. "All my photos of Lily are on it. Every photo from this trip."

Jackson nods, writing it down. "We'll find it. Theatre staff usually turn in lost items quickly."

Claire leans forward; the dizziness returns like an unwelcome guest. "The photos—they're important. There's one from this morning, Lily at breakfast on the balcony. Her hair was messy, and she was eating a croissant." Her voice breaks. "I need those…" she trails off.

Jackson watches. "We'll need you to stay close—in case we find her, or if she tries to come back."

Claire nods, but she can't imagine ever leaving this office. Searching, the ship feels unbearable. She wants to be everywhere at once, yet not at all.

Jackson says, "I know this is hard, but we need you to stay calm. Anyone we should contact for you?"

She shakes her head. "No. It's just us." The truth feels like a razor in her throat. "Her father—he's not in the picture." She says it to fill the silence, to make the facts line up. The real truth: she doesn't know who to call. No one would care about this as much as she does.

Jackson stands. "I'll check with the patrol myself." He leaves, footsteps soft on tile.

Claire is left with Torres, who resumes typing, half-watching the screens. She tries to slow her breathing, but every cell in her body screams with adrenaline. Her head aches, but she barely feels it. The only real sensation is the cold in her hands and the hollow scrape in her heart.

She stares at the monitors—life without Lily in every frame. She wants to tear the screens off the wall. She wants to be inside them, searching every pixel. She tries to focus on what comes next, but the future is a black hole. She doesn't remember how to plan.

Torres speaks without looking up. "They're checking the kids' club. Sometimes kids wander there, even at night."

"Lily doesn't know how to get there." The words escape before she can stop them. "She's three. Too small."

Torres shrugs, as if all children are the same. "Kids surprise you."

Claire almost laughs, but bites her tongue tasting blood. She doesn't want to cry in front of him. She digs her nails into her palm, counting the seconds, counting the places Lily could be. It doesn't help.

Jackson returns, no smile. "No sign yet. They're expanding the search."

Claire tries to ask if she can help, if she can look, if she can do anything, but the words won't come. Her voice is lost. She feels herself tipping toward the edge, the place where nothing makes sense. She wonders if she's dreaming. If this is what her brain does after trauma —makes up a crisis, a puzzle she can't solve, punishment herself for being gone too long.

Jackson sits again. "The search will go through the night. We'll find her."

The promise is empty, but she clings to it, desperate. She wants to believe in the power of systems, that the world can organise itself and set things right.

Claire sits in the metal chair, watching the monitors, waiting for the universe to correct its mistake. She imagines Lily at every hallway's end, behind every door. She tries to summon her back by sheer will. Faces flicker on the screens—a passenger, a child, a crew member. Claire's heart leaps each time. But it's never Lily. Not yet.

Her head throbs with every second, but she barely notices. The world has shrunk to this office, the cold metal chair and the glow of the screens.

A tap on the keyboard, the click of a mouse. Torres works with the focus of a person who wants to be anywhere but here. Claire tries to track his screen through the reflection in the monitor glass, but the image is a smear, faces and rooms doubled and blurred. She looks away, nausea rising, then back again. She doesn't want to miss anything.

Torres frowns, not a big frown, just the slight crease of a man used to systems that don't fail, suddenly confronted by one that might. He glances at Jackson, then Claire, then the screen again.

Jackson notices. "What's wrong?"

Torres lowers his voice, but not enough. "Only one registered in the cabin."

Jackson raises his eyebrows. "You sure?"

Torres clicks through screens, double-checks, then nods. "Only one. Holloway, Claire. No second guest, no child listed."

The air thickens. Claire's scalp prickles.

"That's not right," she says, the words small and sharp. "She's on the reservation. We checked in together. The room had—" She searches her memory for the attendant's name from the previous evening, but it's gone, vanished like every other useful fact. "The steward saw us. That first night when he came to talk."

Jackson's focus sharpens. "Could there have been a check-in error? Sometimes these things happen."

"No," Claire says. "No, that's not—" Her brain is slows, like a computer with too many windows open. "She was just there. Asleep when I left. You can check staff, cameras—" Her hand flutters toward the wall of screens, but it's pointless.

Torres looks at Jackson, then Claire. "Do you have her sail pass card?"

Claire fumbles for her purse, tips it over, spilling its contents—gum wrappers, a broken pencil, two lip balms, her own card, tangled receipts. She searches for the second card, the one with Lily's name. It's not there. She flips every item, checks every pocket. Her hands sweat.

Jackson says, "Sometimes cards get left in the cabin. Maybe she took hers?"

"No," Claire says, but the memory slips away. Did she hand Lily the card? She wouldn't give it to a three-year-old—or did she? Did she leave it on the bedside table? She can't recall the morning, only colours, noise and Lily's voice saying, "I want to do it myself, Mummy," every time they passed a door.

Torres turns his screen toward Jackson. A form with Claire's name is open. Jackson scans it, nodding at the bottom. "She was in medical. Head injury. This is the concussion patient?"

Torres says, "Yes, sir."

They look at Claire as if she might break.

She feels it, a sharp brittle edge running through her. "This isn't—I'm not—" She wants to say crazy. She wants to say, "I know my own child." But she's can't find words that will matter. She's never been good at defending herself, at proving the truth of things she just knows.

Torres is gentler now. "You're sure you were traveling alone, Miss Holloway? No one else joined you? No one who might have—"

"My daughter," Claire interrupts. Her throat is raw. "Lily May Holloway. Three years old. Dinosaur pyjamas. She's missing, not imaginary."

Jackson's tone is measured. "We're not suggesting—"

"You are," Claire says. "You think I'm—" She can't finish. Her body shakes, not from fear, but the sense that the ground has shifted, the world a tilted room and she's sliding toward the wrong end.

Jackson's radio crackles. A voice reports the deck sweep is negative for unaccompanied children. No sign of a child matching the description. The pool deck is clear, the play area locked, the lounges empty. The voice is businesslike, unaffected.

Claire clings to the words. "You have cameras. You can check the cameras."

Jackson nods. "We will. But we need to confirm details first. When did you last see Lily?"

"I already told you," Claire says, voice rising. "She was in bed. Her cat doll. The green hair thing. I—" Her vision blurs and doubles. The world fades to grey and white.

Torres stands, pulls a small bottle of water from a drawer. "You should sit," he says, though she already is. He hands her the bottle, but her hands shake too much to unscrew the cap. Jackson does it for her. She drinks. The water is cold, thin, tasteless.

Jackson asks, "Have you eaten tonight?"

She shakes her head. She doesn't remember. She doesn't remember anything. The forgetting makes her want to throw up. She presses a hand to her throbbing temple, the pain sharpening to a pinpoint in the blur.

Torres returns to the computer, types something. Jackson watches, careful now. "Does Lily have a favourite story?"

Claire nods, grateful for something familiar. "Dinosaurs. I tell her stories about them. She likes Steggy best. Stegosaurus. When we stop in New York next week, we are planning to visit the museum. She's obsessed. Wanted to bring her rain boots, even though I told her it wouldn't rain."

Jackson says, "That's good. Helpful." But his face remains blank. He glances at Torres, who shrugs.

Torres tries again. "If you remember anything else, please let us know."

Claire's vision edges with white. The lights are too bright, the air too thin. She closes her eyes, but the afterimage worsens. The world swimming behind her lids, colours and faces bleeding together.

She hears Jackson on the phone, measured. "She's disoriented, possible post-concussion. Proceed with caution."

The world doesn't tilt—it splits. Claire slips, her body cold, clammy, light. She hears her voice, distant and hollow: "I'm not crazy. She was here. She's real."

No one answers. Only sound is the hum of the fluorescent lights, keyboard taps, and the low, sympathetic murmur of two men who have stopped believing her.

She wants to scream, but the breath won't come. Clinging to the desk, knuckles whitening, she waits for someone to say it's all a mistake.

But no one does.

Jackson clears his throat, careful now, every word a stepping stone over a minefield.

"Sometimes the system doesn't update right away," he says. "It's possible Lily's card is still in the admin queue. Or maybe there was a check-in error at embarkation. These things happen more often than you'd think."

Claire grabs at the explanation like a lifeline.

"So, she's here. She must be. It's just a computer problem." Her voice is brittle, but there's a flicker of relief. She almost laughs, but the sound won't come.

Jackson leans forward, hands folded.

"We'll do a thorough search. I'll go over the logs myself. If Lily is anywhere on this ship, we'll find her." He gives a look to Torres, who nods, unsmiling.

"I'll also talk to the cabin steward and see if anyone remembers seeing her."

Torres stands, straightens his shirt, and readies a clipboard.

"We just need you to wait in your cabin. In case she comes back. Sometimes kids hide, then show up when they're sure it's safe."

"Okay," Claire whispers. She means to sound determined, but her voice is paper-thin. "Yes. I'll wait."

Jackson softens his tone.

"Can I get you anything? Water, something to eat?"

She shakes her head.

"Just Lily."

He offers a small smile; the kind used for people who are not expected to smile back.

"We'll keep you updated. Use the phone if you remember anything else."

Torres hands her a printout of the two reports: one for the missing phone and the other for the missing child.

"They will call your room if your phone turns up," he says.

Claire tucks the pages into her purse, careful not to crease them. She stands, finds her legs unsteady. Jackson opens the door for her, gesturing her out. The corridor is silent and clean, its lights flickering in uneven waves. The world narrows to the rectangle of carpet at her feet.

Torres follows her out, a silent escort. His shoes squeak on the tile. Jackson watches them go, and Claire knows he's already forgotten her face, replaced it with the next person's crisis.

They pass a family in the hallway, two parents, three kids, all alive, loud, and real. One child glances at Claire, then turns away, very tired and ready for bed. She wonders if she ever felt that safe. If Lily ever did.

The walk to the cabin feels endless. The doors all look the same; the numbers melt into each other. Each step reminds her that she is the only one who remembers Lily. Her memories churn: Lily's voice, her laugh, the way she curled around Thomas. Claire tries to hold the details together, but they start to fragment, slipping out of reach. What if she made a mistake? What if she left the door unlocked? What if she never brought Lily here at all?

Torres walks behind her; a reminder that she is being observed. She straightens her spine, tries to look like someone who hasn't lost her mind. Her headache pulses, sharper with every stride. The ship rocks beneath her, gentle but relentless, a lullaby with teeth.

At the cabin door, Torres pauses.

"We'll let you know if we hear anything." His eyes linger on her, searching for something she doesn't have.

Claire steps inside. The room is exactly as she left it. The air is stale. There is no sign of Lily, not even a hair on the pillow, not a footprint on the floor.

She turns back to the door, but Torres is already gone. The hallway swallows the sound of his retreat. She closes the door, locks it out of habit. The click is too loud, too final.

Claire stands in the middle of the cabin, glancing furtively around the room, desperate for proof she isn't alone. She waits for the phone to ring, for the universe to correct itself.

But the only sound is the drone of the air system, and the slow, unsteady beating of her own heart.

CHAPTER NINE

Claire sits on the edge of the bed. Her head throbs with each heartbeat, sharp and mean, unlike the dull hum that lived there before. She presses the heel of her hand to her temple and tries to focus, but the cabin spins, a slow carousel of confusion and pain.

She listens for Lily, so intently that the rest of her senses go blank. There is no child's voice, no scuff of rain boots, not even the quiet tick of the nightlight. Only the air system's endless drone and the low whine of her own breath. The urge to scream is animalistic, but she chokes it down.

The beds are wrong. It takes her a full minute to realise it, as if the world has shifted imperceptibly, a single pixel at a time. She stares at the mattresses, the way they touch, the way the line between them flush and perfect, as if they've always been one bed, not two. But she knows. She knows. In the morning, there were two beds: one for her, one for Lily. She still pictures the gap between them, occupied by a bedside table at the top, the way Lily's blankets trailed off the edge, the plush tail of Thomas the cat dangling like a lure. But the gap is gone; the beds are jammed together with mechanical precision, the covers smoothed and tucked in a way Claire never does.

A shiver runs up her arms. The same cold she felt in the security office. The same hint of someone watching. She tries to ignore it, to focus on something real. She stands, knees buckling, and forces herself to walk the length of the room.

Her first instinct is to look under the bed. She half-expects to find Lily curled there hiding like she sometimes does at home when she wants Claire to "find" her. She crouches, bracing herself against the nausea, and lifts the edge of the blanket. The under-bed space is empty. No toys, no hairbands, no tangle of pink boots. No sign that a child ever set foot here.

Claire's hands start to shake. She yanks opens the closet so hard they rattle in their tracks. She expects a mess—tiny shoes, discarded t-shirts, the green dinosaur dress that Lily refuses to take off. Instead, the closet is immaculate. Her own dresses hang on one side, spaced evenly, untouched. On the shelf, a single suitcase, zipped and upright. She paws at it, unzips it, expecting chaos, clothes and toys tossed inside, but it's perfectly packed with her things, rolled and folded as she did it at home. Lily's backpack is gone. The spare pyjamas are gone. The stuffed animals, the collection of dino figurines, the colouring book with the bent cover—all gone.

She backs away from the closet, a howl gathering in her chest. She clamps a hand over her mouth, just in case.

Next, the drawers. She yanks them open, one by one, not even bothering to be careful. The first drawer is full of her underwear, arranged in neat rows. The second holds her t-shirts and leggings, her phone charger, the novel she never read. No tiny socks. No child's nightgown. The third drawer is empty, a void that mocking her with its perfect, blankness.

She staggers to the bathroom. The little toothbrush she bought for Lily—pale green, soft-bristled, with a dinosaur decal—is missing. Only her own brush stands in the glass. She checks the shower, trash can, medicine cabinet. Nothing but her own things, ordered and sterile.

Claire leans against the cool tile and lets herself sob. The sound is strangled, almost silent—a private breakdown she refuses to share. When she pulls herself upright, her vision swims, and she clutches the counter to steady herself.

She stumbles back to the bed, running a hand over the surface. The sheets are tight; the pillows arranged in perfect symmetry. No dent where a small body might have slept, no indent from the weight of a plush toy. She grabs the mattress and heaves it up, desperate, half-mad. Nothing underneath but plywood and air.

She pulls open the suitcase again, more frantic this time. She upends it, spilling her clothes onto the floor, rooting through every pocket and compartment. No sign of Lily. No pyjamas, no swim goggles, no sticker sheets. Even the old band-aid Lily insisted on saving is gone.

The room tilts. It isn't just the ship's gentle sway. It's the world itself, shifting on its axis, trying to dislodge her. She puts a hand to the wall, slides down to the carpet, and sits, hugging her knees.

The air smells wrong. She remembers the morning—how the cabin was thick with the scent of croissants and apple juice, the faint undercurrent of sunscreen and child sweat. Now the air is clean, artificial, empty.

Claire claws her way back up. She searches the drawers again, hoping for a miracle. She checks the pockets of her own jeans, the lining of her purse, the seam of her jacket. She even searches the small gap between the bed and the wall, but finds only a single strand of her own hair, clinging to the baseboard like a thread of lost time.

The panic is a living thing. It paces with her as she circles the room, again and again, searching for proof that she isn't alone, that she isn't losing her mind. But there is nothing. No crayon mark on the desk, no fingerprint on the mirror, no accidental puddle of juice on the carpet. The room is a museum exhibit, preserved to suggest that no child ever existed here.

She moves to the window and rips back the curtain. The view is black ocean, speckled with distant ship lights, the wake of their own vessel a white scar across the water. She leans her forehead to the cold glass, breathes in, breathes out, fighting for air. Her head throbs with a new violence, the pain behind her eyes sharp as a blade.

She tries to reconstruct the day—every detail, every moment with Lily. She forces herself to remember the breakfast on the balcony, the art class, the splash of pool water on Lily's face, the pizza on the deck at sunset. Each memory is vivid, too real to deny. But the evidence is gone. Only the memory remains, and she can't be sure it's enough.

She tries to remember the morning—did she have a second sail pass card? Did the room steward really see Lily? Did she talk to other parents at the art class, or only watch from a distance? Was there ever a green hair bobble, or was that just a story she told the security officer?

Claire sinks to the floor, her hands shaking so hard she can't uncurl her fists. She feels the ship sway, the movement stronger now, almost violent. The room pitches and yaws, the walls closing in. She closes her eyes and tries to remember Lily's voice, but it fades, as if erased, one word at a time.

The panic settles into a cold, hard certainty. Her head throbs. The world is rewriting itself, page by page, and she is powerless to stop it. She opens her eyes and sees the perfect, sterile room, arranged for a single occupant—and wonders if it has always been this way.

* * *

Claire pulls herself up on the edge of the desk. Her legs barely respond; sweat slicks her hands. The room feels even smaller than before, the ceiling pressing down on her. She stares at the phone, willing her fingers to move.

The number Daniel gave her is written on a slip of paper, tucked under her sail pass on the nightstand. She dials it, fumbling with the buttons. The first ring feels like a gunshot. The second, a countdown.

"Security, this is Jackson."

Her voice barely works. "It's Claire Holloway," she says, her own name feeling foreign on her tongue. "You said to call if—" The words stick. "I need someone to come to my cabin."

There's a pause, the kind that makes it clear he doesn't remember her immediately. Then, "Of course, ma'am. Are you all right?"

"No," Claire says, the truest thing she's ever admitted. "I need someone now. Please." Her voice shakes. "Something's wrong."

She expects questions, demands for explanation. Instead, he says, "Stay put, I'll be there soon."

She hangs up but doesn't wait. She dials housekeeping, jabs the button until it connects. The woman who answers has a gentle accent Claire can't place. "How may I help you?"

Claire tries to sound authoritative, like someone in control. "I need housekeeping, right now. My cabin—" She gives the number, double-checks the plaque on the wall, hoping she's not hallucinating that too. "Something's been cleaned that shouldn't have been."

The voice wavers. "I will send your room steward, yes."

"It's urgent," Claire says. "It's an emergency." She wants to add, *it's life and death*, but the words won't come.

"Yes, ma'am," the voice says, then clicks off.

She drops the phone. It clatters to the floor, as she starts tears through the room again. The same drawers, the same closet, the same bathroom cabinet. If she can just find one thing—one sock, one band-aid, even a crumpled napkin with Lily's scribble on it—it will all be okay. But everything is gone, as if the room reset itself while she wasn't looking.

She checks the trash can. It's empty, lined with a fresh bag. She could swear she dumped half a juice box in there before dinner, with Lily's straw sticking out at a ridiculous angle. Gone. She checks the mini-fridge, where she left half a banana for Lily's breakfast. Only the untouched water bottles and a single can of Sprite, lined up like soldiers. She pulls out the can, cracks it open, and sips. It tastes like nothing.

The knock comes as she's crouched, checking under the bed again. She stands, legs shaking, wiping her hands on her thighs.

She expects Daniel, but finds a young man in a neat vest and pressed pants, clearly pulled from his bed in the middle of the night. His name tag says "Miguel." He looks cheerful, bright-eyed, and ready to help.

"Housekeeping, ma'am," he says, smiling wide. "You called?"

Claire nearly laughs. "Yes," she says, her voice a mess of relief and hysteria. "Thank you for coming." She lets him in, then closes the door behind him with too much force.

Miguel surveys the room with professional detachment. "What can I do for you?" His English is good, but the consonants are soft.

"My daughter's things are missing," Claire says, watching for a flicker of confusion in his eyes. It's there, just for a second, but he recovers.

He smiles, as if she told a joke. "Maybe she hid them? Sometimes the little ones do this, yes?"

"No," Claire says. "They're gone. All of them. Her backpack, clothes, shoes—" She gestures at the closet, at the empty drawer. "And the beds. They were separate this morning. Why are they together now?"

Miguel's brow furrows. "Beds?" He looks at the arrangement, then back at Claire. "I do not touch the beds. Only after checkout, or if you ask for different. Was this not good?"

Claire shakes her head, feeling her pulse pounding at her throat. "It's not what I want. I want it how it was. Two beds. My daughter had her own."

Miguel seems genuinely lost. He walks to the closet, opens it, and steps back, as if inviting her to inspect. "This is how I find it, ma'am. No change." He runs a hand over the smooth surface of the comforter. "Maybe you would like, I call my manager? Or we bring extra cot?"

"No!" Claire hears her own voice, shrill and shaky. She tries to pull it back, to sound calm. "I want you to tell me what happened to my daughter's things."

He glances around, then at the ceiling, as if searching for cameras. "I have twenty rooms today, ma'am. I go in, I clean, I go out. I no change the beds around. If things are missing, maybe lost in laundry, yes?

Maybe lost in the shuffle." His hands circle like a tornado, as Lily would describe it.

Claire steps closer, desperate an answer. "You saw them, right? You saw her dress, her toys, her little green toothbrush?"

Miguel's smile fades. He shakes his head slowly. "I not remember. Maybe only the normal," he says. "Only your things." He pauses; sympathy mixed with confusion. "Maybe you want I look for the lost and found? Many things go there."

She doesn't know what to say. She wants to grab his arm, shake him, force the truth out. But his expression is so honest, so blank, she can't. She just stands, hands shaking, as he offers her a comforting, practiced smile.

"We can check lost and found, yes?" he says again, as if it's the solution to everything.

Claire turns away, unable to meet his eyes. She grabs the phone, dials security again, and hands the receiver to Miguel. "Tell him," she says. "Tell him you don't see her things."

Miguel is startled but obedient. "Hello, yes, this is Miguel in cabin housekeeping. Yes, yes, I am here now." He listens, glances at Claire. "She says daughter's things are missing. But I see only the normal." He pauses, listens some more, nods. "Yes, I wait here. Yes, I show you when you come." He hangs up, shrugs helplessly.

They stand silent for a few minutes. Miguel tries small talk—towels? Turn-down service? Claire ignores him, pacing, opening drawers again, as if the act itself will conjure the missing things.

Another knock, Daniel, tired, tie loosened, face drawn. He steps in, nods at Miguel, and asks Claire directly. "What's happened?"

She unloads everything at once—the beds, missing pyjamas, empty closet, toyless suitcase. Words come out in a raw, urgent rush.

Daniel listens, then turns to Miguel. "Can you confirm this?"

Miguel nods, gestures to the bed and closet. "Always like this, sir. I do not touch."

Daniel asks, "Have you seen a child in this room? Or her things?"

Miguel shakes his head, eyes wide. "Only the lady, always. No child."

Claire's heart pounds so loud she can barely hear. She stares at Daniel, willing him to see her truth. But he looks tired, like someone who's seen too much and wants to see less.

He turns back to Miguel. "Thank you. You can go."

Miguel hesitates, then leaves. The door closes heavy.

Daniel sits on the bed's edge, rubbing his eyes. "Miss Holloway," he says softly, "I checked the records. No one else is booked in this room. No record of your daughter on the ship's manifest."

Claire shakes her head, refusing. "That's not possible. She was here. I have pictures. I—" But the words die, because the phone is gone, the evidence is gone, and she knows how it sounds.

Daniel's face is kind, almost gentle. "Sometimes, after trauma, the brain—" He stops, tries again. "Do you want to see the doctor? I can call her."

"No." The answer is automatic, desperate. "I want you to find my daughter."

He nods, though she sees disbelief. "I will keep looking," he says. "But maybe you should rest." He stands, walks to the door, pauses. "If you remember anything else, call me. Or come to the desk."

She doesn't answer. She stands in the middle of the cabin, listening to the door click shut.

She tries to hold onto her memories, to keep them safe, but they feel slippery, unreliable. She walks to the window, looks out into the endless dark. Lights on the horizon blur together. She almost hears Lily's bright insistent voice, but when she turns around, the room is silent.

She sits on the bed, not knowing what else to do, waiting for morning.

CHAPTER TEN

Daniel Jackson sits at the edge of his chair, elbows pressing into the fake wood veneer of the security office desk. The wall of monitors casts shifting light over the clutter: half-filled forms, pens leaking ink onto his fingers, and an untouched cup of ship's coffee gone cold. Most feeds show empty halls, fluorescent-lit and silent like the rest of the ship at this hour. A few display distant, slow-moving shapes: crew returning from duty, a late-night couple drifting arm-in-arm, a lone passenger pacing a deck beneath stadium lights.

Daniel pinches the bridge of his nose, letting the headache crest and recede. He blinks, then checks the report on the screen before him. Subject: Holloway, Claire. Incident: Reported missing child, unsubstantiated by manifest or crew. Noted as post-fall concussion patient, treated and released. Jackson reads it three times, waiting for the details to rearrange themselves into something that makes sense. They don't.

He dials medical's extension, his thumb numb with exhaustion. Two rings, then Dr. Reyes answers, her voice crisp yet distracted.

"Reyes here."

"It's Jackson," he says scanning his own reflection in the blacked-out screen of a dead monitor—the tired sag of his eyes, the stubble shadowing his jaw after every fourteen-hour stretch. "I need to consult about a passenger. Holloway, Claire. Cabin 8612. You treated her earlier?"

A pause. The hum of machinery in the background.

"Yes, concussion from a fall in the theatre. I discharged her with instructions to rest and monitor for symptoms. She refused to stay. Why?"

He taps the keys with the edge of his nail, spelling out her name repeatedly in the report window. "She's contacted us twice since then. First to report a missing child. Then, a few minutes later, to claim her daughter's belongings had been tampered with. I went with a steward to check the cabin, he says there's no sign of a child. No toys, no second toothbrush, not even the bedding's disturbed. I checked the manifest myself. Holloway's a solo ticket. No child listed, no second guest on file." He says it flat, mechanical, but inside he feels a small twist, a tension he can't justify.

"I spoke with Torres earlier. Is she still insisting there's a child?" Dr. Reyes's voice sharpens, alert.

"Absolutely convinced," Daniel says. "Insists the girl is three years old, named Lily. Has a complete description down to the pyjamas and rain boots. She remembers exact details, but nothing checks out. Crew reports seeing her alone; Torres says CCTV shows her alone. I'm not seeing any evidence of the kid, but..." He trails off, unsure how to phrase the rest.

"But the subject is distressed," Reyes says. "Is she aggressive?"

Daniel shakes his head, then realises it's a phone call. "No, not at all. Upset, yes. Unstable, maybe. But her concern feels real, not staged. I don't think she's acting or angling for a scam. She seems... lost."

Reyes is silent for a long moment. "Concussive episodes can cause memory disturbances. Confabulation, even. Sometimes people invent details to fill gaps. It's rare, but I've seen it before. Trauma can unearth all sorts of things, even full scenarios. Did you administer any cognitive tests?"

Daniel shakes his head. "No, that's your area. But I saw the reports. She passed the orientation and recall tests initially, but became disoriented under stress. With us, the first interview, she was lucid, just scared. The second time, she couldn't track the timeline and kept insisting we were the ones mixed up. So, similar experience."

Reyes nods thoughtfully. "Standard tests only tell part of the story. Under stress, the brain can behave unpredictably."

He glances at Torres, who's just logged off for the night, leaving the office quiet except for the buzz of fluorescents. The air feels colder, the corners of the room darker.

"How bad is it?" Daniel asks, softly. "Are we talking like, a breakdown?"

Reyes's voice drops to confidential. "I don't have enough data, Daniel. But given the pattern, I'd like to assess her in person.

Preferably with a witness, and preferably tonight. The worst thing we could do is let this escalate, for her or for us. Can you have someone bring her to Medical?"

"I'll arrange it," Daniel says. "But she's locked herself in her cabin. Says she won't leave in case her daughter comes back. I can send a nurse to knock."

Reyes sighs, tired but resolute. "If she resists, let her know she can either come in willingly or be escorted. I'll be here all night."

Daniel lets the silence hang for a second. "Thanks, Doctor. Sorry to wake you."

"You didn't," Reyes says. "These things don't keep office hours." The line goes dead.

Daniel sets the phone down. He looks again at the manifest: Claire Holloway, age thirty-two, occupation blank, next of kin blank. Booked alone, traveling solo. He pulls up the file photo from check-in. She's smiling, barely, the camera catching her in a moment of forced composure. No child visible. No evidence of anyone else.

He writes the log update, words careful and precise. He'll send it to the bridge, to the morning shift, to anyone who needs to know.

Before leaving, Daniel stands and walks to the monitor wall, scanning grainy footage of the decks. For a moment, he wonders if the cameras are even real, if they've always shown the world this empty and strange. Then he rubs his eyes, blinks, and everything snaps back. People are just people, and the rules are what keep them safe.

He keys in the notes for the next shift, then leans back in his chair. The bones in his neck pop. There's nothing more to do now but wait.

Claire storms through the cabin, convinced she can still prove the world wrong. She yanks open the nightstand drawer for the third time, clawing past the ship's stationery and safety cards. Dropping to her knees, she sweeps her hands under the bed, searching for a missed sock, a crayon, the soft weight of a plush cat. Nothing. She stands, dizzy, hands bracing the edge of the desk.

She whispers, "She was here," as if saying it again will summon Lily back, turning absence into presence. Her mind replays the day in excruciating detail: the colour of the juice box, the sound of giggles on the balcony, the sharp, happy whine of "Mummy, look!" But here and now, there is only the flat hum of the air conditioning and the sterile glow of the overhead lights.

A crisp, certain knock interrupts. Claire freezes, her heart jerking against her ribs.

She doesn't want to answer, but she does. She opens the door a crack, enough to see a woman in an impossibly white uniform, blonde hair wound into a stern coil at the back of her head. Her hands rest perfectly still on her clipboard.

"Miss Holloway?" the nurse says, voice pitched to soothe but sharpened by long practice. "I'm here for a wellness check. Dr. Reyes is concerned after your earlier accident."

Claire tries to close the door, but the nurse's foot wedges neatly in the gap. "You're not supposed to be here," Claire says, voice thin as paper. "I need to be here. In case—in case Lily comes back."

The nurse waits, exactly as long as it takes for the words to lose power. "It's not optional," she says, with practiced softness. "Dr. Reyes needs to confirm your safety. Just a brief visit to Medical, then you're back. Five minutes."

Claire shakes her head, fingers digging into the door. "I can't leave. What if she needs me? What if— you don't understand, she could come back. If she wakes up—"

The nurse glances past Claire, scanning the room, assessing. "I understand you're frightened," she says. "But you had a concussion. You may not realise how serious it is. If you refuse to come, Security will be notified. I really think it's better to walk with me now. Please."

The please is a formality, the final warning before escalation. Claire feels her breath tighten, a wet animal panic building in her chest. "Can't you just do it here? I'll answer anything. I'm fine. You can see I'm fine—"

"It's policy," the nurse says. "You know how these things are." She tries a gentle smile, that doesn't reach her eyes. "You'll be back before you know it. Just to check the basics. Blood pressure, balance, a few questions. Then you're released. If your daughter returns, she'll be waiting for you here."

A lie, and Claire knows it, but she's trapped. If she resists, there will be more people. More questions. A report that follows her forever. She thinks of the security man. Officer Jackson. Daniel. How he looked at her with that blank, tired pity. She thinks of Lily, the promise she made never to leave her alone. The horror of it crushes her, but the nurse's gaze never wavers.

"I have to leave a note," Claire says, voice trembling. "In case— in case she comes back and I'm not here. I can't— please, just a minute. I know she can't read, but if she comes back, she will know it's for her."

The nurse doesn't roll her eyes, but she might as well. "Of course, Miss Holloway. I'll wait in the hall."

The door closes. Claire grabs a sheet from the desk and scribbles: "Lily, I had to go for a checkup. Stay here, Mummy loves you. I will be right back." She folds it once, twice, and props it against the phone. It looks stupid, childish, but it's all she has.

Her hand shakes as she opens the door again. The nurse stands ready, professional, but her posture is less patient now. Claire steps into the corridor, the world suddenly larger, colder, and less forgiving. She glances back, memorising the shape of the room, the way the shadow falls across the empty bed.

The nurse leads her away, footsteps in perfect sync. Claire looks straight ahead, refusing to cry.

Behind her, the door swings shut. Inside the cabin, the note waits in the silence.

The corridor outside Claire's cabin is a tunnel of pale light, the carpet a faded stripe that seems to lead nowhere. The nurse walks ahead, her steps measured and silent. Claire follows, her legs uncertain, body still resonating with the last frequency of panic. The ship's gentle sway no longer feels gentle. Every subtle shift in the floor knocks her off-balance, as if the world has turned unsteady just for her.

A man returning to his cabin, unsteady on his feet after a late night and too many drinks, nods politely at the nurse and lets his gaze linger too long on Claire. She wonders how she must look—hollow-eyed, dishevelled, a woman pulled from her own disaster and paraded through a world that doesn't care. The nurse ignores the man's stare and keeps moving.

They pass closed cabin doors. Behind them, televisions glow; voices spill out—laughter, fragments of music, the low, sweet moan of a saxophone. For the other passengers, it's still a holiday. A vacation. Claire tries to imagine slipping back into that world: tomorrow's breakfast on the balcony, Lily's curls damp from the shower, the two of them laughing about nothing. But the ache in her head grows with every step. The memory is slick, impossible to hold.

She counts the doors, tracks the fire exit signs. The ship is a machine, its passageways endless and predictable, but it feels like a trap. At an intersection, the nurse gestures for her to turn. Claire stays a half-step ahead, the nurse always close enough to catch her if she falls.

"Are you all right?" the nurse asks, quietly.

"Yes, thank you," Claire replies automatically. Then, after a pause: "How much farther?"

"Just down here. Then the elevators," the nurse says. "You're doing fine."

It sounds like something you'd say to a child who can't swim, and Claire resents her for it. She searches for a reason to turn back. But there's nothing. No miracle. No Lily. Just the endless hallway, the distant sound of someone shouting at a television, and the tightening band of pain around her scalp.

A group of passengers gathers outside a lounge, drinks in hand, chatting under ship's manufactured midnight. Their laughter bubbles up, bright and careless. One woman glances at Claire, then quickly looks away, uncomfortable at the sight of a patient in the land of the well. The nurse moves faster, ushering Claire past, as if shielding the world from Claire's grief.

They reach the elevators. The brushed steel doors are polished so finely Claire sees herself reflected, split and doubled by the panel. She studies the image: hair once shining, now stringy and dull; dark half-moons beneath her eyes. She barely recognises herself. She wonders if Lily would.

The elevator dings open. The nurse presses the button for Deck 2—Medical. The doors close, and the world contracts.

The descent is fast, but to Claire it feels infinite. The headache intensifies. Her knees wobble. She grips the rail, afraid of collapsing, of humiliating herself further. In the reflection, the nurse watches her—one eyebrow raised, a tic of judgment so faint it might be imagined.

The doors slide open into a different world. Cold blue walls, a paler floor, every line clean and sharp. The hallway is deserted but for a digital sign flashing "QUIET ZONE: MEDICAL." Even the air feels clinical, cool, heavy, laced with a chemical tang.

The nurse swipes her card. A soft click. "This way," she says.

Claire steps through. The senses sharpened by the starkness, by the way the space devours sound.

Inside is a narrow waiting room. Chairs line the wall beneath posters about hydration and sun safety. The only art: two framed ocean prints, perfectly aligned. A glass partition separates the desk from the rest of the room. Beyond it, a row of closed doors, shelves of medical supplies, nothing out of place.

The nurse checks her watch, then gestures. "Dr. Reyes will be with you shortly. Please sit, if you like."

Claire doesn't like. But she sits. The chair is harder than it looks, the armrests polished to a clinical shine. Her hands tremble in her lap. She fights the urge to reach for her phone, because right now it doesn't exist. The headache pulses, a warning light in her skull.

Somewhere inside the medical bay, a machine beeps, steady and low. The sound tunnels into Claire's spine. She wraps her arms around her waist, folding inward, trying to shrink the world to something she can bear. The nurse stands sentinel at the door, her face composed, a statue in white.

The antiseptic smell is stronger here. Claire hates it. It's the smell of bad news. Nausea rises again. Her cheeks flush hot. She clenches her jaw, unwilling to give the nurse, or anyone, the satisfaction of seeing her crack.

A door opens. Dr. Reyes appears, tablet in hand, silhouette sharp beneath the fluorescent lights. She speaks to the nurse in a voice too low to catch. The nurse nods and leaves.

Dr. Reyes turns to Claire, unreadable, and gestures for her to come.

The threshold is cold beneath her feet. The room beyond is colder still. Claire steps through, and the door shuts behind her with a final, irrevocable click.

Dr. Reyes sits at a metal table, hands folded around a tablet, her expression so carefully neutral it borders on defiant. The consultation room is smaller than the waiting area, colder, more exposed. Medical diagrams cover the walls: vessels, nerves, and cross-sections of organs rendered in sharp blue and red. The fluorescent light is relentless. Claire's breath fogs in the chill. She makes herself sit upright, arms pressed flat against the rigid plastic of her chair, legs crossed and clamped together, a picture of composure she doesn't feel.

Dr. Reyes glances at the chart, then at Claire.

"I want to start by confirming your basic orientation. Name, date, location?"

"Claire Holloway. March twenty ninth. Oh—after midnight, so the thirtieth." Claire pauses. The year stumbles on her tongue, but she catches it. "2025. We're in the ship's medical bay."

The doctor nods, swipes a finger down the tablet.

"Can you tell me what happened earlier tonight, in your words?"

Claire flexes her hands in her lap.

"I went to the theatre. I fell. I hit my head. I don't remember anything after, until I woke up in the medical bay."

Dr. Reyes hums, as if making a private note.

"How are you feeling now?"

"I have a headache. Some nausea. Mostly I'm tired. I just want to get back to my cabin."

"You were disoriented when you arrived here," Dr. Reyes says. "Do you recall the time between the fall and waking up?"

"No. I told you that." Claire's voice is sharp. She tries to soften it. "It's just blank."

The doctor ignores the edge.

"Any dizziness? Vision changes? Trouble with words or memory lapses?"

"Just the headache. And I guess I'm…" Claire's tongue catches. "I'm scared. I can't find my daughter. I know you think she's not real, but I remember her. I remember everything."

Dr. Reyes nods, jotting something on the tablet.

"We'll get to that. First, I need to do the neuro checks again." She stands, wheels a battered stool to Claire's side, and shines a penlight into her eyes. "Follow my finger," she says, and Claire does.

"Any double vision?"

"No."

The doctor holds up two fingers.

"How many?"

"Two."

"Smile for me." Claire forces a smile; more grimace than grin.

"Good. Any numbness in your face, hands, or feet?"

"No." The word clings to Claire's teeth.

Dr. Reyes returns to her seat and consults the tablet again.

"Any history of head injury, seizures, or blackouts?"

"No."

"Any medications—prescription, over-the-counter, supplements?"

"Just vitamins. And Panadol for the headache."

The doctor's face doesn't change.

"Alcohol or recreational drugs in the last forty-eight hours?"

"God, no." Claire's hands ball into fists, knuckles pale and rigid.

Dr. Reyes taps at the tablet.

"You reported a missing child—Lily, age three. When did you last see her?"

"In our cabin. She was asleep. I left for the show. I was only gone an hour. Maybe less."

Dr. Reyes sets the tablet down, just far enough away that Claire can't see the screen.

"How long have you been on the ship?"

Claire has to think.

"We boarded yesterday. It's our first cruise."

"Was Lily with you at embarkation?"

"Yes." The answer is instant, automatic.

"Did anyone else see her? Friends, family, staff?"

Claire blinks.

"Yes. The steward. He said she was cute." She waits for the lie to register, but the doctor's face stays unmoved.

"Anyone else?" Dr. Reyes asks.

Claire tries to reconstruct the day.

"At the art class—other kids were there. The pool deck, too. The girl with green hair—she played with Lily, I think. We went to the pizza place for dinner. Got takeout. She ate three slices. Got sauce all over her pyjamas."

Dr. Reyes waits.

"Any names for these witnesses?"

"No. I wasn't— I didn't get their names." Claire feels her skin flush, hot under the fluorescents.

"Did you take pictures? Most parents do. Especially on vacation."

Claire bites her tongue.

"My phone is missing. Lost it during the fall. But I had pictures. There's one from breakfast—Lily in her pyjamas."

Dr. Reyes steeples her fingers.

"What's your social media handle? We can check for recent activity."

"There won't be..." Claire shakes her head. "I haven't posted anything. I didn't get the Wi-Fi package. I wanted it to be just us."

"What about her father?" asks the doctor, gently. "We should call him and let him know."

Claire's head throbs. "He's not in the picture. He doesn't even know about her. I— I never even told him I was pregnant." The confession hangs between them, raw and ugly.

Dr. Reyes says nothing, but Claire hears the implication: If the father exists, why isn't he here? Why is no one calling? Why is there only you?

The silence presses in.

Dr. Reyes shifts gears. "How's your sleep since boarding?"

Claire shrugs. "Fine. A little restless. The ship moves more at night than I expected."

"Any difficulty falling asleep or waking up?"

"No."

"Nightmares?"

Claire hesitates. "No. Just the usual weird dreams."

Dr. Reyes glances at the wall clock, then back to Claire. "Can you tell me a little about your mental health history? Any previous episodes of anxiety, depression, or mood disorders?"

The question lands like a slap. Claire's mouth goes dry. "No."

"Any hospitalisations for psychiatric care? Any time you felt you needed help?"

"No." The word is a fist.

The doctor's face softens. "And before this cruise? Any major stressors in your life? Work, relationships, loss?"

Claire's gaze flicks to the door, then back. "I don't see how that's relevant."

"Sometimes these things become relevant," Dr. Reyes says. "Even if they don't feel that way now."

Claire swallows hard. "We had a rough year. Lily being two was hard, three is harder. My business almost went under. But I managed. I always manage." She can't look at the doctor as she says it.

Dr. Reyes makes a note. "You mentioned that Lily's father doesn't know about her. Why not?"

"I didn't tell him." Claire's voice is brittle. "He doesn't get to know. He left me when I miscarried the last time. He doesn't get to be a parent when it's convenient."

"And your family?"

"They're not in the picture." Claire's nails press crescent moons into her palms.

"Any history of childhood trauma? Abuse, neglect, instability?"

Claire lets out a sharp, bitter laugh. "You think this is about my childhood?"

"I'm just collecting information," Dr. Reyes replies.

"Well, don't bother. I grew up fine." Claire's body is rigid, her arms locked tight across her chest.

The doctor leans forward slightly. "You said you remember everything about your daughter. But you also said you lost time after your fall. Have you ever experienced something like that before? A blackout, or a time when reality felt uncertain?"

Claire thinks of the first week after her miscarriage, how days blurred and the world felt both too loud and too far away. She shakes her head. "No. Never."

"Any family history of mental illness? Alzheimer's, schizophrenia, anything like that?"

"No." It comes out harsher than she intends.

Dr. Reyes nods, then waits, as if giving Claire space to fill the silence.

Claire's jaw aches from clenching. She tries to look away, but her gaze keeps drifting back to the doctor's steady eyes, to the blank glass of the tablet.

"Why do you keep asking me the same questions?" Claire says at last. "Why are you trying to catch me out?"

The doctor folds her hands. "Because, Miss Holloway, we have a missing child that nobody remembers. A child who isn't on the manifest, who doesn't appear in any photo, who no one on this ship has seen. That's unusual. I need to rule out every possibility—including neurological or psychological causes."

Claire's vision edges with black. "I'm not crazy."

"I never said you were." Dr. Reyes lets the silence stand, lets the denial echo. "But concussion, especially combined with stress, can lead to memory distortions. Confabulation. Even hallucinations."

Claire shudders. "I know what's real."

"I believe that you believe it," Dr. Reyes says, softly.

Claire's body curls inward. "I can't do this if no one believes me. I can't— I can't be the only one who remembers her."

"You're not alone," the doctor says. "That's why I'm here."

Claire stares at the posters on the wall—diagrams of the brain, the circulatory system, the anatomy of the ear. She tries to focus on the facts, to rebuild the world from basic principles.

"My head hurts," she says. "I need to go. I need to check the cabin."

Dr. Reyes stands. "I'll clear you, but I want you to come back for a follow-up in a few hours. I also want to give you some lorazepam, to help you sleep. You need your energy."

Claire stands too, legs trembling. "If I leave, can I come back? Even if it's the middle of the night?"

Dr. Reyes smiles, the first genuine smile of the night. "That's what we're here for."

Claire hesitates at the door. "You think I made her up. But I remember her. I remember everything."

"Memory is a strange thing," Dr. Reyes says, quiet and measured. "It protects us, even when it hurts us."

Claire nods, unsure if she's agreeing. She grips the door handle, her knuckles whitening, and leaves.

In the corridor, she stands alone, dizzy, the chill seeping through her bones. She walks back toward her cabin, the world both too bright and impossibly thin, and wonders if it will ever feel like home again.

She doesn't make it three doors down before the nurse finds her again —the same white-uniformed shadow, polite but immovable.

"Dr. Reyes has a few more questions, if you have a moment," she says. "She'll keep it brief."

There is no room for refusal. The nurse's eyes don't leave Claire as she escorts her back.

This time, Dr. Reyes waits in a different office. This one more for paperwork than examination. It is windowless, the single chair across from her desk smaller and lower than before, a clear message about who holds authority.

There is no preamble. Dr. Reyes gestures for Claire to sit, then immediately launches in.

"I've checked our records and I want to revisit some of your answers, Miss Holloway. With your permission, of course."

Claire sits, but she doesn't relax. She folds her arms tightly across her body, ankles locked together, body angled away from the desk as if ready to flee at any moment.

"What is this? Another test?"

"Not a test," Dr. Reyes replies. "A clarification. You said you left Lily alone in the cabin, correct?"

"Yes," Claire says, voice tight as piano wire. "She was asleep. I told you."

"Do you remember locking the door?"

"I always do. Always."

"And the balcony?"

Claire's patience is razor-thin. "Locked. She couldn't open it. She's three."

Dr. Reyes types a note, slow and deliberate.

"You say she's three. But your booking is for one. The manifest lists a single passenger. Our records of embarkation show only you."

"It's a mistake." Claire's voice rises. "I was with her. She had her own card, her own bed, her own everything. Ask the steward. Ask—"

She stops. She cannot remember the name. "He saw us."

"We did," Dr. Reyes says. "He remembers you, but not your daughter. And there's no evidence of Lily anywhere in your cabin."

Claire's jaw locks, her fingers dig crescents into her arms.

"Are you calling me a liar?"

"I'm asking if you've ever experienced memory distortion, or events that felt real but later proved not to be. Even under stress?"

"No." The word hits like a brick.

Dr. Reyes doesn't blink. "You had a miscarriage previously. Is that correct?"

It's a trap and Claire knows it, but she can't sidestep fast enough.

"Yes. Just before Lily. What does that have to do with anything?"

The doctor looks up, gaze unwavering. "Sometimes, after trauma, especially unprocessed trauma, the mind creates coping mechanisms. These can be vivid, persistent, even overpowering. I'm not saying this is your fault, or that you're doing anything on purpose. But it's a known phenomenon."

"You think I invented my own daughter?" Claire's voice is so loud, it echoes off the linoleum.

Dr. Reyes keeps her tone level. "No. I think you love your daughter very much. But grief isn't linear. It can take on a life of its own."

Claire lurches to her feet, the chair scraping hard against the floor. She paces the small rectangle of space, breath coming in ragged gasps.

"This is insane. She is real. She was here. She—"

The doctor doesn't interrupt. She lets the anger crash and recede.

Claire whirls. "My daughter is real. She's three years old. She loves dinosaurs. She eats more pizza than any human should. She never goes anywhere without her ragdoll cat, Thomas. She wears her rain boots even when it's dry. These aren't things I made up. These are her."

Dr. Reyes makes another note.

"You described a miscarriage earlier, that it was four years ago, and that Lily's father doesn't know she exists. Is that correct?"

Claire can't answer, not aloud. Her face crumples. Her mouth twists in a silent sob that she swallows whole.

"Don't," she says. "Don't do this."

"I need to understand, Miss Holloway. For your safety, and for the safety of anyone who might be involved." Her tone is gentle but absolute.

"If Lily is a part of your trauma, we need to address it now. Before something worse happens."

Claire shakes her head so hard her hair whips around her face.

"She was here. She was with me. I took pictures, I—"

But her phone is gone. The evidence is gone.

She clings to the memory, to the certainty, but it's slipping, like sand through closed fists.

Dr. Reyes closes the file. The tablet clicks shut.

"This isn't uncommon, especially when grief is unresolved. Some people experience it as a haunting. Others as a phantom limb. For some, it's a living, breathing child."

Claire stares at her, wild-eyed. "She's not a ghost. She's my daughter."

Dr. Reyes lets silence settle, giving it weight.

"We are going to help you, Miss Holloway. But we need you to be honest about what you're feeling. Not just the fear. The loss. The loneliness."

Claire sags back into the chair, all fight gone. She looks down at her hands, at the tiny half-moons embedded in her skin.

"If I admit she isn't real... does that mean I never get to see her again?"

"No," Dr. Reyes says softly. "It means you get to let her go. When you're ready."

For a moment, the world is so quiet, Claire wonders if it's stopped altogether.

She wipes at her face, trembling. "I'm not ready."

Dr. Reyes stands, comes around the desk, and places a business card in front of Claire.

"If you need anything, day or night, you call me. That's not a formality. You are not alone."

Claire's voice is hoarse. "I can go now?"

Dr. Reyes nods. "But I want you to stay close to your cabin. Get some sleep, if you can. We'll check on you in the morning."

Claire takes the card with numb fingers. She rises, unsteady, and leaves the office without a word. In the hallway, the lights glare too brightly, and the walls seem to tilt as she walks, but she keeps moving. Her mind splits in two: one half replaying every moment with Lily, the other a blank white void, aching in its silence.

She opens the door to her cabin, half expecting emptiness. But the note she left for Lily remains, propped against the phone, untouched.

Claire sinks onto the bed, the card pressed to her palm, and tries to recall her daughter's face. The harder she tries, the further it slips away.

She sits in the dark, clutching at the memory, and waits for morning.

CHAPTER ELEVEN

Claire wraps herself around the last memory, knuckles white in the dark, and lets her body yield to the fatigue that's built up like static. She doesn't plan to sleep. She plans to wait—eyes wide, pulse slow, ready for the next sound. But sleep comes anyway, crawling up from the base of her skull, blooming behind her eyes.

At first, there is only the pressure in her chest and the salty taste of tears. She feels the mattress tilt, the faint rumble of the ship, the ache that lingers in every joint. Her thoughts scatter and reform, scatter again. She clings to the shape of Lily's voice, the curve of her daughter's smile, the way her hair stuck to her cheek after swimming. She repeats it, a litany, until the edge of the world softens and gives.

In the dream, she wakes to sunlight and the warm, yeasty scent of croissants. Lily sits across from her on the cabin balcony, knees pulled up, face dappled by shadow through the rails.

"You missed the sunrise, Mummy," Lily says, grinning. Her mouth is ringed with orange juice, the glass cold and sticky in her hand. "You have to watch next time."

Claire reaches across and wipes the juice from her daughter's face. Her skin is warm, alive, soft as any morning before. She wipes her hands and feels the pulse in Lily's wrist, the knuckles, the faint resistance of bone.

"You always wake up before me," Claire says, and Lily's laugh rings out, bright as a bell. Clare can't remember why she was ever afraid.

But as she moves to hold her daughter, the sun flickers. The sky flattens, its colour draining. The balcony tilts, becomes a cold steel deck. The croissants vanish, replaced by something grey and bland.

Lily's face blurs at the edges. Her eyes stay bright but the pupils swim, drifting in and out of focus.

"Did you see it, Mummy?" she repeats, but the words are off, too slow, too loud, as if underwater.

Claire tries to answer, but her tongue won't move. The deck grows colder. The scene slips. The railings are bars now, thick and shadowed. Lily's chair is empty. The glass of juice tips, spills, and vanishes before it hits the floor.

A snap, a stitch in the dream. Claire is somewhere else, a splash of turquoise, the sharp smell of chlorine. Lily is in the pool, hair plastered down, eyes squeezed shut, paddling furiously.

"Watch me!" she shouts, her arms windmilling. Claire's heart leaps. She leans in, holds out her arms, feels the impact of Lily's body slam into her chest. The water is cold, and Lily's laughter is loud enough to fill the sky.

But as she lifts her daughter from the pool, the weight is wrong. Lily is too light. Her skin as slippery as a fish. Claire looks down, only a bundle of wet towels, a ragdoll cat, nothing else.

Lily's voice echoes from across the deck: "Come on, Mummy!" Claire turns, but sees only heat shimmer on concrete, the pool empty but for a floating dinosaur toy.

She calls Lily's name. The sound comes out muffled, like a hand pressed over her mouth. She calls again, louder, and the sky pulses with each repetition. The pool tiles rearrange into a checkerboard. The lounge chairs lean inward, legs tangled. The umbrellas turn inside out, caught by a wind that wasn't there before.

She blinks, the scene shifts.

The bar-turned-art-room: wild, bright, alive with colour. Children in paint-splattered aprons dip brushes and shriek with joy. Lily stands at an easel, hand smudged green and blue, working a mess of strokes onto a page.

"It's a sea dinosaur," she announces, the pride in her voice a physical thing. "It's for our cabin."

Claire tries to join her, but her feet won't move. The carpet is glue, thick and elastic. Each step is an age. When she finally reaches Lily, the painting is gone, the paper blank.

Adam's voice buzzes like static. "What a wonderful imagination!" He's looking past Lily, past Claire, at someone or something neither of them can see.

Claire reaches out to touch Lily's shoulder, but her hand passes through. The room falls silent. The other children vanish. The paint jars are sealed; the brushes dry as bones.

"Mummy?" Lily asks. Her face is suddenly older, eyes too wide. "Where did you go?"

Claire tries to answer, but her jaw clicks hollow. Panic swells, hot, sour, electric. She forces herself forward, tries to gather Lily up, but the space between them grows each time she moves. The distance stretches, infinite. She screams. The sound disappears into the thick, blank air.

Now darkness.

A corridor lined with flickering recessed lights. The carpet, always blue, stretches longer than it should. Claire runs: feet slapping, hair in her eyes, hands clawing at the walls. She is alone. Her body aches, heavy and limp, but she pushes on, calling Lily's name at every turn. All the doors are identical. Closed. Silent. Indifferent.

She opens one.

A cabin: empty beds, stale air, the balcony closed. A note on the desk: "Back soon, love Mummy."

Claire tears it to shreds. She yells. Only her fear answers, echoing back.

Another door: the ship's theatre. Empty seats, the stage awash in pale, flickering light. A flyer at her feet: "Elton John Impersonator, One Night Only." She tries to laugh, but the sound chokes. She searches the aisles, the shadows. Nothing. Just the low hum of the speakers and distant, mocking applause.

Again, she moves. The ship shifts, sways. The world tilts.

Now the dining room. Lily sits at a tall table.

"Tiny toast!" She shouts, reaching for croissants. They vanish before she can touch them. The table stretches, becomes a conveyor belt, whisking her away, through a tunnel of blinking lights and mirrors.

Claire chases. Always too slow. Always a second behind. Her own limbs betray her. She watches Lily shrink, a dot, then gone.

Underwater now.

The pressure crushes. The cold is absolute. Lily's face appears, distorted by the current, eyes pleading. Claire kicks, arms burning, desperate to reach her. But the water turns to syrup. Her body slows, motionless, suspended. The light fades. Lily's voice becomes a faint ripple, then silence.

She floats in darkness. No up, no down. Just the weight of grief. She tries to cry. No tears. Tries to speak. No voice. Not even a name.

Time folds.

Memories flicker. Backward. Sideways. Never the same. Lily is at her side, then a shadow, then only a laugh, a word, the trace of juice on a glass that never was. The loop spins faster, shards of colour, fragments of pain.

The final dream is the worst:

Claire sits in the cabin, lit only by a thin stripe from the hallway. She knows with animalistic certainty, that Lily is behind the door, calling for her. Claire claws at the lock. Her hands are rubber, slipping from the handle. The voice fades. The light dies. The door never opens.

Claire wakes, but only partway.

Somewhere between the dark and day. Her body is lead. Her mind is blank. She tries to move. Can't. Tries to scream. The air is too thick.

In that liminal space, Claire feels Lily's hand in hers. Small. Cold. Gone.

She floats in the nothing, waiting for the world to begin again.

Claire surfaces from the dark with a gasp, like someone who's been drowning for hours. Her eyelids cling shut, only peeling open when she forces them, and even then, the world blurs at the edges. The room is bright. Too bright. A sterile kind of morning that makes her want to hide. Her limbs are heavy. Every muscle aches. Her tongue sticks to the roof of her mouth, sour and thick.

It takes a moment to remember why she hurts. Then, it hits: Lily, is gone. Certainty, then the spiral. She bolts upright, clutching the sheet, scanning the room for proof that it was just a nightmare. That Lily is asleep, drooling on the pillow, her breath warm and damp against the blankets.

But half the bed is made. The far side of the mattress is untouched, the pillows smooth. No dinosaur pyjamas. No green hair bobble. No Thomas the cat. Not even a crumpled colouring page or a single glitter sticker left behind. It is all hers now. Only hers. The room is too neat. Too empty. Her suitcase stands where she left it, zipped tight, nothing disturbed.

The clock reads 07:13. She doesn't know how long she slept, or if she slept at all. It could have been an hour or a year. She touches her face, feels the pillow's imprint, the staleness of a night spent breathing too hard. Her fingers tangle in her hair, and she doesn't recognise the feel of it.

She tries to reconstruct last night: security, the office, the nurse, the doctor, the words that sliced and bled. They said they'd follow up, send someone, check on her. But the hallway is silent. No footsteps. No phone calls. No apologetic knock on the door. Just the ship, humming along, the floor vibrating with its own eerie certainty.

She waits. One minute. Two. She watches the corridor through the peephole. Just an endless row of doors. She half expects to see the nurse with the coiled hair and clipboard, but there's nothing. No sign she was ever real.

She dials. The numbers feel clumsy beneath her fingers. The front desk answers, voice chipper and polished. "Guest Services, how may I help you?"

Claire tries to keep her voice steady. "Hi, this is Claire Holloway, cabin 8612. I'm checking on— I filed a report last night. About my daughter. She's missing. I haven't heard from anyone."

A pause. Then the same neutral tone. "I'm sorry, ma'am. Can you clarify the issue?"

"My daughter. Lily. She's three. I spoke to security, and medical staff, but I haven't had any updates. No one's come by. Is there any news?" Her words splinter. She hates how desperate she sounds.

The receptionist hesitates, "I'm sorry, Miss Holloway. I don't see a record of a missing child on your account. Did you wish to file a report now?"

Claire blinks. The headache creeps back up behind her eyes. "I did file it. They took down her name and description—they said they'd check the cameras. I talked to a man, Daniel something, and the doctor —Reyes. I—" She stops, forces the tremor out of her voice. "Can you check, please?"

She's put on hold. Tinny music fills the silence. Claire drums her fingers, fast, faster, until her skin stings. She watches the clock, watches the numbers change, time slipping like a trap.

The line clicks back in. "Thank you for holding, Miss Holloway. I've spoken with my supervisor and security. There's no record of a child linked to your cabin or name. I can send someone to assist if you'd like to file a formal report."

Claire swallows. "I already did. I just—" She slams the receiver down.

She sits, staring at the desk, her hands shaking too hard to form a fist. She rakes them through her hair, tugging at the roots, hoping pain might clear her head. It doesn't. She stands. Sits. Stands again. Paces the room's short length. She checks the closet, the bathroom, yanks back the shower curtain, half expecting Lily to pop out giggling, "Surprise, Mummy!" It's stupid. But she can't stop.

She pulls the mattress off the bed. Underneath: dust, a spare blanket, folded military-tight. She tears through the drawers, through her clothes, through every seam, every pocket, searching for something, anything, proof that Lily was real. There is nothing.

The anxiety comes in waves, tight and cold. Her hands twist at the hem of her shirt, fidgeting until the fabric warps and wrinkles. She paces again, bare feet marking a path in the utilitarian carpet. Outside the window is bright. The sea endless. The sky a cloudless blue. The world is beautiful. And unconcerned.

She thinks of leaving. Storming down to the security office. Demanding answers. But her legs won't move. Instead, she perches at the edge of the bed, chin in her hands, watching the clock.

The minutes tick by. The world doesn't notice. The air stays clean. The ship stays steady. And nothing changes.

Not for a long, long time.

The phone rings just as Claire's hands go numb on her knees. The jolt cuts straight through the hush like a siren. She snatches the receiver before it can ring again, heart pounding in her throat.

"Hello?" Her voice breaks.

"Hello, is this Miss Holloway?" The caller's tone is friendly, upbeat, tinged with an Australian accent. "This is Hayley from Customer Services. I'm calling about your phone?"

For a moment, Claire is frozen. Her pulse hammers like a drumline.

"My phone," she echoes, gripping the handset tighter. "Yes. You found it?"

Hayley laughs, a neat little trill. "We think so! It's a silver iPhone, right? Clear case with blue stars? It turned up in the theatre last night, but the battery was dead. We're charging it in the back office now."

Relief crashes through Claire. She almost sobs. "Thank you. Thank you. That's it. That's my phone."

"Perfect!" Hayley chirps. "I'll need you to stop by the desk and unlock it for us, just so we can verify ownership before release. Is that okay?"

"Yes," Claire breathes. "Yes, absolutely. How soon can I come?"

Hayley clicks her tongue thoughtfully. "Give it, say, five to ten minutes to charge up enough for you to access it. Just come to the Customer Services desk with your sail pass card."

"I'll be there," Claire says quickly. "Thank you, Hayley. You have no idea how much—" She stops. She almost laughs at the hope in her own voice, the desperate animal joy of it. The phone is everything. The phone is proof.

Hayley signs off with a final "See you then!" and the line goes dead.

Claire clutches the receiver, knuckles white, adrenaline sparking in her chest. She holds her breath, afraid it might all vanish if she exhales. Her phone. Her pictures. Lily. Real. Saved. Waiting.

She stands too fast, her legs buckling, and stumbles to the bathroom.

The mirror startles her. Pale face red-rimmed eyes, sweat-damp hair. She looks less like a woman than a half-finished sketch. But a smile forms—fragile and new, and she watches it take hold.

She strips off the old shirt, turns the shower on full blast, and steps in before the water warms. The cold is bracing, a slap to the senses. She scrubs hard, as if panic and doubt are stains she can remove. Her hands shake. She keeps going.

She skips washing her hair, dries quickly, dresses, and ignores the tremor in her fingers as she pulls on her socks.

The ship is awake now. Outside the cabin window, the world is neon blue, cloudless. Sunlight shards off the water, so bright it stings. Voices drift in from the corridor: a family heading to breakfast, a steward rolling a cart, a child's laughter. Claire listens, nails biting into her palms, hoping for a voice that sounds like Lily's.

None comes.

She snatches the cabin phone and dials the numbers Daniel Johnson gave her last night. With every ring, she's more certain—she is not crazy. Her memories are real. The photos will speak.

No answer. Five, six, seven rings, then voicemail.

"Daniel, it's Claire Holloway. They found my phone. Guest Services just called. I'm heading there now." Her voice quickens. "It has all the pictures of Lily on it. All the proof. Meet me there as soon as you can." She falters, breath catching. "This changes everything."

She hangs up, hands trembling with a cocktail of hope and conviction.

She grabs her sail pass card and checks the mirror again. The woman reflected back is unkempt but resolute. Her eyes blaze with certainty.

The corridor feels shorter. Her steps are quicker, surer. The ship's sway barely registers as she makes her way toward the elevators.

She rehearses: "Here. Look. My daughter. Lily. She was here with me. This is proof." She will say it with a steady spine and unbreakable voice. She will be heard.

Outside, the hallway is bright and teeming. Passengers drift by. The ship awake in a way it hasn't been for hours. She merges with the current, shoulders squared.

Every step brings her closer to the truth. To her phone. To her daughter.

This time, she will not return empty-handed.

CHAPTER TWELVE

Claire pushes upstream through a pod of retirees in matching hats headed to breakfast. The hallway outside Guest Services buzzes with noise—children darting between legs, guests disputing charges on their account. None of it touches her. Her world has narrowed to a single, hard line between herself and the counter.

Guest Services is designed to look welcoming: clean white desks., polished wood trim, oatmeal-coloured walls, meant to soothe the nervous and the lost. The room is bright, almost too bright, and the staff's fake smiles are turned up to full.

The woman waiting for her is younger than Claire expected. Maybe twenty-five. Platinum hair, a tan too flawless to be natural. Her name tag reads HAYLEY, decorated with a small Australian flag. She's the kind of person cruise lines hire in bulk: tireless, cheerful, capable of reciting a script even under gunfire.

"Hi there! You must be Claire?" Hayley beams, hands folded on the counter.

"Yes. My phone?" Claire's voice is strained, sharp. Her own voice irritates her.

Hayley's smile flickers but rebounds. "One sec—let me just check the charging dock." She takes two steps to a cubby in the wall and returns with a silver iPhone in a clear case with blue stars. It's unmistakably Claire's. "We've given it a bit of juice, but it's still pretty low," Hayley says. "Can you unlock it for me, just to confirm?"

Claire snatches the phone, her hands unsteady. The screen lights up. Only 6% battery. The passcode prompt glows. Her thumb hesitates, then keys in six digits. The phone unlocks with a buzz.

"That's great, thanks so much!" Hayley chirps, as if their interaction is over. "If you need a charging cable, we can lend you one—"

"No. I just—thank you." Claire cuts her off, already backing away, eyes locked on the phone.

She doesn't look where she's going. She finds an empty chair by the dolphin mural on the wall and sits. The plastic is sticky against her legs. The phone is an anchor. She cradles it, ignoring the burn of her own embarrassment. Around her, the world becomes white noise. Hayley has moved on, her voice bright as a new penny.

Claire opens Photos. She expects a flood of colour, of proof. The app takes a beat to load. For a second, her reflection stares back at her from the screen, wild hair, shadowed eyes, uneven face.

Then the photos appear.

The first is from boarding day: a shot of the gleaming ship taken from the terminal. Then a blurry selfie, Claire squinting into the sun, the bow of the ship in the background. The stateroom with one king bed. A series of balcony shots: endless sea, flawless digital blue.

She swipes, waiting for Lily to appear. But Lily never does.

There are shots from the muster drill: a crowd on the deck, crew in bright orange vests, Claire's own arm stretched into the chaos. The pool deck, tiled floor, a line of towels, a paper cup of lemonade on a lounge chair. No Lily. No pink boots, No dinosaur dress. Not even a stray hair bobble.

A coldness pools in Claire's belly. She flips to the next day: breakfast on the balcony—croissant, fruit, sunlight sharp. A photo of the art class flyer. A blurry snap of the children's art room—tiny easels, empty. No Lily.

She scrolls faster. Lunch on the pool deck, a burger and fries, a Pepsi can, the shadow of her hand. The Elton John impersonator's flyer. A photo of the theatre stage before the lights went down. Then, a bathroom selfie—lipstick intact, smile uncertain.

Stateroom, evening: one bed perfectly made, a towel folded into a swan, a chocolate balanced on the pillow. No toys. No colouring books. No pyjamas.

The coldness rises into her throat. Her heart pounds. She scrolls back, frantic, searching for the photos she remembers: Lily at the muster drill, Lily with a juice box, Lily painting. The memories are vivid, immediate—and missing. Every image is food, scenery, empty space. Not one contains her daughter.

Claire checks Favourites. Just two landscape shots and a cat meme. Recents. All Photos. Camera Roll. Same sequence. No trace of Lily.

She scrolls further back. Weeks before the cruise. Her apartment. A potted plant, new running shoes, wine, takeout. Only her own face, captured in selfies. A flight confirmation. A calendar. A grocery receipt.

No toys on the floor. No crayon marks. No highchair. No child.

Claire's hands tremble. Her vision narrows. She flips the phone over, as if the case might explain the disappearance. Blue stars wink back up at her, indifferent.

She tries to breathe. The air won't go in. Her pulse roars in her ears. The room tips sideways.

A memory breaks through—Lily at breakfast, hair a mess, mouth sticky with orange juice. Claire can see it, taste it. She remembers her laughter, her little hand gripping hers, the argument about the rain boots. She remembers.

She blinks. The photos don't change.

She looks up. Guest Services hums with life. No one notices her unravelling.

Claire's clutches her mouth. A sharp whine escapes. She opens her call log. No missed calls. No texts. Nothing from a babysitter. Nothing from anyone.

She opens the Notes app. She searches for evidence: lists, reminders, anything. There's only work to-dos, a note about renewing her passport.

Nothing about Lily.

Dizziness rolls through her. She stands. The chair scrapes back. Her knees almost give.

She stares at the phone, her reflection ghosting in the glass. She doesn't recognise herself.

She wants to throw the phone. To smash it. But she clutches it tighter, as if it might anchor her to reality.

She stares at the dolphin mural and wonders why she thought she would find Lily here.

She stands for a long time, breathing in shallow gasps, until the room sharpens again.

Hayley is smiling, helping another guest. The world moves on, indifferent.

Claire looks down at the phone again. It won't change. The evidence is cold, simple: every memory is just that—a memory. There is no proof. No trace. Only the ache of knowing what is gone.

She leans on the wall, legs shaking, and waits for the world to tilt back.

It never does.

It is Daniel who finds her, both a relief and a humiliation. He spots her from halfway down the corridor. He's a tall, not in uniform, but in dark jeans and a polo shirt. His head is bare, the neat practicality of his hair making him look older, yet softer than she remembered. His eyes scan the room, land on Claire, and narrow with concern. She's the only person in Guest Services looking utterly broken.

He crosses to her in three long steps. "Miss Holloway? Claire?" His voice is low, but carries.

She tries to answer, but her throat locks. She can only shove the phone toward him, the evidence trembling in her hands. "Look," she manages. "Look at it. I don't understand—"

Daniel takes the phone, carefully avoiding touching her more than necessary. His hands are large, warm, and steadier than hers. "What's going on?" he asks, already scanning the home screen and then the gallery.

"It's wrong," Claire says. "The pictures—they're all wrong." The words tumble out too fast, jammed together. "I took photos. So many. She was in every one. There were videos. Of her. Of Lily. But now—"

She stops, breath gone. She wants to grab his arm, shake him, make him see the empty space where her daughter should be.

Daniel's brow furrows. "You're saying the photos are missing?"

"Not missing. Just—" She can't explain it in any way that makes sense. "Look." She points at the first shot: the ship at port. "I took that to show her. She was standing with me. I told her about the lifeboats." She swipes to the next—the stateroom. "She was here. I took a picture of her on the bed—there were two. She wore her dinosaur pyjamas." She swipes again, hard, to the breakfast shot. "That's her croissant. She smeared jam all over the table. I took it to send to my mum, but she—" Claire stops. She doesn't remember if she ever actually meant to send it.

Daniel is calm. Too calm. He scrolls through the photos himself, methodical. "When did you last back up your phone?" he asks. "Maybe the pictures are still in the cloud, but not downloaded here."

"I don't use the cloud," she says. "I back up to my computer at home. It's all supposed to be here. Always here."

Daniel tries the Albums tab, then Recently Deleted. Only two images appear: screenshots, both of an art class registration page. He looks at Claire. "These are the only deleted files."

"It's not possible," she says. "I took a video of her at the pool. Photos of her having fun. I told you all about it. You wrote it down. You had a description—"

He holds the phone between them, as if presenting a witness. "Claire. This is what's on the phone. Nothing else."

She wants to scream at him, to tell him he's not looking hard enough. Instead, she rips the phone from his hands and flicks to Recents. She scrolls to the pool deck photo, the one with the lemonade. She points at the shadow of her own hand. "She was right there. You can see the gap. She was right there. It— it changed." Her voice rises, people nearby turning to watch.

Daniel keeps his voice steady. "I believe you took these pictures. I just don't see any children in them. Maybe the phone glitched. Maybe they didn't save."

She shakes her head, wild. "No. I saw them. I remember her. She wore a pink swimsuit with a dinosaur on it. She made friends with a girl named Sophie. She got sunburned. I put cream on her before bed." Claire is crying now, not loud but constant, a leak she can't patch. "How can she not be here?"

Daniel puts a hand on her shoulder, light as a whisper. "Claire, you're exhausted. You hit your head. Sometimes the brain—"

"Don't," she says, a plea, not a warning.

He tries anyway. "Sometimes it fills in the gaps. It happens after trauma. Especially if you're alone, especially if—"

"Don't say I made her up," she says. "Don't you dare."

Daniel lets go of her shoulder. He looks around the room, as if searching for backup. The other staff watch, but don't intervene. Hayley stands behind the counter, eyes flicking between Daniel and Claire, uncertain.

Daniel leans in, soft but firm. "No one's saying you lied. No one thinks you did anything wrong. But this isn't proof of anything. It's just a phone, and it's empty."

She wants to throw the phone, to smash it. Instead, she swipes to the home screen and scrolls through every app—Photos, Messages, Facebook. She types Lily's name in the search bar. Nothing. She opens Contacts, looking for a number saved as Babysitter or Art Class or even Mum. No luck. She checks Calendar for an event— "Lily's

Birthday," "School Play", but the entries are all work, errands, dentist appointments, reminders to water the plant. The phone dies. She will need to charge it to keep searching.

She feels Daniel watching, waiting for her to see it herself.

She tries to remember if she ever called her mother, spoke to another adult about Lily last week, last month. She recalls the art class, the instructor's voice, but not the face. Parents at the pool who never spoke to her. The pizza place, the waiter's smile, but he smiled at everyone.

She is losing her grip. Her mind frays at the edges.

Daniel says, "Claire, you need to rest. I'm off duty now, but they're still looking. I will keep looking. We can talk more when you've slept."

"I don't need sleep," she says thin and empty. "I need her back."

He sighs, not unkind. "Come on. I'll walk you to your room. You can call Medical if you want. I would suggest you do. But for now, take care of yourself."

Too tired to argue, she lets him guide her down the hallway past the mural of dolphins and the parade of people who avert their eyes. He walks beside her, a gentle shadow, never touching but always just close enough.

They reach the elevator. She doesn't remember the ride, only the silence, and the way Daniel checks his watch, then her, as if calculating.

At her cabin, he waits as she fumbles with the sail pass card. She gets it wrong twice. He takes it, taps it on the sensor, and hands it back without a word.

She steps inside. He stays in the hall, watching, making sure she doesn't collapse.

"I'm sorry," she says, not knowing why.

He nods, understanding everything and nothing. "It's okay. I'll check in later."

He waits until she closes the door, then she hears his footsteps fade.

She sits on the bed's edge, phone clutched in her hand, staring at the black screen. For a long time, she waits for something to change, for evidence to reappear, for some proof that she isn't crazy.

But the phone stays blank. The room stays silent.

She gazes out at the vast ocean, her own reflection staring back from the balcony glass. The waves roll by, carrying the world away, and she feels torn between a longing to drift with them and a deep-rooted need to stay anchored where she is.

CHAPTER THIRTEEN

Claire stands in the centre of her cabin. She doesn't turn on the lights. The balcony floods the room with enough brightness, the sun ricocheting off the white ship, reflecting off the dark screen in her hand.

She plugs her phone into the charger by the bed. The connector makes a muted click, the same as at home, but here the sound feels wrong. It is a click of finality. The phone vibrates, once, twice, a pulse beneath her thumb. The battery icon flickers to life, red at first, then white. The lock screen brightens with her own face.

She almost drops the phone.

The photo is one she doesn't remember taking. Or maybe she does. She stares at herself, backlit by the blue of the sea, squinting, hair flying, a half-smile on her lips. She is alone. The space beside her is empty, vast as sky. No shadow, no hint of a child's hand, no accidental crop of a dinosaur-print sleeve.

The phone vibrates again. The motion travels up her hand, through her arm, settling somewhere behind her breastbone. She thumbs the screen, unlocks it, and the gallery opens on the same image: herself, alone, horizon perfectly level behind her. She cannot stop looking. The memory she has does not match the one on the phone.

It should be Lily beside her. That morning, the two of them on the promenade, her daughter squinting against the sun, face sticky with jelly and joy. But the phone only shows Claire, awkward and unsmiling, a woman captured by accident.

She flicks to the next image. The stateroom, taken from the threshold. There should be two beds, one with Lily's toy cat, the other with the novel Claire never touched. But the photo shows only a single king-size bed, made up perfectly. She checks again. No toys. No crayon marks, no stray sock. Not even her own suitcase. Just the tight, clean corners of a hotel sheet, the absence so sharp it lances through her.

Her mouth is dry. She sits on the edge of the bed; the phone cradled in both hands.

The third photo is of the pool deck. Loungers lined up like dominoes, each one vacant. No sopping wet child running toward her, no pink boots, no shriek of *Watch me, Mummy!* The sun glares off the water, a band of white so bright she has to look away. She blinks, trying to clear the spots from her vision.

Her hands tremble. She steadies them on her knees, but the phone shakes anyway, as if vibrating with its own private message.

She scrolls faster. Pizza on a plate. A view of the water from the top deck. A flyer for tonight's show. Generic holiday photos that could have been taken by anyone. Not a single image contains Lily. Not a single image contains evidence that a child ever set foot in this room, this ship, this life.

Claire breathes in; the air feels thin and metallic. Her chest hitches. She zooms in on the photos, hunting for the artefacts: a blur of movement, a reflection in a window, a child's hand reaching for her own. She finds nothing. She checks the Recents album, then the trash. Nothing. She checks every folder, every album, every single byte the phone contains.

There is no Lily.

The ship shifts under her, a subtle roll that sends her head spinning. The floor seems to tilt; she grips the bed to stay upright. The phone slips, nearly falling, but she clamps it hard in her palm.

Her vision swims. She opens Messages. The last text is from a work colleague, weeks ago. She searches for "Lily" in Contacts, Notes, in every field the phone will allow. Nothing. Her hands go numb. The phone suddenly feels too heavy, a stone in her lap.

She looks around the room, desperate for a reality check. The cabin is as bare as in the photo: no toys, no kid-sized shoes, no colouring books. The desk is neat, the closet closed, the air sterile.

She wants to scream, but her voice won't obey. Instead, she squeezes the phone until her knuckles ache, willing it to transform, to yield a different truth.

The ship's hum fills the silence. She counts her own heartbeats, fast and uneven. The light from the phone paints her face in ghostly white, and her reflection in the dark window looks more like a stranger than herself.

She sits, unmoving, the phone burning in her hand, and waits for something to change.

Nothing does.

The memory comes without warning, like a drop in pressure, a crack in the hull.

The ship, the phone, the room—they are gone.

She is back in the hospital. Not the clean, ship-shape white of this cabin, but the blue-green of medical scrubs, the yellow stain of old linoleum, the sharp, wet stink of antiseptic. The walls sweat. The lights press too close to her face.

Her body is split open. She hears herself screaming, but the voice is someone else's. Gloved hands are on her, rough pinches from a blood pressure cuff, the dull pressure of a lure in her hand. A bright line of pain runs through her, hip to hip. She blinks and her vision is wiped clean. Her mouth tastes like pennies and disinfectant.

A doctor hovers over her, face blurred by a surgical mask. The voice is all syllables and no comfort: "I'm so sorry, Miss Holloway. The baby didn't make it." The words press through her ears, settle behind her eyes, burn the memory into bone.

She tries to breathe, but her chest feels full of rocks. She tries to move, but her arms are strapped by wires and tubes. A mechanical beep, sounds, precise and constant, meaning her body is still alive even if everything inside is not.

The room grows colder. The nurse calls someone on the phone, the receiver wedged between ear and shoulder. "She's stable, but she'll need observation," the nurse says, as if Claire is not already a ghost.

She wants to scream, to punch, to break everything. She wants someone to hold her hand, to tell her it will matter again, but the room is empty except for the bodies doing their jobs.

She comes to in a hospital chair, her hands clawing at the thin paper blanket. Marcus sits across from her, knees apart, elbows on his thighs. He looks everywhere but at her. The TV in the corner plays a game show with the volume off. His hair is perfect, his shirt too crisp. He checks the clock on the wall, then his watch, then the floor.

He says, "They said you'll recover fully." Not a question, not an offer. A statement to file away.

She says, "It hurts," but the words are too small for him to hear.

He looks at her with the same expression he uses on conference calls, the one that means I've already moved on, I'm only here to close the loop. "I need to go," he says.

She wants him to cry. She wants him to shout, to break a chair, to hate the world for what it did to them. Instead, he stands, slow and heavy, and walks out the door.

The next memory: home. The curtains closed, the apartment dark except for the light of the fridge as she opens it, stares inside, finds nothing she can eat. The milk is sour. The apples are soft. The only thing that feels real is the ache in her lower abdomen, the void where a child once was.

Marcus leaves for work every morning, returns after dark, sits in the living room with the laptop propped on his knees, never looking up. There are no conversations, only noises—shoes on tile, the shush of water in the shower, the shuffle of papers. He sleeps on the couch, then in the guest room, then not at all.

She tries to reach him. She sits beside him on the sofa, shoulder to shoulder, and says, "I need to talk." He nods but keeps his eyes on the screen.

She says, "I miss her," and his jaw twitches. He says, "She didn't exist." He says, "We need to move forward." He says, "I don't know what you want from me."

She wants to say, "I want you to hurt," but she knows that's the one thing he cannot do.

The last memory: the suitcase by the door, perfectly packed, the zipper a surgical scar. He left their relationship weeks ago, and now he leaves her life for the last time. He does not say goodbye. She stands in the hall, socks on cold tile, arms wrapped around herself. The only sound is the click of the door as he leaves.

She sits at the kitchen table and listens to the silence. She counts the hours until sunrise, then the minutes, then the seconds. The world goes on, uncaring.

In the cabin, the flashback recedes, but the pain lingers, bright and jagged. Claire slides off the bed, her back to the frame, her knees drawn to her chest. The phone lies on the carpet, forgotten.

She cannot breathe. The walls are too close. The air is wet and cold; her skin prickles with sweat. She wraps her arms around her legs, trying to make herself smaller, trying to vanish into the thin space between heartbeats.

She thinks of Lily, of the phantom weight of a child in her arms, of a voice she will never hear again. She thinks of Marcus, of the way he never looked back, of how the world made it so easy to forget.

She buries her face in her knees and shakes.

The ship rocks, a gentle roll. She does not move.

She sits for a long time, knees pulled to her chest, the phone cooling on the carpet by her foot. Time folds in on itself. Only the hard edge of the bed frame presses into her shins, the deep ache in her belly where pain and shame have nested.

She tries to think, but every thought slips away.

Then Dr. Reyes's words rise in her mind, sharp as glass: "The mind can create elaborate scenarios to protect itself from pain." The echo is impossible to shake. Claire wants to punch the memory away, but the voice is inside her, woven tight.

She looks up. For the first time, she really sees the cabin.

There is only one water glass on the nightstand. One towel hangs in the bathroom, folded with the ship's logo perfectly visible. Only one set of toiletries, her own toothpaste, her own deodorant, nothing with dinosaurs, glitter, or child-sized packaging. The slippers by the bed are both adult-sized.

She stands on legs like rope and walks to the closet. She opens it. Only her own clothes hang there: two sundresses, a swimsuit, a cheap rain jacket. She feels along the rail, searching for something, anything, small enough to be Lily's. But the wood is smooth and empty.

Her eyes sting. She kneels and opens the bottom drawer. Nothing but a pair of flats and her running shoes stuffed with rolled socks. She opens the suitcase she packed for both of them. Her own shirts and jeans, folded neat. No pyjamas with cartoon prints, no pink boots, no dinosaur backpack.

She checks again. Her hands fumble through the layers, searching for a tiny sock, a bright hair bobble, a worn toy cat. She finds nothing but her own packing cubes and her own desperate hands.

The urge rises, irresistible. She rips the sheets off the bed and inspects the mattress for indentations, for the shallow mark of a child who slept there. The bed is flat as a board, cold to the touch. She checks under the frame, the dustless expanse between mattress and floor. There is nothing.

She stands in the middle of the room, sweat freezing on her skin. She paces to the bathroom and opens the medicine cabinet. Only her pill bottle. Only her own painkillers. She remembers teaching Lily to brush her teeth, the taste of bubblegum paste, the fight every morning to get her to spit and not swallow. But the brush is gone. Only her own blue-and-white brush stands alone in the glass.

She staggers back to the bedroom. The world shrinks, closes in. She sees herself in the mirror, eyes hollowed out, hair clumped to one side. She looks like someone who has been awake for days. She looks like someone who has lost her mind.

She tries to remember the last real moment with Lily. Not a dream, not a flashback, not a story told to someone else. The details flicker: Lily laughing on the balcony, her face haloed by the morning sun, the way she snorted when she giggled too hard. The way she cried after falling in the pool, the way Claire wrapped her in a towel and sang the song about brave dinosaurs until she calmed.

Were those moments real? Or did she make them, piece by piece, to fill the hollow the world left her?

She wants to remember Lily's smell—the mix of sunscreen, apple juice, and sweat. She wants to remember the exact sound of her laugh. She wants to believe that a three-year-old ever called her "Mummy." But the memories turn soft, slippery. She cannot grasp a single one.

She stands by the bed; one hand braced on the mattress. She feels the pressure of her own fingers, the pulse in her palm. She breathes in, and the air is flat and flavourless.

The room is empty. The room is always empty.

She drops to her knees, presses her face to the carpet, and weeps.

The sound is raw—not even a sob, just a series of small, wet gasps. Her body shakes with the force of it. She hugs her arms around her stomach, the same way she did in the hospital, the same way she did when Marcus left, the same way she did every time the world threatened to take everything away.

She cries until there is nothing left to come out. No more sound, no more tears—just the shudder of her own breath, over and over. The ache in her gut becomes a single, burning point, the memory of something lost so long ago she wonders if it was ever real.

She lies there, curled on the carpet, the ship rocking her with its endless, gentle motion. She does not move.

There is only the hum of the engine, the dark, and the empty space where her daughter should be.

CHAPTER FOURTEEN

The afternoon arrives as like idea, not a reality. Claire lies where she fell, a question mark at the bed's end, one arm curled beneath her chest, the other pressed to her stomach as if holding herself together. The rough carpet scratches her cheek; her tongue is thick with the taste of stale saliva. She hasn't moved since shortly after dawn.

No clock is visible from this part of the room. The light filtering through the curtains is thin and stale, barely different from the night before. Claire's body is cold from inactivity, but she doesn't shiver. Her jaw aches from clenching too hard. Her eyelids are swollen, lashes stuck in little clumps, the glue of dried tears holding them together.

She hasn't changed clothes. The shirt she's lying in is creased and sour under her arms, the sweat from her collapse mixing with yesterday's deodorant poorly washed off this morning—forming a smell she knows will cling to her for days. She hasn't eaten. The water bottle on the desk is half-full; she considers crawling to it, but the thought evaporates before it forms.

She doesn't look at her phone at first. When she does, the lock screen glows, fully charged. It's her own face, caught in that accidental moment on the deck, but she can't stand to look at it. She turns it over, screen down, and lets it slide onto the carpet. No reminders. No evidence.

Time comes in lumps. A distant clang of a service cart rolls down the corridor, but she doesn't flinch. A woman's laugh drifts through the air vent, distant as if from another world. The ship's movement is so constant that she can't calm seas from rough. It all feels the same now.

She hears her breath, shallow and slow, the drag of air through tired lungs. Once, she tries to stand, but her legs refuse. She folds smaller, wraps her arms around her knees, waiting for the next thing to go wrong.

Hours pass unnoticed. Then a knock, a gunshot in the quiet.

The sound vibrates through the metal door. Once, then softer again, as if the knocker regrets the intrusion. Claire blinks, her sticky eyelids pulling tight. She doesn't want to answer. Doesn't want to see anyone.

A third knock. Then a voice. "Claire? It's Security Officer Daniel Jackson. Are you awake?"

She hates the hope sparked by his voice. Hates that it's him and not someone else. Hates that she can't ignore him. She knows he won't go away until she opens the door.

She pushes herself upright, arms wobbling. Her knees are numb, toes prickling as blood returns. She stumbles, half-crawls, to the door, using the bed and the wall for support.

Her reflection catches in the closet mirror: hair clumped to one side, dry, colourless lips, red-rimmed, hollow eyes. She looks like someone held together by threads—one word away from unravelling.

She wipes her face with her shirt's hem, but it only worsens things. Steading herself against the wall, she unlocks the door.

The door opens with a hiss. Daniel stands there, hand still raised to knock, posture relaxed but eyes sharp. He drops his hand after a quick glance, jaw tightening barely. His smile is careful, practiced.

"Afternoon," he says, as if it's a normal day, she is a normal woman in a normal room.

She tries to answer, but words stick. All she manages is a nod—feeling like a confession.

He hesitates, a quiet calculation in his eyes. "You missed breakfast and lunch," he says. "Thought I'd check in."

She almost laughs. Instead, she grips the doorframe, waiting for what he came to say.

Daniel glances into the cabin, the mess on the floor, unmade bed, towel bunched on the bathroom tile. Then back to her face, exhausted, probably dehydrated, one bad conversation from a meltdown.

She expects judgment, but his voice is gentle. "Want to walk with me to Medical? The doc's been asking. Just to check in. You don't have to stay."

Claire shakes her head, not refusing, just disbelieving. "I'm fine," she says, surprised by the hoarse unfamiliar voice. "Just tired."

Daniel leans against the wall, arms folded. Not in uniform— the same dark jeans, but now a blue shirt, sleeves rolled up. He looks like a civilian, but his stance is pure security: wide, balanced, ready.

"That's what the doc said you'd say," he replies with a faint smile. "She also said it's standard after a head injury to do follow-ups. It's not punishment. Just care."

Claire sways, a tremor rising from ankles to hips. She wants to refuse, to sink back into her hole, but the way he waits is final. She won't win.

She pulls the door open wider. "Give me a minute," she says, voice almost normal.

Daniel steps back, giving her space. "I'll be right here."

She closes the door, rests her head against the cool metal. The ship's movement pulses stronger now, engines vibrating through her ribs. Slowly, she changes into a fresh pair of jeans and a long-sleeved shirt smelling of laundry soap. She runs her fingers through tanged hair.

No glance at the phone. She slips her sail pass into her pocket and opens the door before she can change her mind.

Daniel's exactly where she left him, hands in his pockets, eyes scanning down the corridor like checking for threats. He straightens when he sees her, offers a small, encouraging nod.

They walk in silence. Claire tries to keep pace, muscles leaden. Each step feels like her last. One hand trails the wall for support.

The corridor is empty, but life echoes everywhere—the clatter of dishes from the dining hall, child's laugh behind a closed door, the hum of air systems pushing last night's regret out to sea.

Daniel glances at her, but doesn't speak. He matches his stride to hers, slow and measured. When she stumbles at the first turn, he puts a hand under her elbow, just enough to catch her balance, then releases.

"You didn't have to come," she says, eyes down.

He shrugs. "It's my job to look out for passengers."

She almost snaps, almost tells him she's not his problem, but the words wither. Instead, she says, "Sorry for the mess."

He shakes his head. "Seen worse. Had a guy last year who locked himself in his room for four days—made a fort out of towels. Took three of us to talk him out."

Claire manages a small but genuine smile.

"Did it work?"

"In the end," Daniel replies, "people can get weird at sea."

Claire thinks of Lily, how the world twists when you can't tell up from down, truth from lie. She wonders how many aboard this ship are quietly losing their minds, just out of sight, behind neat white doors.

The walk feels endless. At the elevator, Claire's legs threaten to give out, but Daniel steadies her with the lightest touch. He presses the call button and leans against the wall, pretending not to notice her shaking.

The elevator arrives, empty. They step in. The silence is absolute. The doors close, and for a moment Claire is certain she will suffocate.

She focuses on the numbers, watching them tick down: 8, 7, 6… She doesn't remember which floor Medical is on, but trusts Daniel to know.

"Do you want me to stay with you?" he asks softly.

She considers. "You can if you want… yes," she says, surprised by how much she means it.

The doors open, and the cold blue of the Medical Deck rushes in. The lights are brighter here, the air sharper. Claire blinks; her eyes sting.

Daniel leads, neither too fast nor too slow. At the turn to the Medical Bay, he pauses and lets her take the lead. She freezes at the threshold, gripped by the memory of last time—Dr. Reyes, the questions, the feeling of being x-rayed to her soul.

She hesitates. Daniel leans close, just enough for her to hear.

"You got this," he says.

She looks at him, at the soft crinkle of lines by his eyes, and finds a little strength in them.

"Yeah," she says. "I guess I do."

She pushes open the door and steps inside.

Inside the Medical Bay, the cold hits immediately. It's a different cold than the air outside, a manufactured chill, the kind meant to keep bacteria at bay, forcing every breath to taste of chemicals and distant menthol. The walls are so white their edges blur. The only colour comes from a poster about norovirus and the navy blue of the waiting chairs, arranged with geometric precision.

Claire barely has time to sit before Dr. Reyes appears, dressed as before: white coat over dark slacks, hair slicked into a severe bun. She looks neither rested nor tired, as if fatigue is a concept that simply does not apply to her.

"Miss Holloway," she says, voice smooth and practiced. "I'm glad you came."

Claire perches at the edge of the hard chair, hands folded in her lap, sleeves tugged down over her wrists. Her jeans slide against the plastic. She avoids looking at her reflection in the glass panel to her right. She doesn't want to see how fragile she has become.

Dr. Reyes glances at a clipboard, though it's only a formality. Her eyes remain on Claire.

"How have you been since last night?" she asks.

The question is clinical, but the undertone is genuine. Claire considers lying, but it would take too much energy. "I didn't sleep," she says. "I haven't eaten. My head hurts. I don't remember what I'm supposed to do next."

Dr. Reyes nods. "That's not uncommon after a traumatic episode. Has the headache gotten worse?"

"No," Claire admits. "It's just… there."

The doctor sits, crossing one leg over the other. She balances the clipboard on her knee but never glances down. "I've been in touch with my colleagues on land. I want to talk to you about something called false memory syndrome," she says, as if ticking an item off a checklist.

Claire tenses. The muscles in her arms tighten. She fights the urge to interrupt, to tell Dr. Reyes that this is all a waste of time, that she already knows what is real and what is not.

But the doctor continues, her tone gentle but inexorable. "Sometimes, after a head injury, especially when there's underlying stress or a history of loss, the mind can create memories that feel absolutely real. These aren't delusions, not in the classic sense. They're more like stories the brain tells to make sense of pain. The technical term is confabulation."

Claire's mouth goes dry. "You're saying I imagined Lily."

Dr. Reyes tilts her head, like a teacher when a student finally asks the right question. "I'm saying it's possible the events you remember didn't happen the way you recall, that your memories, vivid as they are, might be your mind's way of protecting you."

"I remember everything," Claire says, her voice nearly a growl. "I remember giving birth to her. Her first tooth. The way she said 'dinosaur' when she was barely talking. Her smell. Are you telling me all of that is fiction?"

Dr. Reyes does not smile. "No. I'm saying your brain is doing exactly what it was built to do: make sense of overwhelming loss. It's not a failure of character. It's not your fault. In fact, it's a sign that your mind wants to heal, even if the process is painful."

Claire shakes her head. "I took pictures," she says, voice shaking. "I told you—"

"And those pictures aren't there," Dr. Reyes replies, calm and direct. "I've seen this before, especially after grief. People remember entire lives, relationships, years of events. The memories are precise, textured, emotional. But the outside world doesn't match."

"It's not the same," Claire insists. "You weren't there. I remember the labour. Holding her for the first time. How she looked at me."

Dr. Reyes lets the silence bloom, then says, "Have you ever considered that the pain of your loss—the miscarriage, the breakup— never really left you? That you found a way to hold on by giving yourself a reason to keep going?"

Claire tries to stand, but her legs betray her. She slumps back into the chair; hands knotted in her lap. "So, this is it," she says. "I'm crazy. That's your answer."

"No," Dr. Reyes says, so firm the word vibrates. "You're not crazy. You're hurt. There's a difference. You're also not alone. Many people experience what you're going through, especially after loss or trauma. The head injury may have worsened, but it didn't start this."

Claire blinks hard, fighting tears. She does not want to break down in front of this woman, this stranger who seems to know everything about pain but nothing about what it costs to live with it.

"So, what do I do now?" she asks, voice barely a whisper.

The doctor folds her hands. "When you get home, I want you to see someone—a psychiatrist or trauma counsellor. I can recommend several. This is treatable. It will take time, but you will find your way through it."

Claire tries to imagine going home. She pictures her apartment, the sun through the windows, the silence of rooms with no child in them. She pictures her own hands, small and useless, unable to hold on to anything real.

She looks up at Dr. Reyes. "How do you know this will work?"

The doctor softens, just a fraction. "Because I've seen it work. Because the mind is capable of healing, even after it shatters. You just have to give it the space, and the time."

Claire nods, not because she believes it, but because she cannot think of anything else to do.

Before Claire can stand, Dr. Reyes reaches into a shallow drawer and retrieves a pamphlet, freshly printed on the laser printer, its edges crisp. She holds it by the spine, two fingers pinching the paper as if it might burn her.

She slides the brochure across the table. It stops an inch from Claire's hand.

The title is bold black on white: "When Trauma Makes Us Forget What's Real."

Claire's vision flickers over the words. She doesn't touch the pamphlet right away. Instead, she stares at the cover: a blurry image of a woman looking into a fogged mirror, her own face doubled, indistinct.

Dr. Reyes says, "It may help to read about others who've experienced the same thing. Sometimes knowing you're not alone is the first step."

Claire nods and picks up the pamphlet with trembling fingers. The paper is thin, matte, unsubstantial. She flips to the first page, eyes darting over the text. Each word carries a specific weight.

"Trauma can fracture memory, creating stories to shield us from pain. These narratives may become as vivid as true recollections, often including rich sensory detail and emotional significance."

Claire's throat tightens. She reads on.

"Individuals may recall entire relationships, years of imagined experiences, or the presence of loved ones who never existed. These memories are not delusions, but part of the mind's healing mechanism, a defence forged in necessity."

She hears her pulse pounding, louder than the doctor's voice. Her hands shake so hard the pages rattle. She scans the next paragraph, searching for proof that her case is different, that Lily is not just a name conjured to fill the absence.

"Confabulated memories can arise spontaneously, especially during periods of stress or emotional vulnerability. The onset may be abrupt, often triggered by loss or physiological shock to the brain. The individual remains unaware of the fabrication, experiencing these events as absolute truth."

A coldness fills her chest, the same cold as the hospital, the empty apartment, the months she spent holding her own pain at arm's length.

She thinks of Lily's voice, bright and immediate, the way it filled the world and made everything else secondary. She remembers every time Lily reached for her hand, every sticky-fingered embrace, every whispered *love you, Mummy*.

She thinks of the photos that were never there, the toys that never made it into her suitcase, the hair bobble she could never find when she needed it.

She closes the brochure, not gently. It bends under the pressure of her grip. She wants to scream at Dr. Reyes, demand she prove a negative, to show her exactly where memory ends and story begins.

But the doctor remains silent, waiting.

Claire's breathing grows shallow and fast. The chair's edge bites into her thigh. Her vision tunnels, the white of the room closing in around the edges.

Dr. Reyes reaches for a glass of water and slides it over. The surface trembles, catching the fluorescent light in a shiver.

Claire ignores the glass, staring at the bent pamphlet cover, at the fractured woman on the front.

She wonders what it would feel like to simply accept this, to let go of the insistence that Lily is real, to admit that her own mind has betrayed her. She wonders if that would be better or worse than living with the possibility that she has lost her daughter twice, once in body, once in memory.

She can still hear Lily's laughter, clear as a bell.

She sits very still, fingers whitening around the paper's edge, as the world tips sideways and the hum of the ship grows louder, drowning out the truth.

Dr. Reyes stands. "I'll be here if you need anything else. Take care of yourself, Claire."

Claire doesn't remember leaving the medical bay. She doesn't remember Daniel escorting her to the elevator, through the hallway, or the walk back to her cabin.

She only remembers the words, echoing in her head: stories the brain tells to make sense of pain.

She wonders if this is what healing feels like. She wonders if she will ever know the difference.

CHAPTER FIFTEEN

The upper deck is deserted. Wind slaps at the metal benches and tugs at every loose corner. The fake teak of the walking track gleams slick with spray; each lamp along the railing is shrouded in salt residue, dimmed by the dull glow of the ship's own light pollution. The only movement is the ever-present vibration beneath her feet—the rumble of generators, the slow churn of turbines, the endless, hungry effort of pushing more than three hundred metres of steel through water.

Claire doesn't know how she arrived here. She remembers the elevator, the hollow ping as the doors opened on Deck 15, the way the carpet gave way to cold, artificial wood just beyond the glass windbreak. She remembers the silence, not the absence of sound, but how every noise seemed to fall straight into the sea, as if the world had muted itself.

Now, she paces. She doesn't mean to, but her body craves motion, a constant to keep her thoughts from settling. Her arms are cold beneath a thin long-sleeve shirt; she left the stateroom without a coat. She hugs herself tight, shoulders hunched against the wind, marching back and forth along the stern promenade. Her hair whips her face in wet, angry streaks.

She counts her steps, times her breath. An obsessive rhythm to it: twenty-two steps from one end of the section to the other, three seconds to turn, twenty-two steps back. She cannot stop. If she pauses, the world will flood her.

At the edge, she grips the railing with both hands. The metal is numbing, so cold it burns. She squeezes until her knuckles whiten, then pale further, to the colour of bone. Below, the wake fans out in two violent stripes. The ocean is black but alive, gnashing foam teeth, furious and endless.

Claire stares into it, waiting for something to look back.

Sometimes, if she blinks, she sees movement at the periphery. A child's shape, small and darting, a shock of brown curls caught in the deck lights. But when she looks directly, there is only empty track, the line of unused deck chairs lashed to the railings, the dome of a disused pool cover slicked with night moisture.

She doesn't know how long she stays. The ship moves, but she does not. Her body aches with cold and exhaustion, but she cannot let go. The wind scours her, raising lines of goosebumps along her arms. Her lips feel split, the salt stinging every micro-fissure.

A shadow moves just beyond the outermost lamp. Claire snaps her head around. She is ready for nothing, no one.

But it's her.

Lily runs ahead, barely touching the ground. Her dinosaur-print dress is dark, but the neon stripes on the hem catch the light with every bounce. Her pink rain boots are absurdly clean, impossible with their history. She rounds the corner of the deck, head turned over her shoulder, mouth open in laughter. Her voice is sharp and high, a note Claire recognises at the molecular level: "Mummy, catch me!" She is out of reach, but the sound is close, just below the level of hearing, a vibration in Claire's own chest.

Claire's legs move without permission. She follows, nearly slipping on the wet planks. Her vision narrows to the point of the running child, the flash of bare arms, the flick of a green hair bobble. Nothing else exists. She rounds the corner, past the stairwell, past the shuttered gelato stand. The deck is empty.

The air in her lungs turns solid. She bends at the waist, hands on her thighs, and dry-heaves. The taste is bitter, chemical, laced with memories of hotel mouthwash and cheap white wine.

She straightens. Her vision swims, but she keeps going. The next deck section is even more deserted, the lamps spaced farther apart. Her shadow stretches huge, projected onto the white hull in wild angles. She chases it, hoping it will resolve into Lily's. She knows it won't, but her body is not interested in logic.

At the bow, the wind doubles in force. She braces her feet apart to keep from being blown sideways. She clings to the railing, her hands sticky with cold and something else, grease, or tears, or both. The horizon is abstract, a border between void and darker void. She can't tell where the sky ends and the water begins.

Lily appears again, this time on the starboard side, moving with impossible speed, feet barely touching the ground. The girl stops by the lifeboat station, pivots, and raises one arm in salute.

"Mummy!" she calls. "I'm right here!" The voice is real now, brighter than the ship's lights. The echo travels the deck, bounces off the hull, multiplies and fades.

Claire's chest feels hollow. She opens her mouth to call back, but the wind steals her breath. She staggers, then runs, boots slapping, arms pumping hard.

She rounds the final curve, the bridge looming above. For a split second, she sees Lily—so clear, so alive, standing at the very edge of the promenade, framed in blue and black.

Then the child is gone. Only the railing, the ocean, and the gap remain.

Claire falls to her knees, unaware of the impact. She wraps her arms around the bottom rail, presses her face to the metal. Her cheeks are wet. She can't tell if it is from the spray, or the wind, or her own tears. The ocean roars below, swallowing every sound.

"Maybe I dreamed you," she whispers. The words are stripped of meaning by the wind. "Maybe I made you up." She digs her nails into the salt-crusted bar, willing it to answer.

For a moment, she pretends Lily will step out from behind the next pillar, grinning, calling for her. For a moment, she is sure the story will end differently.

But nothing happens.

Her hands are numb; her knees locked in a pain that promises to outlast the night. She lets her head fall forward, pressing her forehead to the rail. The world shrinks, then shrinks again.

A horn sounds, deafening and close, a warning blast from the bridge, a signal to whatever waits in the dark ahead. The whole ship shudders; Claire feels the vibration deep in her skull.

She lets go, stands unsteadily. The wind is relentless, a living thing. She wipes her face with the back of her hand and turns her eyes upward.

There is no moon; it's hidden by the clouds. The sky is blank, a stretch of black so total that it feels like a dare.

She stands at the railing for a long time, waiting for the hallucination to return, to finish what it started. It doesn't. The night goes on, uncaring.

Claire hugs herself, teeth chattering. She retraces her steps along the empty deck, her shadow tall, thin, and unrecognisable.

As she walks, she catches herself whispering a lullaby, one she can't remember learning, one she can't imagine ever not knowing. The words vanish in the wind, the tune shredded by the sea.

CHAPTER SIXTEEN

The pizza bar is never truly empty. Not even after midnight, when the main dining room closes and the drunks slouch toward their cabins, leaving only crew on break, insomniacs, and the kind of parents who'd rather feed their kids pizza than wrestle with bedtime. The air smells of scorched flour and fake basil, the ovens burning hot enough to mask the industrial chill of the air conditioning. The vinyl booths are sticky at the seams, and harsh lights spotlight every flaw, every spill, every fingerprint on the glass.

Claire hesitates at the threshold, blinking against the sudden, surgical brightness. The shift from night deck to food court leaves her squinting, head pounding. She feels hungover, though she hasn't touched a drop in weeks. The ship moves beneath her, not a roll but a slow, uneven pulse that makes her knees ache.

Only a few patrons linger at this hour: a table of teenagers in matching jackets, heads down over their phones; a middle-aged couple splitting a pitcher of flat beer, avoiding each other's gaze; two men in staff polos, talking quietly over the remains of a meat-lover's special. No one notices her.

She steps to the counter, standing back as a crewman in white gloves wipes down the sneeze guard in exaggerated circular strokes. Behind him, the ovens glow with promise and heat. The server on duty is a young man, late teens, hair cropped short and stiff with product. His name tag reads BEN and something in his eyes makes him look both exhausted and immune to the fatigue that haunts everyone else on the ship.

He meets her gaze and offers a practiced smile. "Evening, ma'am. Or morning, I guess. What can I get you?"

"Just—" She clears her throat, voice gravelly from sleep deprivation. "A slice of cheese. Please."

He nods, grabs the biggest slice from under the lamp, slides it onto a paper plate with the precision of someone who's done this a thousand times. "Anything to drink? Water, soda, maybe a little coffee to keep you going?"

She shakes her head, then changes her mind. "Actually, coffee. Black."

Ben pours from a pot that must be hours old, and slides the cup across the counter. "That'll do it," he says, turning to the next customer.

She thanks him, then finds a booth near the window. She sets the plate down, staring at the cheese as it congeals in the cold air. Her hands tremble, and she doesn't know if it's exhaustion, adrenaline, or something else. Pressing her palms to the tabletop, she wills them to steady.

This is where she and Lily got their pizza last night. She remembers it vividly: the bright lights, the sticky booth, her daughter clambering up to the edge of the seat grinning at the promise of unlimited pizza while they waited for their takeaway to eat on their balcony. Lily wore her dinosaur dress that night. She insisted on feeding the first bite to Thomas, the ragdoll cat, smearing tomato sauce across the toy's stitched whiskers.

Claire can almost hear Lily's sharp "Mummy, it's too hot!" and see her blow on every bite with the exaggerated seriousness of a three-year-old determined not to burn her tongue. The memory is sharp, immediate, but the booth across from her is empty, the paper placemat pristine, not a trace of crayon or juice spill.

She tears a bite from her slice, chewing mechanically. The cheese is rubbery, the crust hard as plastic, but she forces it down. She tells herself she needs the energy, that she is rebuilding, that every bite is a step toward normal.

She watches Ben behind the counter, clearing trays and stacking plates, wiping surfaces with the same tired precision. He moves like a ghost, silent and invisible unless directly engaged. When no one else is at the counter, she stands and approaches, plate in hand.

"Can I ask you something?" Her voice sounds too loud in the empty space.

Ben glances up from the register, one eyebrow raised. "Sure thing. Need another slice?"

"No, I—" She hesitates. "I was here last night. Around six. With my daughter. A little girl, three years old, curly brown hair, dinosaur dress. You must have seen us."

Ben's face stays neutral, but a flicker of discomfort crosses his eyes. "Ma'am, I work the late shift. There are lots of families, lots of kids. Sorry, I don't remember every guest."

She presses on, desperate. "But you have to remember Lily. She called you the pizza boss. Asked if you had any tiny toast, and you gave her a breadstick instead. She dropped her juice box, and it rolled under the counter."

He looks down, pretending to check a smudge on the countertop. "That sounds cute, but I'm sorry. I wasn't on then. I see hundreds of people a night. Unless you're a regular, or make a scene, faces start to blur together after a while."

Claire feels her cheeks burn. "But we were here," she insists. "I have a picture." Her hands shake as she pulls up the gallery. The only photo from that night is of the pizza—a close-up of cheese and sauce, nothing else. No Lily. No juice box. No dimpled smile. The emptiness of the photo makes her dizzy.

Ben waits, polite but unmoved. "It's a nice pizza," he offers, and the words sting more than they should.

She scrolls faster, showing him photos from the trip: the deck, the pool, the stateroom. In every one, she is alone. She wants to scream, to throw the phone, to shatter the screen to force the truth out of it. Instead, she stands there, phone trembling in her grip.

Ben shifts, uncomfortable. "Is your daughter missing?" he asks, voice lowering. "Do you need Security?"

"No," she says. "Yes. I don't know. They said—" Her throat closes. "I just need to know if anyone else remembers her. That's all."

He sighs, setting the rag aside. "Ma'am, it's a long cruise with many sea days. People get tired, things get mixed up. If you lost something, I can check Lost and Found. If you're worried about your kid, I can call Security. But I really don't remember a little girl in a dinosaur dress."

Claire wants to argue, to push, but the words are gone. The oven's hiss fills her head, drowning out everything else.

She mumbles a thank you, backs away from the counter, nearly trips over an empty chair. The world seems tilted, the lights too bright, the sounds too sharp. She sinks back into her booth, clutching her phone, staring at the pizza photo until the image blurs and swims.

She is alone. She has always been alone.

The booth across from her stays empty, and the cheese on her plate growing cold and stiff.

She tries to sit still, but her body won't cooperate. The seat vibrates beneath her, every muscle keyed up as if braced for impact. Claire stares at her phone, flicking through empty evidence, willing a photo of Lily to reappear. It doesn't. Only cheese pizza. Only the ocean. Only herself reflected over and over in cold glass.

After a minute, she stands and returns to the counter.

Ben is loading the last few slices into the warming drawer, head down, but he glances up as she approaches. This time, his eyes are wary, guarded.

"Sorry to bother you again," Claire says, but her words are already sharp. "Are you sure you don't remember? It was last night. Little girl, brown curls, dinosaur hair bobble. She called you the pizza boss. You gave her extra olives because she said they looked like eyeballs."

He doesn't look away, but the smile is gone. "I really wish I could help," he says, voice flat. "But I just don't recall. I didn't start till ten. Maybe you have the wrong night? Or maybe someone else was working."

"No," Claire snaps. "It was you. You were wearing the same shirt. You gave her a sticker, right there before we took our pizza to our room." She points at a spot on the counter, a faint circle where the adhesive left a ghost.

Ben shrugs, then glances over her shoulder at the other patrons. "A lot of kids like stickers," he says. "Sorry."

Claire feels the heat rise in her face. She wants to lean over the counter, to shake him, to make him remember. Instead, she turns to scan the room for an ally, anyone who might have seen.

The teenagers look up, then look away, their faces blank behind the blue glow of their screens. The couple at the beer pitcher mutter to each other, lips barely moving. The crew have left; only dirty plates remain.

Claire's voice rises without her meaning it to. "There were other people here that night. They must have seen us. Someone must remember—" She stops herself, breath coming fast.

Ben takes a half-step back, then gestures toward the kitchen. "I can call my supervisor if you want. Maybe she remembers something."

"Yes," Claire says, "yes, please." She tries to sound calm, but her hands drum a wild rhythm on the counter.

Ben disappears through a swinging door, and she hears muffled voices from the kitchen. She presses her palm to the glass, trying to steady herself, but her reflection swims, features distorted by the curved sneeze guard.

The room feels smaller, brighter, as if the lights are dialling up with every second.

The supervisor comes out a moment later, wiping her hands on a towel. She is older, early forties maybe, with dark hair pulled into a low bun and a name tag that reads "ELISE." Her eyes are quick and clinical, appraising Claire before she speaks.

"Can I help you?" Elise says, voice calm, with a slight accent Claire can't place.

"I was here with my daughter," Claire says. "Last night. She's three, brown curls, dinosaur dress. We sat in that booth." She points, hand trembling. "I need to know if you remember us. Please."

Elise's smile is soft but distant, the way people smile at customers who might tip into madness at any moment. "I do remember a little girl with a dinosaur shirt," she says after a pause. "But I see a lot of them, you know? Dinosaurs are very popular these days."

Elise nods, like someone marking time until the right moment to exit. "Is your daughter missing?"

"No!" Claire's hands clench into fists, nails digging into her palms. "She was here. She was with me. But now—" She stops, unable to finish.

Elise's eyes flick to Ben, then back to Claire. "If you need to talk to someone, the medical bay is open all night. Security, too. They're very good. Sometimes, when people get tired or—" She lets the sentence dangle.

"I'm not tired," Claire says, but it's a lie everyone knows. "I just need you to remember. Please. She's real. She was here."

Elise gives a gentle, rehearsed smile. "I believe you," she says. "But I can't say for sure. Maybe you should get some sleep? It's easy to get confused at sea. Everything blends together after a while."

Claire's chest tightens. She feels the attention from the other tables— the teenagers sneaking glances, the couple whispering behind their hands. She is the spectacle now, the unhinged woman at the pizza bar. Her face burns.

She backs away, muttering, "I'm sorry," over and over. She nearly knocks a chair down, catches it at the last second and leaves it askew. The room tilts, and she grabs the edge of a table to steady herself.

Behind her, Elise and Ben exchange a look—the kind that means they'll remember her after all. Just not in the way she hoped.

Claire flees down the corridor, the lights and the noise chasing her. She does not look back.

The corridor outside the pizza bar is mercilessly bright. The floor feels soft, but the overhead lights are harsh, unblinking. Claire leans against the wall, sucking in air as if she's just run a marathon. Her face is wet; she wipes it with the back of her hand, but the tears keep coming, stinging her skin.

For a moment, she can't remember where she is, or why. The world narrows to a corridor, white, blue, and endless, with doors on either side that never open. Her heart hammers. She sinks down, sliding until she sits on the carpet, knees pulled tight to her chest. She hides her face and tries to make herself invisible.

A couple rounds the corner, maybe the same from the pizza bar, maybe not. They slow as they pass her, stepping wide. She hears one whisper, "Poor thing," and the other murmur something that might be "drunk," "sad," or "crazy." Their voices carry down the hall, fading into nothing.

She hugs her legs, rocking. For a moment she imagines Lily here, curled beside her, head heavy on her shoulder. But there is only empty space. Only the echo of her own ragged, sharp breathing.

She wants to vanish. She wants to undo the last hour, the last week, the last four years. She wants to be a person with a real life, a real daughter, and a real chance at getting home in one piece.

She forces herself up, bones creaking, head spinning. Stumbling forward with hand on the wall, she walks slowly. The corridor seems to stretch ahead, longer than she remembers. She is alone.

As she moves, the doubts close in. What if they're right? What if there never was a Lily? What if the memories are just stories her brain made up to fill the silence? Every step forward is an argument: Yes, I remember. No, I don't. Yes, she was here. No, she wasn't.

The carpet blurs. The walls lean. She blinks hard and keeps moving.

She reaches her cabin door and stands with her hand on the handle. She hesitates, afraid of what she might find—or not find—inside.

She closes her eyes and thinks of Lily: the smell of her hair, the sticky warmth of her hand, the way she said, "Love you, Mummy" in the dark. She holds the memory, tight, refusing to let it dissolve.

She opens the door. The room is empty.

She steps inside, and the silence is total.

CHAPTER SEVENTEEN

Morning arrives without kindness. Light seeps in around the blackout curtains, the same numb, grey-white glow as every morning on the ship, but to Claire it might as well be the inside of a headache. She doesn't know when she fell asleep, or for how long. She wakes with her face pressed into the pillow, jaw throbbing, cheek stuck to a damp spot. For a moment, she stays like that, eyes closed, trying to float, trying to hold the day at bay.

But the memories begin anyway.

She is standing in the pizza bar, pleading with the server, her hands empty. She is on the promenade, chasing a blur of green hair bobble down a corridor. She is in her own cabin, searching under the bed for the body of a child who was never there. Her mind replays the sequence, out of order, skipping and doubling back like a bad DVD. She wants to stay in the fog, but panic forces her up.

She sits up in bed, knees drawn to her chest, and takes stock. The room is as she left it: suitcase gaping open, dirty clothes in a heap, water glass half-full on the desk. No toys. No stickers. No crayon scrawls on the walls. The desk surface is smooth and clean, save for a faint ring from her own mug. The other half of the bed is untouched. She runs her hand over the sheets, the fabric stiff and cold, still creased from the last time housekeeping tucked it in.

There is nothing of Lily here. Not even the smell.

She stands, every muscle screaming, and wobbles to the bathroom. The light is harsh, unforgiving. She looks at herself in the mirror: puffy eyes, raw lids, hair clumped in ragged curls. She hasn't brushed her teeth. She does so mechanically, staring at the mirror, willing it to show someone else. She rinses, spits, and catches her own eye.

"Get it together," she whispers, and the voice sounds like someone else's.

She dresses in yesterday's clothes, still faintly damp with sweat. She doesn't care. The ship's movement is stronger today; she braces herself on the sink, then the wall, then the doorframe as she makes her way to the small desk. She drops into the chair, grabs her notebook from the drawer, and slaps it down on the surface. She has to do something, or she will lose what's left.

It's the travel journal. She bought it weeks before the trip, a splurge from the stationery store. She meant to fill it with memories for Lily: "This is what we did, so you never forget." The cover is teal, soft to the touch, with an elastic band holding it shut. She cracks it open. The first page is blank. She stares at it until her eyes sting, then picks up the pen.

She writes the date at the top of the page. The numbers look wrong, the year unfamiliar. She pauses, then presses harder.

31 March 2025

She starts to write.

She writes fast, handwriting tight and spiky, pressing so hard the ballpoint gouges the paper. She writes about the train to Southampton, how Lily kicked the seat in front and sang "Twinkle Twinkle" until the man turned around and glared. She writes about the hotel, the way the elevators smelled like old fruit and how Lily jumped on the bed until security came up and told them to keep it down. She writes about boarding the ship, how Lily screamed with joy when she saw the water slide on the top deck.

She writes about the dinosaur-print dresses. She lists every one: the blue one with T. rex, the yellow one with triceratops, the green one she wore so many times the fabric started to pill. She describes how Lily would refuse to wear anything else, how she would stand on the bed and roar at Claire until she gave in.

She writes about the hair bobble, the green one with the plastic stegosaurus on it. How Lily wore it every day, even to sleep. How she cried when it snapped, and how Claire fixed it with clear nail polish and a paperclip, then spent hours online searching for a replacement and bought every one she could find. She draws a picture of the bobble in the margin, careful lines, even though she has never been good at drawing.

She writes about "tiny bread." The way Lily called toast that, how she would refuse to eat anything unless sliced into rectangles and called by the 'right' name. She writes about the night they ordered pizza and Lily fed the first bite to Thomas, her ragdoll cat, then licked the tomato sauce off the toy's nose.

She fills half a page, then another, and another. Her hand cramps, but she does not stop. She skips lines, runs sentences together, invents her own shorthand to keep up with her urgency. If she slows down, she is sure the memories will drain away.

She writes about Lily's voice: "She sounded like a bird, like a whistle, like a tiny ambulance." She writes about how Lily said "I love you, Mummy," not as a question but as an announcement. She writes about the smell of Lily's skin, a mix of sunscreen, apple juice, and sweat. She writes about the night Lily threw up on the deck and Claire cleaned her with a towel that still smelled like bleach.

She writes about the pool, the art room, the pizza bar. She writes about the fight in the hallway, how Lily stomped her foot and said, "I can do it myself." She writes about the moment she looked away, just for a second, and Lily was gone.

Her writing is not neat. The lines jump the margins, curl around the edges, twist into little knots at the end of paragraphs. Sometimes she switches to all caps. Sometimes she leaves out verbs or whole words, or just scrawls a single phrase over and over, filling the white space as if afraid of leaving any blank.

She writes until her hand aches, then switches to her left. The ink smudges. She does not care. The room is silent except for the scratch of the pen and the rumble of the ship's engines below. The air is stale, recycled, thick with the memory of hundreds of people who breathed it before her.

She pauses, presses her fingertips to her temples, rubbing the skin in hard circles. She looks up and around, half-expecting Lily to appear at the end of the bed, to ask for juice or the iPad or a story. But the room is empty. The silence is so complete it hums.

She goes back to the journal.

She writes about the first day, the orientation, the woman at the kids' club who called herself "Bubbles." She writes about how Bubbles showed Lily the games, how she called her "sweet pea," and bent down to tie her shoes. She writes about the crafts project, how Lily glued googly eyes to a paper plate, then asked if she could bring it home.

She writes about the doctor, Dr. Reyes's voice, the cold medical bay and the word "confabulation." She writes about the pamphlet, about being told that everything she remembers is a trick, a story, a wound that never healed.

She writes about the phone, about the empty photos, the ghostly gaps where Lily should be. She writes about the feeling of being erased, of standing in a crowd and realising no one can see you, no one ever did.

She writes about the time Lily almost drowned, how she pulled her out of the bathtub and held her for an hour, sobbing, heart pounding. She writes about the time Lily hid in the laundry basket and Claire tore the apartment apart looking for her, convinced she was gone forever. She writes about the panic, the relief, and how her own mother used to say, "You always expect the worst, don't you?"

She writes until the pages stick together from the sweat on her palms. She writes until her head spins, her stomach growls and her eyes blur so she can hardly read her own words.

She is hunched over the desk, shoulders bunched to her ears, body curled protectively around the notepad as if someone might take it away. The urge to hide it is overwhelming. She glances over her shoulder, checks the door, then slides the elastic band tight around the journal, tucking it into the drawer as if locking away a part of herself.

She sits back, arms limp at her sides, breathing in the smell of paper, ink, and her own desperation. The silence presses in, thick as a pillow over her face.

She pulls the notebook out again, just to check that it's real, that the pages are still there, that she can read the words. She flips through fast, looking for something to catch her, to prove it wasn't just a dream. The words shimmer on the page, urgent and strange, but they are hers.

She bends over the book, pressing her face into the spine, whispering the details to herself over and over.

"She loves dinosaurs. She calls toast 'tiny bread' because she likes it cut small and croissants 'tiny toast' because when you slice it crosswise the little discs look like toast with a dark outside and lighter middle. She wears her green hair bobble every day. Her cat is named Thomas. She loves me, and I love her."

She whispers until her throat hurts. She whispers until the words run dry.

She stays curled over the journal, hands ink-stained, body stiff, listening to the hum of the engines and the echo of her own voice.

In the hush of the cabin, it is the only proof she has.

* * *

She can't keep still. The words in the journal don't hold her. Even as she traces the letters with her finger, the memory of writing them blurs, as if the ink fades from the page the moment she looks away. She tucks the notebook carefully into the desk drawer, closes it so softly it barely makes a sound, and turns to the next line of defence.

Her phone.

She grabs it from the side table, her hands slick. The battery is nearly full, but the charge icon blinks like a warning: this is your last chance. She unlocks the screen with the facial recognition, and the lock screen dissolves into the grid of apps. For a moment, she just stares at it, thumb hovering above the glass.

She opens Photos.

She has done this already, but there must be a mistake. She scrolls back, searching for evidence. The day before, and the day before that. Selfies, her own face, always alone. No Lily reflected in sunglasses, no blur of a child running past. She flips to Albums, tries the search bar: "Lily." No results. She tries "dinosaur," "pizza," "cat," "Thomas." Nothing.

Her breathing shallows; the air in the room suddenly feels thin.

She checks Messages, scrolling through threads. She searches texts to her mother, her ex, even old friends she hasn't spoken to in years. All recent communications are work, logistics, shipboard notices about safety drills, or room service. She searches "Lily," "daughter," "kids' club." Still nothing. Her inbox is clean, almost surgically so.

She checks Notes. Maybe she left herself a reminder, a packing list, something. The most recent note is from a month ago: "Boarding passes, sunscreen, charger, book." She scrolls back further, finding only shopping lists and half-finished drafts for client emails. Nothing about Lily, nothing about the trip except a single reminder to "bring art supplies."

She searches the browser history. It is a graveyard: weather updates, cruise ship deck plans, a brief detour into dining room reviews. She searches "Lily" again, thinking maybe she Googled something about a rash, or a fever, or what to do if a child goes missing at sea. Nothing. The only mentions are stray search results for "lily pad pool float" and a Wikipedia page about a plant she doesn't recall reading about.

She goes to open the Email app. Hope flickers—maybe the booking confirmation, the welcome packet, the itinerary she remembers printing for both of them. But the app is gone, uninstalled the week before the trip. She told herself it was to avoid work distractions, to give herself "space." She tries to redownload it, but Wi-Fi demands a password she does not have. She slams her thumb on "Cancel," but it doesn't help.

She checks the App Store. The trash. The "Recently Deleted" folder in Photos, just in case. Empty.

She checks Recents in Calls. The last few calls are work-related before she—no they—left for the trip. No one else. No calls to her mother, the babysitter, or anyone.

She sits back in the chair, the phone slippery in her hand, and stares at the wall. The engine hum is louder now, vibrating through her bones.

She checks Photos again. She swears there were pictures. So many pictures. She remembers Lily in the pool, Lily wrapped in a towel, Lily making a face at the camera while eating pizza. She can see it clearly, like a dream. But the photos are gone. Not even a stray sock, no shadow in the background.

She scrolls faster, her thumb cramping. She checks the dates, timestamps, metadata, desperate to find a glitch. Blank spaces where pictures should be. In some, her expression is off, she is looking at something out of frame, eyes crinkled in laughter with a child. But the frame is empty. The laugh is a private joke.

She starts to shake.

She checks Settings. Maybe parental controls, a hidden folder, a bug. She restarts the phone. Unlocks it again, Repeats the steps, hoping this time it will be different.

She opens the journal app, hoping for a note about Lily. The only entry is from two days ago: "Don't forget to tip the steward. Guest Services closes at 9." Nothing else.

She tries to remember the booking the trip. Sitting at the computer, Lily in her lap, mac and cheese smell on her fingers. Selecting "two guests," remembers checking "child under twelve." The excitement. Lily clapping when the confirmation email came.

But there is no email. There is no record.

She drops the phone on the bed, the sound muffled by the comforter. For a moment, she wants to throw it out the window, to send it spinning into the blue, let the sea take it. She stands, her legs barely supporting her, pacing the room, rubbing her arms.

She turns back, snatches the phone from the bed, checks one last time—every app, every menu, every possible cache or backup or folder.

Nothing.

Her hands go numb. The phone feels like a block of ice in her palm.

She sits at the bed's edge, knees apart, elbows on thighs, phone held between her hands like a prayer. She tries to remember Lily's voice, the precise sound of her laughter, the exact words of their last conversation. She can remember everything about her, and nothing at all.

The cabin is silent. The phone screen goes dark. She turns it on again, staring at the blank reflection of her own face.

She whispers Lily's name. It sounds wrong.

She checks the Photos app once more. Scrolls back to the very first image ever saved on the phone. A photo of herself in a hotel bathroom, hair wet, face unlined, eyes wide and hopeful.

No baby pictures. No birth announcements. No record anywhere of the girl she swears she held in her arms.

She sets the phone on the bed, staring as if waiting for a confession. Her body feels hollow, skin tight. She can't breathe.

She picks the phone up again. Repeats the search. Every step. Every menu. Every folder.

Nothing changes.

She presses the phone to her chest, desperate to feel something through the cold.

The room is so quiet she hears the pulse of her own blood, the whisper of her breath, the sound of her mind giving way.

She curls around the phone, as if it can protect her.

It is the only thing left.

CHAPTER EIGHTEEN

The hours slip by unnoticed. Claire comes to at her desk in, hunched over the teal travel journal, a line of dried drool tracing the crease of her wrist. The new words on the page swim and twist, unreadable. She wipes her mouth, trying to orient herself. It's late afternoon; when she peeks past the curtain, the sun is flat and unfriendly on the ocean, a cold grey that makes time impossible to place. The ship is quiet for once. Maybe everyone at lunch. Or maybe everyone is dead and has floated away.

She closes the notebook, the elastic snapping satisfyingly, then tucks it in the drawer. For a moment, she just sits, listening for any sign of Lily—her breath, her giggle, the muffled stomp of boots from the bathroom. Nothing. The far side of the bed is empty, sheets straight as a hospital cot. No trace of pyjamas, no toy cat, not even a forgotten juice box under the table. It is as if she never existed.

A knock at the door, rapid and bright, shreds the silence.

Claire freezes. Her heart climbs into her throat. The knock comes again, insistent. "Housekeeping!" a voice sings, high and confident.

She moves to the door but doesn't open it right away. Through the peephole, she sees the steward: tall, olive-skinned, black hair slicked back, smile primed and waiting. He rocks back and forth on his heels, a bundle of towels draped over one arm.

She opens the door. He springs into action.

"Good afternoon! Miss Holloway, yes? I am Miguel. I make up your room." He sweeps in with practiced authority, already moving toward the bed, eyes scanning for signs of disorder.

Claire steps aside, body rigid, unable to trust herself to speak. She watches him strip the bed with quick, precise movements, a dance choreographed by repetition.

He glances over his shoulder. "Will you need extra towels today? Or —" he gestures, in a half circle, "new sheets? Or just the usual service?"

Claire's voice is paper-thin. "Did you see a child with me?"

Miguel blinks, brow furrowing in polite confusion. "A child?"

Claire steadies herself on the edge of the desk. "My daughter, Lily. She's three—curly brown hair, a little loud, always wearing dinosaur clothing and pink boots. You must have seen her with me. We checked in together. She was here, always getting in the way."

Miguel's expression sours slightly, searching for the right answer, flipping through some internal manual. "I... I tell you the other day. I only see you, Miss Holloway. Maybe I make mistake? But on my list, only your name." He nods quickly, apologetic, as if that might help.

Claire's breath quickens. She steps between Miguel and the exit, blocking his retreat. "No, you must have seen her. She leaves her things everywhere—stickers, colouring books, toys. You never picked any up?"

Miguel's hands flutter nervously. "No, ma'am. Room always very neat. I think maybe you keep good care. I only do turndown bed and change towels."

He edges past her toward the bathroom. Claire follows, too close.

Miguel opens the door, checks the shower, then the little shelf where the toiletries go. "I bring you new shampoo today?" He holds up the mini bottle like a trophy.

Claire ignores the offering. "You never saw her? Not once? She was with me."

Miguel pauses, eyebrows raised. "I am sorry, but no, I do not remember your child. Maybe I meet her and forget, but—" He shrugs. "I do twenty rooms every day. Sometimes, I forget a face."

Claire's hands shake. She looks past him, into the bathroom mirror, seeing herself—a gaunt, sharp-edged woman, eyes bloodshot and rimmed with doubt.

"Can you check your records?" she asks. "There must be a list. A manifest. You have to know who is in each room."

Miguel straightens, sensing the shift. "Manifest says only one. I check again, if you want."

He wipes his palms on his trousers, edges toward the door, but Claire plants herself in front of it, blocking his exit.

Miguel's eyes dart, calculating. "Miss Holloway, I only wish to help. If your daughter is missing, you should talk to Security. I am only room steward."

Claire's desperation leaks through. "No. You're not listening. She's not missing. She's gone. No one remembers her but me. You must remember something. Anything."

Miguel's grows careful, wary. "I only see you, Miss. Every day. You very quiet, always alone. No mess. No noise. I think you maybe enjoy the peace."

Claire lets out a ragged laugh. "That's not possible."

Miguel glances at his watch. "Maybe you travel with another person and she visit other room? Or maybe… someone pick her up for club?"

"Kid's club," Claire mutters. "She was supposed to be there this morning. But they won't remember her either."

Miguel's mouth sets in a thin line. "Sometimes, guest switch room and not tell us. Maybe you find her on pool deck? I can make announcement, if you wish."

"She's three," Claire says, voice breaking. "She wouldn't go anywhere alone. She needs me."

Miguel backs away, hands raised, towels held like a shield. "I am sorry. I only want to help. If you remember anything, you call Guest Services, yes?" He tries to sidestep her, but Claire doesn't move.

"Wait," she says, "the first night. When you introduced yourself. I was putting Lily to bed. The door was open, the shower was running. Are you sure you didn't see her then?"

Miguel freezes. For a moment, he looks genuinely uncertain. He chews his lower lip, eyes unfocused.

"I… maybe? But the door was closed, and I hear only water." He shrugs again. "I do not look inside. Is private. You understand?"

Claire does not understand. But she nods anyway.

Miguel's face relaxes, relieved. "Maybe you call Security. Maybe they help you find her." He gestures with the towels. "I come back later to finish service, okay?"

She steps aside. Miguel leaves quickly, almost running, the smile gone from his voice.

The door clunks shut behind him. Claire sags against it, panic pooling in her chest. She can still smell the ghost of Lily's soap in the bathroom, still hear the echo of her daughter's laugh in the shell of her memory.

She fumbles for her phone, opens the gallery, flips through the photos again. Nothing. She zooms in on the reflection in the bathroom mirror, searching for a fragment of Lily behind her own face, a smudge of colour, a shadow.

She finds nothing.

But now there's a new thread: the shower, the closed door, the possibility of Lily hiding just out of sight.

Claire latches onto it, hands trembling with hope and dread.

She has to see the manifest. She has to check the logs. There must be a record somewhere.

She will not let Lily disappear so easily.

She finds Miguel two doors down, wrestling a fresh set of towels onto the cart. She grabs his arm, not gently. He jumps, startled, then forces a smile. It wavers at the edges.

"I need to see the manifest," Claire says, her voice is so calm it surprises even her. "The one that says who's in this room. Now."

Miguel looks down at her hand, then at her face, reading something dangerous in both. "Miss Holloway, this is not—"

"I'm begging you," she interrupts. "I just need to see it. Please."

He hesitates, glancing down the hall both ways. The corridor is empty, but he keeps his voice low, conspiratorial. "This job sheet is not for guests," he says, but as he speaks, he digs into his vest pocket. He pulls out a folded sheet, creased and sweat-stained, the edges softened from handling. He holds it just out of her reach.

"Is only for staff," he repeats, as if that will shield him from what's coming next.

Claire snatches the page, tearing it from his grip.

She unfolds it. The lines swim at first, her eyes sting, wet with tears, the words blurred by her grip. She blinks, focuses, and finds the line for her room: 8612. Holloway, Claire. One adult. No other names. No mention of Lily. The column for "children under twelve" is blank.

A nausea rises in her throat, sour and alive. She scans the other rooms, searching for Lily's name on a different line, hoping it was misfiled, misplaced. There is nothing.

Miguel stands very still, hands fidgeting at his sides. "Is always just you, Miss. I check every day."

Claire's mouth is dry. "That's not possible. There were two beds the first night. There was a second bed for Lily. It was made up with little chocolates on the pillow. You remember that?"

Miguel's face twists, apologetic. "No, Miss. Always one bed. Always." He glances at the paper in her hand. "Maybe you remember different? But I never change beds. Is always set before guests arrive."

She feels a chill creeping up her arms, settling cold in her spine. "You never saw toys? Pyjamas? Anything for a child?"

Miguel shakes his head firmly. "No, Miss. Only your things. Very tidy, always. I remember because is not so usual."

She looks at the page again. Her vision tunnels, the corridor closing in around her.

"May I have it back, please?" Miguel asks timidly.

She hands it over, fingers numb. He folds the paper quickly and neatly, stashing it back in his pocket.

He lingers for a moment, as if waiting for another order, another version of the truth, but Claire has nothing left to say.

Miguel backs away, cart rattling, footsteps quick. At the end of the hall, he glances over his shoulder, his face a mix of pity and relief.

Claire leans against the wall, the cool surface grounding her. She feels hollow, as if her own name on the list is a lie, a placeholder for a ghost.

She slides to the floor, legs pulled to her chest, and staring at the spot where Miguel disappeared.

There must be another answer. There must.

Her hands won't stop shaking.

She is about to lose herself entirely—mind looping, fingers numb, thoughts flickering in and out—when a name surfaces, sharp as a splinter beneath the skin.

Petra.

It hits so suddenly that Claire drops her phone, the device bouncing once on the mattress before skittering to a stop at the edge. The name floats there, inexplicably buoyant: Petra. Or—she blinks—Bubbles. That's what the kids called her. Bubbles, from the kids' club, the woman who smiled at Lily and called her "dino princess," and bent down to tie her shoes with practiced, gentle hands.

The memory is so clear it stuns her. The clean scent of sanitiser in the kids' club lobby, the walls plastered with hand-drawn sea creatures, the background clamour of children. She hears Petra's voice copying Lily's favourite phrase: "That's a roarsome t-shirt! Did you bring a dinosaur aboard too?" Lily beaming, clutching Thomas to her chest. Petra knelt beside her, close enough that their heads nearly touched, helping her glue coloured paper scales onto a cardboard stegosaurus.

This is real. Not the soft-edged lie of photos or the fading script of a journal entry. This is muscle memory, a lived moment. For a second, Claire almost laughs with relief.

She sits upright, swings her legs off the bed, and presses her palms hard to her thighs to steady herself. Her body feels flushed and hot, as if she's just surfaced from underwater. She repeats the name in her head: Petra. Bubbles. Petra. Bubbles.

It is a thread, and she grabs on.

She stands, wobbling, and pulls her hair back into a rough ponytail. Her hands shake, forcing her do it twice. She grabs the sail pass card from the desk and slides it into her pocket. She checks her reflection in the mirror: eyes bloodshot, skin pale, but her jaw set, her lips tight with purpose.

She grabs the phone—her heart skips as she picks it up, afraid even now to let it out of reach—and tucks it into her back pocket. She doesn't bother with makeup or a clean shirt, but pauses at the door to look back, ensuring the journal is hidden, safe in the desk drawer.

She opens the cabin door.

The hallway is the same as always: a muted run of blue and cream, the carpet pattern looping in lazy waves, the air cool and filtered. Housekeeping carts line the far end, vacuum cleaners humming in the distance. Claire walks fast, head down, avoiding eye contact. Her muscles are tight, every step a fight against the inertia of the past two days.

She takes the elevator to Deck 12. Standing in the corner, arms wrapped around herself, the elevator feels like a capsule, cut off from everything outside. She uses the brief privacy to whisper Petra's name again, repeating the words like a spell: "Bubbles. Kids' club. Friday afternoon. She saw us. She saw Lily."

When the doors open, the corridor floods with noise—kids shrieking, parents shouting, the sharp ding of arcade machines from the game room next door. The smell of chlorine from the pool deck seeps in through an open side door, and for a second she's right back in the memory: Lily clutching her hand, bouncing with excitement at the thought of the craft table, stickers, markers, and Petra's warm, accented voice.

She walks to corridor's end, passes the "Adventure Club" sign with its cartoon octopus, and stops before the glass doors. Through them, she sees the familiar set-up: a front desk with its tidy row of cubbies, bulletin boards crowded with children's artwork, kids running circles around beanbags. A young woman stands at the desk, head down sorting forms into a colour-coded tray.

Claire pushes the door open. The sound hits her like a wave. The woman looks up, startled, and for half a second Claire's heart seizes—because it isn't Petra.

It's a different woman, younger, with bleached blonde hair in a short, spiky cut. The name tag reads SHANNON. She smiles at Claire, professional but empty. "Hi there! Can I help you?"

Claire's mind stutters. She tries to find the script, pull the memory into the present. "I'm looking for Petra. She works here? The kids call her Bubbles. Hungarian, I think."

Shannon's smile doesn't waver. "Oh! I think I know who you mean. Bubbles! She's off now but will be back for the night shift." Her tone is perfectly neutral. "Did you want to leave a message, or—?"

"No," Claire says, too fast. "I just—I just need to talk to her. It's important." Her hands go slick with sweat. "What time is her shift?"

"Seven o'clock," Shannon says, without checking the schedule. "She's always here for art hour. You're welcome to wait, or come back later."

Claire nods, backing toward the door. Her heart pounds so hard she can feel it in her ears.

"Is there anything else?" Shannon asks.

Claire shakes her head. "No. Thank you." She tries to smile, but it doesn't stick.

She stumbles into the hallway, feeling raw, her skin buzzing with anticipation and dread. She checks her watch, just after four. Three hours until art hour.

She paces the deck, trying to walk it off, but the nervous energy only builds. She tries to sit in the library, but her foot taps uncontrollably against the carpet, drawing dirty looks from an elderly couple at the next table. She wanders the promenade, watching the sea slide past, rehearsing what she will say to Petra when she finally finds her.

"She'll remember," Claire whispers. "She has to remember." She crafts the conversation in her head: "You saw her, right? My daughter? Lily. She wore the dinosaur shirt. You helped her with the craft project." The words are shaky, but all she has.

She checks her phone twice, then three times, making sure it's charged, making sure the sail pass is still in her pocket. She finds herself outside the Adventure Club again, staring through the glass, watching the clock.

At seven on the dot, the doors open and kids come pouring in, a tide of colour and noise. At the back of the group is Petra—tall, dark hair pulled into a messy ponytail, eyes quick and bright. She bends to greet the children, her accent unmistakable as she rounds them up: "Come on, my little monsters, we have painting to do!"

Claire nearly bursts into tears at the sight.

She waits until Petra is free, until the kids settle at their stations. She approaches the desk, body taut, hands curled into fists to keep from shaking.

"Petra?" she says, voice breaking.

Petra turns, sees her, and tilts her head. "Yes? Can I help you?"

"My daughter—Lily," Claire says. "You helped her with the stegosaurus last time? Brown curls, dinosaur shirt, her cat is Thomas?" She waits, praying, willing Petra to pull the memory up.

Petra smiles, puzzled. "I'm sorry. I don't remember. Was she in our group this week?"

Claire's vision blurs. She fights to keep her voice steady. "She was here. On the open day. With me. You called her dino princess. She liked the green hair bobble. You helped her tie her shoes."

Petra's face softens. She looks genuinely sorry, but also genuinely confused. "I'm sorry," she repeats. "I work with so many children. Sometimes they blend together. If you want, I can check our sign-in sheet for her name?"

Claire's whole body goes rigid. She forces a smile. "Yes. Please. Can you check?"

Petra flips through a clipboard, finger tracing down the lines. "No Lily Holloway," she says. "Do you have her sail pass card? Maybe I misspelled it."

"No," Claire says, "it went missing along with her."

Petra scans again, slower. "No, I'm sorry. No Lily at all." She looks up, concerned now. "Is she missing? Should I call Security?"

Claire shakes her head, a single, violent jerk. "No. Thank you. You've been— thank you." She turns and walks away, barely hearing the children's calls or the words of apology that Petra tries to offer after her.

She walks until her legs give out, until she finds herself on an empty part of the deck, the wind ripping at her hair, the cold biting her arms. She stands at the railing, gripping the metal so hard her knuckles ache.

The last thread is gone.

She stares out at the endless, indifferent ocean, waiting for the memory to fade.

It doesn't.

CHAPTER NINETEEN

There is a rhythm to silence, and Claire has learned it well. The quiet in her room is not peace but a living thing—a pulse stretching every second until it aches. The hum of the ship is a low, permanent fog that never lifts. The curtains are drawn. She sits on the edge of the bed, staring at the wall where sunlight diffuses into nothing.

Her hands are unsteady. The notebook lies closed on her lap, the elastic pressing a hard groove into the cover. She presses her thumbs against her temples, then into her eyes, willing herself somewhere else. But everywhere else is worse.

Lily is gone. No toys, no clothes, no food stains; no sign she was ever here. No one remembers her: not the room steward, not the woman at the kids' club, not a single witness in the pizza bar. Even the records say Claire checked in alone. Only Claire's own mind clings to the shape of a child who once filled every waking minute.

If she moves, she will break. So she does not move.

The first knock is soft. The second is not.

She jerks upright, her heart a fist in her throat. The suddenness—the realness—slams through the wall of silence like a thrown stone. She blinks, wipes her face, and looks at the door. For a second she thinks it's a hallucination, a ghost. But then the knock comes again, measured, professional.

"Miss Holloway? Security."

It's him, the one who found her in the corridor after the first night. The one with the steady voice, who never looked away. She does not remember his name, only the sense that he was the last person on this ship who didn't treat her like she was already gone.

She doesn't want to answer. She doesn't want to see him, or anyone. But the idea of him standing in the hallway, waiting, is unbearable. She stands, her legs slow to respond, and walks to the door.

She opens it an inch, using the chain as a leash. His face is there, right at eye level, the same tight-cropped hair, the same badge on his jacket. He holds a paper bag in one hand and a tablet in the other.

"Evening," he says, his voice calm, someone who knows not to push. "Do you have a moment?"

She nods, or maybe just tips her chin forward. She doesn't trust her voice, not yet.

He waits for her to open the door further. When she does, he shifts so his badge and uniform are more visible, as if to reassure. He does not smile.

"I'm Daniel Jackson. Security Officer," he says. "We spoke the other day." He pauses, taking her in—her hair still wet from the shower, the old shirt, the hollows under her eyes. "I hope I'm not interrupting."

"I wasn't doing anything," Claire says, voice thin.

He looks down the hall, then at the tablet. "I wanted to check in. There was an incident report today from the pizzeria overnight." He glances at her, gauging the impact. "Also, a couple of concerned calls. Housekeeping. And kids' club." He stops, letting her fill the rest.

She tightens her grip on the door. "Are you here to make me leave?"

Daniel shakes his head. "No, ma'am. Nothing like that." The bag crinkles as he shifts it from one hand to the other. "I just want to make sure you're alright. It's… a rough cruise for a lot of people."

Claire laughs, but it's just a burst of air from her nose.

He nods, as if she made a point. "I'm supposed to offer counselling services. Or a medical check, if you want." He glances at the bag, then back at her. "But I also brought dinner, if you're interested. I figured you might not want to go to the dining room."

She stares at the bag like it might be a bomb.

"I'm not hungry," she says, but her body betrays her; her stomach folds in on itself at the smell, something warm and greasy, pasta or bread or both.

Daniel's eyes are dark, not the hard kind of dark, but the kind that's used to watching people unravel. "You mind if I set this down?" he asks, lifting the bag. "I'll leave it outside if you'd rather."

She looks past him, down the hallway, half expecting someone else to appear. But they are alone. The corridor is as sterile as her room, the only colour coming from the flash of the exit sign.

She opens the door fully, then steps aside, her body caving around the space she leaves for him.

He enters without hesitation, but not with the arrogance of someone used to being invited in. He moves carefully, placing the bag on the desk, the tablet beside it. He glances once at the bed, at the neatness of the sheets, then at the notebook in her hand.

"You can sit," she says, not looking at him.

He takes the chair, spinning it so he can face her but not too close. He sets his hands on his knees, the gesture almost deliberate.

There is a silence, not the hollow kind, but a waiting one.

Claire rubs her palms against her thighs, trying to wipe away the tremor. "I know what this is about," she says. "You think I'm having a breakdown."

Daniel holds her gaze. "That's not my call." He chooses his words with care. "But people are worried about you. The staff, the other guests. They don't know how to help."

She closes her eyes for a second, then opens them again. "No one remembers her. Not even the ones who saw her. Not even..." She shakes her head, unwilling to say it out loud. "It's like she's been erased."

Daniel waits, the space between them dense with things neither will say. He gestures at the notebook. "Is that for her?"

She nods. "It's all I have."

He sits forward, elbows on his knees. "May I ask? Your daughter— can you tell me about when you last saw her?"

Claire digs her nails into her palm. "Saturday. In bed. She was wearing her dinosaur pyjamas. Just before I left to go watch the show. I was only meant to be gone an hour." The memory stabs her, sharp and useless. "She was asleep. And then..." She shrugs. "She's just gone."

Daniel does not write this down. He doesn't even pretend to.

"You believe me?" she asks, almost a whisper.

He waits a beat, then: "I believe you lost something important." His voice is careful but not unkind. "I believe this is real for you."

She wants to scream at him, to throw the bag of food at his head, to demand he dig through every cabin on the ship until Lily is found. But instead, she just sits, shoulders shaking with the effort not to fall apart.

Daniel stands, moves to the desk, and pulls two containers from the bag. He opens one, the smell of tomato and basil filling the room. "Eat something," he says. "It'll help."

She hesitates. "Are you going to watch me?"

He shakes his head. "I'll go if you want. Or I can stay. Your choice."

She wants to tell him to leave. She wants to beg him to stay.

She picks up the fork and eats. The pasta is hot, too salty, but she doesn't care. She doesn't remember the last time she ate.

Daniel sits in silence, not touching his own food, watching her but not staring. For a long time, they listen to the silence, waiting for it to change.

But it doesn't.

They finish the meal on the balcony. Claire carries the containers, Daniel following with two forks and a bottle of water. The salt wind cuts the air, sharp and damp, but she prefers it to the confinement of the cabin. The sky is still light, though the sun has slipped behind a thin strip of cloud, turning the ocean's surface a metallic grey. Below, the wake stretches to infinity, white foam scribbling on slate.

Claire sits with her feet tucked beneath the thin deck chair. Daniel takes the other chair, angling himself sideways to face both her and the horizon. For a while, they eat in silence, only the scratch of fork against plastic and the low, throbbing hum of engines far below. Occasionally, voices drift up from a distant deck, laughter, or the shrill yip of a child, but it is always fleeting.

When her container is empty, Claire sets it on the table, draws her knees up to her chest and wraps her arms around them. She stares at the horizon, blinking hard. Daniel watches her—not with the predatory patience of a therapist, but like a man waiting for something he cannot name.

Eventually, he says, "Tell me about her."

She doesn't answer at first. The words catch in her throat, raw as rope. But the sea is vast, and there's nowhere else for the words to go.

"She's three," Claire says flatly. "Her name is Lily. She loves dinosaurs. She calls toast 'tiny bread' and croissants 'tiny toast.' She wears the same green dress every day, unless I hide it. She has a stuffed cat named Thomas; she can't sleep without him. She talks all the time, even in her sleep."

She stops, pressing her chin to her knees.

"Go on," Daniel says softly, his words almost lost to the wind.

Claire closes her eyes. "She hates loud noises. She covers her ears, but only with her fists. She's afraid of the drains in the pool. She says they 'eat the water.' She— she wanted to see real dinosaurs. She thought there might be fossils on the ship." The words come quickly now, desperate. "She likes apple juice and hates eggs. She has a scar on her forehead from falling off the couch last Christmas. She laughs like a duck. She—" Her voice breaks.

She covers her mouth, but the sound escapes anyway.

Daniel waits, letting her fill the silence at her own pace.

Claire breathes slow and ragged. "She called me 'Mummy' even when she was mad at me. She used to say, 'I love you, Mummy,' then bite my finger like a joke. I think she was worried I'd forget." She laughs—a wet, choking noise. "It's funny. She was always afraid of being forgotten."

Daniel nods. "She sounds incredible."

Claire blinks away tears, embarrassed by the mess. "I know you think it's not real. That's what everyone says. But I remember her. Every minute."

"I believe you," Daniel says simply, not performative.

Claire looks at him, searching for mockery, but his face is only tired. The wind lifts a lock of his hair, and he smooths it back absently.

He says, "I've checked every record we have. The manifest shows only your name. Guest Services has no note of a child." He lifts a hand, a peace gesture. "But that doesn't mean I'm giving up. If you say Lily was here, I'll keep looking."

She hugs her knees tighter. "You must think I'm insane."

He shrugs. "A lot of people get weird at sea. The brain does strange things when it's untethered." He looks out at the ocean, then back at her. "Sometimes people lose themselves a little. Sometimes they find something they didn't know they were missing."

She does not reply. The ache in her chest is back, dull and familiar.

The silence grows, then Daniel speaks again, softer. "If you remember anything new," he says, "anything at all—let me know. Even if it seems impossible. This is my direct line." He leaves a card on the desk. His name is handwritten on it. Daniel picks up the empty containers, stacks them, and stands. "If you need me, anytime, call the number on the card," he says.

"For what it's worth," he says, "you're not the only one who feels alone on this ship." He lets the words hang there, then leaves.

She watches him go. The sliding door closes behind him with a click, leaving her alone with the wind, the low growl of the ship, and the memory of her daughter's laugh.

The empty chair across from her feels too small for an adult. She pretends, just for a moment, that Lily is sitting there, swinging her legs, waiting for Claire to tell her a story.

The illusion fades, but the ache does not.

She sits on the balcony until the stars come out, and the only sound left is the endless, indifferent rush of the sea.

When she comes in from the balcony a few minutes later, the room is cold and still. She expects Daniel to be gone, but he remains, standing in the corner, with his hands in his pockets. He doesn't look at her immediately, as if granting her permission to reassemble herself before being seen.

She walks to the sink, splashes water on her face, and dries it with the stiff hand towel. The light over the mirror casts her skin in a sallow hue, her eyes ringed with deep, exhausted purple.

Daniel clears his throat. "I'm still on duty," he says, "but if you're up for it, there's a magic show in the theatre tonight. It's kind of a tradition on these crossings. Helps take your mind off things."

She dries her hands, folds the towel twice, and sets it on the counter. "A magic show?"

He shrugs precisely. "It's not bad. I can walk you down, if you want. Or just leave you to it. No pressure."

She almost says no. She almost says she's lost interest in every human comfort, every bit of entertainment. But then she looks around the room—the neat bed, the empty space where Lily's things should be —and realises that another hour alone will break her in half.

She nods. "Okay. I'll go."

Daniel relaxes gradually. "It starts at eight. We should head down now if you want a good seat."

She checks her watch, more out of habit, than a need. She doesn't care about the time. She cares only about surviving the next hour.

She puts on her shoes, grabs her sail pass card from the desk, and slides it into her pocket. She hesitates, scanning the room. She almost expects to see Lily's jacket hanging from the back of the chair, or the green dinosaur bobble left on the nightstand. There's nothing—not even a stray sock.

The ache wells up again, deep and mean.

At the door, Daniel waits, with one hand on the handle. He watches her with the careful patience of someone used to leading the wounded through unfamiliar places.

She takes one last look around the room. She tries to memorise the bedspread's pattern, the colour of the walls, the view from the window. She tries to fix it all in her mind, just in case it vanishes next.

"Ready?" Daniel asks softly.

She nods.

They step into the corridor. The world outside is brighter, louder, alive with the motion of other lives. They walk side by side, silently, past clusters of passengers in pressed shirts and bright lipstick, past crew who nod and smile but never look directly at her.

At the elevator, Daniel presses the button and stands slightly behind her, a bodyguard without the pretence. The ride is short. The doors open on Deck Five, and the theatre glows ahead, all red carpet and gilt trim, a line of people already snaking into the hall.

She hesitates at the entrance, the press of strangers suddenly overwhelming. But Daniel gestures unobtrusively toward the side aisle. "There's a balcony. Quieter. Better view."

They climb the stairs and find seats near the back, away from the crowd. The room smells of perfume and popcorn, with a faint, spicy aftershave lingering from the men in the front row.

Claire sits, hands clasped in her lap, trying to blend into the seat. The lights dim. The hum of anticipation rolls over the crowd, a living thing.

Daniel leans close. "If you want to leave, just say the word."

She nods, eyes on the stage. The curtain trembles as the show begins, the magician's voice big and booming, a parody of command. The tricks are obvious, but the audience gasps and laughs anyway. Claire tries to watch, to let the sleight of hand work its spell, but her mind drifts elsewhere.

She thinks of Lily, how she would have loved the coloured scarves, the rabbits, and the silly patter. She tries to remember her daughter's laughter, but the theatre's noise drowns it out.

For a second, she wishes she could vanish, too, to slip between worlds and find the one where Lily is waiting.

Daniel sits beside her, not watching the stage but her face, as if searching for signs of cracks.

When intermission comes, he offers her a bottle of water. She takes it, drinks, and feels the cold hit her stomach.

"Thanks," she says.

He doesn't reply, just gives a small, understanding smile.

When the lights dim for the second act, Claire forces herself watch. Daniel left at intermission to check in with the office. She lets the show wash over her—a tide of colours and noise—and for a few minutes she feels almost weightless.

Afterwards, when the theatre empties, Daniel meets her at the exit. They walk back to the cabin in silence. Daniel waits at her door as she fumbles with the sail pass, her hands clumsy and slow.

"If you need anything tonight, just call" he says.

She nods, then steps inside.

She stands for a long time in the middle of the room, listening to the ship, to the low rumble of the engines and the faint laughter drifting down the corridor. The ache in her chest is still there, but less sharp.

She sits on the bed, retrieves the teal notebook from the drawer, and runs her hand over the cover.

She doesn't write. Not yet.

Instead, she closes her eyes and tries to remember Lily's face—the precise shade of her eyes, the sound of her voice. She holds it there, refusing to let it slip away.

Outside, the ship moves forward, cutting a line through the indifferent dark.

Claire lies back and lets herself drift, just for a while, on the memory of her daughter's laugh.

CHAPTER TWENTY

She stands again, aimless. The bathroom is a box of mirrors and chrome. She turns on the shower, waiting until steam ghosts the room and beads form on the glass. She strips, dropping each piece of clothing in a heap on the tile, and steps into the water. The heat shocks her, too hot at first, but she forces herself to endure it. She closes her eyes, lets the spray pummel her scalp, her shoulders, the ridge of her spine. She washes slowly, methodical. She lathers shampoo into her hair until her scalp tingles. She scrubs her arms, her chest, her thighs, hard enough to leave streaks of red.

The steam erases the mirror; her reflection gone except for a blurred oval at the centre. She stares into it, searching for herself, but all she sees is colour and movement, the outline of a woman melting at the edges. She cups her hands under the hot water and pours it over her face, again and again, until her skin burns and her ears ring.

She stands under the spray until the water shifts from punishing to numb. When she finally turns it off, the air feels cold, raw. She towels herself dry with rough white terry, ignoring how it scratches her skin. She wraps her hair in the towel, then sits naked on the closed toilet, waiting for her breath to slow. Her body shakes, but not from cold.

She dresses in pyjamas—soft cotton, loose at the knees, fabric faded from too many washings. The pants slide on easily; the shirt sticks to her damp skin. She wants to feel comfort, but it registers as nothing. She leaves the towel on her head, wrapped tight, as if holding her skull together.

The bed is an expanse of white, sheets crisp and flat. She lies on her side, pulls the duvet up to her chin, and waits for the shivering to stop. The hum of the ship is constant, but beneath it she hears faint footsteps in the corridor, the distant clang of a service cart. The world is busy, somewhere. In here, there is only the slow, uneven rhythm of her own heart.

She stares at the wall, eyes wide open. The digital clock on the nightstand blinks 22:09 in red, then 22:10. She imagines Lily in this bed, curled up against her, little feet poking under the covers, hair smelling of soap and sleep. She imagines the sound of her breathing, the weight of her small hand on Claire's arm, the heat of her body pressed close. She tries to remember what it felt like to be needed, to be anchor, orbit, and sky.

She hugs a pillow to her chest, squeezing it tight. The pressure is a poor substitute for a child's embrace, but she holds on anyway, willing herself not to let go.

The tears start slow, silent. They leak from the corners of her eyes and slip down the side of her nose, pooling at her temple, soaking into the pillowcase. She does not make a sound. She is careful, as if the world might overhear her and send someone to intervene. But the more she tries to contain it, the worse it gets.

Her body shakes, muscles tensing and releasing in spasms she can't control. Her teeth chatter, jaw clenched so hard it aches. She bites the edge of the pillow, stifling any noise. Her whole body is a fist, knuckles whitening, lungs burning from the effort not to sob. But eventually the control breaks, and she gasps, the sound guttural, torn from somewhere deep.

She presses her face into the pillow, muffling the noise, letting it take her. She cries hard, ugly, the kind of crying that leaves her dizzy and hollowed out. She thinks of Lily—her face, her voice, the way she would say, "Mummy, don't cry," then touch Claire's cheek with sticky fingers. She thinks of the emptiness of the room, the impossibility of remembering and forgetting at the same time.

When it's over, she lies flat on her back, arms limp at her sides, breath ragged. Tears have left tracks down her face, cold and sticky. The pillow is damp, the sheets twisted around her legs. The room feels even quieter now—the silence absolute.

She closes her eyes. For a long time, she does not move. Sleep creeps in slowly, a sedative at the edge of consciousness. She lets it take her, grateful for the blankness, for the promise of even a moment's peace.

She dreams, but the dreams are just noise, shapes and colours, the taste of salt, the ache of loss echoing through her chest.

She sleeps until the ship's morning song blares over the intercom, snapping her awake.

* * *

The ship's PA clicks on at exactly 8:30, piping in a soft, synthetic chime and a woman's voice.

"Good morning, guests! We hope you had a restful night. Breakfast is now being served in the main dining room and the buffet. Today's forecast: clear skies, gentle seas, and a full day of activities."

Claire is already awake, blinking at the dull ceiling, her mouth lined with the taste of old salt. The room is blue with early light, shadows on the wall like bruises. She has not moved from the spot where she landed last night. Her left arm is numb, fingers tingling as she peels it away from the pillow. The tears from the night before have dried, leaving her eyelids swollen and tight.

She considers rolling over and pretending the world does not exist when a knock at the door splits the air. Not tentative, but brisk and certain—two sharp raps, then silence.

She pulls herself upright, the blanket dragging after her. Her head aches, her mouth dry. She shuffles to the door in bare feet, not caring how she looks, and squints through the peephole.

A young man stands outside, pressed into a pale green uniform, dark hair slicked to his scalp. He balances a tray with both hands, his posture military-precise. Claire opens the door just enough for the tray to pass.

"Room service," the attendant says, his accent neat and practiced. "Special delivery for Miss Holloway."

He does not look at her face, only at the tray, as he places it on the table by the door. "Enjoy," he says, already retreating. He hands her a small, folded note, the paper thick and folded to a perfect square.

The door closes with a clunk. For a moment, Claire is stunned by the suddenness of it all; the light, the food, the touch of the note in her hand.

She reads the note, recognising the blocky script at once.

Enjoy the tiny toast.

-D. Jackson.

Her throat catches. She does not cry but feels tears pressing behind her eyes, pressing forward, hungry for any excuse. Instead, she lays the note flat on the desk, smoothing the creases with her thumb.

The tray holds a single croissant, two slices of melon, a cluster of grapes, and a glass of orange juice sweating on the coaster. The croissant is hot, the paper napkin underneath gone translucent with butter. She sits at the desk, facing the window, and pulls the plate close. The chair is stiff, the upholstery slick under her thighs. She does not turn on the lights; the morning is enough.

Outside, the sea is a brushed-steel plate, sunlight bouncing off the surface in random flashes. Far below, she can see the lower deck, already dotted with passengers in pastel activewear, all purposeful strides and swinging elbows. A family passes by, two adults, a girl in pigtails, a boy dragging a backpack, and Claire watches the girl stumble and giggle, the parents catching her by the hands and lifting her mid-stride. The sound does not travel up to the window, but Claire can imagine it: the high-pitched squeal of a child happy to be airborne.

She picks up the croissant. It flakes instantly, shedding a drift of crumbs onto the plate. She tears it in half, watching steam curl from the centre. The smell is good, better than anything she remembers eating in days. She takes a bite. It is warm, soft, sweet with a bitterness at the edge, and she chews with her eyes closed, focusing on the sensation and nothing else.

She tears the croissant into small pieces, almost instinctively, the way she used to for Lily, small, easy bites, nothing big enough to choke on. She piles the pieces on the napkin, then eats them one by one. The habit is so automatic it takes her a moment to realise what she is doing.

She looks at the other half of the croissant and imagines it in Lily's hands, the buttery ridges pressed flat by impatient fingers, the crumbs caught in the curve of a smile. She can almost see her there, perched on the desk chair, legs swinging, eyes fixed on the next bite.

"Tiny toast, Mummy," she would say, every syllable a celebration.

The pain is sharp but brief. Claire lifts the glass of juice and drinks, the acid burning her throat. She sets it down with a shaky hand, then turns her eyes back to the window.

On the deck, the family has moved on, replaced by a pair of women walking arm-in-arm. They are older, their hair grey and cut short, their bodies moving in careful sync. They pause at the railing, look out over the water, then lean into each other, heads touching. Claire wonders if they have children, if they have ever lost something so central it rearranged every atom in their body.

She stabs a piece of melon with the tiny plastic fork chewing it without tasting. The grape cluster is perfect, each orb tight and gleaming, but she cannot bring herself to eat one. She pushes them to the edge of the plate, then circles them with the fork again and again, until a shallow groove forms in the napkin.

She glances at the note. Enjoy the tiny toast. She traces the words with her finger, pressing hard enough to leave a dent in the paper.

She eats the rest of the croissant in silence, eyes fixed on the sunlight, her mind empty except for the mechanical acts of chewing, swallowing, and breathing.

When the food is gone, she sits very still, hands folded in her lap, waiting for the ache to subside.

It does not.

She rises, puts the tray in the corridor, then closes the door behind her. She stands with her back to it, staring at the note still on the desk.

She is not hungry, not even a little, but she wishes there were another croissant to tear apart, another small ritual to carry her through the morning.

Instead, she sits at the desk, pulls open the travel journal, and readies herself for the next battle: the fight to remember.

The notebook is where she left it last night: teal cover, elastic stretched to near breaking, edges already smudged from days of use. Claire opens it, flips to the first blank page, and tries to remember how to begin. The pen feels heavier than expected; it leaves an oily smear on her fingers as she clicks it open.

She writes the date at the top. 1 April 2025. The numbers come out shaky, misaligned. She pauses, then writes LILY in all caps, underlining it three times. The ink feathers at the edge, bleeding into the grain of the paper.

She doesn't waste time on a greeting, or an introduction. She dives straight into the memory, as if she might lose it unless she pins it down immediately.

She writes about the hospital. The first time she held Lily. She writes about the weight, two point eight kilograms or six pounds, three ounces, but also the heat of Lily's body, the damp sweetness of her breath. She describes how the nurse lifted her, one hand under the head, the other beneath the back, and how that was the last time she trusted anyone else to hold her daughter safely.

She writes about the days at home, the cracked window in the apartment, the way the sun pooled on the rug at three in the afternoon. Lily's crib. The mobile with the moon and stars. How the spinning made Claire dizzy to watch though Lily never took her eyes off it. The nights when Lily wouldn't sleep. The hours spent rocking, humming, whispering any words that came to mind. Every song she can remember, lullabies, Beatles, even Christmas music in July.

She writes about Lily's first smile, the grimace that she convinced herself it was love even when everyone said it was gas. The first tooth. The first fever. The first word. ("Mum-mum," though the paediatrician insisted it didn't count.) The nappies with the blue indicator line, and how Lily would scream if it was even a shade off white.

She flips the page without checking for neatness.

She writes about food. How Lily adored mashed banana, then despised it. How she spat peas with perfect aim but devoured sweet potato like it was all that existed. The fight over sippy cups. The long battle to get her to drink anything but breast milk. The time she hurled the bottle at the wall so hard it left a mark.

She writes about Lily's walk. Her waddle. The fall. The bump on her forehead that never fully faded. The time she climbed the sofa, arms raised in triumph, then toppled off and burst into tears. The time Lily hid in the laundry basket for nearly an hour, silent as a secret, while Claire tore the apartment apart, only to find her curled under a pile of clean towels, giggling.

She writes about Lily's voice. High, raspy, always too loud. Her favourite words— "dino," "kitty," "no"—each a universe of meaning. The green hair bobble with the plastic stegosaurus. How Lily wore it even in sleep, refusing to let Claire remove it. The daily battle over shoes, mornings spent begging Lily to wear anything but the pink rain boots.

She writes about the art. Stickers plastered to the walls and fridge. Paper plates turned into monster masks. Crayon lines defying the colouring book. The pride in Lily's face as she showed off her creations, her whole body swelling with the need to be seen.

She writes about Thomas, the cat. How Lily carried him everywhere, tail dragging, shoved into backpacks, baskets, strollers. The time he had to be washed after a juice box incident. How Lily sat vigil by the dryer, face pressed to the door, waiting for the cycle to finish.

She writes about the apartment. Too small when Lily was angry. Too big when she was gone. The fights—over bedtime, snacks, the TV remote. How every argument ended with Lily's arms around her neck, her voice thick with tears: "Sorry, Mummy. Sorry."

She writes about the cruise. The train to the port. Lily's fascination with the automatic doors. How she insisted on pressing the button for every floor. She writes about boarding, the way Lily clung to her, nervous but excited, the way her eyes grew wide at the sight of the pool, the water slide, the endless horizon outside the glass.

She writes about the pool deck. How Lily stomped in her boots despite the heat. Shrieked with laughter at the spray from the fountains. Wore her life jacket even in the cabin. The pizza bar. Late-night slices. Lily calling the cheese "stretchy" and dangling it from her mouth to make Claire laugh.

She writes about the crafts at the kids club open day. The woman with the accent helping Lily glue paper feathers to a cardboard dinosaur. Lily announcing to the whole room: "I made this for my Mummy." The sticker Lily got from the staff, and how she refused to stick it anywhere but on her own hand.

She writes about the night Lily disappeared.

She writes about the moment she returned. About the silence. About the way her own voice echoed down the hallway when she called Lily's name.

She writes about searching. The corridors. The decks. The endless repeating blur of doors and carpet. The security guard's careful voice, his eyes never quite meeting hers. The disbelief. How no one remembered Lily. How even the photos vanished.

She writes about the ache in her arms. The absence of weight. The ghost of Lily's laugh in her ears.

She writes until her hand cramps; fingers locked around the pen. She switches to her left. The handwriting collapses into a jagged scrawl, but she doesn't stop. She writes until the page curls under her fist, until the ink bleeds through, the elastic snaps and the cover flops open, and pages fold over each other.

She writes about the fear. Of forgetting. Of losing the memories. Of imagining it all. She writes about the doctor. The pamphlet. The crushing possibility that the mind can create a child just to avoid the grief.

She writes about Lily's laugh. How it sounded. What triggered it. She writes it again and again. Lily's laugh. Lily's laugh. Lily's laugh. Until the words distort, lose meaning—then regain it when she starts again.

She loses track of time. The light shifts from pale blue to silver to grey to darkness. She doesn't notice the hunger or the ache in her back. Only the ship's rumble, a neighbour's knock, the slow slide of night through the blackout curtains.

Her hand is a claw, ink-stained and trembling. But she keeps going. Afraid that if she stops, the memories will fracture, escape through the cracks, and dissolve into the air, as if they were never real to begin with.

She writes a note at the bottom of the page:

REMEMBER: LILY. GREEN HAIR BOBBLE. DINOSAUR DRESS. TINY TOAST. CAT IS THOMAS. DON'T LET HER GO.

She draws a box around it. Double lines. The pen tears the paper. She circles it, again and again, trying to make it permanent.

When she finally sets the pen down, her fingers won't straighten. Her knuckles are white. Her nails are bitten raw. She flexes her hand, wincing, and rests it gently atop the notebook, as if it might slip away without her.

She looks at the page, at what she's written, and tries to see it as proof. As evidence. As something solid in a world that won't stay still.

She thinks of the breakfast croissant. The note from Daniel. How even the smallest things can carry a person through the day.

She closes the notebook, smooths the cover, and places it at the centre of the desk. She leans back in the chair, shoulders burning, and stares at the teal rectangle, willing it to hold the truth.

She waits for the next thing to break.

The next knock comes just after dusk: three slow, deliberate taps, muffled by the thick cabin door.

Claire pauses mid-step between the desk and the bed, notebook in hand. She wipes her ink-stained fingers on her thigh, and opens the door a crack.

Daniel stands there holding a tray with two domed plates and a sweating bottle of water. He looks tired, dark stubble shadowing his jaw, but offers a careful smile.

"Evening," he says. "I brought dinner. Thought you might want somewhere quieter than the dining room."

She steps aside to let him in. He moves with quiet ease, setting the tray on the desk, and lifting away the metal covers: pasta in a light sauce, wilted spinach, and a chunk of bread. It's more than she's eaten all day.

"I hope you like it," he says, pouring water into plastic cups. "Apparently, it's the chef's best effort."

She almost laughs. "Thanks," she says, her voice scratchy from disuse. "I wasn't sure I'd eat at all. And thank you for breakfast."

Daniel nods and carries the plates to the balcony, gesturing to the deck chairs. "Best view on the ship," he says. "If you can ignore the wind."

The sun is nearly gone; the sky bruised with purple and gold. The sea below shimmers like shifting glass, each wave catching slivers of light. Claire settles into a chair, tucking her bare feet beneath her. Daniel sits beside her, not too close, and places the plate on her lap.

They eat in silence at first. The pasta is barely warm, but Claire finds herself hungry, twirling forkfuls and swallowing without effort. Daniel watches the sea, his profile outlined by the fading sun. He eats slowly, chewing each bite with focus, like it's his job.

After a few minutes, he speaks. "You were writing when I got here. Was it about Lily?"

Claire nods, eyes on her plate. "I don't want to forget her. It feels like if I stop thinking about her, she'll disappear for good."

Daniel is quiet in a way that doesn't press. When he does speak, it's soft. "What was she like as a baby?"

The question catches Claire off guard. She sets down her fork and thinks. "She was... intense," she says. "Right from the first night. Wouldn't sleep unless I held her, and even then, barely. She hated baths. But she loved my voice, even when I didn't have anything to say."

Daniel smiles, a faint crease at the corner of his mouth. "Sounds about right."

"She had so much hair," Claire goes on. "The nurses joked she'd come out with a full head of it, but no one expected curls." She mimics twisting an invisible lock. "She'd grab my finger with both hands, like she was anchoring herself."

"What about lullabies?" Daniel asks, eyes on the horizon. "Did you sing to her?"

Claire chuckles, quietly embarrassed. "Always. Sometimes I made up words just to get her to settle. Her favourite was 'You Are My Sunshine.' I sang it every night, even when I didn't mean it."

Daniel turns to her, face open and unguarded. "Kids pick up on what's real," he says. "Even if it's not pretty."

Claire looks away, blinking against tears. She takes a long sip of water.

"She was a handful," she says. "A real little monster. But she was mine."

Daniel's voice is gentle. "Tell me more."

Claire breathes in, letting the sea air calm her. She talks about the early mornings, the bottles, how Lily would only nap in the car. She recalls her first steps, how she toddled into the kitchen, fell, and got back up again, determined. She describes storybooks, how Lily insisted on the same one every night, finishing the words before Claire could.

She remembers the green hair bobble, the dinosaur dress, the pink rain boots. The crafts, the stickers, pizza nights. Lily's stubbornness, her laughter. The way she refused to say "please" but never forgot "thank you."

And the last day, how ordinary it was. How quickly everything changed.

She tells Daniel everything. Because it feels like the only thing left to do.

He listens. He nods sometimes, smiles other times. He never interrupts. Never rushes her. When she falters, he waits.

The sky deepens from gold to blue to black. The ship's lights flicker on, casting long reflections in the wake below. Claire looks at her empty plate and realises she has eaten every bite. She dabs her mouth with a napkin and laughs, surprised.

"I guess I was hungry after all."

Daniel grins. "The sea air," he says. "Or maybe just the company."

They sit in companionable silence, watching the night settle over the ocean. A breeze rises, clean and cold. Claire shivers in her thin pyjamas. Daniel stands, offering his jacket. She shakes her head. She wants to feel the cold. Wants it to remind her that she's still here.

After a while, he collects the dishes, stacking them on the tray. He hesitates at the door.

"If you ever want to talk—or just sit out here—I'm around."

Claire nods. "Thank you. For listening."

He closes the door softly behind him. The ship hums. The water glows with reflected light.

Claire remains on the balcony long after he's gone, legs pulled to her chest, head resting on her knees.

The cold seeps into her bones, but she does not move.

She thinks of Lily. Of the stories she told. The shape of the loss stays sharp, but somehow feels less suffocating.

She lets the night fold around her, carried forward by the ship's endless motion, ready for whatever comes next.

* * *

She doesn't know how long she stays on the balcony. The night is all motion, salt wind, engines, the slip of water far below. The conversation with Daniel settles in her bones, not a comfort, but a brace against collapse.

When the cold finally drives her inside, the cabin is set for evening: lights dimmed, corners softened, the bed turned down again as if for someone else. She runs her fingers along the edge of the notebook but doesn't open it. Wrapped in the blanket, she perches on the side of the bed and stares at the wall, waiting for time to pass.

A knock at the door startles her. Daniel stands there, sleeves rolled to his elbows, hair mussed by the wind. He leans in the doorway; one hand braced against the frame.

"Up for a walk?" he asks. "There's a violinist in the theatre tonight. Word is she's better than the magician. I think you should get out for a bit."

Claire almost refuses. Only a moment ago, she'd wanted solitude. Now, the idea of being alone again makes her stomach twist—and his easy presence feels like something she can't quite let go of.

"Okay," she says, voice thin. "Let me get dressed."

They walk side by side through the corridor, neither speaking. The ship is awake now: passengers in pressed shirts and sparkly dresses, perfume and aftershave thick in the recycled air. Laughter and music drift from the cocktail lounges. A man in a tuxedo stumbles past, arm in arm with a woman who throws her head back and laughs, sharp and sudden. No one looks at Claire, but she feels their glances anyway, hot and invisible, like fingers on the back of her neck.

She hugs herself, arms wrapped tight, steps small and precise. Daniel doesn't touch her, but walks close—his presence a buffer against the tide of strangers.

Near the elevators, the crowd thickens, a knot of people waiting for the doors to open. Claire tenses, shrinking against the wall. Daniel notices, angles his body to shield her, placing himself between her and the others. They wait in silence, the air heavy with cologne and anticipation.

When the elevator arrives, the car is already half full. Daniel gestures for her to go first. She steps in, back to the wall, eyes on the glowing numbers overhead. The ride is short but suffocating. At each stop, more people squeeze in, their chatter filling the small space. Claire breathes through her mouth, steadying herself.

On Deck Five, the doors open to a flood of noise and light. The theatre lies ahead, framed by a grand archway and red velvet ropes. Ushers in crisp uniforms direct the crowd, pointing people to their seats with practiced ease.

Just as they reach the entrance, Daniel's radio crackles to life. He winces and pulls it from his belt.

"Security to Officer Jackson. We've got an incident in the Meridian Bar. Need you down here, over."

Daniel sighs, barely audible above the din. He glances at Claire, apology written in the tight set of his jaw.

"Duty calls," he says. "Will you be okay?"

Claire nods, but her fingers twist in the hem of her shirt.

"I'll be fine."

He starts to turn, then stops. "If you want, I can meet you here after the show. Or you can call my number, if—" He breaks off, gives a small, awkward wave, and disappears into the crowd, already speaking into the radio.

Claire stands at the threshold of the theatre, uncertain. Passengers stream past: couples, families, old friends in matching cruise shirts. She feels both invisible and painfully exposed, like the only one without an anchor.

For a moment, she thinks about leaving. She imagines walking the decks alone, cold air biting her skin, the vast dark of the open ocean pressing in from every side.

But something stubborn holds her there. She steps forward, following the line of bodies into the theatre. The space is cavernous, every seat angled toward the stage, the air tinged with the musk of old carpet and anticipation.

CHAPTER TWENTY-ONE

The theatre is filling quickly with patrons eager to see the violinist. Claire enters through the back, heading toward the balcony Daniel showed her the night. The darkness is thick, but not complete. Stripes of dusty light cut across the room to guide people to their seats. She blinks, letting her eyes adjust. The plush seats stand in rigid rows, untouched and uniform. On the stage, a single microphone glints, waiting.

Her stomach twists. The balcony holds memories of last night with Daniel, but she doesn't look. Not yet. Instead, she moves forward, drawn by an unfamiliar urge toward a new purpose. She moves down the centre aisle, the carpet so soft it drinks the sound of her steps. Suddenly, she walks with urgency, as though she might dissolve if she stops.

She counts the rows: one, two, five, ten. The space is vast, built to hold over a thousand. Every seat aimed at the same point on the stage; the room itself is a machine of attention. She glances at the theatre entrance behind her, no one lingers; everyone is moving toward the seating near the stage, leaving only the faint flicker of green safety lights marking the exits.

She turns left, finds the staircase. It's wider than she remembers, the carpet clean, the chrome railing cold from a distance. She stares down for a long time, her mind blank except for the dull thump in her chest. Her hands twitch, craving something to hold.

She inhales deeply and takes the first step. The tread yields beneath her, dense but forgiving. Still, every vibration echoes in her knees. She pauses on the landing, places a hand on the rail. It's colder than she expected. She squeezes, leaving a faint, greasy print behind.

She remembers the last time: the theatre full, sound bouncing off every surface. The smell of perfume, the urge to escape before the crowd blocked the aisles.

Her legs wobble, but she forces herself on. One step. Two. She halts. There it is: the exact spot she fell. The memory hits so hard it splits her vision. There's the step, the shoe, the precise angle of her ankle twisting. The phantom pain flickers in her joint, more surprise than agony.

She remembers falling. But she remembers it wrong.

Her breath quickens. The air bites cold at her lungs. She steps back, hand glued to the rail. Eyes closed, she replays it all, frame by frame.

The theatre was packed. Laughter. Applause. A woman brushing popcorn off her lap. Claire stood near the top of the stairs, watching the early leavers file out before the encore. She moved quickly, wanting to beat the rush. Her hand slid along the railing, slick with something—sweat? Cleaner?

She remembers the weight of her own body, the tension in her legs.

Then—something else. A push. Subtle, but undeniable. A pressure at her lower back, just above the tailbone. Not an accident. Not a stumble. Not a slip.

A hand. Steady. Intentional.

She gasps. The sound ricochets up the stairs and into the cavernous dark. Her grip tightens until her fingers ache. She turns. The aisle is empty.

Then the aftermath: the slow-motion fall, the tug of gravity, the snap of her chin trying to catch the descent. Blurred faces. The taste of blood. The wet tang on her tongue. The crack of her skull on the hard floor.

And—just before she hit, she turned, looked up, and saw a shadow receding. Not a face. Not a person.

She shivers. The heat drains from her skin. Her knees falter, but she forces them straight.

At the top of the stairs, she grips the rail, memory crashing into her. She breathes deep, slows her pulse. She lets go, wipes her hand on her pants, and steps back.

She whispers, "I didn't fall."

The words hang in the air, then vanish.

She stands frozen, staring at the spot where she landed, mind spinning.

Someone pushed me.

Now she knows. The memory has snapped into clarity. She feels it in every nerve.

She thinks of Lily, how her daughter always looked back to make sure Claire was close, how she laughed and ran and never let herself be caught.

She thinks of the empty cabin, the vanished photos, the strange campaign to convince her that Lily never existed.

She wonders who wanted her to fall. Who wanted her to forget.

She stands at the top of the stairs, the knowledge growing heavier by the second.

She didn't fall.

She was pushed.

The world tilts and stutters. Claire stands frozen at the top of the stairs, her hand clenched around the cold metal rail. Her skin prickles, every hair on her body standing to attention. A high, thin whine rings in her ears, like a siren heard underwater. The back of her head throbs, as if she'd hit it only moments ago.

She replays it. Not just the fall, but the moment before. The heat of someone behind her. The brush of fabric at her back. A faint scent, aftershave or cleaning fluid, or both. The memory flickers, jumping in and out of focus, like her mind wants to see it but can't bear to.

Someone was behind her. Not just present, moving with her. Pressing into her space. Then, the pressure: hard, brief, perfectly placed. Not an accident. Not a stumble. A push. Deliberate. Cold.

She tries to breathe, but her throat clamps shut. Her chest is tight, squeezed by invisible hands.

She thinks of all the times she felt eyes on her since boarding the ship. The too-friendly smiles from strangers in the corridor, the way staff would glance at her and then away, the sense that someone always knew where she was, even before she did.

She remembers the day at the pool. The woman with the clipboard who called her by name. The man at the pizza bar who swore he'd never seen Lily. The kids' club worker who insisted her daughter was never there. A chain of denials. A campaign to make her doubt herself.

And now—the push.

Her hands shake. She presses her knuckles to her mouth, biting down on the pain, willing her body to still. But her heart keeps hammering, wild and insistent.

Another detail surfaces. The moment after the fall, when she looked up through the blur of tears and blood. A shape at the top of the stairs. Not a face, just a silhouette. Perfectly still. Watching.

She'd thought it was shock, or guilt, or the confusion of a crowd. But now she knows: it was satisfaction.

She wants to scream. She wants to tear the theatre apart, seat by seat, until she finds the one who did this. But her legs won't move. She's rooted to the spot, held by fear and fury both.

She forces herself to let go of the rail. Her fingers leave damp, angry prints on the chrome.

She glances behind her, half-expecting to see someone standing there. The aisle is empty. Still, she keeps looking, again and again, unable to shake the sense of being followed.

She backs away from the stairs, each step careful, deliberate. She moves up the aisle, then sideways, then up another row. As if distance alone could keep her safe.

Her mind spins. Who would want her to fall? Who would want her gone? The answer arrives. Fast. Logical. Terrifying.

Whoever took Lily.

She remembers how the world erased her daughter. How no one believed. How even the photos and records vanished. It was all connected. Someone had gone to great lengths to make Lily disappear. To make Claire doubt her own mind.

But she hadn't doubted. Not really. Not in her bones.

Now, she knows.

She stands in the darkened theatre, breath quick and shallow. She wipes her palms on her pants, checks the exits, the shadows, every place a threat could hide.

She is not safe here. She is not safe anywhere.

She wants to run to Daniel. To tell him what she's remembered. But trusting anyone on this ship feels suddenly absurd. She doesn't know who to believe. Who's real. Who's part of the plan.

She closes her eyes. Just for a second. And pictures Lily: the stubborn set of her jaw, the dimple in her cheek, the way she stomped her foot when she didn't get her way.

The memory doesn't fade—it sharpens.

Someone took her daughter.

She opens her eyes. The lines of the world sharp, hard, unshakeable.

She is done being afraid.

She leaves the theatre. Steps into the corridor. Does not look back.

She knows the truth now.
And she will not stop until she finds Lily.
Whatever it takes.

CHAPTER TWENTY-TWO

The wind on the upper deck is a living thing. It howls through the gaps in the safety glass, drives needles of salt air into every crack in her skin. Claire leans into it, letting the cold burn her face, because it's better than what waits behind her eyes. Her hands tremble on the railing, but she can't make herself let go.

She counts the people on the deck. Thirty-two if you include the bartender, thirty-three if the shape at the far end is real. Most are clustered around the pool, sunburned flesh pressed against plastic loungers. They laugh, scream, order drinks, oblivious to the world ending one deck above. Claire moves through them like a ghost, unseen until she brushes too close and gets a flinch, a dirty look, a muttered word.

She scans every face, searching for Lily's hair, Lily's dress, Lily's boots, but the crowd offers nothing but strangers. Some smile, reflexive, reptilian. Some glare, not bothering to hide the judgment. A child shrieks near the hot tub, her voice knifing through Claire's head so sharp she almost blacks out. The girl is maybe six, not even close. Claire wants to grab her by the shoulders and demand: *Have you seen her? Have you seen my daughter?* But the words tangle and die.

She paces the length of the deck. Her body is all angles, bones knocking together in protest. She feels like she hasn't eaten since yesterday; her stomach is a clenched fist. It doesn't matter. The hunger feels deserved.

Someone in a white jacket steps in front of her. Claire jolts, heartbeat slamming up into her throat, but the man just wants to know if she'll try the drink of the day—mango something, 'very fresh, very happy.' His smile is fake as plastic, eyes flickering to her hands, to her face, and away. She shakes her head, steps around him, fights the urge to run.

She remembers the push. The hand at her back, the precision of it. The blank space where a face should be. Her mind runs through the memory again and again, like a dog gnawing bone. It's real. It happened. She was not clumsy. She was not weak.

Her brain offers up a new terror. Maybe Daniel wasn't helping her. Maybe he was watching. He has access to the cameras. He always showed up at the right moment, always so calm, so understanding. Maybe he's the one who wants her to think she's crazy, to make her doubt everything so when she finally loses it, they'll say she did it to herself.

She laughs, short and sharp, and the wind eats the sound before it can land.

She keeps walking. A trio of teenagers pass, heads down in a screen-lit huddle. One glances up and grins at her, no, not at her, through her. Like she's not even there. That's worse than being seen.

The deck narrows by the mini-golf course, forcing her close to the glass. She watches the sea, endless and empty, and for a second, she wonders what would happen if she climbed the rail and let the wind take her. She would vanish. No one would remember. The world would keep spinning, no gap left behind.

But Lily is still here. Somewhere. Claire can feel it, a splinter under the skin. She closes her eyes, and there's Lily's hand in hers, sticky and warm, the way it was on the first day. She remembers the exact weight of it, the damp print it left on her palm. She remembers Lily's laugh, the specific pitch, the way it rose and fell in three quick bursts, never quite the same as on the recordings.

She opens her eyes. The memory dissolves in the dark of the night.

She keeps moving, not because she wants to, but because stopping feels like dying. Her feet drag her past the buffet, the gym, the empty shuffleboard courts. Everything is too clean, too bright. She wants to find a dark corner and crawl inside, but there are no dark corners on this ship. Only people, always people, watching, waiting.

As she rounds the next bend, she spots Daniel. He stands by the lifeboats, talking to another officer. His posture is easy, casual, but his eyes never stop moving. He sees her, nods once, then goes back to the conversation. Claire ducks behind a pillar, breath caught in her lungs. She waits, counting to ten, then twenty, before emerging.

Daniel is gone.

She hurries past the spot where he stood, half-expecting to feel a hand on her back, to be shoved again. Nothing happens. She is alone.

The world spins a little, but she keeps going. She needs to circle the ship, again and again, until something gives. She needs to find the weak spot, the crack in the illusion, the proof that Lily was real.

She reaches the bow, wind screaming now. She clings to the rail, stares into the void, and dares the world to take her.

But the world does not care. The ship cuts forward, splitting the sea into perfect halves, leaving nothing behind but a white, frothing wound.

She waits for the dizziness to pass, then pulls herself upright.

There is more searching to do.

There's a thump in her chest, slow at first but then hard and steady. Claire retraces her steps; eyes fixed on the artificial seams between the boards. Every few yards, she glances over her shoulder. No one follows. Still, she can't shake the feeling of a camera lens tightening on her.

At the mini-golf course, the world turns bright and noisy. Children shriek over missed putts. Parents sip beer on cartoon-green benches. Claire wants to walk past, to let the noise roll over her, but then she spots a splash of yellow beneath the third bench.

A small rubber duck.

She stops so fast it jolts her knees. For a moment, she stares. The duck lies face up, the beak lopsided, one eye slightly higher than the other. A tiny paper tag is tied around its neck with string.

Her legs go numb.

She crouches, ignoring the stab of pain in her thighs, hand hovering just above the duck. The tag reads, in a childish font: "Cruising Ducks —keep or hide, you decide!"

Her heart slams against her ribs.

She remembers: Lily had wanted to find a duck so badly. She talked about it every day before the cruise, begged Claire to search the decks "just one more time." She called it the mission, made up stories about where the ducks went, who found them, what happened if they never came back.

Claire picks up the duck. The plastic is cold. She turns it over, searching for a signature, a clue—anything. The tag is laminated. The string is new. No handwriting.

She presses the duck to her chest. The force nearly folds her in half. She fights to breathe evenly, but tears push behind her eyes. She holds tighter, willing herself not to break in the middle of the ship.

A memory surfaces: Lily at the buffet, sticky fingers tracing circles on a tray.

"Maybe they don't want to be found," she said, solemn. "Maybe the ducks are hiding from the big people."

She'd hidden under the table and quacked until Claire dragged her out. Even then, she didn't stop laughing.

Claire wants to crawl under the bench and scream.

Instead, she wipes her eyes on her sleeve and sits hard. The duck rests in her lap.

A shadow passes over her feet. She looks up. A crew member with a broom, waits silently, then offers a tight, polite smile and moves on.

Claire turns the duck over again. Something about it feels wrong, off in a way she can't explain.

It's too new. Too perfectly placed.

As if it was waiting for her.

As if someone knew she'd come.

The thought hits her like a blow.

She's being watched. She's being tested.

The duck is a plant. A signal. A message: We know what you're looking for. We know you won't stop.

She shoves the duck into her pocket, stands, and strides toward the bow.

Her chest blazes. Her pulse pounds.

Every face is a threat. Every glance, a warning.

Did Daniel leave the duck?

To bait her? To use it later?

Or is it worse? Something orchestrated from a place she can't see.

She touches the duck in her pocket, fingers brushing the hard edge of the tag. She tells herself it's real. That Lily was real.

But she can't stop looking over her shoulder.

The world is closing in.

All she has left is a plastic toy and the memory of her daughter's laugh.

She walks faster.

The walk to her cabin is a gauntlet.

Claire presses herself flat against the wall whenever someone rounds a corner. The crew move in efficient packs, all smiles and name badges, but she sees the calculation in their eyes: the one who logs her on a clipboard, the one who pauses just a second too long at her face, the one with the radio who glances at her, then whispers into the static.

She ducks into a side stairwell when she hears laughter. Up close, the walls are paper-thin, the carpet damp where it meets the tile. She counts the steps—twelve down, three to the left, seven more to the right—and slips past a couple in matching shirts arguing about the pool schedule. She keeps her head low. No one stops her.

At her door, her hand shakes so hard she drops the sail pass twice. She wipes her palms on her pants, taps the card on the sensor, and listens for the soft click before pushing through. She slams the door, throws the deadbolt, and drags the chain across with trembling fingers.

She stands with her back against the door for a full minute, listening for footsteps.

There are none.

The room is a freezer. She fumbles with the thermostat, cranks it up until the air turns thick and wet. She peels off her jacket, tosses it on the bed, then yanks the curtains shut in one hard motion. The lights of the ship vanish. Only the yellow of the cabin lights remain, humming and sharp.

She pulls the 'Do Not Disturb' sign from the desk and hangs it outside. The act feels pointless, but it's a rule—and she's desperate for any sense of order.

She checks the lock three more times before she's satisfied.

She paces. The duck is still in her pocket, pressing into her hip, a constant reminder. She sets it on the desk, her hands lingering on its plastic surface.

She examines it like evidence. A scratch, a mark, a hair, a fingerprint, anything. She turns the tag over and over, checks the string for an out-of-place knot. She even tries to open the bottom, pries at the seam with her nails, but it doesn't budge. She peers through the tiny hole in the beak, in case someone drilled a camera inside. Nothing.

She squeezes it. The duck gives a weak, pathetic squeak. She listens to the echo. Then she smells it, sniffing the beak, the belly, the string. Just plastic. Faint chemicals. Maybe a trace of chlorine. She licks her thumb and rubs the tag, half-expecting invisible ink to rise.

Nothing. Not a single secret.

Victory surges, then vanished. In its place: doubt.

What if this is exactly what they want? What if the real message is in the act of finding it? Or worse, what if it's a warning—proof they know where she is, what she's thinking, what she's lost?

She sits on the bed, duck in hand, and rocks. The motion is muscle memory—years ago, sleep-deprived. Lily a newborn refusing to close her eyes. Claire would pace the living room, baby on her chest, humming under her breath, swaying until one of them gave in.

She blinks. The memory flares, too bright. For a moment she's there, in that too-warm apartment, surrounded the smell of spit-up, milk, and laundry. Lily curled against her heart. She holds the duck tighter, as if it might stir with life.

The phone rings on the nightstand. She jumps, nearly drops the duck, and stares at the screen: SECURITY and a four-digit number. She ignores it, afraid of who might be on the other end.

She stands, duck in hand, and walks to the suitcase. She unzips it, burrows to the bottom, and pulls out a soft, faded t-shirt. She wraps the duck inside, tight, and tucks it into the far corner beneath extra jeans and a half-rolled sweater.

She closes the suitcase, clicks the lock shut, and drags it to the foot of the bed.

She sits, arms around the case, chin on her knees, eyes on the door.

She will not sleep. Not yet.

She will watch. She will wait. If they come for the duck, they'll have to go through her first.

The night stretches. Minutes bleed into hours. She counts the sounds in the hallway—the squeak of a cleaning cart, the thud of footsteps, the muffled laughter of strangers. Each time, she tenses, heart racing, ready to defend her prize.

Near morning, her body betrays her. She slumps, still clutching the case, eyelids fluttering, mind drifting toward a place where the world makes sense and Lily is safe, waiting for her with a plastic duck in each hand.

She dreams of nothing but yellow and the ache of still holding on.

CHAPTER TWENTY-THREE

Claire wakes up wrong. Every muscle is locked, her jaw clamped tight, fingers curled so fiercely her nails have left angry half-moons in her palms. Sweat crackles on her scalp, and a damp patch on the pillow beneath her cheek. Her first thought is a scream—Lily—but it catches behind her teeth. By the time her eyes focus on the ceiling, the name has already lost its sound.

The cabin is dark, save for a thin slit of light at the base of the blackout curtain, narrow as thread but relentless. She listens: the rumble of engines, the hiss of ventilation, the high-pitched whine of the air conditioning that never stops. Beneath it all, her pulse pounds, slow and heavy, a metronome for panic.

Her head throbs. Not the dull echo of a fall, but something urgent, an animal gnawing at the base of her skull, pain pulsing in waves. She tries to sit. The room tilts. She sags back to the bed, eyes squeezed shut until the vertigo subsides.

The clock blinks 05:43 in blurry red, two dots pulsing like a warning. She was up most of the night. The body remembers. The body keeps the score.

She takes inventory: nothing broken, nothing bleeding. She flexes her hands, wincing at the ache in her knuckles from days of writing. Her left ankle is stiff, a souvenir from the fall, but she can wiggle her toes and press her foot down without fireworks of pain.

She breathes, slowly, trying to slow her heartbeat. It doesn't help.

The suitcase waits at the foot of the bed. She drags it closer; the wheels hum loud in the quiet. She opens the zipper with care. Inside the duck remains, wrapped in a burial shroud of t-shirt, yellow beak poking through the fabric like a bad joke. She lifts it out, cold plastic in her hands. It doesn't squeak. She kisses the beak to her lips, for a second, then slips it into the robe pocket.

She stands with a creak of bone and steps into the bathroom. She locks the door. Then checks the lock again. She runs the water, not for need, but for noise. Sitting on the closed toilet, she breathes until the fire behind her eyes cools to a simmer.

Memories return in shards: the push at the theatre, the duck at mini-golf, the sterile cabin, the missing photos. The sense of surveillance. The prickle on the back of her neck in every corridor. Daniel. The staff. All of them smiling. All of them helpful. All of them pretending not to see.

She says aloud, "They're hiding her. They must be. Why erase the evidence? Why plant the duck? It's a message. A warning. They want me to stop looking. They want me to forget."

In the fogged mirror, her reflection is alien: hair wild, pillow lines etched into her face, a yellowing bruise blooming at her temple. She barely recognises herself. It doesn't matter.

She showers quickly, dresses in yesterday's clothes. She avoids the closet's empty half, the shelf where Lily's boots used to rest. She doesn't look at the untouched pillow beside hers.

She squeezes the duck in her fist and slips it into her pants pocket.

She opens the door a crack, listening. Silence. A check through the peephole confirms it: no one. Only sunlight crawling across the carpet.

She steps into the corridor.

She walks fast, but not too fast. Head down, eyes on the carpet, hands stuffed deep in her pockets. She skims the wall, counting doors, glancing up, only to check for cameras or crew.

This is no longer paranoia. It's survival. Every whisper. Every shuffle, every hiss of a rolling cart sets her nerves screaming. But she keeps going. She has to.

She takes the stairs. Each landing, she pauses. On Deck Six, a steward folds towels with robotic precision. Claire waits for his back to turn before slipping past.

She imagines Lily laughing, running ahead in this hallway. That hurts more than her ankle, more than her head.

At the end of the corridor, another crew member, this one in maintenance blue, keys into a supply closet. He meets her eyes. She freezes. He nods, then looks away. She notes his gloves, his access card on his belt. She files that away. Details matter.

She merges with a group of older women in matching floral shirts, trailing behind their chatter to mask her movement. When they veer toward the spa, Claire dashes for the next intersection.

She hates being seen. But being ignored might be worse. Every uniform is a warning: she is a problem. A liability.

She pauses at a water fountain, lets the cold shock of it cleanse the taste of fear. She sets the duck on the rim, then takes it back.

She keeps moving.

She doesn't know her destination, only that staying still isn't safe. Not while they're watching. Not while Lily is still out there.

She descends another staircase. Then another. The lower decks smell different: less like cologne and pool chlorine, more like oil, metal, the funk of too many people pressed into too little space. Lights flicker, corridors narrow.

Then: a security officer ahead. Not Daniel. Older. Broader. Military stillness. He stands with his hands behind his back, legs spread in a stance that says "do not approach." Claire recoils into shadow.

She waits. He doesn't move.

She considers retreat. But the nowhere is safe now.

She recalls the duck. The note. Keep or hide, you decide. She wishes it were that easy.

She steps out, slow and steady. "Just looking for the laundry room," she rehearses. It's a weak line, but it's all she has.

The officer meets her gaze. She flinches. He says nothing.

She walks on. Skin crawling. Door after door after door.

Eventually, the tension fades. A fraction. She exhales.

She's improving. She's surviving.

At the end of a blank hallway, she rests a hand on the wall. Breathes.

She closes her eyes. Thinks of Lily. Her hand. Her scent. Her warmth.

She opens her eyes.

If they want to hide her daughter, they're going to have to try harder.

The next floor, three, is a dead zone. No voices, no music, not even the scrape of cleaning carts. The air feels different here, drier, less perfumed, with a faint tang of metal and bleach. The walls are white, aggressively so, and the carpet is cheaper grade: the plush gone, the pattern faded to the colour of hospital scrubs. The only décor is a series of safety signs and a faded evacuation map in three languages.

Claire moves quieter now, senses stretched thin. Her shoes make less noise on this carpet, but her pulse drums like a bass in her ears. She stops at every junction, listens. When nothing moves, she counts five slow seconds before continuing.

She is far from the heart of the ship. Here, the guest rooms are fewer, the doors farther apart. Most of the cabins have their 'Do Not Disturb' signs out, a clear signal no one is coming or going. It feels abandoned. Like the aftermath of a party everyone forgot to clean up.

The lighting changes as she moves aft. Overhead, soft yellow bulbs give way to harsher fluorescents, each humming with the ship's secrets. The ceiling drops a few inches, air ducts visible like silver veins running the corridor's length. The floor dips, just barely; she realises she's walking lower than before, just above the waterline, maybe.

She wonders if Lily is here, somewhere just out of sight. Locked behind a door, waiting for her mother to find the key. The thought keeps her moving.

She checks every door as she passes. Most are guest rooms, locked tight. Some are utility closets, their handles cold and unyielding. At the hall's end, a service cart sits abandoned, a single towel draped over its edge like a flag of surrender. She glances back, but the hallway is empty. Nothing behind her but fluorescent ghosts.

She turns the corner and spots the door at once: wider, heavier, painted a flat institutional grey. A placard reads "Crew Access Only." Below, in smaller print, "No Guests Beyond This Point." The sign is new, the edges sharp, but paint around the handle is chipped and worn. People touch this door. They go through it often.

It is open. Not much, just a sliver, but enough to spill a bar of icy blue light spill across the carpet. The light is wrong, too bright, too clean, and it slices the dim hallway in two.

Claire stops. Her body goes rigid, hairs on her arms bristling. She glances left, then right. Nothing. No witnesses.

Her heart pounds. She wants to run to the door, but her legs are locked. She stands there, every nerve electrified, afraid to move, afraid to breathe. The duck is a cold weight in her pocket.

She steps closer, slow and careful. The light grows stronger, the hum louder, drowning out every other sound. She stops a foot from the door, ears straining. On the other side, a voice—low, guttural, then gone. She thinks she hears footsteps, too, quick and even, followed by the hiss of a closing hatch.

She waits, counts to ten, then places her hand against the door. It is cool, almost wet. She leans in; the crack wide enough to see through.

The world beyond is nothing like the rest of the ship. No carpet, just vinyl flooring and painted stripes. Walls are lined with pipes, wires, panels blinking red and green. Overhead, fluorescent bulbs buzz like hornets, casting sharp shadows on the floor. The corridor runs straight and narrow, a spine of metal and smooth panels fading into shadow.

People move here, but not like guests. Fast, focused, never stopping. Some wear uniforms, some coveralls, but all walk with purpose. They pass each other with clipped nods, carrying crates, pushing bins, none looking up, none speaking unless they have to. It's a machine, every person a gear.

Claire watches, not breathing, afraid that even a sigh will draw attention.

A woman rounds the corner, face pale under cold light, arms stacked with boxes. Behind her, a man in black walks with a tablet pressed to his chest, muttering into an earpiece. Further down, two figures pause at a junction, heads bent in hurried conversation. One laughs, but it's a knife-blade sound, quickly swallowed by the ship's noise.

There is something else: a tension in the air, a sense that everything here balances on a thread. Every motion precise, every glance calculated. No one wastes time. No one is here by accident.

Claire feels hairs rise on the back of her neck. She thinks of Lily—small, soft, terrified, lost in a place like this. She tries to picture her daughter in the maze of pipes and wires. Her stomach turns to water.

She wants to step through, follow the current and see where it goes. But her body won't let her. Not yet.

Instead, she pulls back, slow and careful. The door whispers shut behind her. The click is deafening.

She stands in the empty hallway, heart racing, the crew corridor's echo burned into her eyes.

She knows what she has to do.

Claire presses her face against the small glass panel on the door, straining to decipher the shadows lurking in the depths below. What secrets do those rooms hide? Her heart races when her eyes lock onto something strewn and forgotten, shoved against the corridor wall—Lily's unmistakable green dinosaur hair bobble. Urgency surges through her as she realises this is where her daughter is.

She reels back, heartbeat lodged in her throat. Then she realises she's not alone.

A man stands less than a metre away, having appeared from the side passage so silently he might as well have been waiting there all along. He's tall, around forty, with skin stretched tight over sharp cheekbones, and hair buzzed close to his skull. The white of his uniform glows blue in the corridor light. A badge is stitched on his chest, a name in black thread, but Claire can't focus on it because his eyes are two perfect chips of glass, and they are locked on her.

She tries to speak but finds only gravel in her throat.

"This area's restricted," the man says, every syllable clipped and exact. "Please step back."

The accent is hard to place, neutral, flattened by years of corporate hospitality, but there's nothing friendly in his tone. He holds his hands out, palms forward, the universal sign for "Do not come closer."

Claire nods slowly, and steps back, one pace, then another. The duck in her pocket presses into her thigh. She looks down, tries to muster the sheepish smile of a lost tourist, but adrenaline burns hot in her cheeks.

"Sorry," she says, voice brittle. "I was looking for the laundry. Got turned around."

The man does not blink. "Laundry is on Deck Eleven, midship. Passenger facilities are clearly marked. If you need assistance, ask at Guest Services."

He does not move until she is three metres away, then pivots and swipes a card across the panel beside the door. It's a small, black rectangle, barely wider than a thumb. As the card makes contact, a red LED blinks once, then turns green. The door hisses open, a sliver at first, then wider, and the man steps through, giving her one last look before the door glides shut behind him.

Claire stands in the empty hall, head buzzing.

She has seen exactly what she needed: the panel, the light, the card kept on a retractable belt clip, easy to grab but secure. The way the man waited for her to back off, never taking his eyes off her. The rules here are simple, but absolute: you need a card. You need to look like you belong.

She breathes through her nose, jaw clenched so tight her teeth ache. She tries to remember every detail: the angle of the swipe, the speed of the light, the way the man's eyes stayed fixed on her until the last possible second.

She walks back down the corridor, hands in pockets, head down. She turns a corner, waits five seconds, then peeks back. The door is closed. No sign of the man. No sound but the low, electric hum of the ship's arteries.

She doesn't know how to get a card—not yet. But she knows what to look for, and what to do when she finds it.

The fear is still there, a living thing inside her. But it's smaller now, boxed in by the new shape of the problem. She moves quicker, all the pain in her head replaced by a clear, metallic drive.

She's not going back to the cabin. She's not going to sit and wait for someone else to solve this.

If Lily is anywhere on this ship, she's behind that door.

And soon, Claire will be too.

CHAPTER TWENTY-FOUR

The world is fluorescent and harsh. The lights on Deck 4 never truly shut off, but in the early morning they flicker and pulse making the world seem less real, more manufactured. The shopping promenade is supposed to be "the heart of the ship," but right now it feels like a dead vein, stores shuttered, kiosks empty, digital directory screens the only things alive.

Claire walks the length of the deck three times before seven a.m. Her pace is steady, measured. She keeps to the right, eyes forward, feet whispering on carpet that's designed to mimic waves. Her hands are buried in her pockets, shoulders hunched, trying to make herself smaller. She counts the cameras; those built into the fake art-deco wall sconces and the ones disguised as smoke detectors. There are more than yesterday. Or maybe she just never noticed them before.

The only people out this early are crew: a woman in a green housekeeping uniform, pushing a silent cart stacked with bleach and clean towels; two maintenance techs in navy jumpsuits, working at the base of an escalator; and a single security officer making rounds, his jacket unzipped, radio on his shoulder hissing static. They don't look at her. They never do. It's as if she is transparent, only half-written into the ship's script.

But she knows they're watching. Always.

The pain in her head is a minor character this morning. The bruising from the fall is now a low-grade throb behind her ear, not a warning, just a fact to acknowledge and move past. She moves in straight lines now, less likely to drift or sway. The world is sharper, like the contrast slider pushed too far. She welcomes it.

She pauses at the glass doors of The Emporium, the largest store on the ship. Inside, shelves are still half-lit, mannequins in resort wear frozen mid-strut. She checks the hours posted in three languages on the door: opens at eight. She does the math in her head, recalibrates her plan, then moves on.

At the coffee kiosk, two baristas set up pastry displays in silence. Claire lingers, pretending to examine the menu, but really watches the corridor's reflection in the glass, counting people behind her. She tracks the cleaning staff's pace, noting which ones are working and which ones are just moving through. She files away the pattern.

She buys a black coffee, no milk. The woman hands it over without a smile, eyes flickering over the name on her sail pass card before moving on. Claire carries the cup to the far end of the promenade, sits at a banquette upholstered in teal vinyl, and watches the world.

She makes a list in her head:

1. Disguise.

2. Access card.

3. Distraction.

The first is easy. She has money, and the Emporium has two mannequins dressed in cruise-logo hoodies and hats. She only needs ten minutes and the right size. The second will be harder, but not impossible—she's seen the way the staff carry their cards, forgetting to tuck them into their badge reels after swiping. As for distraction, she is a mother: improvisation is the only thing she's ever been good at.

A family with three children enters the promenade, all wearing matching cruise t-shirts. The youngest, a girl with a wild mop of hair, is mid-tantrum, stamping her feet and howling at the injustice of no ice cream for breakfast. Claire feels a flash of envy at the noise. She wonders what it would be like to scream in public, to let it all out, to demand what you need.

She drinks the coffee, the burn on her tongue grounding her in the moment. The caffeine sharpens everything a step further.

She checks her watch. 07:27. Thirty-three minutes until the Emporium opens. She finishes the coffee, tosses the cup in the trash, and walks the deck's perimeter again.

On the second lap, she sees the same security officer by the art gallery. He's pretending to read the digital display about a "Featured Artist of the Week," but really scans the deck, eyes darting person to person, never lingering more than a second. She wonders what he writes in his report. She wonders if there's already a file on her: Holloway, Claire. Subject exhibits unusual behaviour, avoids eye contact, walks in loops. Possible risk factor: prior incident with guest services, known medical history (see MedBay report from three nights prior).

She pulls her phone from her pocket, pretends to check messages. Battery low. A single notification from the cruise app: "Friday is Port Day! Don't forget your shore excursion tickets." She deletes it. She opens the camera, flips it to selfie mode, and uses the screen as a mirror.

Her face is drawn, skin pale except for the bruise by her ear. Her hair is a mess; curls matted against her forehead. She ties it back with a hair tie from her wrist, pulling hard enough to make her scalp scream. She looks like a woman with nothing left to lose.

She watches the barista at the coffee kiosk. When the woman leaves the counter to restock cups, Claire moves in, fills a napkin with sugar packets and grabs a plastic spoon. No plan for these yet, but it feels right to collect them.

Back at the banquette, she waits.

At 07:58, the Emporium lights click on. The manager, a tall man in a red vest and too-white teeth, unlocks the door. He flips the OPEN sign, checks his watch, then disappears into the back. Claire stands, wipes her hands on her jeans, and walks over.

She's the first customer. The man returns, smile ready, and greets her in a voice honed by years of retail training. "Good morning, ma'am! Can I help you find anything today?"

"Just browsing," she says flatly. She moves past him, toward the row of logo wear. Her hand runs along the rack, feeling for sizes. She grabs a large navy hoodie with the ship's name in white block letters, and a matching baseball cap. She slips them over her arm, then scans the racks for something else—maybe sunglasses, maybe a scarf—but decides it would look too much.

She drifts toward the back, eyes on the convex mirror mounted in the corner. She sees the manager watching, hands folded over his belt. She gives him nothing, no hint of nervousness.

At the counter, she pays with her sail pass card. The sales associate, Anna, makes small talk about the weather, and how lucky she is to have a clear day today. Claire nods, gives her a tight smile, and says, "Thanks." She tucks the bag under her arm and heads for the exit.

She turns to leave, but something catches her eye. Next to the register, stacked low on a white display table, is a row of toy ships, model replicas, about a foot long, with real rigging and tiny cannons glued to the decks. The box is sealed with a round sticker—security, probably—but it draws Claire's attention, and she realises she might not need the access card after all. A small tag under the display reads: 'Perfect gift for your junior sailor!'

The word 'junior' hits her like a kidney punch. For a split second, she sees Lily's face, almost three years old and glowing, hands pressed to a toy-store window, begging for a plastic stegosaurus. The feeling is old and raw. She lets it pass, then picks up the ship.

She carries it to the register, forcing herself to smile. "Almost forgot. My daughter's obsessed with boats," she says, and is surprised at how steady her voice sounds.

Anna's eyes soften. "Good taste," she says. "My son tried to sail his in the bathtub. Didn't end well." She scans the box, then slides it into a separate bag. "If you need gift wrap—"

"That's okay. She'll want to open it right away."

Anna hands over the bag. "Hope she likes it," she says, and this time there's no question it's genuine.

Claire nods, then leaves.

Outside, the deck is filling with more people—retirees with lanyards, couples in gym clothes, a few staff in crisp uniforms. The world is waking up, but Claire feels herself fading into it, less a person and more a data point on a graph.

The promenade is busier now. The coffee line is six deep; a crew member sweeps crumbs from the carpet while another polishes the brass railings. The families from before have multiplied, small children darting between adults, voices rising and falling like a tide.

Claire walks slowly, eyes on the carpet. She hugs the bags to her chest, making herself as small as possible. At the edge of the shopping deck, she spots the security officer again. This time, he's not pretending to be interested in art. He stands with his back to the wall, arms folded, face scanning the crowd with calculated indifference.

She turns her head away, drifting toward a jewellery store with glittering displays in the window. She presses her face close to the glass, pretending to be fascinated by a row of watches, but keeps the officer in her periphery. He checks his phone, glances up, and moves on. Only then does Claire let herself exhale.

She clutches the bags tighter; the toy ship wedged against her ribs. She feels the round tamper sticker under her thumb, remembers the plan: catch the door when it is open, block the latch with the sticker, make it look like nothing happened and the door is closed like normal.

The headache pulses behind her eye, but she welcomes it. It means she's alive, means her senses are firing.

She glances at her watch. 08:18. She has maybe forty minutes before the halls fill with excited travellers. She wants to be in and out before anyone notices.

She heads for the bathroom on Deck 14, near the running track—not the closest by any means, but the one she's chosen deliberately. This one has two entrances, one from the interior corridor and another facing the deck. Perfect for a quick change.

She picks up her pace, every step rehearsed and mapped. She doesn't look back.

She is almost there.

The buffet buzzes like a hive. By nine a.m., every table will be packed. Tourists in board shorts and sandals swarm the steam trays, herding kids and piling plates high with scrambled eggs, sausage, and pastries. The air is thick with a dense, sticky-sweet smell, but Claire barely registers it.

She moves through the line with practiced indifference, hoping someone will notice her. She grabs a small white plate, lifts a croissant from the pile, and pours a glass of orange juice. No second trips, no excess. She's here to be seen, then become invisible.

Scanning the room for a table with a view of the exit, she settles near a fake potted palm. Sliding in, she tucks the toy ship bag under her feet, and bites into the croissant. The pastry flakes, dry and a little stale, but she chews and swallows, her jaw working on autopilot.

She drinks the juice in three quick sips, letting the acidity clear her mouth. Her fingers drum a nervous rhythm on the table as her eyes sweep the room. She counts nearby staff: three bussers, two breakfast chefs, one manager in a pressed white shirt. None look at her. Then again, none look at anyone for more than a second.

She finishes the croissant, wipes her hands on a napkin, and lets her gaze slacken for a moment. The buffet noise overwhelms her: children squealing, cutlery clattering, the whir of the juice dispensers. She imagines Lily here, feet dangling off the chair, hands sticky with jam, face bright and open.

Closing her eyes briefly she imagines Lily's hand in hers. The memory gives her a sliver of strength.

She opens her eyes. The room remains unchanged. The plan is still in motion.

She checks the clock on the wall: 08:41.

Standing, she slides the plate and glass onto a bus cart, and picks up her bags. She moves toward the exit, eyes on the floor, slipping out without a word.

In the corridor, she slows. A woman running errands, nothing more. She carries her bags like they are the most important things in the world.

She moves toward the next phase, each step measured, heart pounding so hard she feels it in her teeth.

She doesn't hesitate.

Not now.

The bathroom is empty when she enters. The lights hum with the same artificial insistence as everywhere else, but the air here is tinged with bleach and something citrus. She checks both entrances twice, then ducks into the last stall, bolts the door, and kneels on the cool tile. Her breath comes fast, then slows as she counts her tools.

She opens the plastic bag and pulls out the hoodie, the cap, and the toy ship. She lays them in a careful row on the closed lid of the toilet. Sliding her sail pass card from her jeans, she tucks it into the hoodie pocket.

She rips off the tags and wriggles into the hoodie. It smells new, and chemical, like it's never been worn. The sleeves are too long, but that's good, it covers the bandage on her wrist and the scratches from the other night. She tugs her hair into a low, loose knot, jams the cap on tight, and checks herself in the small mirror above the sink.

It's like looking at someone else. The woman in the glass is pale, hollow-eyed, but she could be crew, guest, or nobody at all. The hoodie and hat erase her. She likes the feeling.

She moves quickly, tearing the sticker off the model ship box with her thumbnail. It comes away clean, a perfect circle of blue. She rolls it sticky-side-out and affixes it to the inside of her sleeve, out of sight. She returns the toy ship to the bag, for later. For Lily. If it's still here.

She breathes in through her nose, out slow. The sounds of the ship are muffled here, just the rush of air through the vents and, distantly, the thud of someone jogging the running track above. She listens for footsteps, waits a long minute, then cracks the stall door.

Still empty.

She checks the mirror again. This time she looks herself in the eyes, and forces herself to remember: You're doing this for her. For Lily. For the child no one else remembers, the one who has been excised from the world by forces she can't name.

The duck. The memory comes sharp and clean, as if Lily is whispering it in her ear: "Find the ducks, Mummy! The mission isn't done until you find them all." The toy is still safe in her pocket, a totem, a proof of existence that no amount of denial can erase.

Claire closes her eyes, holding the memory tight. She imagines Lily in the crew corridors: afraid, alone, but alive. Waiting for someone to break the rules, to smash the system, to find her.

She snaps her eyes open. She's ready.

She jams her hands into the hoodie's front pocket, grabs the model ship bag, and leaves the stall. At the sink, she runs cold water over her face, wipes away the shine, and dries off with a scratchy paper towel. She tucks the model ship under the sink up against the wall. She will return for it later. Claire checks both entrances one last time, then steps into the corridor.

The plan is set. She will exit through the exterior door, circle down to the lower deck, wait for a crew member to open the access, then block the latch with the sticker.

Time to go.

She steps out the external door into the morning light. The air is crisp and sharp, and she sets her sights on the next phase.

She does not look back.

She thinks of Lily, face turned up, freckles across her nose, a single curl stuck to her cheek with strawberry jam. She hears the echo of "I love you, Mummy," said just once, so fast you could miss it. The ache in her chest is a wound she cannot suture, but it's also a compass, pointing her toward the only thing that matters.

She reviews the plan: buy a coffee to use as a distraction, go down the back stairwell, wait by the crew access, cover the latch with a sticker when the door opens. Move fast, stay low, look like you belong.

She opens the door a crack and listens. A woman's voice in the corridor, laughing, then fading away. Nothing else.

She breathes once, twice, then steps out.

The running track is busy with morning joggers and walkers. She enters the crowd and walks, the cap pulled low, the hoodie disguising her frame. She swings her arms, not too much, just enough to look like someone on a tight schedule.

Strolling past the bustling bar, she pauses and orders a rich, aromatic coffee. The server, swift and practiced, expertly brews countless cups during this busy hour. She offers him a grateful smile, the warmth of the café enveloping her senses as she savours the moment. After a quick scan of her sail pass card, she turns and gracefully exits, the comforting scent of freshly ground coffee lingering in the air behind her.

At the stairwell, she checks over her shoulder. Still nothing. She pushes through the heavy door and moves down eleven flights, each step counted, each landing scanned before she rounds the corner. The hum of the ship's machinery is louder here, a constant shudder through the steel and air.

At the bottom, she waits in the shadow of the landing. She checks the crew access door: grey metal, a chipped handle, the reader blinking red. Now to wait.

She will find Lily.

No matter what.

CHAPTER TWENTY-FIVE

The cup stays hot for exactly four minutes. Then it turns lukewarm, the cardboard sleeve growing soft under her grip, the plastic lid fogging up with sweat. Claire leans against the wall by the crew access door, coffee cradled in both hands as if it might burn her if she lets it slip. She counts seconds by heartbeats, breathes in the rich bitter scent and tries to ignore how her pulse races faster than the seconds on her wristwatch.

It's cold on this landing, colder than elsewhere on the ship. The corridor hums with low-frequency air, blowing up from the machinery below. Bare walls stretch blank except for a few maintenance instructions in stencilled blue. The door is just as she remembered: industrial grey, paint chewed from the edges, a scab of rust at the bottom right corner. One small window. The only motion is her breath, steaming faintly in the artificial chill.

The cup is a prop, and a shield. She keeps her chin tucked low so the brim of her new cap casts her face into shadow. She pulls the hood up around her neck, the navy fabric forming a halo stamped with the cruise line's logo. The sweatshirt swallows her whole, sleeves rolled to fists, body lost in fabric. From a distance, she doesn't look like a woman. She doesn't look like herself.

Above her, the stairwell is empty. To her left, the deck stretches into a dead end: just a locked supply closet and a neatly looped fire hose looped in its case. The carpet here is thin and patched, faded by years of bleach. She rocks on her heels and waits.

Every few minutes, a sound breaks the silence: footsteps overhead, a burst of laughter from the guest deck, a muffled PA announcement piped through the hull. Once, a steward in blue walks past on the landing above, pushing a cleaning cart stacked with boxes. He doesn't look down. She counts his steps until they fade.

She flexes her hand inside her hoodie sleeve, feeling the circle of sticky plastic pressed flat against her palm. The sticker is soft now, the adhesive warmed by her body. She checks again, thumb sliding over the surface, reassuring herself that it's still there.

She glances at the door, then back at her cup. The surface ripples as her hand shakes.

She's been here for eleven minutes, maybe twelve. She knows if she waits too long, she'll start to lose her nerve, but patience is the point. Let them come to you, she used to say to Lily, when they played hide-and-seek in their old apartment. Be the prize, not the seeker.

She pictures Lily crouched behind the sofa, a socked foot poking out, hair wild and grin even wilder. For a second, her heart aches so sharp she nearly gasps.

Then the door rattles.

It's subtle, just a tap of metal on metal, but it floods her with adrenaline so hot her skin prickles. She steps back, presses herself to the wall, feigning disinterest. She angles her face so the cap shadows her features and lifts the cup in a practiced, casual motion.

The door vibrates once, then again. The red LED by the handle blinks green, and the latch clicks. The door swings outward on a slow hydraulic arm.

A man emerges, reading something on his phone. He's younger than the last, face smooth and sleep-puffed, jaw shadowed by the start of a beard. His white uniform is untucked, a badge on his chest, but she doesn't need the name.

He steps out, head down, scrolling with his thumb, nearly walking straight into her. Claire pivots, angles the coffee outward as if startled. She times it down to the second.

"Oh—shit, sorry!" he stumbles back as the cup collides with his arm.

The coffee sloshes, a brown arc across his sleeve and pants front. Some of it splatters onto the floor, some onto the toe of his shoe. The heat shocks him out of his phone and into full, frantic awareness.

"Jesus. I—shit. Did I burn you?" he asks, dropping the phone to paw at his shirt.

Claire feigns surprise, but her hands are steady, her voice pitched perfect.

"It's fine. My fault, really," she says, setting the cup down on the carpet with a trembling hand. "You good?"

"Yeah, just—" He grimaces, shakes out his arm, wiping at the worst with the edge of his shirt. "Not my best morning, I guess." He looks up, meets her eyes, then looks away just as fast. "Sorry again."

"No worries," she says, eyes tracking every move. The door behind him hasn't closed fully. The hydraulic arm is slow, deliberate, giving her a five-second window to act.

She shifts her weight, rubs her palm against her thigh, and slips the sticker out of her pocket. His attention is glued to the stain.

She crouches as if to pick up the cup. In the motion, she palms the sticker and presses it firmly over the latch, a quick, careful press.

She straightens, holding the now-empty cup.

He glances at the door, sees it drifting shut, and sticks his foot out to hold it open.

"I can get you another coffee," he says, earnest, cheeks brightening with embarrassment. "Seriously. You want to come with? There's a barista just up those stairs."

She puts the cup in her other hand, shakes her head, ducks her chin further under the cap. "Thanks, but I'm running late. I just—" She glances at her watch, shrugs. "Gotta get back."

He nods, relieved. "Yeah, same. They'll kill me if I'm late again." He laughs nervously, then brushes past her. "Again, so sorry."

He holds the door for her anyway, like an afterthought, even as he moves down the hall and pulls out his phone again. Claire steps up to the door, slow, letting it close almost all the way, just as he turns the corner.

The sticker works perfectly: the latch doesn't extend into the metal strike plate, leaving the door looking securely closed, but it isn't. The indicator flashes red, a single lazy blink, then nothing.

She glances up the corridor. No one's watching.

She slides the empty cup into the rubbish bin by the stairwell, wipes her hand on her sleeve's inside, and steps through the door.

Inside, the world changes.

The crew corridor is lit in unkind blue-white, the floors a patchwork of metal and vinyl, the walls scored by years of movement. Pipes run along the ceiling, some wrapped in insulation, some sweating beads of condensation. The space is narrower, louder, the air filled with the clatter and drone of hidden machinery.

The noise is sharper, more real than anything in the guest spaces. Every step echoes, not in emptiness, but against the constant work of the ship. There's no carpet. Every surface is designed for utility, for speed. Signs point everywhere and nowhere at once: "Laundry—Aft," "Mess," "Electrical Room—No Unauthorised Access."

She checks behind her. The man is gone.

She breathes slowly, letting relief settle into her bones.

This is it. This is where they would keep her.

She checks her pocket—duck still there, still a totem—and starts down the corridor.

Each step feels lighter than the last. The cap is still low, the hoodie still loose, but she no longer needs the disguise as armour.

She has passed the first test.

The door swings closed behind her, whispering shut over the sticker.

She is inside.

And she will not leave without Lily.

CHAPTER TWENTY-SIX

The corridor behind the crew access door is nothing like the guest areas. It is a throat of cold metal. The kind of place built for utility, not comfort. Claire steps in and the door sighs shut behind her, locking out the last hint of carpet and simulated sunlight. Ahead, the passage is lit by fluorescent strips spaced too far apart, throw harsh circles of light on the grey floor, leaving islands of shadow in between. Her breath fogs in the cool air. The wall at her back vibrates with the steady, living hum of the ship.

She moves. Her shoes slap the metal grating, louder than she wants, every step a dare. On both sides, the corridor is lined with storage cages: wire mesh bins packed to bursting with folded linens, boxes of bottled water, shrink-wrapped flats of canned vegetables. A stray handcart stands at an angle, blocking half the passage. Its wheel squeaks when she nudges it aside. The sound echoes, unashamed.

She expects alarms, or an intercom voice, or the sudden appearance of a security officer. Nothing. Only the hush of forced air and the distant, arrhythmic clank of machinery.

The further she goes, the more the world changes. The smell, first: pure disinfectant, so strong it makes her eyes smart, mixed with an undercurrent of machine oil and the off-gas of plastic. The air is denser, as if every atom is packed with warning. Then the temperature: the climate control is aggressive here, the chill meant for machines, not people. It stiffens her joints, makes her hands ache.

There is no attempt at hospitality. The signage is purely functional, black letters on white tape: LAUNDRY, WASTE, MAINTENANCE, ELECTRICAL. The hallways branch and double back, a geometry designed to hide, not guide. She slows to memorise the turns, fingers twitching at each intersection, afraid she'll lose herself in this maze and never find her way out.

At the end of the first corridor, the passage splits. To the right, the floor slopes down. A sign points to "Service Level B," and below it, a list of numbers—4, 6, 9—none of which mean anything to her. To the left, a heavy fire door is wedged open with a chunk of blue foam. Beyond it, the lighting changes to a sickly green, as if whatever is back there lives under a different sun.

She hesitates, then moves left. The door swings with her, and for a second, she sees her own reflection in the narrow glass: hair hidden by the cap, eyes wide, the navy hoodie swallowing her neck and shoulders. She looks like a vandal, a stowaway, someone who shouldn't exist. She likes the feeling.

A sharp noise snaps her focus. Up ahead, voices, men's voices, close, clipped, not English. She ducks to the side, heart pounding, and squeezes between two rolling bins. The space is barely wider than her hips. The plastic side presses cold against her thigh.

The voices grow louder, then fade. She risks a look: two men in blue coveralls, their arms full of cardboard, walking fast and not even glancing her way. They're gone in a flash. She lets herself exhale, then listens, counting to ten, before emerging.

Her foot slips as she moves, and pain jolts up her left leg—her ankle, the old injury, the reminder of the fall. She sucks in a hiss of air, biting back a curse, and waits for the pain to recede. It doesn't, not all the way, but she can stand on it. She can keep moving.

The corridor narrows and slopes again. A new sound emerges, softer but relentless: water, maybe, or the hiss of steam. She follows the noise, limping slightly, fingers trailing along the wall for balance.

As she rounds a bend, the world opens. A small foyer, more like a holding pen, with three doors and a battered bench. Above the bench is a faded chart of the ship's decks. The guest floors are painted in bright, tropical colours; the crew decks are marked in institutional grey, with lines and arrows like the branches of a nervous system.

A crash from the next corridor, metal on metal, the rattle of a dropped tray. Claire tenses. The sound comes closer, then a figure blurs past the doorway: a woman, tall, hair pulled into a tight knot, face hidden. She doesn't see Claire. The woman is gone before the echo dies.

Claire edges forward, peering around the corner. Empty. She presses on, hugging the wall, checking every few steps for the shadow of pursuit. She feels the throb of the ship through her soles, as if the engines themselves are urging her on.

The next corridor is lit by naked bulbs caged in wire. It feels like a tunnel, or a vein, or a coffin. She walks faster, ignoring the complaint of her ankle and the burn in her lungs. She rounds another turn and finds herself in another corridor, long and empty.

She listens. Nothing. She moves.

Halfway along, her breath catches. She leans against the metal handrail, sweating under the hoodie despite the chill. She pulls the duck from her pocket, just to feel its weight, the shape of the mission. She squeezes it until her palm aches, then tucks it away.

Another fire door, this one closed. She presses her ear to the metal, listening for signs of life on the other side. Silence, or as close as this ship ever gets.

She opens the door a crack.

The corridor beyond is even narrower, the walls close enough to touch both at once. More storage bins, more sealed crates. The lighting is harsher, every imperfection in the floor picked out in brutal relief.

She moves, counting her steps, marking each alcove and turn. Every time she hears a noise, a cough, a laugh, the drag of something heavy, she freezes, heart in her throat, and waits until the world is safe again.

She remembers Lily, her voice bright and wild: "You can do it, Mummy. Be brave."

The deeper she moves, the harder it becomes to track time. In the crew corridors, every passage looks identical; bare metal, battered carts, the same industrial signage. The lights flicker in rhythm with the ship's heartbeat. The air hangs thick, electric with the promise of disaster.

She rounds a corner and freezes.

A sound. Not machinery, nor the low voices of crew, but something sharper, lighter. It cuts through the haze like a wire. A child—definitely a child—chatters in quick, shrill bursts. The words are muffled, impossible to make out, but the cadence is unmistakable: a child telling a story, or reciting a song, or inventing a world from nothing.

Her body goes rigid. For a moment, she doesn't breathe.

Is it Lily? The possibility slams into her so hard she nearly drops to her knees.

She edges closer to the wall, her pulse pounding in her temples. She closes her eyes, tuning out everything but the voice. It comes and goes, sometimes fading, sometimes so close it might be behind the next door. It's impossible to tell if it's real or a trick of memory, if she's tracking something through the metal or just hallucinating from hunger and hope.

She clings to the wall, moving slowly, scanning every vent and seam for signs of movement. She expects a camera at every junction, a watching eye, a silent alarm ready to trip. Her hands sweat through her sleeves; she wipes them on her hips, then checks over her shoulder. Nothing.

She follows the sound, letting it guide her deeper. At a junction, she hesitates, certain the voice comes from the left. The corridor narrows, the shadows lengthen. More doors now, all heavy and painted, some with warning signs, others with only numbers.

She inches forward, careful not to let her shoes squeak. The voice grows louder here, almost singing. She presses her ear to a door marked "STORAGE - 17A." The metal is cold, vibrating with the ship's energy, but beneath it she hears a giggle, high and piercing, followed by a string of nonsense syllables.

She sags against the door, dizzy. It has to be her. It has to be Lily.

Or it's nothing. Or a trick. She bites the inside of her cheek hard, forcing herself to stay grounded.

She weighs her options. Opening the door could trigger an alarm, alert every crew member nearby. Hesitating risks losing the voice, swallowed by the ship.

She tries the handle, just a touch, enough to confirm it's locked. She listens again, nails digging into her palm. Faint footsteps approach, rhythmic and soft, each step echoing softly through the still air like whispers on the wind.

She holds her breath until the echo fades.

She straightens, checks the door again. It opens.

Claire pauses just past the threshold, her back to the door. It's another corridor. Her heart pounds a double kick in her chest, one beat for fear, one for hope. She waits until her breath steadies, then moves forward, hands deep in the pouch of her hoodie.

The blue-white light buzzes overhead, flickering in a way that summons every memory of hospital waiting rooms and school basements. Pipes snake along the walls, some thick and scabbed with insulation, others delicate as veins.

She listens for voices. For a long minute, there is nothing but the chorus of the ship, air, motors, the judder of something large turning far below. She closes her eyes, focuses, filtering for the one frequency that matters. The silence is total.

Then: a sound. Faint but real. Not an adult voice, but lighter. Higher. Not a word, but maybe a syllable, or the end of a laugh.

She turns left, toward it.

Doors line the corridor, all alike. She counts them as she goes, hoping she'll need the number on the way back. But even as she does it she knows she won't, this isn't a place built for return trips. Every turn is subtraction, not addition.

The next junction comes fast. She nearly walks into a man in a blue jumpsuit, bent over a box of tools. He glances up, eyes flicking to her face, then away. He doesn't ask questions, doesn't slow his work. She guesses there are a hundred people in this warren at any time, and anonymity is a kind of mercy. She keeps walking, her pace quickening.

The corridor splits. One path is straight, the other a sharp dogleg to the right. She chooses right, less for strategy than for certainty that straight lines lead to nowhere important.

She checks behind her. No one follows.

At first, only the ambient thrum. Then comes another sound, clearer now: a peal of laughter—definitely a child. It's gone in a second, but it's enough. She slips out from her hiding place and into the next corridor.

A hard, adult footstep clatters behind her. She flattens against the wall, heart in throat. The noise approaches, then passes: a pair of women in housekeeping uniforms, both carrying bulging linen bags. They don't see her.

She lets the air out of her lungs in a slow hiss, then keeps moving.

With every turn, the corridors grow more alike. Every junction a duplicate of the one before, and she loses track of her own path. She tells herself to be rational: ships are built for efficiency, not beauty. But the sameness feels personal, like an insult, like a dare.

Cold sweat breaks on her neck. She shakes out her hands, willing them to steady.

She stops at a four-way junction and tries to orient herself. A strip of white tape on the floor reads EVAC 4. A lifeline, maybe, or just more noise. She turns left, hoping.

At hall's end is a door, heavier than the rest. She tries the handle. It's locked. She stares at it, mind blank. Then she hears the voice again, closer now, the shriek of a child, echoed and multiplied. This time, there are two voices, both laughing, both gone before she can fix them in her head.

She slumps against the door, body folding into itself. Fatigue hits sudden and hard, a flood that makes her want to lie down and sleep forever. She shakes it off, wipes her face, and keeps moving.

Deeper in the ship now, the crew spaces have given way to a kind of institutional limbo: painted steel, flickering light, floors sloped just enough to trip the unwary. There are fewer doors. Each one she passes, she stops and listens, sometimes pressing her ear to the painted steel. She hears nothing, or maybe just the imagined rhythm of her own pulse.

A corner. She takes it too fast and almost collides with a woman in a security uniform. For a split second, they lock eyes.

The woman frowns. "Are you lost?"

Claire shakes her head; voice stuck in her chest. "Looking for the mess," she manages, low and flat.

The woman looks her up and down, gaze snagging on the cap, the hoodie, the lack of ID. "Wrong side," she says pointing up. "Second right, then left at the end. Someone will show you."

Claire thanks her, then doubles back, counting steps before ducking into the next supply closet.

The closet is cramped, stinking of bleach and something sour. She hunches on a crate, listening through the thin wall to the woman's footsteps as they fade.

She sits a long minute, hands balled in her lap, breathing slow and shallow. She pulls the duck from her pocket, runs her thumb over the seam. It squeaks, barely audible, but the sound soothes her. She puts it back.

She checks her phone. No signal. Battery at eight percent. She clicks it off, stuffs it deep in her jeans.

She stands, wipes her palms on her thighs, and opens the closet door.

The voices are gone, but now she hears something else: a faint, rhythmic clang, like pipes being struck far away. She follows it—left, then right, then left again—as the corridor narrows to barely more than a shoulder-width. The air grows warmer.

The corridors double back on themselves, repeating dizzy loops. She passes the same safety poster three, maybe four times. Every turn is a dead end or a trap. The only way is forward. Always forward.

Her ankle throbs. Her head swims. She cannot stop.

She listens, desperate for the voices, but now all she hears is the drumbeat of her own feet and the gasping breath in her ears.

She rounds a final corner and stops, blind with exhaustion.

The corridor ahead is dark. But in that darkness, she hears the voice again.

It's Lily. She knows it.

She moves toward it, every step a dare to the world that would take her daughter.

She will not stop. Not now. Not ever.

She is deeper in the ship than ever before. The way back is gone.

But somewhere ahead, a child's voice, calls for its mother.

And Claire will answer.

CHAPTER TWENTY-SEVEN

The corridor narrows and cools, then banks hard left beneath a sign so faded the arrows are ghosted out. Claire traces the sharp edge of the wall with numb fingertips. The air smells like oil, old sweat, and something she can't place, like the inside of a plastic bag left baking in the sun.

She's deeper in the ship than ever, each turn peeling her further from the world above. Every passage looks identical, designed to be invisible. No one has cared how these spaces appear. Crew pass by in ones and twos, moving with the half-trot of people late for a meeting or a smoke break. No one meets her eyes. That's good. The disguise is working. Or maybe she is truly invisible.

Once she nearly collides with a man in a jumpsuit pushing a dolly loaded with boxes. He grunts but doesn't stop. She spins out of away, her heel skidding on linoleum, twisting her ankle, hard. She limps, teeth clenched so tight her jaw aches.

She rounds a corner and enters a wider corridor lined with doors every few meters. Some are propped open by bins of folded laundry; others are stencilled with numbers or abbreviations she doesn't understand. At the far end, a door hangs open, spilling a bar of fluorescent light onto the floor.

Beyond is a break room. She hears the buzz of a vending machine, the murmur of a television set to cartoons, and the low hum of voices. Crew only, obviously, but no one guards the threshold.

She stands a few paces from the door; shoulders pressed to the wall. The pain in her ankle pulses brightly but it's nothing compared to the ache in her chest. She waits, listening, filtering the sounds for the one she needs.

A child's voice. It's there—a word, a song, something childish and alive. Not a tantrum's whine. Something softer.

She moves into the doorway, slowly carefully. She peers in, eyes searching for the threat, the pattern, the trap. She expects a room full of men, or maybe women, all hunched over tables, slurping noodles and checking their phones. There are three people, but they're scattered: one asleep at the table, head pillowed on folded arms; another leaning against the vending machine, scrolling his phone, his lips moving silently. Neither looks up.

The third is a child, about three, curled on a sagging couch by the wall. Wrapped in a grey blanket, knees drawn to her chest, hair dark and shiny under the harsh light. The TV is turned low, showing an old cartoon with round-faced animals and too-bright colours. The girl watches, eyes heavy, drifting closed in the pause between flickers.

Claire's heart stops. For a moment the world blanks out, every sound dropping away. She sees only the girl's shape, the line of her cheek, the roundness of her fists clamping blanket's edge.

It's Lily. It has to be Lily. No other possibility.

Her throat makes a low, animal and she's across the room before she knows it.

"Lily," she says, then louder, voice cracking on the second syllable. "Lily!"

The girl startles awake. Blinking at Claire, uncomprehending, then shies backward against the couch's arm. Her face is moon-pale, eyes wide and scared. Claire drops to her knees, hands shaking, trying to gather the child up, to wrap her in long empty arms.

"Lily, it's me. Mummy's here," Claire says, words dissolving in her mouth. She hugs the child, holding on as if the room spins, as if loosening her grip will sweep her away.

For a split second, the girl goes still. Then she screams.

The sound flays the skin off the world. A shriek so high it stuns every nerve in Claire's body. The girl thrashes, heels kicking, fists battering Claire's shoulders. "Mama! Mama!" she shrieks, the accent all wrong, the word strange in her mouth.

Claire's mind fractures along old fault lines. She hears Lily, she feels Lily, but everything about this child is wrong. Not just the look, but the smell—the shampoo is cheap, not Lily's fruit-scented kind. The skin is cooler, the breath not as sweet. Even the weight is off. This girl is lighter, almost hollow.

She holds on anyway—until the child bites. Tiny, sharp teeth sink into the meat of her forearm, jolting her back to the room.

The vending machine man looks up, phone forgotten, face flickering through shock, then anger, then fear. He yells something Claire doesn't understand. The man at the table jerks awake, sees the scene, and stands so fast his chair tips over.

"Mama! Mama!" the girl howls, thrashing like a netted fish.

Claire lets go. Her neck is red with crescent marks where the girl's nails dug in.

The girl scrambles off the couch, feet bare, blanket trailing behind. A woman tears through the door and snatches her into her arms. Both mother and child wide-eyed in terror. She shouts, a torrent of syllables, Tagalog or something close. No translation needed. She demands to know what Claire did to her daughter.

Claire kneels on the stained carpet, panting. The pain in her arm is nothing compared to the hollow in her chest. The two men stare at her, silent.

The mother looks up at Claire, her expression worse than any accusation: a mix of loathing and pity, an open question about what kind of monster would lay hands on a child. Her lips hiss sharp words that Claire understands anyway—*Don't touch her, don't come near, don't ever, ever.*

Claire stands slowly, rubbing her neck. She wants to say sorry, but the word doesn't come. She backs toward the door, never turning her back to the men.

She stumbles into the corridor, blinking. The world tilts. She leans against the wall, breathing hard, eyes blurring with tears that refuse to fall.

She slides to the floor, legs numb.

There is no Lily. Or there is, but she is nowhere Claire can reach.

She sits in the cold, waiting for the world to make sense.

It doesn't.

CHAPTER TWENTY-EIGHT

It happens fast. The memory of the girl's scream still echoes in Claire's head when the door slams open with such force the handle cracks into the plaster. Four security officers—white shirts, black slacks, radios hissing pour into the corridor. The lead man points at Claire and his voice is a weapon: "Get on the ground!"

She flinches, tries to stand, but they're already on her. Hands clamp onto her arms, shoulders, neck. She hits the linoleum knee-first, the impact bruising. Someone twists her wrist behind her back. Another yanks her hair and shoves her face to the floor. Her cheek is pressed into grit and old stains, hot breath bouncing back at her.

The girl sobs, the mother wails, holding her child with one arm while waving the other at the officers. Tagalog, rapid and sharp, but the meaning is clear: *monster, thief, crazy.* Claire shakes her head, tries to speak, but a knee in her back steals her breath. She tries to say "Lily," just that, but her voice is a wheeze.

Someone zip-ties her wrists. The plastic bites deep, skin scraping raw. Time slows, then rushes back. She's hauled upright, biceps screaming, frog-marched to the door. A hand claps over her mouth. She bites hard, but teeth slide off thick fingers. She is nothing in their grip.

In the next corridor, the officers move as one. They slam her shoulder against the wall, force her head down, shove her forward. Crew members in the hall scatter, eyes averted, faces gone slack with fear. Someone radios ahead: "Subject in custody. Female, guest. Heading to security."

Daniel is there. Not in front, but in the second row, face bloodless, jaw tight. He doesn't look at her at first. Then, as they drag her around the next corner, their eyes meet. Claire spits one word: "Daniel!" It's a plea, a warning, everything.

He blinks, but the mask returns. "Just breathe, Claire," he says, not for her, but for the officers, the camera, the record.

They double-time it through the ship's arteries, no carpet, no windows, just cold vinyl and overhead pipes and the stink of burnt coffee from unseen break rooms. The further they go, the more her mind unravels. She's a puppet. Her feet barely touch the floor. Her arms, numb and throbbing with each jolt.

She tries again. "I wasn't—she's not my—" But the words go nowhere.

The lead man, older, eyes as cold as coin, leans in. "Save it. You talk to the chief." His grip is surgical, calibrated to hurt but not break.

At the next door, two more officers wait. Standing at parade rest, hands behind backs, eyes forward. One is the woman from before, the one who found Claire lost in the crew passage. Now she stands taller, her face blank with the satisfaction of seeing a problem neutralised.

The security door is grey steel, heavy, designed to keep things in or out. It buzzes as they swipe their badges, then swings wide on greased hinges. They shove her inside. It's less an office, more a holding pen: metal bench, table bolted to the floor, walls the colour of an overcast sky. They really do have a small jail cell on the ship.

They seat her hard in a chair; the zip-tie still biting. For a moment, everyone just stands there, breathing heavy.

Claire's voice is raw, but forced up. "I wasn't trying to take her," she gasps, "she looked like—"

The chief, a woman with her hair slicked into a bun and the aura of someone who's seen every kind of trouble, raises a hand. "You'll have your turn," she says, flipping open a leather-bound notepad. Her pen ticks like a metronome. She glances at Daniel. "Jackson, incident report."

Daniel steps forward. His voice is ice, clipped and precise. "Subject found in unauthorised crew area, physical altercation with minor child and parent. Resisted apprehension."

He won't look at her. She watches the side of his face, the muscle twitching in his jaw. She wants to scream, but the room is too small. The mother and daughter wait just outside the glass partition. The girl is quiet now, clinging to her mother, eyes fixed on the floor.

Another officer reads from her sail pass card—her name, cabin, then from his tablet, her history. He says it aloud, as if to remind the universe that Claire Holloway is a problem, not a person.

Claire's legs twitch. Her heart hammers inside of ribs. She tries again. "It's a mistake. I was looking for—" She hesitates, then spits it out: "My daughter. She's missing. No one's helping me."

Silence.

Then the chief says, "You attacked a child. That's a crime everywhere."

"I didn't—I thought—"

"Not your child. Not your business." The chief's voice is flat, uninterested. She snaps her notebook shut. "You're in holding until we get the captain's call."

Daniel doesn't say a word.

They cut the zip-tie, only to cuff her wrists in front instead—plastic again, but thicker this time. Blood trickles down her thumb.

They leave her on the bench. Officers file out, Daniel last. He hesitates at the door, opens his mouth, maybe to say her name, maybe to explain, but the chief calls his rank, and he's gone.

Claire is left alone with her shame, her wrists, and the echo of Lily's name in her ears.

Her face is wet. She doesn't remember when she started crying.

She stares at the ceiling, unblinking.

She waits for the next humiliation to arrive.

It takes forty minutes for the next thing to happen. The steel bench is too cold, the cuffs too tight. Claire shifts, wrists burning with each movement, the plastic digging in until it feels like part of her. She could scream, but there's no point. The cameras in the corners blink red; the glass partition is her only company.

She stares at the mother and daughter on the other side of the glass. The girl is still, eyes closed, the mother's arms coiled around her like barbed wire. Neither has moved since they arrived. The mother rocks gently, whispering something into the child's ear, eyes fixed on a point above Claire's head. There's no hatred there, only a dead calm, the resignation of someone used to worse.

The security chief returns, accompanied by two people: the interpreter, slim and nervous, lanyard around his neck, and Daniel, shoulders hunched, face set like a prison door. The chief doesn't look at Claire. Instead, she opens the door to the holding pen and says, "We're going to talk now."

She gestures for Claire to take a seat across the table. The cuffs remain on.

The interpreter sits to one side; the mother and daughter opposite. The little girl has stopped crying but hides her face in her mother's sleeve. The chief introduces the interpreter, then the mother, then the girl, but not herself. Claire catches their names but they slide off her like oil. She's too numb, too empty.

The chief starts, voice careful. "This is your opportunity to explain. We're recording. Interpreter, you are to translate everything exactly."

The interpreter nods, his English clear but mechanical. He asks the mother something in her language, listens, then turns back to the room.

"She says her name is Ana. She works in the laundry," he says, gesturing to the woman's uniform. "This is her daughter, Mia." He doesn't look at the child as he says it.

Ana begins to speak, soft at first. Her words are liquid, fast, tumbling over each other. The interpreter listens, face blank, then translates:

"She says she knows she did something wrong by bringing her daughter on the ship. But she had no choice." Pause. "Her husband— Mia's father—was hurting them. At home in the Philippines. He beat her, and Mia. There were police, but he has family in the government. No one would help."

The mother's hands clench on the table, knuckles white. The interpreter glances at her, then continues.

"She got the job in laundry because it was the only way out. She left the country legally, but Mia wasn't on the paperwork. Mia couldn't be. So she made a plan."

Ana's voice gains speed, urgency. The interpreter's voice stays steady:

"She hid Mia in the laundry bins, and the storage rooms. She taught her to be quiet. For the first three days, Mia stayed in the cabin they share with two other women from the laundry team. The others helped. They gave her food, let her out only at night. Mia never left the crew areas. Never went where passengers could see."

The mother is crying now, but she keeps talking. The interpreter's hands shake, but his words are still clear:

"She thought if she could just finish the contract, get to Canada, she could apply for asylum. She wanted to save her daughter." Another pause, longer. "She says she is sorry. She never meant to hurt anyone. She did not expect a passenger to come into the crew break room and try to take her daughter. She did not know what else to do."

Silence. Even the hum of the ship seems to cut out.

The security chief looks at the mother, then at Claire, then at Daniel. Her face is blank, unreadable.

Claire feels the air in her lungs freeze solid. The logic of the last few days reorganises; every paranoia and wild story now hollow compared to what's in front of her.

She shakes her head. "I thought—" But the words are nothing.

The interpreter translates for Ana. The mother bows her head, not looking at anyone.

Daniel's face is not blank. It's contorted, broken at the edges. He rubs the bridge of his nose, then clears his throat.

The chief addresses Claire. "Did you understand what was said?"

She nods. "I'm so sorry," she says, but it's too small. It's nothing compared to what's been done.

The chief turns to Ana. The interpreter relays the message.

The mother just holds her daughter tighter.

The interpreter adds, voice almost a whisper: "She says if you need to call the authorities, do it now. She only asks that you let her stay with her daughter."

Claire's face burns. She wants to crawl under the table, vanish, anything. She stares at the floor.

The room falls silent when the interpreter finishes. Ana's story, every word of it, lies across the table like a lifeless thing. No one moves. Daniel stares at the tabletop, his hands balled into fists. The security chief taps her pen, each tap landing like a warning.

After a pause, the chief says, "That's enough. Remove the restraints."

Daniel is the one who does it. He pulls out a pocketknife, saws at the plastic, and frees her arms. His fingers linger on Claire's wrists a beat longer than necessary, as if willing her to meet his gaze. She can't. Her skin is scored and purpled, swollen where the bands dug in too tight.

She sits with her hands in her lap, not touching, not moving, not breathing if she can help it.

Ana wipes her face with the heel of her hand. The little girl clings tightly to her mother's neck, eyes staring blankly ahead. The interpreter murmurs a few soft words. Ana doesn't respond.

The security chief stands. "That will be all for now. You will all remain here pending Captain's call."

The interpreter leads Ana and the girl from the room. Claire keeps her head down as they pass, the shame so thick she can barely see. She wants to apologise, wants to explain—*It wasn't meant for you.* But her mouth feels full of rocks.

In the heavy silence that follows, the officers speak quietly, trading guesses about what to do next. Daniel stands apart, leaning against the far wall, his face tight and unreadable. He folds his arms, then unfolds them, then folds them again. Every time he catches Claire's eye, he looks away first.

Claire hears fragments from the staff huddle:

"Reporting requirements—"

"…maybe Immigration if they—"

"The captain has to decide."

"…company policy, but it's unclear…"

She wants to believe someone will show mercy. But she knows what the world is like for people like Ana. She knows what happens to women who try to run.

She traces her finger over the grooves left by the cuffs, the marks a map of where she's been.

When the chief leaves, Daniel finally steps closer.

He keeps his voice low. "You okay?"

She laughs, a hollow, empty sound. "No. Are you?"

He shrugs. "Doesn't matter. Just—take care of yourself."

She wants to ask what happens now. She wants to scream, beg, undo what's been done. But she sits, hands folded in her lap, staring at the table.

Daniel leaves. The room empties again.

She sits for a long time.

Eventually, she starts to cry.

No one comes in. No one tells her to stop.

She stays that way until her hands stop shaking.

She stays that way until there's nothing left.

CHAPTER TWENTY-NINE

It's the brightness that hurts her first. The world swims behind a membrane of light and pain, every edge burning sharp where the fluorescent panels rake across the ceiling. Claire blinks, but the glare pierces clean through her eyelids, straight into the throb at the centre of her forehead.

She tries to move her hand, but it's slow. A weight presses on her wrist. She looks down: an IV line snakes out from the crook of her elbow, taped down so tightly it puckers the skin. Her other arm is draped in a rough blanket, not the kind you'd find in a guest suite. Hospital grey, linty. It smells faintly of plastic and bleach.

The hum is constant here. It fills her bones, a deeper vibration than anything on the passenger decks. She tries to sit up, but a clamp of pain locks her neck to the pillow.

"You're awake," someone says. The voice is soft, almost rehearsed. Not a doctor—too familiar. She blinks again, the world resolving into patches of blue and white.

Daniel sits beside her bed. He's in uniform, sleeves rolled, hair tidy except for a single lock gone wild above his left eyebrow. His posture is perfect: hands folded, back straight, legs anchored wide in the plastic chair. But his knuckles are white, gripping the edge of the seat.

He nods, nothing more. His mouth is a thin line.

She wants to ask where she is, but the answer is everywhere. She knows a medical bay when she sees one—the taste of nothing on her tongue, the endless hum, the tastefully blurred prints of ocean landscapes tacked to the walls.

Movement in the corridor is a blur: white coats, blue scrubs, shadows sliding past the frosted glass. Daniel says nothing else, just sits there, eyes fixed on her face, waiting for her to remember.

She does.

She remembers the break room. She remembers the woman and her child. She remembers the way the world tipped sideways when they dragged her through the crew corridors, Daniel's voice somewhere behind her, telling her to breathe, comply, let them handle it.

A hiss of air, then the soft click of a latch. The door swings open, and Dr. Reyes enters.

"Miss Holloway." The tone is neither questioning, nor greeting.

"Yeah." Her voice is a scrap of sandpaper.

"I see you're lucid. Excellent." Dr. Reyes glances at the monitors—pulse, blood pressure, oxygen—and makes a note without breaking stride.

Daniel stands as the doctor enters, moving back two paces as if he's supposed to be furniture, not witness.

The examination is brisk, professional. Dr. Reyes flashes a penlight in Claire's eyes, checks her tongue, asks her to squeeze both hands, to wiggle her toes, to follow her finger left and right. The hands are gentle, the voice never sharp, but there is no comfort in the touch. Only measurement, only data.

"Do you know where you are?" the doctor asks.

"The ship's medical bay."

"Which day is it?"

Claire blinks, tries to conjure the calendar. "Tuesday. Or—Wednesday? Is it still the same day?"

"Close enough." The doctor makes another note. "You've had quite a shock, Miss Holloway. Do you remember why you're here?"

A flicker behind the doctor's head: Daniel, eyes narrowing just a fraction. A tiny shake, barely there. Claire blinks, uncertain.

"I— there was an incident." She tries to sit up, and this time the pain is duller, contained. "With a child."

The doctor nods once. "You were found in the crew passage, in a break room, physically restraining a minor. The mother was—understandably—distressed. Security intervened. You knocked your head again in the scuffle." She pauses, scanning Claire's face for something, then adds, "You also refused sedation, and attempted to leave the MedBay after regaining consciousness."

"I don't remember that."

"It's not uncommon," Dr. Reyes says, scribbling. "Disorientation after head trauma, especially combined with emotional stress. Are you aware of any other episodes like this? Memory loss, blackouts, confusion?"

Claire wants to say no. The word sticks to her tongue, sour and heavy. She remembers the voids in her timeline, the hours lost in her cabin, the minutes that stretched and snapped in the theatre, the entire day spent circling the decks in a trance. She remembers the dreams, and the way Lily's voice sometimes sounded as if it came from inside her own head.

"I— I'm not sure," she manages.

Dr. Reyes does not react, does not comfort. She makes a note.

"I see," she says. "Do you recall any recent emotional distress? Bereavement, trauma, major life changes?"

Daniel is in the corner now, eyes pinned to a smudge on the wall. He does not look at her. She remembers the last real conversation they had: on the balcony, the night air sharp, the memory of Lily so bright it made her ache. She wants to say Lily's name now, but the doctor's gaze is surgical.

"I lost my daughter," Claire says, voice barely above the hum. "She was taken. No one believed me."

For the first time, Dr. Reyes's face softens. Not sympathy— something closer to confirmation.

"I'm sorry, Miss Holloway. I truly am." The doctor's tone is careful, not cold. "But we've searched the manifest. Interviewed every staff member, every child here. There is no record of your daughter ever being on board."

A pulse of anger shocks her upright. "That's not possible. She was here. I have—" She reaches for her phone, then remembers. The photos no longer exist. Her hand closes on empty blanket.

"Sit," says Dr. Reyes, and the force in the word makes Claire's knees go soft. She sinks back.

"You experienced a traumatic loss previously. The evidence suggests your condition—your delusions—have escalated from the head trauma. This is not uncommon. Isolation, disrupted routine, sleep deprivation—they can all contribute. In your case, I believe it's compounded by prior trauma."

Claire feels the world tilt again. "You think I imagined her."

"I think you need help, Miss Holloway. Professional help. When we dock in New York, you will be met by a psychiatric evaluation team. Until then, I am authorising constant observation and restricted access to passenger areas."

Behind the doctor's back, Daniel's face is carved from stone. He catches her eye. His hand flickers at his side, a gesture so small she almost misses it: open palm, then a slow, careful close. Shut up. Don't argue.

She doesn't.

Dr. Reyes stands. "You will rest here for one more hour. Security will escort you to your cabin after. Do not attempt to leave or you will be sedated. Do you understand?"

Claire nods. The doctor leaves, the door shutting with a hush of air.

Daniel waits until the footsteps fade.

Then, soft as paper, he says, "I'm sorry."

She doesn't answer. She stares at the ceiling, at the patterns in the foam tiles, at the endless white, until her eyes burn and the world blurs again.

She knows what comes next.

But she also knows Daniel is still here, waiting for her to see the signal.

She files it away, deep in her chest, where they can't take it from her.

She waits for the hour to pass.

The second hand ticks louder than her pulse. Each jerk of the red needle cracks like a gunshot in the quiet. Claire lies flat on the bed, arms folded over her belly, legs straight as a corpse. The blanket they gave her is too short, her feet freeze in the cold air, but she doesn't move to fix it. If she keeps perfectly still, maybe the pain will pass her by.

Daniel is the only other person in the room. He sits exactly where the nurse told him—one meter from the head of her bed, not blocking the monitors, hands in his lap. He doesn't try to speak. He doesn't shift. If he blinks, she misses it. The only things that move are the clock, the ache in her head, and the slow creep of grief under her skin.

She waits for the doctor to return. That is the rule: no talking, no leaving, no medication. Just observation. It's like being on display—a museum piece in a glass case, except the only visitors are those already convinced of what you are.

The hour passes in slices. Every minute is a test. Sometimes she tries to match her breath to the rhythm of the ship's motion. Sometimes she lets her mind go blank and watches the patterns in the acoustic tile above. Sometimes she looks at Daniel, just to see if he is still there, still real.

When Dr. Reyes returns, it's with a clipboard and a new pen.

"Miss Holloway. Are you ready to talk?"

Claire's throat is raw. She nods, the motion small.

The doctor sits at the foot of the bed, one hand on her knee, the other poised to write.

"Let's go over what happened, starting with the break room."

Claire digs her fingers into the blanket. Her nails bend back, pain a lifeline.

"I heard a child," she says, voice flat as the table. "I thought it was my daughter."

Dr. Reyes nods, makes a note. "But when you got there—"

Claire wants to vomit. "It wasn't her. It was someone else. I grabbed her. I thought she was in danger."

"Do you remember what you said?"

"No." She can feel Daniel watching her, but she doesn't look up.

"You insisted she was yours. That the crew had taken her from you. You became agitated, physically violent." The doctor glances at the sheet, checks off a box. "Can you explain why you did that?"

The words build behind her teeth, but when she opens her mouth, nothing comes out at first.

Then— "I don't have a daughter." Her face flames. The silence after is almost beautiful.

Dr. Reyes smiles, not unkindly, but with the satisfaction of a solved equation. "Good. What made you realise this?"

"I think the fall," Claire whispers. "Maybe it made me… I don't know. I started seeing her. I remembered things wrong." She wants to take it back, but the words are already out, and she feels her heart crumple around them.

"That's a very important realisation," Dr. Reyes says. "Many people in your position—"

"Can I go now?" Claire asks. She doesn't mean to sound desperate, but it's all that's left.

"One more hour," the doctor says. "You're making progress, but we need to ensure you're safe before you return to your cabin."

Daniel hasn't moved. She sneaks a glance and sees his jaw flexing, tight with something between relief and guilt.

The doctor stands. "You're doing the right thing, Miss Holloway. We'll talk again in an hour." She leaves, and the door clicks shut.

Claire lets herself cry. Not the sobbing of the last room, not the rage or the wild grief. Just a silent, wet river that runs down her face and soaks the edge of the blanket. The tears pool in her ears, drip to the pillow, and cool fast on her skin. She wipes them away with the heel of her hand and stares at the ceiling until the tiles swim.

Daniel sits through it. He doesn't flinch or look away. He waits, like before, for her to be done.

The second hour is slower than the first. Her body aches from stillness, her mouth tastes of old pennies and shame. She listens to the clock, but now every tick echoes her confession: I don't have a daughter. I never did.

When the nurse comes in to unhook the IV, she does it in silence. She hands Claire a pill cup with two white tablets, 'for the swelling,' and watches as she swallows them, checks her mouth for compliance then leaves.

 Daniel stands. He looks at her, and this time he lets his face soften.

"Just hold on," he says, voice almost gone. "It's not over."

She wants to ask him what he means. She wants to ask if he believes her, or if he ever did. But the words are heavy, and she is too tired to lift them.

Instead, she nods.

At 16:00, Dr. Reyes returns. She moves quickly; clipboard tucked under one arm like a shield.

"Miss Holloway," she says, not unkindly, "you're cleared for discharge. Your chart is updated. You are to rest, stay hydrated, and avoid further incidents."

Claire sits upright, steady now, the trembling in her limbs replaced by a dense numbness. She nods once.

The doctor runs down a list, voice crisp. "You will be escorted to your cabin. You are not to leave unescorted, nor may you attend group events. Security will check on you every four hours. For your safety, a team member will be stationed outside your door. Should you need medical assistance, press the button on your phone and someone will attend."

Claire meets her eyes. There's no accusation, not anymore. Only the finality of a closed file.

"Yes, Doctor."

Dr. Reyes turns the clipboard for Daniel, having him sign something. The transfer of custody, Claire thinks, as if she's cargo. They don't touch. The doctor leaves, and the silence echoes after her.

Daniel helps her up, not with a hand, but by stepping aside and letting her stand on her own. The medical gown is gone, replaced by her own clothes, neatly folded at the end of the bed. She pulls them on: jeans, t-shirt, hoodie. The fabric smells of her, but not the way she remembers. All the warmth is gone, replaced by the sharp detergent scent of the laundry facility. Her shoes feel tight.

They walk the corridor together, side by side. The halls are empty at this hour, but every intersection feels haunted by the possibility of an audience. Daniel keeps a respectful distance, neither guard nor friend, but something in between.

As they reach the main corridor, the world changes. Passengers move in clusters: families, couples, retirees, all busy with the business of vacation. Claire feels their eyes on her. Some glance away immediately; others let their gaze linger on the bruise at her temple, the fresh tape on her arm. The whispers are faint, but she catches her own name, the stuttered "That's her," or "Is she okay?" The echo follows her, all the way to the elevator.

Daniel presses the call button. They wait in silence.

The doors open to reveal a cluster of women in yoga pants, all clutching smoothies and laughing too loud. The laughter stops when they see her. Claire steps inside. The women press to one side, all smiles and apology, but the shift is unmistakable. She wants to tell them she is not contagious, but the words would only make it worse.

At her deck, Daniel guides her out. The corridor is quieter here, but the silence is different: not absence, but anticipation. They reach her door. A uniformed officer stands by the frame, hands clasped at her waist. Young, dark hair pulled back tight, eyes sharp.

"This is Officer Martinez," Daniel says. "She'll be taking first watch."

Martinez nods, expression neutral. "If you need anything, just ask. We'll do our best."

Claire says, "Thank you," and means it. The door opens with a beep, and she steps inside.

The first thing she notices is the emptiness. The room is clinically neat, every surface wiped clean. The bed is made. Still one, not two. The small chair by the window is bare, the table cleared of all but a laminated safety brochure. Nothing is out of place, but also nothing belongs.

No dinosaur pyjamas on the bed. No trail of croissant crumbs on the floor. No backpack, no toys, no hint of Lily anywhere.

Claire stands in the centre of the room, hands at her sides. She half expects a voice to call out: "Mummy! Look what I found!" or the sudden shriek of a three-year-old's laughter. Instead, only the muffled shuffle of the officer settling in outside.

She walks to the bed and sits on the edge. The blanket is cool, the sheets too tight. She runs her hand along the space beside her, searching for a dent in the mattress, a curl of brown hair, a lost button, any sign that a child ever existed here.

Her hand comes back empty.

She lies back, arms folded across her chest, and stares at the ceiling.

The ache is dull now but deeper than before. It fills her up, marrow to muscle, settling in the places once reserved for hope.

She closes her eyes.

She tries to remember Lily's face, the way her mouth would crumple when about to cry, the sound of her feet in the corridor, the smell of her hair after a bath. But the images are thin, ghostly. Even the memory of the duck is fading, the edges blurring until it's just another toy, easily forgotten.

A knock at the door. Martinez's voice, calm and practiced, "Just checking in. Everything okay?"

"Fine," Claire says, not moving.

"Let me know if you need anything."

The door clicks shut. The room is silent again.

She stays on the bed, counting her breaths, letting the world fade in and out.

She stares out the window, watching the ocean churn below. The water is grey, endless, always moving but going nowhere.

She wonders if this is what the rest of her life will be, the same room, the same silence, the same absence, every day a little more empty than the last.

She closes her eyes, and tries to remember.

But already, the details are slipping away.

She waits for night to come. For the next check-in, for the next order, the next protocol, the next hollow hour.

She waits.

She waits.

She waits.

CHAPTER THIRTY

The night has a texture to it. Claire stands barefoot on the balcony, skin numbed by the wind, clutching the cold metal rail until it indents her palms. Far below, the Atlantic surges and slaps against the hull, a sound like bones grinding, relentless and unfeeling. The ship's white lights are shuttered here, the only glow coming from the running lights above and the sickle of the moon, snagged in a torn fist of clouds.

She tilts her head back and closes her eyes. There's salt in her nostrils, in her hair, under her nails. The taste of it settles on her tongue, acrid and animal. She breathes in, out, in again, matching her breath to the slow exhale of the sea. Her mind runs through the events of the last ninety-six hours, each one a separate laceration, none fully closed.

Sometimes she wonders if she is already overboard, just a pale smudge on the water, and the rest is her body playing catch-up. There is no difference, she thinks, between the hollow in her chest and the darkness that eats the horizon.

Inside the cabin, the light is set to its lowest, a syrupy amber that leaves the corners black. The chair by the bed is empty. The desk is cleared of all but the laminated safety card, which she's memorised. The bed is made, four pillows stacked two-by-two, the second set as smooth as the day she boarded. There is no mess, no trace of a child.

She pushes up onto her toes, arching her back until something pops and the ache becomes clean. It's almost eight. She wonders when they will send her food.

A knock, soft but sharp, slices the air.

She flinches, half-expecting the door to burst open and a white-coated nurse to drag her off by the elbow. But it's only a quiet knock from the corridor. She lingers out on the balcony, a beat too long, then steps inside and lets the sliding door whisper shut behind her. The noise seals out the sea, leaving only the low murmur of the ship's life support and the tick of the air vent. She wipes her hands on the hem of her shirt, then crosses to the door and peers through the peephole: Daniel, still in uniform, tray balanced in one hand, the other tucked behind his back. When she unlocks the deadbolt and opens the door, he nods at her once, the gesture mechanical.

Daniel doesn't smile, but his face is easier than it was in the clinic. He holds out the tray, a single plate under a silver dome, a tall glass of water sweating onto a paper coaster, and a folded napkin with metal cutlery tucked inside.

"Dinner," he says. His voice is a degree warmer than the corridor outside.

She glances at the officer stationed by her door. It's not Martinez. The new guard is young, hair clipped close, face flat as a shut window. He doesn't acknowledge her, doesn't even look up from his phone.

Claire gives him a long, deliberate stare anyway. The old paranoia flickers. Then she takes the tray and steps back.

"Thank you."

She sets it on the desk, peels off the dome. Fish, rice, green beans sliced lengthwise and lined up in militant rows. The smell is pleasant, but the sight of it makes her stomach clamp. She pours the water, careful not to spill.

Daniel waits in the doorway, hands folded, eyes roaming the cabin for anything out of place. There is nothing to find.

She picks up the fork, slices off a corner of the fish, and chews it without tasting. Her throat is raw from hours of silence. She wonders if Daniel has been briefed, if he's read the new file—Holloway, Claire, possible psychosis, suicide risk moderate. She wonders if he's supposed to watch her eat, to make sure she doesn't choke or cut herself.

"Did you want something?" she asks, low.

He tilts his head. "Thought I'd check in. Mandatory security checks every four hours, remember?"

She stabs at the beans, arranging them into a small picket fence along the edge of the plate. "You could have just asked."

He exhales, more tired than annoyed, and leans back against the door. "I know."

She can't decide if the word is an apology or an admission of defeat.

She eats three more bites, each one slower, letting the minutes stretch until the pressure in the room thins out. Daniel doesn't move. The new officer in the corridor is a statue.

"Is Martinez off shift?" Claire says, not turning around.

Daniel shrugs. "She's fine. They rotate every two hours."

Claire nods, filing it away. The beans squeak under her teeth, and she grinds them down with the molars, savouring the noise. She drinks half the water in one go, wiping her mouth with the back of her hand.

The silence hangs. She feels Daniel's gaze, the way he keeps her in his periphery, measuring the tension in the air like a surveyor. She wonders how many breakdowns he's witnessed, how many guests he's talked down from the edge.

She wonders if he's still following the script, or if this is his own invention.

He says, "How are you?"

The question is so bland, so useless, that she almost laughs. But the edge of his voice is rough, and she sees the line between his brows.

"Fine," she says, swallowing hard.

He waits.

She puts the fork down, wipes her hands on the napkin, and turns to face him. The room is too small for this, but she doesn't care.

"Do you want the real answer?" she asks.

He crosses his arms, gaze steady. "If you want to give it."

She looks past him, at the seam in the corridor carpet, at the edges of the world that have been shrink-wrapped around her. Then she looks at her own hands, the skin dry and starting to crack around the knuckles. He steps further in, allowing the door to click closed behind him.

"I lied to the doctor," she says, voice so quiet it almost isn't. "About the memory, about—everything. I said what I had to so they'd let me out."

Daniel nods, once. Not judgment, not surprise. He just waits.

Claire presses the tips of her fingers together, watching the way the blood pools and blanches beneath the skin.

"I know how it sounds. I know what it looks like." She shrugs, helpless. "But I remember her. I remember Lily. I remember holding her hand, and the smell of her hair, and the way she would always insist on picking the croissants with the most chocolate."

She shakes her head, bitter. "But I can't prove it. Not a single fucking thing. They scrubbed the photos. They changed the records. They are watching me. My brain isn't broken; I get it."

The room is so quiet that the vent fan sounds like a jet engine.

Daniel's voice is soft, but grounded. "You think you're being watched?"

She almost laughs, but the sound dies in her throat. "Aren't we all?"

He gives her that much. He does not try to convince her she's wrong, or right—nothing at all.

"I'm not going to do anything stupid. That's why I lied. I said I'd comply, and I will. I'll smile at the nurses and let your people check on me every four hours. But I'm not going to stop hoping, or looking. Not while there's a chance."

Daniel absorbs her words. He shifts his weight, then steps slowly closer to her, keeping his hands visible—a gesture not lost on her.

"I don't think you're crazy," he says.

She wants to believe him. Wants it so badly it aches.

"I might be," she whispers.

He shrugs again, more human this time. "Doesn't mean you're wrong."

She stares at him, measuring. "You think Lily's out there?"

He looks at the floor, then the ceiling, then at her, then lets his gaze drop back to the carpet. "I don't know. But if she is, I think you're the only one who can find her."

A pulse of heat flares in her chest. Hope, maybe—or just the last gasp of adrenaline.

"Why are you telling me this?" she asks.

He rubs the back of his neck; the skin reddens under the friction. "Because I've seen a lot get lost on ships," he says. "Most of it stays lost."

She picks up the fork again, turning it over and over, the metal slick with condensation.

"What do you think I should do?" she asks.

He hesitates, then offers a faint smile. "You already know."

She wants to believe that, too.

The new officer in the hallway clears his throat—a low rumble signalling time's up. Daniel straightens, brushing invisible dust from his uniform.

"Try to sleep," he says. "We dock in New York in two days."

She nods, the motion heavy.

He opens the door, steps into the corridor, and is gone.

She finishes her water. The rest of the plate sits, untouched.

She walks to the balcony and opens the door again. The wind has grown harder, the world outside is all black and silver.

She leans on the rail, feet planted wide, eyes on the horizon.

She thinks on Daniel's words, lets them sink deep into her bones.

She closes her eyes—just for a moment.

She waits.

She waits.

She waits.

But she does not let go.

CHAPTER THIRTY-ONE

Morning is a razor, sharp and thin. Claire stands on the balcony, wrapped in a blanket stolen from the foot of the bed. Her bare feet are cold on the composite flooring, the sea air wrapping around her ankles like ice. It tastes of salt and distant rain. The horizon is an iron bar stretching from nowhere to nothing.

She tightens the blanket at her neck; knuckles pale against the fabric. Her body aches; sore, stiff, brittle as old paper. She cannot remember the last time she slept. It doesn't matter. The ocean pays no mind to her exhaustion.

The water isn't blue. It is gunmetal, layered in bands that ripple and cross and snarl against each other. The ship leaves a bruise of wake behind, but the surface heals in moments, the wound vanishing as if it never was. Occasionally, a crease in the water catches the light and flashes white, then fades back to grey.

She watches the movement for a long time, eyes fixed, pupils pinched small in the new light. She doesn't blink unless she has to. Each breath is measured and held, as if rationing the minutes until sunrise.

Inside, the air hums with recycled warmth. On the balcony, there's only wind, the slap of water, and the slow burn of the sun dragging itself over the edge of the world.

A knock at the door—sharp, quick, then three seconds later, a softer repeat: standard ship cadence, customer service version. Claire doesn't answer right away. She waits, counting down from five, then turns and steps inside.

The room is exactly as she left it: perfectly made bed, a single dent in the pillow, the air heavy with cleaning fluid and the faint memory last night's fish dinner. The knock comes again, a polite escalation.

She pulls the blanket tighter, then opens the door.

A uniformed attendant stands on the threshold, tray balanced at waist height. He's young, expressionless except for the upward flick of his eyebrows, a gesture of deference. The tray is heavy with breakfast —bright fruit, pale pastries, a pot of coffee.

"Good morning, ma'am," he says. "Your breakfast. Management asked me to let you know the delivery fee has been waived today." He smiles politely but tiredly, as if he's nearing the end of a long shift.

Claire takes the tray without speaking. Its weight is more than she expects. She steps back, letting the door drift shut.

She sets the tray on the desk, then stands over it, arms limp at her sides. She studies the arrangement for a long time, as if expecting it to change. The coffee steams gently from the spout. The fruit is cut into precise wedges and cubes, each glistening. The pastries come in three kinds: one chocolate, one almond, and one glazed with a clear, sticky coating.

She sits and starts with the coffee. The pot is small, stainless steel, heavier than it looks. She pours a single cup, black, then sets the pot exactly parallel to the tray's edge. She lifts the cup with both hands and sips. The coffee is hot, bitter, more acid than flavour. She swallows anyway.

She moves to the fruit, eating melon first, one cube at a time, placing each rind on the lip of the plate. Then the berries—blue, red, dark. She chews them slow, tongue pressing each one to the roof of her mouth until it bursts. She sorts the remaining fruit by colour, then size, then how much she thinks Lily would have liked them.

The pastries remain untouched. She slides the plate to the left, then back to the centre, then nudges it closer to the coffee. She arranges the napkin on the side, folding it in half, then quarters, then eighths.

Her movements are steady, unhurried. Each act of sorting, of dividing, of stacking keeps the world from spilling apart.

She takes another sip; the mug trembles in her hand, but only a slightly.

Through the glass, the ocean keeps moving. The sun is higher now, but its light doesn't reach inside. It only sharpens the shadows.

Her eyes drift from desk to window, then tray, back to window. She repeats the circuit, not expecting anything new, but because the rhythm helps. If she watches long enough, maybe she'll catch the world breaking.

She pushes the fruit plate away, then pulls it back. She plucks a single orange slice from the edge and holds it to the light. The flesh glows translucent, a thin web of veins running from rind to centre. She eats it in two bites.

She wipes her hands on the napkin, folding it again.

The knock, the tray, the coffee, the eating—it's all a sequence, a pattern. She feels safer inside it. She doesn't remember the taste of the food. She doesn't want to.

After a while, she stands and carries the tray to the corridor. She sets it on the floor outside the door near the waiting security guard. She offers him a weak smile, then adjusts the position of the tray. Satisfied, she returns inside.

On the balcony, the wind has picked up. The blanket is damp at the hem where it brushed the metal railing. She wraps it tighter and sits, folding her legs beneath her.

The ocean is endless. The ship moves through it as if it isn't there. The sky is blank except for the sun, a low white smear above the horizon.

She fixes her eyes on the line where water meets sky. She dares it to change.

She sits for a long time, the blanket wound tight, cold creeping up her legs.

She waits for something to happen.

But nothing does.

The sun is higher when she moves. The blanket is heavy on her shoulders, the damp turned to chill in the shadow of the upper deck. The white of the hull below is blinding, so Claire fixes her gaze on the deeper blue of the water.

She loses time, measuring nothing but the movement of the sun and the slow shrink of shadow. The world is silent except for the hush of wind over the glass and the ships' steady heartbeat.

She doesn't go inside, not even to use the bathroom. Her body is too tired for need. She sits, waits, trying not to think about the hunger knotting under her ribs.

The next knock comes at noon. Three sharp taps, then a pause, then a single rap—different cadence, new attendant.

Claire stands, bones aching, and opens the door.

This one is older. He wears the same uniform, but the name tag is clipped crooked, and the tray is balanced with practiced ease on his hip. He smiles without effort.

"Good afternoon, miss. Your lunch." It's a silver tray with a shining domed cover. "Sign here, please." He slides a receipt forward, pen already clicked open.

She signs without reading. Her name looks foreign in her own hand. The attendant thanks her, then leaves, stepping crisply and silently on the carpet.

Claire carries the tray to the balcony, setting it on the low table beside her chair.

She lifts the dome. The smell is strong, brine and lemon and the faint sweetness of cooked shellfish. The platter is ridiculous: crab legs stacked like scaffolding, shrimp coiled on a bed of ice, scallops gleaming under a tangle of micro-greens. There is bread, sliced thin and toasted to gold. A dish of butter, solid and pale.

She stares at it. The arrangement is perfect, every detail in its place. She could photograph it for an ad.

She breaks a crab leg, splitting it with the nutcracker provided. The meat is white, nearly translucent. She dips it in lemon, then tastes. It is cool, rich, almost sweet, but the flavour is distant, a memory of food more than the thing itself.

She eats slowly, one bite at a time, each motion performed as if someone is watching. She alternates between shellfish and bread, counting out the sequence in her head. She pauses every few minutes, sipping cold, sharp water from the glass.

After a while, she loses interest. The smell turns metallic, the texture clots on her tongue. She wipes her mouth on the corner of the napkin, then folds it over the plate.

She pushes the tray to the far edge of the table, aligning it so that no part hangs over the edge. She presses the dome back in place, making sure it sits flush, then lines up the utensils beside it.

Her hands are sticky. She licks the tips of her fingers, then wipes them again.

The ship rolls beneath her, gentle but constant. The pitch is slight, but enough to sway the furniture, to set the ice cubes in the glass chiming together. Claire curls her toes around the bar at the bottom of the chair and leans forward, elbows on knees, hands clasped tight.

She watches the sea, the endless shifting of colour and line. The horizon is less defined now, the sky hazy with the promise of heat.

A flock of birds trails the ship, riding the slipstream. Their thin, sharp bodies cut the air in perfect arcs. Claire tracks them, eyes never leaving the place where they dip and rise again, skimming just above the waves, always in formation.

She envies the precision, the predictability. The unbroken pattern.

Her body is heavy, gravity a constant, not something to resist but something to sink into. The blanket is bunched around her waist, the sleeves of her shirt rolled to the elbow.

Her tangled hair has been whipped into knots by the wind. She does not bother to fix it. The salt has dried on her lips and at the edges of her nose.

She closes her eyes and leans into the shade. The birds' sound is distant, a sharp cry swallowed by the rush of water. Listening to it, she lets her thoughts drift with the shapes of their flight.

She could sit here forever.

Opening her eyes, Claire looks down at her hands. They are trembling, faint but steady.

She folds them together, then apart, then together again.

The sun is past its zenith now, the shadow of the railing falling across her legs. She shivers, then pulls the blanket back to her shoulders.

The tray sits untouched, the dome shining in the light.

The birds are gone.

The only thing left is the sea.

The day folds into dusk with a long, low shudder. Claire sits inside, knees drawn to her chest on the end of the made bed, watching the sky bruise from orange to purple through the thin seam of her blackout curtain.

She has not moved in over an hour. Her hands are asleep. The taste of seafood lingers in the back of her mouth, tinged with lemon and the memory of cold butter. She feels weightless and anchored at once, body drifting while her mind clings to whatever will not let go.

At six, a knock at the door. Slow, deliberate, three beats only. Daniel.

She stands, smoothing her shirt, and answers.

He's holding a tray in both hands this time, arms tense with the effort of balancing the stack. On top: two dinner plates, a bottle of water, two glasses, two sets of napkins rolled around silverware, a small bread basket. He's shaved since last night, the stubble gone from his jaw, but there is a line of exhaustion beneath his eyes.

"Evening," he says, and waits for her to step back before entering.

He carries it to the balcony setting it down on the table, arranging each element with precision. He lays out the plates, unfolds the napkins, pours two glasses of water, and places the bread in the centre. He doesn't ask if she wants to eat out here, but the gesture is invitation.

She's sitting in the same chair as before, blanket bunched around her waist, hands limp in her lap.

Daniel sits across from her. The angle puts his face in shadow, the sun behind him. For a moment, they just look at each other.

He removes the domes from the plates. Steak and potatoes for him, a vegetarian pasta for her. The smell is warm, almost homey. Picking up her fork, Claire waits until Daniel does the same before starting.

They eat. The silence is absolute, the only sound the scrape of utensils and the rush of wind across the balcony.

Daniel is focussed, small bites, chewing each one fully. Every few moments, he glances at Claire, then looks away before she can meet his eyes.

The food is good, better than lunch, but Claire finds herself pushing the pasta around on the plate, lining up the penne by length, stacking the slices of zucchini, sorting the tomato into one neat pile at the rim.

She takes a bite, chews, swallows. Repeat.

Daniel breaks the silence first.

"Did you get outside today?" He keeps his eyes on the table as he speaks.

She nods. "Stayed out here most of the morning."

He nods, too, as if ticking off a box. "Sun's good for you. Helps you sleep."

She shrugs. "Didn't make a difference."

He sips his water, sets the glass down exactly where it was before. "Did you see the birds?"

"Yes."

"Kind of amazing, how they follow us for so long," he says. "Sometimes I think they don't even know why they do it. Just instinct."

She says nothing, returns to her food.

Daniel eats another few bites. When he speaks again, his voice is lower. "How are you doing?"

Claire chews a mouthful of bread, then wipes her fingers on the napkin. "Fine."

"Really?"

She looks up at him. "You're not my doctor."

He smiles, a little sheepish. "You're right. Sorry."

She finishes the glass of water and pours herself another, the liquid catches the last of the sunset and refracts it across the table.

They eat in silence for a while.

Daniel tries again. "Are you reading anything?"

She shakes her head. "Can't focus. Pages blur together."

"You could try the audiobooks on the TV. That's what I do, when I can't sleep."

Claire makes a mental note, then erases it. "Maybe," she says.

Daniel folds his napkin and sets it on his plate. He laces his fingers together, thumbs moving in small circles.

"I know it's hard."

She looks at the horizon, fading from orange to grey.

"It's not hard. It's just what it is."

He waits. When she doesn't continue, he says, "If you want to talk, you can."

She shrugs. "What's there to say?"

He holds the silence for a few seconds longer. "Fair enough."

They finish the meal without another word. The moon is rising, thin and white like a fingernail. The deck lights below flicker on, illuminating the spray at the bow.

The plates are empty, Daniel stacks them neatly, placing the cutlery on top, and covers the stack with the napkin. He stands.

"Do you need anything before I go?"

Claire shakes her head. "No. Thank you."

Looking at her for a long moment, he nods, jaw working as if there is something left unsaid.

"Okay. I'll be around."

She watches him leave, the door clicking shut behind him.

She sits for a moment, pushes back from the table and stands at the railing. The wind is colder, sharper. She leans into it, letting her hair tangle across her face, breathing in the salt and cold.

The sky is empty except for the moon, the ocean below is black, the surface broken only by the trail of the ship.

Pressing her hands to the rail, feeling the chill seep into her bones, she stares at the water, at the place where the world ends, waiting for something to rise up and fill her.

She closes her eyes and says, softly, "Lily."

The wind snatches the word away, carrying it out to sea.

There is no answer.

She opens her eyes. The ocean is still there.

She stands at the railing until her legs go numb, the moon is high, and the cold has worked its way deep into her bones.

She returns inside, draws the curtain, and sits on the bed, hands folded in her lap.

She waits for morning.

She waits.

CHAPTER THIRTY-TWO

Claire wakes at 7:42, eyes already open. The clock by the bed flashes its numbers in red, always red, always precise, like a warning light. The first thing she does is pull the thin white blanket from the foot of the bed and wrap it around her shoulders. She likes the weight, the way it anchors her to the world. There is comfort in the ritual.

She steps onto the balcony. The rail is wet with dew and salt; she grips it anyway, letting her fingers go numb in the chill. She counts the passing minutes by the sweep of the second hand on her watch, the only thing she still trusts to tell time. The air is cold, but not unbearable. It sharpens the edges of her thoughts.

Below, the ocean churns. It is the same as it was yesterday, and the day before, and every day since she started waiting. The surface is restless, the wind carving ridges that shimmer and vanish in a breath. She tries to track the ship's progress by the movement of the waves, but they betray nothing. No land, no birds, no sign that the world is anything but water.

Breakfast comes at eight, always eight, delivered with the same sequence of knocks. The man on the other side is careful, polite, never looking her in the eye. The tray is set on the desk, its contents different each day but arranged with military precision. Today it's a bowl of sliced melon, two hard-boiled eggs, a croissant, a single orange cut in half. The coffee is in a steel carafe, heavy and hot.

She eats on the balcony. The wind is stronger now, pulling at her hair, but she keeps the blanket tight and peels the eggs with numb fingers. She chews without tasting. The fruit is cold and slick in her mouth. She eats every bite, then lines up the empty shells in a row along the edge of the plate. When she's done, she pours the coffee and holds it with both hands, letting the heat burn through the blanket.

Afterward, she slides the tray into the corridor and nods to Officer Martinez standing watch.

Inside, the room is exactly as she left it. The bed is made, the desk clear, the bathroom door slightly ajar. The air smells faintly of citrus and bleach. The only evidence of life is the faint imprint of her body on the balcony chair, the outline of her heel in the nap of the carpet.

She sits and waits.

At 9:03, Claire tries the door. She eases it open a few inches, just enough to glimpse Officer Martinez still at her post. No chance of slipping past. Claire lets the door drift shut and returns to the balcony, pulse steady, mind already moving ahead.

She watches the ocean for hours. Sometimes she counts the waves; sometimes she counts her heartbeats. She is not sure if this helps, but it keeps her mind occupied.

Lunch comes at noon. The knock is different: three quick then one, the lunch attendant, a code she's learned to recognise. The tray is heavier, the food richer—today, grilled salmon, rice, steamed broccoli. She eats it all. She stacks the empty plates and wipes crumbs onto a napkin, then folds the napkin into a square and tucks it under the fork.

It is only after lunch that she lets herself remember.

She closes her eyes and tries to summon Lily. She begins with the basics: the colour of her hair, the sound of her laugh, the way her hands would seize Claire's shirt when scared. She tries to conjure the exact shade of Lily's eyes—hazel, flecked with green, almost gold in the right light. She tries to hear Lily's voice, but the words run together, melting into nonsense.

She tries harder. She pictures Lily at the breakfast table, face smeared with jam, her tiny fist often clutching the plastic dinosaur. She remembers the pink rain boots, mismatched socks, the dress with a triceratops print. She remembers the softness of Lily's curls, how they would spring loose even after being brushed a dozen times.

But the details resist. Blurring at the edges, shifting, flickering like a bad transmission. Claire fights to keep them in focus, but the harder she tries, the more they slip away.

She opens her eyes, breath sharp in her throat. Sweating, despite the cold, her hands are shaking.

Unlocking her phone, she scrolls through the gallery. At first, the images are as she remembers: photos of the deck, the endless sea, a selfie taken by the pool with her hair wrapped in a towel. She swipes, faster and faster, hunting for the photos of Lily, the ones she took in the stateroom, at the pool, at mini golf. The places where Lily should be.

But Lily is gone. There are no photos of her. Not one.

She scrolls back to the beginning. There is a photo of a bed, perfectly made, with a towel folded into the shape of a swan. There is a photo of breakfast, coffee and fruit and a single croissant. There is a photo of Claire, alone, reflected in the bathroom mirror. She looks tired, older than she remembers. She looks like a person waiting for a verdict.

She stares at the phone until her eyes blur. She wipes her face, but her hand comes away dry.

She peeks through the door again. Still guarded.

Back on the balcony, the air is colder. The wind has shifted, bringing with it a metallic tang, almost bloody. Breathing it in, she holds the scent in her lungs until it burns. She sets the phone screen down on the table and listens to the hum of the ship.

She wonders if she is disappearing, too.

The afternoon passes in pieces. She counts the minutes between the shifts of light, the slow motion of the sun across the sky. She watches the shadows creep along the rail, then fade. She waits for dinner, but it is not time yet.

She sits, blanket tight around her shoulders, hands balled in her lap.

She tries again to remember Lily.

This time, she gets nothing.

She feels the panic start, a low buzz in her fingertips, a tightening behind her eyes. She clamps her jaw until it aches. She digs her nails into the palm of her hand, desperate for something sharp, something real.

She repeats Lily's name over and over, a litany, a spell.

But the name is just a sound now. The meaning is gone.

She rocks in the chair, back and forth, counting each motion, each breath. She counts to one hundred, then to one thousand. She does not stop.

When the sun finally goes down, she opens her hand.

There are crescent marks where her nails bit into the skin. They are already fading.

She stands, blanket trailing behind her, and looks at the ocean one last time.

It is exactly as it was this morning.

It will be the same tomorrow.

Pressing her forehead to the glass, she wills herself to hold on just a little longer.

But the world does not change.

She stays like that until the sky is black, until the first stars appear.

She waits, and waits, and waits.

Her hands don't stop shaking.

The knock comes at 18:11, right on time. Claire is on the balcony, knees drawn to her chest, watching the deck lights flicker to life below. The air has gone sharp again, tinged with ozone, the ship's slipstream flinging salt spray against the glass.

Three slow deliberate knocks at the door. She hears the whir of the key card, the soft click of the lock. Daniel enters without invitation; his voice pitched just above the hush of the ventilation.

"Evening," he calls. His tone is softer than before, edged with fatigue. She hears the familiar scrape of a tray on the desk, the careful rattle as he unpacks their dinner.

She stays outside, still, until he repeats his knocking pattern on the balcony door. He slides it open, careful to minimise the gap, and leans out, his hair windblown, a single wrinkle creasing his uniform shirt at the shoulder.

"Dinner's ready," he says. "It's a good one tonight."

She stands, the blanket falling away from her shoulders. She steps inside and lets the glass close behind her. Daniel has set the table with deliberate care. Two plates each: one of pasta tangled with something green and fresh, the other a neat mound of salad with white cheese shaved on top.

He pours two glasses of water, sets them precisely on the table, then pulls out her chair with a flick of his wrist. The room is small enough that they're nearly knee to knee.

She sits. He waits for her to take the first bite.

She twirls a forkful of pasta, the strands slipping, pooling in a watery sauce. She chews, swallows, tasting nothing. He watches her with the patience of someone who knows not to press.

They eat in silence for two or three minutes, the only noise the scrape of fork on plate and the gentle slosh as the ship pitches. Finally, Daniel lifts his glass.

"To almost making it," he says.

She raises hers, clinking the rim to his. "Almost," she echoes, then takes a sip.

The water is cold and sharp, burning all the way down.

He tries for small talk. "Captain says we're on schedule. Weather's good, just a little headwind. You should see the Statue of Liberty around six, and land just after dawn.

She nods, looking not at him, but at the arc of the water in her glass. She tracks its movement, the way the surface pulls and bends with each tilt of her hand.

"Did you get outside today?" he tries.

"All day," she says, her voice is flat. "I watched the clouds for an hour, maybe more. I counted the wakes from the other boats. I tried to imagine what the bottom of the ocean looks like."

He smiles, a real one. "Dark and cold, I bet. Probably full of lost keys and sunglasses."

She doesn't laugh. "And bodies."

He lets the joke die. "And bodies," he repeats.

A silence builds, thick as velvet. She picks at her salad, tearing the leaves into shreds. She looks at her hand and realises it is shaking. She puts the fork down and presses her palm to her thigh, trying to still it.

Daniel sips his drink, sets the glass down, folds his hands together. He waits for her to say something.

She looks at him. Not through him, not past him. At him.

"I'm starting to wonder if you're all right," she says. Her voice is quiet, but it does not waver. "What if I'm the one who's wrong?"

He doesn't answer, but his eyes tell her to go on.

She tries to organise her thoughts, but they come out in pieces.

"I keep trying to remember Lily's face. The shape of it, the weight of her on my lap, the way her hair smelled after a bath. But when I close my eyes, it's like trying to remember a dream from when you were five. I know she existed—I know she did—but the picture keeps getting fainter."

She rubs her thumb and forefinger together, as if the memory could be conjured by friction alone.

"There used to be photos. Videos. Her favourite shoes, the dinosaur ones. Now, I look, and it's just me. Alone. I went through every message, every photo. I must have checked my phone a hundred times today. There's nothing. It's like she was never there. Like I made her up."

Daniel says nothing, but his hand shifts, sliding fractionally closer to hers on the table.

She takes a breath, holds it, then lets it out slowly.

"When Marcus left," she says, "I thought it was because he couldn't handle me after we lost the baby. I blamed him, blamed myself, blamed everyone. But now—I'm starting to wonder if maybe there wasn't a baby at all. Or maybe the baby was all I had. Maybe my mind just… filled in what my heart needed."

She stops. The tremor has spread to her jaw. Clenches her teeth, she feels the ache at the hinge, the dull throb radiating up to her temple.

"It's getting harder to remember the sound of her laugh," she says, almost to herself. "The way she'd say 'Mummy, look!' every five minutes. That was her thing. She was always so certain I'd care."

Eyes burning, but she blinks the tears back. "I thought losing her was the worst thing that could happen. But forgetting her—having her slip away, bit by bit—that's worse. So much worse."

The words hang in the air, heavy and irrevocable.

She looks at Daniel. For the first time, she lets him see how raw she is. How hollow.

He doesn't try to fix it. He doesn't tell her she's wrong, or that it's all in her head. He just reaches across the table, slow and deliberate, and puts his hand over hers.

He doesn't squeeze. He just rests it there, the weight and warmth enough.

She looks at their hands. The contrast in size, in colour. The certainty of his grip, the way her own hand trembles beneath it.

She lets the tears fall, just a few, not a flood. Letting the silence have the room.

After a while, she picks up her glass with her free hand. She takes a sip, then another.

"Thank you," she says, not looking up.

He nods once, as if he understands exactly what she means.

They finish the meal in silence.

The ship keeps moving. The deck lights flicker and fade, the sky smudged with stars. A ring of water marks the table where his glass once sat, his hand still resting gently on hers. The silence between them isn't empty—it hums, low and steady, in time with the ship's engine, charged with the weight of what's just been said. Something has shifted. Unspoken, but understood.

She doesn't try to remember Lily again.

Not tonight.

Tonight, she lets herself be held, just for a minute, in the gravity of another person.

Tomorrow, she will try again.
But for now, she lets the moment be enough.

CHAPTER THIRTY-THREE

Claire wakes to the taste of steel in her mouth and the distant, relentless sound of horns. For a moment, she isn't sure if it's the ship or some alarm ringing inside her head. The light is thin and watery, and so cold it bites beneath her skin. She pulls the ship's robe over her pyjamas, and steps onto the balcony.

The city is a grey blur, rising in stacked rectangles beyond the wet rail. Fog slices between the buildings, smearing their edges. Below, the ship docks amid a frenzy of uniforms and neon vests. Passengers crowd the rails on every deck, chattering, taking selfies, and blocking the gangways. Over the loudspeakers, a woman's voice reads a list of instructions, pausing every few seconds for emphasis: "All guests may now proceed to the gangway. Please have your sail pass card ready."

Claire stands motionless. The air smells of diesel and salt, with an undertone of sour coffee drifting upwind. She holds her arms tight across her chest, the robe is scratchy, the sleeves already damp at the cuffs. She watches the city, the water, the machinery of arrival.

A knock at the door—breakfast. Claire takes the tray and carries it back to the balcony. A banana, cereal, a sealed yoghurt, and two packets of sugar for the coffee she doesn't want today. She peels the banana with surgical care, as if it might reveal something. It's under-ripe, fibrous, but she eats it slowly, watching the activity onshore.

A gull lands on the rail, so close she can see flecks of dirt in its feathers. It cocks its head, fixes her with one black eye, then turns away, bored. She envies its decisiveness. She wishes she could just lift off, circle the mess below, and then vanish into the white.

Instead, she eats.

On the dock, forklifts trundle in tight, angry circles, stacking and re-stacking pallets wrapped in green plastic. Every third load is a crate, heavy and stamped "SUPPLY" in red, large enough for a grown man to fit inside without hunching. She counts—six, seven, then nine in quick succession. The noise is pure violence: the screech of rubber, the metallic clang of forks hitting steel, the shouts of men in hard hats waving the next load forward.

Claire's mind does the math. If you had to move something—or someone—without being noticed, this would be the way. That's how they got the other little girl in. She presses her hands to the glass, the chill cutting through her skin. Imagining the inside of the crates: darkness, recycled air, the judder of motion with every bump and stop. Trying not to picture Lily curled up in that space, but the image comes anyway, vivid and sharp.

She swallows hard, then takes the yoghurt. The foil lid peels back with a pop. She dips her finger in tasting the bland, almost chemical sweetness. It reminds her of every hospital waiting room, every time she's tried to eat when her stomach was a clenched fist.

She watches the flow of passengers on the pier: a river of colour, children with balloons tied to their wrists, retirees in matching shirts, a bachelorette party in identical tiaras. The security line at the terminal snakes along, undulating with every announcement. Cameras flash. Voices overlap. A woman cries, but it's the happy kind, loud and obnoxious, arms flung around a man too stunned to react.

Claire hates all of them. She wants them to disappear, just for a second, so she can see what's underneath.

She wipes the yoghurt on the rim of the cup, sets it back on the table, and checks the time. 8:26. The first wave of customs inspections should be finishing soon. She rocks on her heels, shifting from foot to foot, the way Lily used to when she was bored or tired or ready to bolt. She waits for the world to slow down, but it never does.

On a small gangway near the back of the ship, a staff member in a white uniform helps a woman with too many bags. The woman's hair is hidden under a wide-brimmed hat, her face lost behind sunglasses bigger than her hands. She moves fast, not pausing to thank the helper, pulling a small child by the arm. The child's feet barely skim the ground, pink sneakers trailing, a blue bandage on one knee.

For a second, time shudders. Claire can't breathe. Her ears ring.

She leans forward, straining for a better look, but the woman is already gone, absorbed by the current of bodies moving toward the escalator to the customs hall. Only the flash of the sneakers lingers—a punch of colour, too quick to process, but unmistakable.

Her breath comes ragged. She squeezes her arms tighter, digging her nails into the meat of her biceps. She wills herself not to move, not to scream, not to let the world see her fracture.

Below, dock workers wrestle the blue-crated load onto a rolling cart. One man pulls a crowbar, prying at nails along the seam. The crate pops open just a fraction, and the worker steps back, shaking out his hand. He laughs, shouts something at the woman on the forklift, but Claire can't hear it. All she sees is the gap, the blackness inside, the way the man hesitates before he looks.

She imagines a child's hand, pale and reaching, pressing through the crack. She imagines Lily's voice, thin as breath, calling out for her. *Mummy, look.*

CHAPTER THIRTY-FOUR

She doesn't think. She just runs.

One second Claire is gripping the balcony rail, the next she's inside, racing across the room. Her mind shreds the intervening steps—unlocking the door, stepping into the corridor, the way the carpet burns under her bare soles. She moves with the velocity of a falling object slamming into Officer Martinez as she passes. There is no hesitation.

The hallway is already crowded with luggage and bodies; an entire week of vacation jammed into a single exodus. She elbows past a family blocking the exit, the father's mouth opens to say something, but the words fall behind her. Every step launches her forward toward the elevators, but the button is lit, the numbers frozen. Five floors up and crawling. No time.

She pivots, heading for the stairwell. Someone shouts, "Hey!" as she shoulders through, but down is her only thought.

Her feet slap the stairs. The carpet is cold, each edge biting into her heel. She takes the first landing in two strides. The robe catches on the next step, almost sends her flying, but she rights herself, ignoring the sharp pain as the belt tears loose. She's half running, half falling.

Second landing, third. The air grows denser, humidity thick from a hundred panicked bodies sweating the space. She can smell herself, the sour tang of anxiety and old detergent. She tucks her elbows in, drops her chin, and runs. Fourth landing, fifth.

The stairwell opens onto a main corridor, this one even more packed. Luggage lines the walls. A toddler sits cross-legged, blocking the centre, and Claire nearly stomps on her. She veers right into the crush of passengers waiting for disembarkation. A babble of voices, a high-frequency whine of a speaker system, and above it all, a familiar voice—

"Ma'am, stop! You need to come with me."

She doesn't look back. She barrels through a knot of guests in pastel sweaters, their hands up in comic defence, faces registering only confusion.

"Claire!" The voice again, closer. She glances back, sees Martinez in full uniform, ponytail slicing the air as she jogs after her. For a second their eyes lock—Martinez's wide with alarm, Claire's burning. "You need to return to your cabin. I'm calling Security."

"Get Daniel Jackson!" Claire screams. It comes out ragged, loud enough to silence the nearest crowd. "Get him. Now. Or get out of my way."

Martinez pauses, a moment of calculation, then goes for her radio. "Control, this is Martinez. I have a situation—Code Charlie—passenger Holloway, Deck Three, forward corridor heading out. She's not stopping. Repeat, she's not—"

A crewman tries to block her with an arm, but Claire goes low, football-style, slipping past. Her robe billows open, the left sleeve dangling. She couldn't care less. She's free.

The PA system crackles: "Charlie. Charlie. Charlie. Deck Three. Midship. Charlie. Charlie. Charlie. Deck Three. Midship." Her name is not mentioned, but she knows it's about her.

She can hear Martinez behind her, the echo of her boots on hard vinyl flooring. "Stop now!" Martinez shouts, "You're going to hurt yourself—"

Claire doesn't stop. She thinks of Lily. Of the flash of pink shoes. Of the way her mouth moves when she's nervous, thumb tucked into the seam of her sleeve. The image fuels her. She can see the finish line.

She bursts out onto the third floor. This is the lower-level gangway, the place where families gather while waiting to leave for their excursion. Chaos—children running, parents screaming, camera flashes going off every few seconds. She ducks behind a service cart, eyes scanning the crowd for the wide-brimmed hat, the blue bandage, the tiny feet.

She sees them. Halfway down the dock, moving fast. The woman is leading the child, glancing over her shoulder every few steps. The hat bobs like a target.

Martinez is right behind her but slows to avoid the crowd. Claire takes the chance, veers right, and leaps the velvet rope meant to corral passengers. She's in the open now.

There is shouting, people jumping out of the way, but Claire doesn't hear them. The world is a tunnel. The end is in sight.

Two more officers try to intercept, flanking her from left and right. She fakes right, then pivots, using a free-standing sign as a shield. It nearly topples, but she doesn't slow.

"Jackson!" she screams, but her voice is lost in the noise.

The woman in the hat is almost at the escalator, the last barrier before the city. She clutches the child's wrist, dragging her. The girl is crying, her voice shrill above the din.

Claire digs for one last burst. Thirty metres away, then twenty. One officer grabs for her, but his grip snags only the empty sleeve of the robe. She wrenches free, the fabric ripping at the seam.

The queue to the bottom of the escalator is a wall of bodies, but Claire plunges through. Her foot slams on something, slicing her heel. She keeps going.

Ahead, the woman and child are running. The hat is gone, yanked off in the sprint. The woman's hair is long, platinum blonde, wild. The girl stumbles, falls, the woman yanks her up.

Claire's bare feet leave prints on the concrete, a trail of blood from her heel. She's gaining. She's so close.

Martinez and the others shout behind her, but Claire hears only her own breath, the wet slap of her soles, the thud of her pulse in her ears.

Ten metres. Five.

The woman glances back, sees Claire closing, and for a second her face is clear, tanned, and familiar. It's Hayley, the Guest Services officer. Everything falls into place. Of course it is.

Claire screams, a wordless roar, and hurls herself forward.

Hayley pivots, shielding the girl, but Claire crashes into them, all three tumbling to the ground. The pain is instant, but she doesn't care. She claws for the child, wraps both arms around her, and rolls away from Hayley's reach.

There is nothing left of her but nerves and muscle. Instinct. The world boils with motion, noise, hands.

The first hand grabs Claire's shoulder, but she shrugs it off, all animal, focused on the child. She grips the girl's arm—small, birdlike, trembling—and yanks her in, sheltering her with her whole body. The child makes soft, half-choked cries, but Claire hushes her, pressing her face to the girl's head, breathing her in, wild and desperate. The scent is shampoo, panic and something else, something so familiar it blurs Claire's vision for a second.

The woman—Hayley, she knows now, no more hats or sunglasses to hide behind—grabs at the girl, shrieking, "Let her go! Let go! You're hurting her!" There's nothing calm in Hayley now, none of that careful, Guest Services polish. She claws for the child, nails raking Claire's wrist, tearing the thin skin until blood wells up and drips onto the girl's shirt.

Security hits like a tidal wave. Two men with arms like corded wire, one reaching for the kid, the other wrapping Claire in a bear hug from behind. She won't let go. She bites, twists her shoulder, and thinks she tastes blood—hers, the officer's, or just her imagination.

"Mummy's here, it's okay, I've got you," she whispers in the child's ear, over and over. The girl gasps, tears smeared across her cheeks, mouth working but no words. Claire tightens her hold, makes herself a wall.

Hayley screams, "She's crazy! She's crazy! That's not your daughter!" Security yanks her back, but she fights too, making guttural sounds that Claire didn't know she had.

Daniel appears suddenly, dressed in civilian clothes, his voice forceful but cracked like he's speaking to a wounded animal: "Claire, Claire, let go. Let go. No one's going to hurt her. You need to let go."

But she can't. She knows if she lets go, it's over.

The child coughs, then manages a single word, almost a question: "Mummy?"

Claire sobs. She shakes, the world hot and blurred, but she forces herself to look at the girl. Something's there, something real, the tilt of the brow, the shape of the chin, the eyes widening in a pattern she recognises. For a moment she's back in the old apartment, Sunday morning, Lily in pyjamas, sunlight turning her curls to warm bronze.

Then hands are everywhere—security, Hayley, Daniel, even Martinez. They pry her loose, bit by bit. Claire clings, shifting her grip to the girl's ankle, then her shoe, the pink sneaker with the triceratops patch. For a second she holds just the shoe, and then even that is gone.

She screams, full-throated, as they wrestle her to the concrete. Her head slams the dock; the world flashes white. She howls, "She stole my child! She stole her! That's my Lily! That's my Lily!" The words echo, bouncing off the cruise terminal walls, picking up other voices—

tourists with phones, crew with radios, an ambulance siren somewhere down the street.

Security flips Claire onto her stomach, wrenches her arms behind her. Plastic cuffs bite so hard her hands go numb. Someone pins her ankles; someone else grinds a knee into her spine. She fights, thrashing, but the world softens at the edges. She's sobs, snotty, loud, ugly, and doesn't care who sees.

She keeps her eyes on the girl, the only fixed point. The child cries, arms limp, but her face turns toward Claire. Confusion and fear mix there, but also something else—a question, an ache, a glimmer of recognition that won't die.

Daniel looms over her, blocking out the sky. He looks like he wants to say something, but his mouth tightens. He leans down, puts a gentle hand on her head, and says, "It's over, Claire. It's over."

She spits at him, can't find words, just makes a noise. He wipes his cheek and looks away.

They pull her to her feet, none too gentle, dragging her toward the ship. She tries to dig her heels in, but her feet slip with blood. She looks back, tries to twist, but one of the guards holds her by the neck, another by the arm. She screams again, hoarse, "You have to listen! That's my child! She's mine!"

Martinez walks beside her, face like stone. "You're making it worse," she says, low. "Just stop."

Claire shakes her head, wild. "You saw her. You know."

Martinez just sets her jaw and keeps moving.

They reach the security office, the same grey door, the same glass. Inside, the world smells sharp with bleach, sweat, and the ozone smell of panic. They dump her on a bench, cuffed and hunched, and slam the door. She repeats "Lily" softly, over and over, like it's a password that will eventually unlock the world.

CHAPTER THIRTY-FIVE

Claire and Hayley are led in from opposite holding rooms, zip-tied and silent. The security office is freezing—too much AC, too little warmth in the lights, the walls, the people. Claire's chair is hard plastic, cutting into her thighs. Her arms throbbing, a dull ache crawling from fingertips to elbow, but she holds herself upright. There's a kind of dignity in refusing to slump, refusing to look like the madwoman everyone assumes she is.

Hayley is across the table, pressed into the farthest edge of her own chair, as if proximity to Claire is contagious. Her shirt is half untucked, and there's a run of mascara on one cheek that she hasn't noticed. She looks pissed, but also, Claire is sure of it, afraid. She drums her fingernails on the tabletop, the click-click a Morse code of barely held panic.

Two security officers are present. The older one, likely in charge, stands by the door: heavy, pale, badge clipped to his breast pocket. His expression is carefully blank. The younger officer sits behind a battered laptop, occasionally typing, mostly watching. Their posture is rigid, impersonal, but the way their eyes flick between Claire and Hayley says they are waiting for the truth to surface.

Lily is here, too. She sits on a rolling chair by the opposite wall, feet not touching the floor. Her hands rest in her lap. A box of tissues and a cup of juice sit untouched on the table in front of her. Beside her stands a third officer—female, older, with the fixed, pinched smile of someone trained to handle children. Lily swings her feet, not looking at anyone.

The room is silent, except for Hayley's fingernails and the groaning from the ship adjusting to the dock. No one is eager to speak. Maybe they're waiting for someone, or maybe they're all hoping this mess resolves itself.

Finally, Hayley breaks the silence, her voice sharp enough to cut. "This is ridiculous. I don't even know why I'm even here. That's my niece. I have the paperwork—"

The door opens. The chief of security steps in and nods to the room, taking her place near the officers without a word.

The senior officer lifts a hand. "Ma'am, please. We're sorting out the facts. There was an incident, and—"

"An incident?" Hayley almost laughs, dry and bitter. "This lunatic tackled me on the dock. She— she hurt me. She terrified my child. Why is she not in a cell?"

The officer doesn't respond. He's heard this kind of outrage before. He glances at Claire, then at the woman beside Lily. The message is clear: hold, wait, observe.

After a beat, the chief answers, calm and even. "You both were. Now you're here so we can figure out what actually happened."

Hayley leans forward, eyes blazing. "If you let her anywhere near my child, I'll have your jobs. All of you. She needs to be medicated, not coddled."

The woman with Lily looks averts her gaze. The younger officer types a note, lips pressed tight.

Claire doesn't rise to the bait. She keeps her eyes on Lily—on her daughter's profile, the curl behind her ear, the defiant jut of her chin. It's like looking through frosted glass: the child is here, alive, but distant, walled off by someone else's story.

Hayley keeps going. "I don't even know who she is. She started following us on the ship, harassing us—"

"I never saw you until the show," Claire says. Her voice is calm, almost detached, but the air thrums with it. "Stop lying. Please. Just stop."

The older officer interjects, voice firm. "Let's keep this civil. Ma'am —" he nods at Hayley, "you say the girl is your niece?"

Hayley seizes the chance. "Of course she is! We have the same eyes, the same—ask her. Ask anyone. You saw how she reacted. She screamed for me. She doesn't know this woman."

Claire speaks directly to Hayley, low and steady. "What's the name on her birth certificate?"

Hayley flushes, then recovers. "You think I'm going to discuss my niece's personal information with a stalker?"

"She's mine," Claire says. "Her real name is Lily May Holloway. Her favourite dinosaur is Stegosaurus. She sleeps with a stuffed cat, named Thomas, he's missing an ear." Her hands flex behind the chair, aching to gesture. "She's terrified of thunderstorms. When she's tired, she tells stories about animals going to space."

Hayley's head shakes in a fast jerky denial. "This is sick. This is so —"

"She hates orange juice with pulp," Claire adds. "She calls it 'lumpy juice.'"

The younger officer blinks, glancing at Lily, who is silently watching Claire.

"Enough," says the senior officer. He turns to Claire. "We have reports—medical and otherwise—that you suffered a head injury. That you've been having... memory issues. That you did this to another child. Is that correct?"

Claire nods. No use denying it.

"Then can you see how this looks?"

"I don't care how it looks," she says, letting her voice rise. "I know my child. You have to listen."

Hayley slaps the table. "This is harassment. I want her charged."

The officer sighs and gestures to his partner. "Let's get statements. One at a time." He turns to Claire. "Do you need medical attention?"

"Only if you let her near my niece again," Hayley snaps. "She's dangerous. She attacked us."

Claire closes her eyes and counts to five. When she opens them, Lily is still watching her, hands arranging the tissues into a line.

"Lily," Claire says, softly. "Sweetie, do you remember what we did before bed the other night?"

Hayley starts to object, but the officer raises a hand. "Let her answer."

Lily doesn't speak right away. Then— "We got pizza." She glances at Hayley, uncertain.

"And did we do something with your hair?" Claire asks.

Lily nods, just barely. "You brushed it. You said it looked nice."

The younger officer consults the screen, then looks at Lily. "That was before you got separated from your mum?"

"Yes," Lily says, but her eyes dart between adults, unsure which answer is safe.

Hayley's smile is brittle. "She's confused. She's tired. You're traumatising her."

"Lily," Claire says. "Do you remember what you told me about the moon?"

A long pause. Lily's lips tremble. She looks at her hands, then at the officer beside her, then finally at Claire.

"That it looks like my shoulder?" she whispers.

Claire feels time stop. "That's right, baby."

Hayley is unravelling. "She's manipulating her. You can't—"

Claire speaks over her. "There's a birthmark," addressing the officer. "On her right shoulder. Shaped like a crescent moon. If you don't believe me, check."

The room stills.

The officer with Lily leans in, speaking softly. Lily slips off her cardigan. The officer gently peels back her collar.

There it is. A perfect crescent, pale against the skin.

Silence. Even Hayley stops mid-word.

The chief officer bends closer, then glances at the other two, who nod, eyes wide.

"It's there," she says. "Exactly as described."

Claire slumps, the fight draining from her. The relief is so sudden she almost laughs.

Hayley's face crumples. The anger is gone, replaced by something raw and afraid. She shakes her head, but the protest is gone from her voice. "That—that doesn't mean anything. It's just a mark. She could have seen it at the pool—"

Claire looks at Lily, who is still sitting quietly, shoulder bared, waiting for someone to tell her what happens next.

The chief straightens up. "Ma'am," she says to Hayley, "I think we're going to need a little more explanation."

Hayley folds in on herself, fists pressed to her temples.

Claire closes her eyes. The relief is a knife, not a salve.

She waits for the next cut.

It doesn't take long for Hayley to unravel. The second the officers confirm the birthmark, the tension in her shoulders dissolves. Her face shifts from hostile to hollow in one breath. For a moment, she looks at Claire—not with the old contempt, but with a wild, empty fear that turns her from an adversary into a child.

She slumps forward, hands splayed on the table, and begins to sob. Not the loud, messy crying of someone who wants to be consoled, but the silent, full-body shudder of a person whose last line of defence has crumbled. Her hair falls across her eyes. She doesn't bother to fix it.

The sound is barely louder than the hum of the ship's ventilation, yet it fills the room, a raw animal noise with no hope left in it.

The older officer moves quickly, snapping a signal to his partner. The younger rises, placing his own body between Hayley and the door. The female officer at Lily's side brings the girl over, one hand gentle on her shoulder. She doesn't resist as she's guided to stand next to Claire.

Claire can't move. She's still bound, hands numb and bloodless from the tight zip ties. Only her voice still works.

"Are you okay?" she whispers.

Lily nods, then looks away. "Are you?" she asks, even softer.

The words almost break Claire open.

The senior officer bends down to cut the restraints. He fumbles for the blade, his hands shaking just enough to betray him. When the plastic snaps, Claire's arms drop, heavy and useless, then tingling as the blood returns. She rubs her wrists. They are ringed in red, raw and damp.

Across the table, Hayley's face is slick with tears. She shakes her head and smears the wetness with her palms. "I didn't want to," she croaks. "God, I didn't—I'm sorry. I'm so sorry."

The female officer moves closer, and sets a tissue box in front of her. Hayley grabs two, balls them in her fist, but doesn't use them.

Claire wants to say something cruel. She wants to scream, to release all the venom she's built up from days of being told she was crazy. Instead, her body vibrates with an exhaustion that runs deeper than the bone.

The older officer sits down beside Hayley, not too close, hands folded on the table. "Ma'am, you need to explain. What's going on? Why did you try to take the child?"

Hayley opens her mouth, but the words caught in the gears of her panic. Finally, she gets one out.

"Money," she says.

The officer nods, unsurprised. "How much?"

"Five thousand. Up front." She glances at Claire, then looks away. "They said there'd be more. After we reached port."

The younger officer writes down every word. The older one asks, "Who? Who paid you?"

"I don't know," Hayley whispers. Then louder, frantic: "I swear, I don't. It was messages. Just messages. No names. No faces." She presses the tissue to her mouth, biting into it. "It started in Lisbon. Guy at the casino, said he knew people who could help me out of my debt. Said all I had to do was… take care of something."

Claire watches torn between disgust and relief.

The officer leans in. "Describe him."

"Tall. Dark suit. Blue tie. He never gave a name. He said I'd get a call when it was time. And I did. The night before we set sail. He said there was a child on board, that I had to get them off the ship, that there'd be people waiting at the terminal. They didn't care which one. If I did it, they'd pay the rest. If I didn't, they'd…"

She stops, hands trembling.

"They'd what?" the officer asks.

Hayley presses the tissue harder to her lips. "They said they'd hurt my family. My mother. My brother. I believed them. They knew things. About me. About where I grew up, about my dad." Her shoulders shake. The tissue shreds in her hands.

The room is so quiet, every syllable lands like a needle.

The female officer comes around the table, kneels beside to Hayley, and speaks in a low, soothing voice. Hayley sobs harder, hunched into herself.

The chief officer turns to Claire, voice gentler now. "We're sorry for the trouble, Miss Holloway. Is there anything we can do for you right now?"

Claire doesn't answer. Her mind races, but her body stays locked in the chair. She reaches for Lily, then hesitates. Afraid the girl will flinch. Instead, Lily steps into her lap and wraps her arms tight around Claire's waist.

Claire buries her face in Lily's hair, breathing deep, smells the faint trace of strawberry shampoo, the heat of her skin, and the wet salt from her tears. She wants to hold her forever, but her arms are weak, so she just rests her chin on the top of Lily's head.

Behind them, the senior officer handcuffs Hayley. The younger officer writes down every word Hayley says, the page filling up with a confession nobody wanted.

Claire rocks Lily gently. She's crying, but silently. The ache in her chest is worse than before, but it's a new kind of pain—a bright, animal need to keep her daughter safe, to never let go.

Hayley's voice rises, desperate, as they handcuff her to the table. "Please," she pleads, "please, you have to believe me. I had no choice. You don't know what they're like. You don't—"

The officer shushes her, calm but firm.

Lily looks up at Claire, her eyes puffy and red. "Are we going home now?"

Claire can't speak. She just nods, pressing her lips into Lily's damp hair.

Hayley keeps crying as they lead her out, her voice echoing off the metal and glass. The officers follow. Their footsteps are hollow. Final.

Now, it's only Claire and Lily. The world narrows to the space between mother and child. For a long time, they don't move.

Claire holds her closer. Lily tucks herself in tight, burying her face in Claire's side.

When the officers return, they're quieter. One of them kneels beside Lily and offers a soft smile.

"You did good, kiddo," he says. "You're very brave."

Lily doesn't answer, but Claire feels her nod, just a little.

They sit like that, wrapped together. The lights are still too bright. The air still too cold. But for the first time in days, Claire feels something like safe.

She closes her eyes and waits for the world to start again.

CHAPTER THIRTY-SIX

The peace breaks with the arrival of police.

They file in two at a time, the glossy black of their boots snapping across the vinyl flooring, uniforms pressed so sharp the seams could cut. Their voices are deep, deliberate, nothing like the cruise staff.

Following are the four security officers from earlier and the kidnapper.

The lead officer surveys the mess: Hayley, cuffed and pale; Claire, bloodied and wild-eyed; Lily, a bundle of limbs and heartbreak. He's not cruel, but there is no warmth in him. He speaks to the officers, voice low. They ask Claire to confirm her name, Lily's name, date of birth. They take pictures—her face, her arms, the bruises from where the guards pinned her. They request permission to photograph Lily, Claire agrees though Lily buries herself deeper into her lap.

Police officers haul Hayley to her feet. Her wrists are already darkening under the cuffs, but she offers no protest. They empty her pockets and bag onto a grey tray: lipstick, phone, staff ID, aspirin, a wallet with less cash than expected, a wad of receipts. Two passports.

One officer opens a passport, flips through, then hands it off. His partner studies the photo, then Lily, then back again. Claire braces for it, expecting the next twist, the sudden reversal—*But this isn't your child. You must be mistaken.* But the officer simply closes the passport and seals it in a clear evidence bag.

The message becomes clear: Hayley is under arrest.

The lead police officer kneels beside Claire. "Is there anyone we can call for you?" he asks.

Claire looks at Lily, silent and buried in her arms. "Just let me stay with her," she whispers.

The officer nods, and signals for the room to clear.

Hayley is last to leave. She glances back once. Her eyes are void. No pleading, no hatred, just empty. She stumbles as she's led away. Claire wonders if her own feet will ever find solid ground again.

Silence returns. The female security officer stays close and watchful.

Time softens. Officers come and go, none asking Claire or Lily to move. A medic kneels beside them. He checks Claire's head and hands, working quickly and gently. He gives her a cloth for her cut palm. The sting is grounding. Proof she's still alive.

Time passes. Maybe minutes, maybe hours. A new officer arrives. His badge marks him as police, not ship staff. He squats beside Claire, hands visible.

"I need to ask you a few questions," he says. "To ensure Lily is safe."

Claire nods, stroking Lily's hair. "Anything."

He takes a statement, where she last saw Lily, what happened on the dock, about allergies or medical needs. His tone is calm. He never doubts her. He takes careful notes.

When he finished, he says, "She'll need to go to the hospital. You too."

Lily whimpers. Claire pulls her closer. "Can I be with her?"

"Yes," he assures. "Every step."

A private car is arranged. The female security officer from earlier hands Claire her phone and wallet, retrieved from her room. She also has two newly issued sea pass cards, for her and Lily. "For evidence, we'll need to keep Lily's things Hayley took," she says, voice almost a whisper. "Let us know what Lily needs. We'll send it to your room."

Claire nods, shaky, and lists essentials—clothes, toys, toiletries.

On the pier, the morning sun is bright, harsh. Officers flank them as they walk past disembarking passengers. A few turn to stare. Someone raises a phone to take a picture, not knowing the story, only seeing the drama of a woman in blood-spattered pyjamas and a child with tear-tracks on her face. Claire shields Lily's face and keeps walking.

They're escorted through customs without delay. A police officer opens the door to an unmarked sedan. The interior is cool, quiet. Claire climbs in, pulling Lily into her lap.

"Hungry?" she whispers.

Lily shakes her head, too tired to speak.

The car pulls away. Claire watches the cruise ship shrink in the mirror. It already feels like something from a nightmare she can't quite believe she survived.

Then Lily shifts and murmurs, "Mummy."

The word undoes her. Claire closes her eyes, tears streaming silently as she presses Lily close.

"Mummy's here," she whispers. "I've got you."

And for the first time in days, she believes it.

At the hospital, they're escorted straight through by a uniformed officer. No waiting room, no delays. Staff move with quiet urgency, and Claire stays close to Lily as nurses check her over. The officer waits just outside the door.

A social worker joins them—professional, composed. She runs through the necessary questions about family, custody, medical needs. Claire answers without hesitation. Nothing surprises the woman. She's heard it all before. Lily earns a sticker for being brave. She presses it onto Claire's hand before curling into her lap and falling asleep.

The officer stays nearby, never obtrusive but always present. Claire doesn't know what comes next, but for now, she holds Lily and listens to the rhythm of her breathing, steady and safe.

She remembers every detail.

She will never forget again.

When Claire steps into cabin 8612, Lily on her hip and a security officer trailing behind, she almost expects the space to shrink, to steal the breath from her lungs like it did the first night. But the room is different now, made unfamiliar by absence and then by return. The king bed has been split—now two singles again, perfectly made, each with crisp sheets and a folded blanket at the foot. Two soft towels lie folded in the bathroom, a row of tiny soaps and carefully arranged hair products resting gently on the sink. Bags of supplies for Lily sit quietly on the floor beside the bed, ready for whatever comes next.

The security officer does a sweep, checking the balcony, the bathroom, and the closet. He gives a stiff nod. "We've been asked to keep a close watch, just to make sure you're both safe. I'll be right outside if you need anything." Then he leaves. Claire latches the deadbolt behind him and flips the extra lock, though she knows it's mostly habit.

Lily is heavy in her arms, still half-asleep from the ride and the exam. She smells of baby shampoo and hand sanitiser. The large hospital wristband is still snapped around her left wrist, taped down so it wouldn't slip off. Claire sets her down on the bed. The child's face is pale, her eyes rimmed in red.

Claire kneels, brushing a strand of hair from Lily's cheek. The softness of it nearly undoes her.

She rises, takes the new towels, and heads for the shower. The water runs warm and fast, a luxury after the antiseptic drag of the hospital. She undresses Lily, carefully removing the wristband, and sits her on the closed toilet while the water heats. The girl doesn't resist, but she doesn't help either. She's limp, silent, eyes tracking nothing.

Claire checks the temperature with her elbow, then lifts Lily into the stream. The girl hunches her shoulders, shrinking from the spray, but allows Claire to lather her hair, wash her all over.

There's a scrape on Lily's knee, a bruise on her thigh. No blood. No bite marks. No lasting visible harm. Claire wants to weep with relief, but she doesn't. She just pours water over Lily's head, as if she could rinse away the lost days.

When they finish, she wraps Lily in a towel and dries her hair with gentle fingers. She dresses her in the softest pyjamas, new ones with green dinosaurs and orange cuffs. The pants are a size too big, but Lily doesn't complain. She just sits, hands folded, watching Claire with wide, unblinking eyes.

There's a knock at the door.

Claire flinches, heart leaping, but she recovers quickly. She checks the peephole.

The captain stands in the hallway, tall and stiff in his formal uniform. The gold braid on his shoulder shines in the fluorescent light. Next to him is a woman in a navy suit.

Claire takes a breath, then opens the door.

The captain bows, deeply, the motion rehearsed. "Miss Holloway," he says. "May we come in?"

She nods, stepping aside. The captain enters, followed by the woman, who is carrying a slim folder and a black notebook. The captain's face is grave, set in lines of apology. He glances at Lily, then at Claire.

"I wish I could express my regret in words," he says, voice low and careful.

"I can't begin to imagine what you've been through. I want you to know how relieved we all are that your daughter has been found safe. I'm deeply sorry this happened aboard our ship. When I took command, I promised every every guest that they were safe here. I'm sorry I failed you."

Claire shrugs. She doesn't know what to say to that.

He tries again. "You are aware the crew member responsible has been removed from duty and turned over to the proper authorities. We are cooperating fully with the investigation and will continue to support you in any way we can."

Claire nods, her voice barely above a whisper. "Thank you."

"If there's anything you or Lily need, day or night, please don't hesitate. Guest Services has been briefed, and I've given them full discretion to prioritise your comfort and privacy. My door is open to you."

The woman in the suit nods and opens the folder. "We can arrange for you to disembark at the next port, with an escort. If you wish to remain onboard, we will provide private security for the rest of the journey."

Claire sits on the bed with Lily beside her. "We'll stay," she says.

The captain nods. "Of course."

He hesitates, then says, "If there's anything else you need—anything at all—please tell us."

Claire almost laughs. She glances at Lily, who stares back solemn and still.

"I need this not to have happened," Claire says. The words escape before she can stop them, but the captain only nods again.

He bows once more, thanks her for her courage, and exits with the woman. The door closes behind them with a soft, final click.

Claire double-checks the locks.

She turns. Lily is still on the bed; knees hugged to her chest. Claire joins her, lets the silence stretch, and finally gives in to the need to hold her. She gathers Lily into her lap, rests her chin on the girl's head. The weight is comfort and penance both.

They sit like that for a long time.

When Lily's eyes begin to droop, Claire shifts her onto the pillows, and tucks the blanket up to her chin. She lies beside her, close enough to feel the tiny puffs of breath on her cheek.

The cabin is quiet. The engine thrums beneath them, steady as a heartbeat.

Claire stares at the ceiling. She tries to imagine what tomorrow might look like. She can't.

She looks at Lily, at the long lashes, the curve of her mouth, the way her small hands rest in small fists on the blanket.

For the first time, Claire lets herself believe this is real. Lily is here. She is safe.

Claire closes her eyes.
She does not sleep.
She just listens to her daughter's breathing and waits for the world
to begin again.

CHAPTER THIRTY-SEVEN

Claire wakes to a new sound in the cabin, a soft, bright murmur that warms the air like sunlight. Lily is humming to herself as she lines up dinosaur toys along the windowsill, freshly dressed in new clothes after their nap. Her shirt is on backwards, her hair still tousled, and her mismatched socks stand out against the pale blue carpet.

Claire sits at edge of the mattress; a blanket draped around her shoulders. She's not cold, but the weight helps. Every surface in the room is scattered with signs of life: a new purple plastic stegosaurus near the trash can, a half-completed colouring sheet tucked under the lamp, Lily's new pink rain boots inverted on the heating vent. The place looks lived-in. Alive.

The opposite of what it had been just hours before. Then, the bed had seemed too big, too perfect. The air had a sterile sharpness to it, an absence of anything warm. She remembers hating the view—a blank slab of sky and sea with nothing to break it up.

Now, it's different. The glass is fogged with breath, and the moon cuts a path through the calm water. Lily's voice bounces off the ceiling, filling dead spaces with melody.

It makes Claire want to cry, but the tears won't come. She's suspended between fear and relief, unsure what the rules are now that the game has ended. She checks the clock: 18:40. Almost dinner time.

Three knocks at the door. Not the brisk, impersonal one of security. This is softer. Claire knows who it is before she stands.

She opens the door, Daniel stands there, balanced in the frame with three dinner trays stacked on one arm. He's in a fresh uniform, shirt pressed, hair damp from a shower. He looks taller than usual, maybe because there's no crisis weighing him down.

He clears his throat. "Room service, for two lovely ladies."

Lily pops her head over the bed, eyes wide. "The nice man!" she squeals, then ducks back down, embarrassed.

Claire smiles, her face aching from disuse. "Come in."

Daniel steps inside, careful to keep the trays level. He takes in the room's cheerful chaos, then delicately sets the food on the desk. A plate for each of them: pasta with red sauce and cheese for Lily, steak and potatoes for himself, and a salad with grilled salmon for Claire. Cloth napkins, silverware, and a tiny carafe of apple juice accompany the spread.

"Figured she might want her own," he says, voice a little rough.

"Thank you," Claire says, and means it.

She helps Lily into the desk chair and nudges the pasta closer. Lily curves her body toward the plate and devours the first forkful with both hands and a satisfied gasp.

Daniel stands awkwardly by the door, hands behind his back. "I'm supposed to check if you're okay," he says. "No protocols. Just... check."

"We're fine," Claire says. She perches on the bed, picking at the napkin. "She's happy."

Daniel nods, relief rippling through his body like a visible current. He looks from Lily to the colouring sheet, then at the window. He avoids Claire's eyes.

Lily raises her head, mouth ringed in sauce. "Are you a policeman?"

Daniel grins, the first real smile Claire's seen from him. "Something like that."

"Do you have handcuffs?"

He pulls a face, mock-serious. "Not right now, but I know people who do."

Lily considers this, then nods, satisfied. She returns to her dinner with focus.

Daniel clears his throat. "I need to talk to your mum for a sec. That okay?"

Lily shrugs, slurps up a noodle, and tunes them out. Claire meets Daniel's eye and raises a brow.

He gestures to the balcony. A silent request. She rises, blanket still wrapped around her, and follows him out.

The air is cold but soft. The wind less biting than the night before. The ship's wake glows white in the moonlight, a path that seems to stretch into tomorrow.

They stand close, not touching. Daniel leaves the door ajar so the sound of Lily's humming drifts outside to meet them.

He looks at the horizon, then at Claire, then back again. "You know it's not over."

She nods.

"They're running a full investigation. Us, NYPD, FBI, Interpol—probably anyone who's ever worn a badge."

"I figured."

"They want to talk to you again. Both of you. It's—" He exhales slowly. "It's going to be a lot."

Claire is quiet. She thinks of the future in cautious steps. Lily's preschool, her job, therapy for both of them.

She says, "Thank you. For believing me."

He flinches. "I didn't, at first. I should have. I'm sorry. I wanted to. I just... didn't."

"It's okay."

"It's not," he says, nearly inaudible. "But I'm going to make it better. If I can."

They stand in silence. The sea is steady, the wind a dull roar. Inside, Lily's calls, "Mummy, can I have more juice?"

Claire turns to go, but Daniel stops her with a hand on her shoulder. It's gentle, but solid.

"I'll leave you to it. Can I come by tomorrow?" he asks. "For breakfast, maybe? I'm off then. I'll bring better coffee."

She smiles. "You can try."

He grins, then steps back. He holds the door until she and Lily are settled at the desk, then retrieves his tray and excuses himself with a salute.

The door closes. The world shrinks to three: mother, daughter, and the night.

Claire pours the last of the juice into Lily's cup. She eats her salad slowly, savouring every bite.

After dinner, she sits on the floor with Lily, building a dinosaur zoo from the pillows.

Later, when the lights are out and Lily is asleep, Claire pulls the blanket up to her chin and listens to her daughter breathe.

For the first time in a long while, she doesn't wait for the world to change.

She just lets it be.

She closes her eyes, and lets herself drift.

* * *

Daniel is early. He knocks at 7:13, just as the sun slices a hard-edged bar of light across the balcony. Claire is already awake—has been for hours, mapping the day's schedule in her mind like a military campaign. She lets Lily answer the door. Watching her daughter manage the world, even in small ways, eases the tightness behind Claire's eyes.

Lily greets Daniel with a whole sentence. "Good morning. We have coffee already, but it's Mummy's kind, so it's not good." She points to the mug of instant coffee on the desk, then to the pastry basket, then to herself. "I ate a tiny toast."

Daniel holds up a white paper bag. "Bet you didn't eat three," he says. "Fresh from the bakery. The ship's best."

Lily's eyes widen. She opens the bag, counts the croissants inside, and looks up at her mother with solemn triumph.

Claire smirks, takes the bag, and sets it by the window. "She wins," she says. "Always does."

Daniel sets two proper coffees on the desk, then kneels to Lily's level. "Do you mind if I talk to your mum for a bit? You can be the boss while we're outside."

Lily considers, then nods. She's busy—her zoo needs rearranging, a dinosaur is due for a nap, and there's a colouring sheet she plans to finish before breakfast ends.

Claire shrugs into a hoodie and follows Daniel onto the balcony. The cold is sharper than the night before, but she prefers it that way. The glass door is left ajar. Lily hums, a thread that ties her to the world inside.

Daniel doesn't waste time. He leans forward, arms braced on the railing, eyes locked on the horizon. "I need you to know the truth. Everything we found."

Claire pulls her hood up, crosses her arms, and waits.

Daniel breathes in, then out. "First off, I want to say—when I saw you on the dock with Lily, I knew immediately. No more doubts. You were right all along."

She nods. It's a comfort, but a hollow one.

"I wasn't on duty at the time," Daniel says. "But I couldn't let it go. I started digging—logs, footage, anything that might explain why no one believed you. I've read all our reports."

He glances at her, then down. "Turns out, the first big gap came right after your fall. I saw you, but Officer Torres took your initial report. He saw the head wound, read the file about your past hospitalisations, and assumed… well… He assumed the rest. He never pulled the CCTV footage like I asked. Just said there was no child."

"Dr. Reyes helped that along," Claire says flatly.

"She did," Daniel agrees. "Torres prompted it, then she told him it was possible—even likely—you were experiencing false memories. They flagged it in the system. After that, no one thought to check beyond the obvious. Every time you reported Lily missing, they wrote it up as another episode."

Claire's nails dig into her palm. "But there were pictures. Videos. On my phone. What happened?"

"After you fell—sorry, were pushed—Hayley took your phone and used facial recognition to get into it," he says. "She didn't just delete them. She used some artificial intelligence app to erase Lily from all the remaining pictures. All of them. Same background, same angle, just no child. It looked perfect unless you really dig."

She grips the railing, knuckles white. "Bitch," she spits.

Daniel nods. "She also found a backdoor into guest records. Our report doesn't give details. She shouldn't have been able to access that to change it. Head Office have people looking into it urgently. That's how she removed Lily from the manifest."

He pauses, lets her take it in.

"There's more," he says. "She gave her ID card master key access. She entered your room, took Lily, then came back and cleared out all her things. Housekeeping logs show a call from your room at 10:22. 'Liquid spill, bed linen needs full change.' She pushed the two beds back together and a different attendant came to do the job. When the job sheet was run the next morning, your usual room attendant saw one guest and one bed, so took the appropriate linen. He wouldn't have noticed the change."

Claire's heart pounds loud enough to drown out the ocean. "She took Lily's things."

"All of it," Daniel says. "They found it in her luggage after security stopped her at the dock. She planned to dump it after handing Lily over."

"Why?" Claire's voice cracks. "Why would she do all that?"

Daniel's face tightens. "She was pulled in by a ring. Child trafficking, they think, but the details are still coming together. She didn't know you. Didn't have any grudge. She just saw a kid—young, not many connections, easy to isolate. When you checked in, she flagged Lily and other children. Then she waited for the right chance."

Claire shivers, more from rage than cold. The days before reassemble in her mind, every joyful moment now spliced with dread.

"She was going to take one of the kids from the club on the last day." Daniel says. "She'd added herself as an adult authorised to collect several children. That evening, you went to the theatre alone. She saw you. Followed you. Pushed you. When you were out of sight long enough, taken to Medical, she used the master key. Lily was asleep. When she woke the next morning, Hayley told her you'd gone to the doctor and she was her aunt looking after her for a while. She said you gave her all the toys so she knew she could trust her."

Claire's stomach churns. "And after—when I started looking—"

"She had control of the story," Daniel says. "Torres had flagged you as unstable. Dr. Reyes signed off. No one actually looked at the footage, until I did yesterday. Torres has been suspended. And when you finally caught up to them at the dock, Hayley just… went for broke."

Claire's eyes sting. She stares at the wake, that endless white rope that ties the ship to the past.

"What happens to her now?" she asks.

"She has been arrested. But she's cooperating," Daniel says. "She naming names, giving up methods. It's huge, Claire. You saved a lot of kids."

She shakes her head. "I just wanted mine back."

Daniel is quiet for a long moment.

"I'm sorry it took this much to make people believe you. I'm sorry I didn't believe you."

She doesn't respond.

He shifts, meets her eyes. "If you want, I can stay with you and Lily as much as I can until we dock. I'll ask to be assigned to you while I'm on duty. After that, I'll make sure you get support—real support—not just a pamphlet and a phone number. I'll even give you my direct mobile number. If you want it, that is."

Claire exhales, a long breath that rattles in her chest. "Thank you."

They stand in silence, the wind on their faces. The sun is higher now. The water blue instead of black.

Inside, Lily draws a dinosaur. She looks up and waves, face smeared with chocolate and contentment.

Claire turns from the rail, moves to the door, and pauses. "One more thing," she says.

Daniel waits.

"I'd love a steak for dinner. With lots of vegetables. Lily will take nuggets and chips."

He grins. "It's a date."

She steps inside. The cabin warmth wraps around her like a safe room.

Daniel follows and closes the balcony door behind him.

They sit with Lily, who's already asking what's for lunch.

The world has changed. But the day goes on.

The next morning is quiet—just the way Claire likes it. No falls, no missing children, no blood in the sheets. No unexpected knocks at the door that tilt the world off balance. Just the three of them, eating breakfast in a room that smells faintly of toast and orange peel.

Yesterday had been fun—a tentative blur of shipboard adventures: mini golf, crafts, a splash in the shallow end of the pool.

Lily sits cross-legged on the desk chair, swinging her legs. She's narrating an adventure for a dinosaur, who is apparently exploring a volcano made of croissants. Her voice is loud and cheerful, but it doesn't grate. Not today.

Claire sips her coffee and watches sunlight play on the wall. Daniel stands by the window, pouring juice into Lily's cup, doing his best to look casual. He fails, but the effort is almost charming.

He takes his coffee black, drinks it fast, then sets the cup aside. Something about his posture is different—looser, like he's given up pretending to be just another face in a uniform.

He glances at Claire, then away, then back again. "I wanted to say something," he says, his voice lower than usual. "For real, this time."

Claire sets her mug down and waits.

He laces his fingers together. "I'm sorry I didn't find her sooner. I saw the signs, but I—" He shakes his head. "I talked myself out of it. Thought maybe I was seeing patterns that weren't there. That's what we're trained to do. But I was wrong."

Lily's croissant volcano erupts, scattering flakes on the carpet. She cheers.

Claire says, "We're here now. That's what matters."

He nods, but doesn't look convinced. "It matters to me," he says. "You matter. Both of you. That night you first had dinner with me on the balcony? I found something I didn't know I was missing."

He says it simply, with no drama, and expects nothing in return. Claire feels the words settle in her chest, a weight and a buoyancy at the same time.

He stands, paces to the window, then back again. "I'd like to keep having breakfast and dinner with you. If that's okay."

Lily looks up, blue frosting on her chin. "He can stay, Mummy."

Claire laughs and claps a hand over her mouth, surprised by the sound.

Daniel grins, sheepish. "That's unanimous, then."

He sits across from her, elbows on the table. The ship lurches slightly, and he steadies his coffee with one hand.

Claire studies him in the light, the soft lines at the corners of his eyes when he isn't pretending to be in charge. She thinks of all the hours he spent searching for Lily, even after the system said to give up. She remembers how he never once told her she was crazy, not even when she was.

She asks, "Why?"

He blinks. "Why what?"

"Why do you care?"

He looks at Lily, then at Claire. "Because the first time I saw you, really saw you, you looked like someone who deserved better. Like someone who could survive anything, but shouldn't have to do it alone."

Heat rises in her cheeks, but she doesn't flinch.

He adds, "I know I'm not the hero you wanted. But I can be the one who stays. If you let me."

Lily makes a dinosaur noise, then goes back to her game.

Claire reaches across the table, and places her hand on his. His skin is warm. His nails are neatly clipped. A faint scar crosses one knuckle.

"You can stay," she says. "For breakfast. For dinner. For after."

He covers her hand with his, squeezes once, then lets go. The touch is brief but it echoes.

They watch Lily for a while, the small body at the centre of a world Claire almost lost.

The ship moves forward. Outside, the horizon curves into a thin, endless line.

Inside, the three of them sit together, the silence deep and comfortable. Lily hums a tune, low and content, her voice the anchor that holds them all.

Claire looks out at the water. Then at Daniel. Then at the child who made her brave enough to be whole again.

She closes her eyes and listens not for danger, but for the sound of what comes next.

CHAPTER THIRTY-EIGHT

ONE YEAR LATER

The gangway is a ribbon of blue carpet stretched between land and sea, soft and insubstantial under Claire's feet. She stands just before the threshold, hand clamped to the steel rail, pulse hammering in the meat of her palm. She knows she's blocking the way, but for now no one seems to mind. The crowd hums with anticipation, luggage bumping ankles, badges swinging on lanyards, the air salted with the promise of departure.

Lily bounces beside her, knees already scuffed, dinosaur backpack bobbing with each hop. Her shirt hangs loose, one side already untucked, and she holds a plush triceratops by the frayed horn. The toy's name is Steggy—at least this week. Every few seconds Lily squeezes the dinosaur to her chest, then swings it out again like a baton, conducting the music in her head.

Claire glances at her daughter, scanning for any sign of distress or nerves, but all she finds is kinetic joy. Lily's eyes are wide, her mouth in constant motion:

"Mummy, are we going yet? Is this the ship? Is it bigger than the last one? Will there be a pool? Will Steggy like the pool?"

The questions trip over one another, but Claire answers every one, even if it's only with a nod.

The line shuffles forward. Behind them, a woman in a sunhat checks her watch. Ahead, a family in matching fluorescent shirts, slogan lost to the crowd, herd twins toward the crew member scanning passes. The Mediterranean wind plucks at Claire's hair, sneaks beneath her collar, laced with the deep, oily breath of the port. Somewhere below, a forklift beeps, the echo rattling the gangway end to end.

Lily is undeterred. She tugs at Claire's sleeve, her voice now a half-whisper.

"It smells like fish, but not the bad kind."

She wriggles the triceratops under Claire's chin.

"Steggy says it's safe. He says we should go."

The moment stretches, and Claire lets it. She inhales, holds the air in her chest, lets it rattle through her like a warning or a song. Her mind still conjures a thousand disaster scenarios: misplaced tickets, wrong ship, wrong day, the sudden vanishing of her daughter's hand in the tide of strangers. But her body is steadier now. She can feel the difference, not absence, but control. The old panic sits in her gut, but it's small, contained. A passenger, not the captain.

She shifts her grip on the rail, wipes the damp from her palm onto her jeans, and bends down to Lily's level.

She meets Lily's gaze, hazel to hazel. For a second the world goes silent.

"Are you ready?" she asks.

Lily beams.

"I'm so ready I'm two times ready. I'm infinity ready."

Claire offers her hand. Lily takes it, strong and sure, her fingers sticky from the grape juice they'd shared in the cab. Together, they move forward. Each step is easier than the last.

At the scanner, the attendant grins, and kneels to Lily's height.

"Is that a dinosaur I see?" he asks, mock-serious.

Lily nods, lifting Steggy for inspection.

"He's a herbivore, so he won't bite."

The attendant winks, waves them through, and the machine gives a satisfied chirp as it reads their passes.

Inside the ship, the temperature drops. Claire breathes deep, letting the cool air clear her head. The transition from land to ship is always abrupt—here, the world narrows to a tunnel. The windows are smudged with the oily film of a thousand crossings. The floor creaks, the whole structure flexing with the wind and the movement of so many bodies, but Claire walks steady. Each footfall is a decision. A small defiance against the undertow of old fears.

Lily chatters about everything she sees: the pattern in the carpet, the colour of the doors, the number of steps to the entrance. She asks if the ship will have pancakes, if pancakes taste different at sea, and if the captain ever gets seasick. Claire answers, sometimes with words, sometimes with a gentle squeeze of her hand.

The entryway is chaos but not the kind that frightens her anymore. Crew members in navy jackets direct families left and right, voices raised but never sharp. The lobby gleams under glass and brass, every surface polished to a mirror. The smell is instantly familiar: recycled air, lemon cleaner, and the faint trace of salt that no amount of scrubbing can remove.

Lily spins in a circle, arms up, Steggy flailing in celebration.

"We're here!" she shouts. "We're on the ship!"

Claire smiles, a real one. She scans the room, mapping exits, noting the nearest staff. But it's automatic now. She doesn't let it control her.

Instead, she crouches and points to the grand staircase, the one with the gold banister and the thick red runner.

"Want to see the pool?" she asks.

Lily squeals and races ahead, dinosaur bouncing against her back.

Claire follows, steps light, posture tall, eyes clear.

It isn't the same as before.

It will never be the same as before.

But it is enough.

And for today, that is everything.

The pool deck is a mosaic of sunlight and water, every inch vibrating with colour and sound. Claire's first step onto the synthetic wood planks sends a jolt up her leg. The air smells of chlorine and ocean, mingled with coconut sunscreen and the faint tang of cleaning spray. Overhead, a lattice of shade panels dapples the crowd in shifting patterns.

Lily sprints ahead, sneakers slapping the deck, backpack bouncing in rhythm. She veers toward the pool, skids to a stop at the edge, and peers into the blue expanse like it's the mouth of a cave. Her voice cuts through the hum: "Mummy, it's so big! Look how deep it goes!"

Claire catches up, breath quick but steady. She squats beside her daughter, tucking a stray curl behind Lily's ear. The pool is rimmed with gleaming tiles; every metre marked with cartoon animals. At the shallow end, a group of kids flings plastic rings into the water, shrieking as they dive after them.

"Can I go in now?" Lily asks, already halfway out of her shoes.

"Let's find a spot for your stuff first," Claire says. "We don't want Steggy getting lost, do we?"

Lily shakes her head, solemn. "Steggy hates swimming. He gets soggy."

They settle at a table just off the main drag, its surface sticky with the sugar residue of previous guests. Claire lines up their bags, checks for towels, scans the deck. No strangers watching, no shadows lurking. She breathes easier.

Lily ditches her shoes and dress, about to leap into the chaos when she pauses, turns back, and wraps both arms around Claire's waist. The hug is sudden, fierce, then gone. Claire's stomach flips, in the best way.

"I love you, Mummy," Lily says, almost as an afterthought.

"Love you more," Claire replies and means it.

Lily bolts for the water. She hovers at the edge for a moment, uncertain, then spots a girl in a neon-green swim cap and runs over, waving hello. Within moments, the two are plotting a synchronised jump, voices already blending into one bright sound.

Claire watches, eyes narrowed against the glare, trying to memorise the shape of Lily's happiness. She doesn't let herself forget how rare it used to be.

The sun is warm almost hot and for the first time in weeks Claire lets her arms go bare. She stretches them across the chair, lets her shoulders drop, lets the weight of the day slough off. Around her, the other passengers are a blur: men in cargo shorts, women in wide-brimmed hats, teenagers orbiting the snack bar like satellites. The noise is high-pitched but harmless. Nothing here can touch them.

Lily is already in the water, squealing with laughter. The girl with the green cap, Maya, as Claire quickly learns, teaches Lily how to hold her breath and count to ten. In no time, they're trading handstands and splashing up at the lifeguard, who ignores them with professional patience.

For a while, Claire just watches. She traces the arc of Lily's arms as they break the surface, the way her hair mats to her forehead, the unselfconscious joy in every movement. A year ago, this would have been unthinkable. A year ago, they would have barely made it out of the cabin.

She wipes her eyes with the heel of her hand, laughing at herself.

"Hey," says a voice, soft but close.

She turns. Daniel stands there, a small backpack slung over one shoulder, his uniform crisp and clean, sneakers looking brand new.

The effect is jarring and perfect. For a moment, she can't remember the last time she saw him in uniform.

"You made it," he says.

"Of course," she replies. "Couldn't let you get all the sun."

He sets his bag down, takes the seat beside her, and immediately shifts it closer. His arm finds her waist with the ease of long practice. He smells of aftershave and clean laundry.

They watch the pool together. Lily surfaces, spots Daniel, and waves so hard she nearly loses her grip on the ring she's holding. She paddles over, dripping, and leans on the edge.

"Daniel! Did you see my handstand?" she asks, out of breath.

"I did," Daniel says. "Ten out of ten. Olympic-level, for sure."

Lily beams, then squints up at him. "Are you going to swim too?"

He shakes his head, mock-sad. "I have to keep an eye on your mum. She might get into trouble."

Lily giggles and splashes water in their direction. "You're silly."

She and Maya vanish beneath the surface, plotting their next trick.

Daniel leans in, kisses the side of Claire's head. "How are you really?" he asks, low.

She leans into the touch. "Better," she says. "Really better."

He squeezes her hand warm, dry, steady.

They sit like that, companionable, for a long time. The sun climbs higher, the deck grows busier, but it doesn't matter. The noise is just noise.

When Lily comes up for air, Daniel stands, stretches, and walks to meet her at the edge.

"Hey, champ," he says, crouching. "I have some news."

Lily blinks water from her lashes. "What?"

He drops to one knee, eye-level with her. "I'm very excited you're on this trip, because it's my last one working on the ship. After this, I'm leaving to become a real police officer."

Lily's jaw drops. "Like in the movies?"

Daniel laughs. "Sort of. But I'll get to help people for real."

Lily considers, then nods, satisfied. "Will you still come over for pancakes?"

He glances back at Claire, grinning. "Every Sunday, if your mum lets me."

Lily does a tiny victory dance, water spraying everywhere. "Yes! Steggy loves pancakes."

Daniel ruffles her hair, then stands, still watching her. "Go have fun, kiddo. You're safe. We're all watching you."

Lily cannonballs back into the pool.

Daniel returns to Claire, sits closer than before, their knees touching. "She's good," he says.

"She's perfect," Claire replies.

They spend the rest of the afternoon poolside, speaking in low voices, letting the world shrink to the boundaries of their table. The anxiety never fully leaves, but it no longer owns her.

They are a family now, stitched together by luck, stubbornness, and the simple act of refusing to let go.

At some point, Daniel says, "Let's take her to the pizza place for dinner. She'll love it."

Claire agrees, already picturing Lily's face when she sees the menu.

She stands, stretches, and helps Daniel pack up the towels. Together, they call for Lily, who comes running, hair wild and eyes brighter than the sun.

They walk the deck together, Lily in the middle with Steggy in one hand, her parents—because that's what they are now—on either side.

Claire glances at the horizon, watches the sky change colour, and realises she is not afraid.

Not anymore.

The restaurant is all glass and gold, polished so brightly it blurs the line between inside and out. The waiter seats them in a window booth, the view slanting over the ship's prow and out to the darkening sea. A linen tablecloth muffles their movements, and every fork or glass placed by the waiters is a small, perfect ceremony.

Lily dives into her pizza with both hands. Within seconds marinara smudges her cheek, and the triceratops settles beside her on the banquette, a napkin tied around its neck. She bounces her feet, keeping time with a tune only she can hear.

Daniel orders wine for himself and Claire, lemonade for Lily. The server brings it in a green bottle, pouring with a flourish that makes Lily giggle. Claire sips, letting the acidity burn away the last nerves clinging to her chest. She glances around, noting other families, couples, lone travellers content in their small silences.

The low hum of conversation comforts her. Plates slide across tables, glasses clink, laughter bursts and fades in waves. Overhead, the dimmed amber lighting casts everything in a warmth that feels earned.

The food is better than she imagined. Claire eats slowly, letting each bite linger, tasting the olive oil, the bite of garlic. Daniel carves his steak with patient precision, savouring every mouthful. They don't talk much at first, content to exist in the moment, in the bubble of sound and light.

Lily's meal disappears at warp speed. Afterwards, she lines up the crusts on the plate's edge, then arranges the napkin into a tent for Steggy. The sun dips lower, throwing a line of fire across the water's surface. Lily rests her head on Claire's shoulder, eyelids fluttering.

"Big day," Daniel says, grinning.

"She'll crash as soon as we hit the room," Claire replies, voice low. "Maybe before."

Lily rallies once for ice cream, but after a few bites, she's done. She curls up next to Claire, head in her mother's lap, dinosaur tucked under one arm. Claire strokes the hair back from Lily's forehead, marvelling at the easy trust, the way her daughter lets go of the day and falls asleep.

Daniel watches them, eyes soft. He reaches across the table, covering Claire's hand with his own. His thumb traces a slow, patient line over her knuckles. "You okay?" he asks, barely above a whisper.

She nods. "Better than okay." She looks out at the horizon, the impossible expanse of blue fading to black. "I don't know if I ever thought we'd get here."

He squeezes her hand. "I did," he says, with just enough joking in his tone to keep it light. "Had a hunch."

She laughs, then covers her mouth, careful not to wake Lily.

The conversation drifts. Daniel asks about her job, how many clients she'll lose by being at sea for two weeks, if she's worried about missing deadlines.

Claire shrugs. "They'll wait," she says. "Turns out, I'm harder to replace than I thought."

He smiles, proud. "Told you so."

She asks about his plans—what comes next, once the ship docks for him for the last time.

"I just want something steady," he says. "Home in the evenings." Then he glances at her, a playful glint in his eye. "Sleep in the same bed. Maybe even have someone to split a pizza with on Fridays."

Claire pictures it: Daniel at the stove, Lily at the kitchen table with colouring books, the world outside receding to a safe, manageable distance. She wants it, more than she expected.

"You can come over for pizza," she says.

He feigns shock. "You cook?"

"Not well," she admits. "But I can order with the best of them."

He grins. "That's all I ask."

Lily sighs in her sleep, a happy sound. Claire rests her cheek on the top of her daughter's head, closes her eyes, lets the moment settle. She feels the gentle roll of the ship, the deep vibration of the engines, the weight of Daniel's hand over hers.

For a long time, that's all there is.

Outside, the sun finally sinks, and the first stars poke through the wash of dusk. The city lights slip behind them, until only the ship and the sea exist.

Claire doesn't look back.

She breathes in, steady and even. The old fear is there, but it's a memory now. A ghost she's learned to live with.

She looks at Daniel, who is still watching her, then down at Lily, soft and warm and safe.

It is enough.

And for the first time, Claire lets herself believe it always will be.

The Nice Boss
A perfect job. A kindly boss. And a secret that won't stay buried.

Emily lands her dream job, with the dream boss. He's calm, kind, and owns a remote cabin in the woods that he allows his staff to use to unwind. But when a colleague disappears without a trace, everything shifts. That quiet kindness feels like a carefully crafted mask, and trust quickly turns to suspicion.
How far would someone go to keep a secret?

In a world where the nicest faces hide the darkest secrets, some truths are more dangerous when they stay hidden.

Hide and Seek
A missing child. A hidden past. And a game that was never meant to be played.

When twelve-year-old Lachlan vanishes near Auckland's historic North Head tunnels, his parents—each with secrets of their own—are forced into a race against time. But as the search deepens, so do the cracks in their carefully curated lives. Was Lachlan playing a game... or was someone playing him?

In a town built on myths and buried truths, nothing stays hidden forever.

Dear Reader,

Thank you for choosing to spend your precious time with my story. Writing this debut novel has been a leap of faith, and knowing it found its way into your hands means more than I can say.

I hope these pages kept you up too late, made you double-check your doors, and question your own memory once or twice. If you enjoyed the ride, do me a favour and recommend it to a friend (but don't ruin the twists, or I might have to write *you* into the next one). And if you find yourself glancing over your shoulder for a while… well, some stories like to linger.

Sleep tight, and thank you for reading.

And don't worry, the next story is already in progress.

Until next time,

Nicola Faulkner